THE BOOK OF
QUINT

RYAN DACKO

Copyright © 2022, 2023 by Ryan Dacko

This edition published 2023

Amberley Publishing
The Hill, Stroud
Gloucestershire, GL5 4EP

www.amberley-books.com

The right of Ryan Dacko to be identified as the Author of this work has been asserted in accordance with the Copyright, Designs and Patents Act 1988.

ISBN 978-1-3981-2247-5 (paperback)
ISBN 978-1-3981-2248-2 (ebook)

British Library Cataloguing in Publication Data. A catalogue record for this book is available from the British Library.

Illustrations by Graham Nolan.

For Robert Shaw and Mary Ure

CONTENTS

PART III

"Now the Lord sent a great fish to swallow Jonah"

Jonah 1:17

PROLOGUE

It broke the silence of the ancient fishing village. A red 2024 Jeep Wrangler rumbled down the only roadway the town had ever known. The vehicle floated to a stop and kicked a cloud of dust across the crooked *Keisel's Car Rental of Amity Island* sign on its dulled metal door. The engine fell silent, returning the village to a serene, inanimate state.

She opened the door, and her shoes touched the sand. She took the time to stare down at them and the footprints they made in the vehicle's shadow.

Did he stand here? If this is the place, he must have walked here for years.

The woman stood at the end of the harbor in front of a vacant lot within a row of crowded fishing shacks and cottages. She walked forward into the space. The long grass of neglect made the lot look out of place. Her legs felt the slender blades of grass graze her skin and she smiled. She knelt to trace the patches of wild beach heather with her fingertips.

A setting October sun cast its last remnants of warmth on her face. She studied the harbor that stretched far out to a distant ocean inlet. Her long, light brown hair caught the fresh breeze hailing from the sea and comforted her. She continued her walk through the plot of overgrown vegetation and rusted nautical artifacts towards the seawall. An old pylon, angled and defeated, stood from the water. Remnants of a long-forgotten dock gripped the pylon's barnacle covered wooden shell. She looked into the green saltwater of high tide and gazed at the reflection.

When she was a little girl, if someone asked *where will you be at twenty-seven?* —this place would never have been her answer. She didn't even know it existed until last year.

He must have kept his boat right here. What's buried down below this water that might be his? These shacks could still be the original ones.

The woman took out a piece of paper from the front pocket of her denim shorts and read the second address. She held her phone up to the harbor to take a photo of silent fishing boats, all dormant and out of use. Another photo of a rusted anchor laying on its side. A worn fishing net draped across its pitted iron. She searched the digital maps and looked up to the small cottage on the hill overlooking the harbor.

That must be it. Harbor Hill Road goes around the back and up there. That's the one.

The climb up the cobblestone road felt good after her long legs had cramped behind the person who slept with the seat reclined on the flight. All the way from Anchorage to Boston with her knees stiff and tired. Then the ferry ride, and the drive across the island. The walk tried to relax her already shaking and nervous hands. She was never good at meeting people. Jim was always the talker.

She approached the cottage with caution. The old screen door sat open an inch. The rusty spring too aged to do its job and pull the door all the way closed.

The woman raised her hand to knock but lowered it. She cried.

Jim, why aren't you here? I can't do this without you. It wasn't supposed to be like this. I'm so nervous and don't know what to say.

The young lady wiped the lone tear from her pale cheek and filled her lungs with a deep breath through the nose. The salt air calmed her. It reminded her of home.

A newfound sense of bravery overtook her, and she knocked on the chipped white paint of the door's frame. There wasn't an answer.

To her left, over the small side yard, she saw the harbor down below. The setting sun lit up the sand and fishing shacks with an orange glow. She turned and stepped towards the back, where the cottage faced the harbor. A small deck of weathered wood extended from the house to overlook the small fishing town. She looked around, and it didn't appear anyone was home. The side windows of the cottage shone dark and empty.

She stepped onto the gray deck and walked to the railing. The warped wood shifted when she placed her hands on it. Rusted nails, loosened from shrinking timbers, failed to hold the rail steady. She looked down towards the back of the harbor and saw the empty lot with the red jeep.

I only ever read about this place on the internet. This was where he lived.

"Can I help you?"

She turned at the sound of the weak voice behind her. On the small bench at the center of the deck, an old man sat with a blanket over his legs. He leaned back against the cedar shake siding of the small cottage and looked at her with tired eyes. His trimmed white beard shined bright in the late afternoon sun.

"I'm sorry, sir. I knocked, but there wasn't an answer."

"That's because there's nobody home."

She looked at the little man and tried to find the right words. His face hung grim and worn.

"Yes, I understand, but…"

"I'm not telling anymore stories. No more hidden camera tricks for your social media. Go find a sasquatch if you want to make a name for yourself."

"I'm not interested in any of that, sir."

"Then what do you want? This is private property."

She fumbled her nervous words from across the deck.

"I was told Hershel Salvatore lives here and I…"

"Hershel Salvatore is dead—passed away back in 2018. I live here now." The old man studied the lady and wondered why she looked back towards the end of the harbor. He leaned forward and straightened the frames of the small, round glasses on his nose.

The woman no longer looked at him and stayed focused on the empty plot in the distance. Her voice grew quiet and reserved.

"I'm not sure why I'm here. My fiancé died at sea last winter, and I felt if I didn't do this now, I never would."

"Do what?"

"See where my grandfather lived."

The old man leaned on his short legs and softened his voice. "It's not every day a young lady from Alaska comes all the way out here looking for Hershel. You might be the first. I didn't think Hershel had any children?"

She turned to the old man and wondered how he knew. He pointed to her shoulder.

"Your sweatshirt says Dutch Harbor on the patch."

The lady felt silly to give away such an obvious clue. She reached into her back pocket and pulled out an aged envelope of yellowed paper.

"No, not Mr. Salvatore. He's the only name I had who may have more information. If he's gone, then it died with him."

The woman pulled a faded photo from the envelope. She stared at the picture and then back at the water. Her silence amplified the distant sound of a fishing boat's horn. Instincts told the old man this wasn't a normal tourist. This one wasn't looking for tales of killer sharks. This woman differed from the others. She looked lost.

"I'm sorry to have been so direct, miss. Years of isolation from the mainland and I forgot my manners. My name is Matt Hooper. I knew Mr. Salvatore."

When I heard his name, I remember the shivers that went up my back. The guy from the stories.

The woman stood in silence. For the moment, words failed her. She looked at him as if he were a ghost. Her blue eyes turned to the photo in her hands as she walked it across the deck towards the old man.

"Mr. Hooper? My name is Rebecca Quint. I believe you knew my grandfather."

Hooper looked down in disbelief at the photo being handed to him. A black-and-white photo of a young sailor with a steel gaze and chiseled chin. The matted paper photo of the man in his United States Navy uniform—curled and creased over its eighty-two years of existence. Hooper's aged hands shook, and his eyes welled up.

"This is the first photo I've ever seen of him. I've been searching for fifty years… half a century."

The old man broke down and wept while looking at the photo.

Rebecca knelt next to him. She wanted to put her arm around him. He struggled to maintain a studious composure—his words certain and direct.

"I've been searching for you, Rebecca. You are the only proof he ever lived. I searched my whole life for anyone to pass on what I have. I'm almost eighty and thought I'd die never knowing the answers to the questions he left. You are the answer. You have no idea."

"What do I have no idea about, Mr. Hooper?"

"You are as close to family as I'll ever have. Everyone else is dead."

Matt Hooper paused while drying the red eyes under his glasses. He fought to focus on the old 1940s Navy photo. He looked into the man's eyes for the first time since 1974.

"You have no idea how grand and large he was. I lost my father at sixteen to a boating accident. Never found him. The ocean just took him. When I met your grandfather—he was everything I needed in my life. A man full of history and information. The toughest captain I'd ever sail under. I was a naive kid and thought I knew it all. Your grandfather saved so many lives. It took him from this world. He died far too soon and the loss was so unbelievably profound. The world lost a source of history and knowledge. Like losing a father all over again. You look just like him. When I look at you, it's like he's alive again. I can't believe it."

"Is it true then? Was the shark as big as they say?"

"It was bigger. He fought it and wore it down. He gave up his life. His boat. I would not have survived if it weren't for him."

"You were in the steel cage? I read the articles and your interviews."

"I was caught inside the cage. The mouth. The teeth. I didn't talk about it for years but, I promise you every day, I relive it. The fear wakes me up at night, then it turns to heartache—for the loss."

Hooper leaned forward. "Don't let any of these people tell you it was a myth. I could tell you all kinds of things that you don't have time for. The scientific community shunned me—they laughed and ridiculed me. They worked with the political machine to silence me. No proof but my own observations and a few others. Nobody can change the facts. I know what I saw. It was their interpretation of those facts that I couldn't control."

Hooper took the blanket off his legs and jumped to his feet. He held out his hand to help her up.

"You are tall, too. Just like him. Remarkable," said Hooper looking up. He handed the photo back.

Rebecca stared at Hooper with amusement. His demeanor switched to an excited state.

"We have no time to waste, Rebecca. There's so much to tell you. I can tell you a whole novel. I can talk to you. The whole novel that's in my head. You need to hear everything. Follow me. I have something to show you."

She tried to keep up with his short, quick steps.

"She was a hundred-and-one, but before she died, she told me about my last name—handed me this photo and the legal papers. A plot of land on an island called Amity."

"So, Hershel wrote to your grandmother? He must have known her name and never told me. Fascinating. He blamed me for many years, said he should've been out there as the third crewman instead of me. I never could convince him otherwise."

Rebecca and Hooper approached the large metal doors at the front of the barn. Hooper unlocked the padlocked chain that wrapped the handle. He tapped in a security code on the box of glowing numbers mounted to the side.

"I can never be too careful these days... all the souvenir hunters and thieves."

My stomach knotted with nerves. Nothing can prepare you for that moment when your entire life takes a turn, and you realize it will never be the same.

"Matt, what is this place?"

Hooper gripped the wide handle to the barn door and looked back at Rebecca.

"Rebecca, the ocean takes everything. I'm sorry for your losses. Most people will never know what it's like to work the water and the suffering that comes with it. You walking onto that deck this afternoon wasn't a random chance. You are the continuation of this story. You are the only one left to continue it?"

"Continue what?"

"His legacy."

Matt Hooper threw open the large door. A polished concrete floor reflected the white lights that hung from the vaulted ceiling. The climate-controlled air vent kicked on in a low rumble.

Before her, a vast collection of artifacts and historical pieces mounted to walls or sealed under pressurized protective glass. A boat's steering wheel. A bent and twisted propeller. Her eyes fell on an enormous set of jaws that hung on the back wall. Large white teeth of a great white shark stared back at her. The lower portion of the jaws charred black with fire damage.

Rebecca stepped forward into the white glow of the LED lamps.

"Your grandfather made a lot of powerful friends in the war, and some powerful political enemies here on Amity. I searched everywhere for any records of his life. They erased him from the local and mainland census records. His military records disappeared. The only document I ever had to prove he was real, a bus log for a Navy boot camp back in 1942. Three initials—RSQ. That's it there."

Hooper pointed to the old handwritten page in a lit display case.

"I only ever found one picture of him. From a microfiche file. I had to sift through a San Francisco dumpster for an hour to find it—an experience I wouldn't wish on my worst enemy. From the San Francisco Chronicle front page in 1951. That's him there."

Rebecca looked deep into the glass case. The scratched photo negative picture of a man standing over three dead sharks shining with the light from below.

"I spent years collecting all this. In 1977, after another great white came around, the town people burned down the fishing shack. They said he cursed this place. His first mate, Hershel, the guy who wrote your grandmother, recovered as much as he could before the fire consumed the rest. The jaws on the back wall are just a few that survived."

Rebecca walked around the large light box to the massive great white shark jaws. Other sets of teeth surrounded it—each wide open and ready to bite.

"Over here, I mapped out the entire debris field of the Orca. Self-financed the side-scan sonar using an underwater drone back in 2014. I dove the wreck a hundred and sixty-seven times. I know everything about her. How she sits on the ocean floor. Which pieces drifted in what direction during the sinking. Even after I knew everything, I found myself drawn out there. Still underwater, it calls to me. It's hard to describe. I recovered everything possible. His captain logs. The throttle controls. The set of tiger shark jaws from the flying bridge."

Rebecca felt a presence when she stared up at the two well-rusted rifles mounted on the wall.

I've seen these before. His hands held these and used them. I only ever saw them in my dreams. The same shape. The color of the wood.

"Those are his two rifles. That one on the bottom was the one Martin used to kill the shark from the Orca before she sank."

"Orca?"

Matt Hooper smiled and turned to the table along the far wall. Under the sprawling collection of nautical charts, marked with location tabs and notes, Rebecca approached the table and its long slab of water-damaged wood. Scratched letters sat covered in a haze of dried green algae:

ORCA

"Your grandfather's boat. This place is all yours, Rebecca. His entire story mapped out, except for some key details. His recovered and restored logbooks. Detailed interviews with his first mate—transcribed and on video. The other survivors who were in the water with him during the sinking of the Indianapolis. I got it all back there on computers and hard copy… volumes of information."

Rebecca Quint looked around in disbelief. Hooper stepped closer and focused his voice towards her.

"It's an experience that changes the way you view life. This story, if told in its entirety—will hit you right between the eyes, and you will never ever forget that experience. You can't let it die."

"I'm just a girl from an island in Alaska. Everything is very simple there, including me."

"No, you are not. You are the next chapter of his life. This is your history."

PART I

1 SLEEP

For the most anemic of moments, Quint fell asleep. He felt so tired, he could taste it. His brain savored in the slumber denied to him for over one hundred hours. His mind shut down and contemplated pure darkness—a delicious slice of death.

Quint's unconscious reflexes continued to keep his body alive, and it drew in a breath. With a deep draw of his lungs, instead of precious air, he felt the cool water enter his mouth. The foreign feeling of water rushing past his throat fired neurons of instinctual survival from his brain, jolting Quint awake in a blast of adrenaline and fear. His head snapped back from the ocean, and he regurgitated the mixture of saltwater and fuel oil that had filled his mouth. A deep inhale of air let him know he was still alive. Quint gagged and struggled to purge that salty liquid death from his mouth while looking around. The nightmare had gotten much worse. In all directions, he was alone.

The gray twilight of dawn broke the blackness of night, and Quint found the horizon. How long had he slept before his face fell forward into the dreaded saltwater? It felt only ten seconds' worth, or maybe ten minutes—no way to be sure.

A thick layer of fuel oil stuck to his hair and covered the cracked skin of his face. The black petroleum got into his eyes when he jumped from the port side during the sinking five days ago and it's plagued him ever since. The oil in his eyes caused them to become bloodshot and swollen, irritated beyond belief. Every blink felt like someone threw sand under his eyelids and it ground away at the corneas. Adding saltwater only made the constant sting turn into severe burning. If he closed his eyes, he felt the scratchy grit. If they stayed open, the ocean breeze caused them to dry and burn. The pain was maddening. His body no longer had excess hydration and couldn't spare any tears to clean the eyes.

Quint placed his hands on his closed eyes and let out a scream of anguish but also despair. His mind admonished itself for becoming weak and falling asleep. He settled on holding his eyes in a grimaced red squint—neither open nor closed. This kept the pain tolerable.

He felt under the black oily water and found the loose strap on the side of his life jacket. Quint held it out of the water for a quick inspection—his knot was still fast. The other end had torn away. How long was he sleeping? How far did the ocean pull him from the group? Why did he let his guard down? These questions, of which he hadn't any answers, haunted him.

The soggy gray US Navy-issued kapok life jacket was waterlogged and only kept his chin above the water. Dr. Haynes told them the vests had a forty-eight-hour rating—long enough for a rescue. They already doubled that, and no rescue was in sight. He tried to scissor kick and lift himself higher in the water. The life jacket weighed him down and he couldn't see anything past a few yards of empty ocean.

The swells picked up again. Quint had to time it right. A wave picked him up, and he shifted in all four directions at the peak. In the dim gray light, he couldn't see anyone. Feeling the gravity of the eight-foot swell dropping him back down to sea level, Quint slapped the water in anger. His heart raced as panic crept in. They come for you first when you are alone—those demons from the deep.

Knowing that the ocean plays visual tricks while it picks you up, other swells can hide things that float in the troughs further away. The memory of his father, showing him this while fishing in rough seas off Nauset beach twenty years earlier, played through his mind. Quint kept trying. He didn't have the strength nor the time to panic.

By the third attempt at catching a peak wave, he saw them one hundred yards off to the east and called out to them. A small cluster of dark objects. Men in life jackets on the outer edge of a much larger group of random clusters of men, also in life jackets—only their heads cushioned between the sea-swollen gray collars showing above the water.

The faint grayish blue of the immediate horizon turned a slight hue of orange. It was almost that time. They strike again at dawn. He knew death was a certainty, unless he could get back to the group.

Quint began to swim.

He reached forward with all his strength—hand over hand, grabbing the water with cupped fingers and pulling himself ahead. His exhaustion turned his muscles into jelly and he had no strength, but the panic-induced adrenaline was a shot of life he did not expect. He kicked and thrashed his bare feet. His Navy-issued dungarees bit into the saltwater ulcers on the skin behind his knees. He ignored the pain, while the stinging in his eyes reminded him to keep his face out of the water.

Twenty-five yards from the group, he could see Jack Cassidy waving and calling to him. Quint looked up and saw Cassidy and Troy Boyd holding onto the piece of floater net for stabilization. They both waved for his attention and then started pointing to the north. Quint turned to his left and saw another head adrift, one hundred feet away. The ocean had a relentless habit of breaking the men from their tight groups and mixing them up during the nights.

Quint didn't want to join another group. Together, they were some excellent fighters, and they all wanted to live until now. They fought hard against the attack at sunset and kept each other alive. However, the conscious act of leaving a shipmate out here alone to die disgusted him and overruled any desire to get back.

The horizon line became a knife-edge of red with an orange glow. Dawn was coming.

Quint didn't hesitate. He lurched in the loner's direction. Was it another suicide? Someone who wanted to give up? If so, Quint prepared himself to curse this guy out for making him expel the extra energy in swimming further away from the meager safety of the group. He would leave him there if the person wanted it. Whoever it was, Quint thought, this guy sure had a good ass-kicking coming.

Quint's shoulders burned from atrophied muscles. The soft ocean-marinated skin under his arms broke and bled from the chafing against the heavy life jacket. Ten yards away, he saw the loner's face.

"Herbie. Herbie, wake up, dammit."

Quint spoke with exhausted breaths as he recognized his friend, Herbie Robinson, eyes closed and head tilted to the side, cradled by the cinched-up life jacket collar. A few more strokes to get within reaching distance.

Memories of them on port calls in San Francisco and Pearl Harbor, hitting the bars, Herbie wooing the ladies with stories of his baseball career playing for the Cleveland Indians, flooded Quint's mind. He only had three or four close friends aboard the ship, and he thought they all had died during the sinking.

Quint continued his struggle through the water and let out a hint of a smile. No matter what happens, at least he will have a friend to talk to while waiting to die.

Quint reached for the outstretched arms of his friend. Even though Herbie's face was covered in baked-on oil and his combed back jet-black hair rested in a dried mess, he looked so much at peace in his sleep.

"Herb, let's go now. We haven't got much time."

Quint grabbed at the sleeve of Herbie's light blue Navy work shirt. Herbie remained motionless. Except upon the tug of his sleeve, he rose higher in the water. Quint looked up at his friend, whose face hung a foot higher above the water than his own. At that moment, Quint's smile dropped—something was wrong. Herbie's arms slung lower now, as the soaked life jacket kept him chest-high out of the water and he bobbed up and down in a rhythmic motion with the sea.

Quint reached out and pushed his friend's shoulder.

"Herb, wake up."

With the push of his fingers, Quint flinched when his friend fell backward and upended. He saw a bloody mess of a stump that was Herbie Robinson's waistline rise from the dark water below. Ripped tendrils of shirt mixed with ghostly white streams of skin and fleshy hose-like intestines. The spinal column pulled to the side and jutted out of the upside-down corpse. Quint stared in horror. He stared at what they left of his friend. Those athletic legs with which his friend would use to generate all the power and torque upon pitching a baseball ninety miles per hour over home plate were now gone.

Quint thought of all the nights after they ran out of money and stumbled back to the ship with matching noble drunken strides. They would always get into some sort of athletic contest. Some nights, it was a sprint down the shadowy Navy pier to the quarterdeck finish line, which sometimes Quint would win. Or maybe an arm-wrestling match over a wooden crate of fifty-five caliber ammunition shells, which Quint would always win. Other times, a potato throwing contest with a target sixty feet away, which Herbie would always win—until they ran out of potatoes or one of the mess cooks started shouting at them. Herbie was an elite athlete, and Quint swore the guy would live forever. All those laughs and memories. He thought of them all in the few seconds it took for the paralyzing shock to wear off upon staring into the violent destruction of blood-drained muscle and flesh.

Quint reached down, felt for Herbie's arm, and re-righted his friend. Herbie's legless torso was eaten to a macabre balance, and no longer heavier at either end—its weight neutralized by what little buoyancy the failing life jacket offered. The corpse flipped with little effort. Herbie's face rose from the water, eyes still closed in a peaceful sleep.

The orange and red of the horizon now broke across the sky and highlighted the stray clouds overhead. Quint stared at the orange light on his friend's face as he reached into the life jacket, feeling for the metal chain that held the identification tags. Quint pulled the metal chain up over Herbie's head, even making sure the tags didn't disturb his face, as if it may wake him up from his slumber. In one motion, Quint placed the chain over his own head—the two metal identification tags clinked together as he stuffed them down the collar of his light blue Navy work shirt. Next, the laborious process of untying the straps that held Herbie's life jacket closed with cramped fingers.

Quint stared at Herbie while removing the life jacket. He slipped one arm at a time out of the vest. Quint's eyes watered and the stinging subsided for a moment—one last gift from the friend who sailed and fought alongside him over the past three years.

With the life jacket removed, Quint held Herbie's hand for a few seconds while they both rose and fell together with the ocean swells. He was tired of saying prayers for the dead and after the ship's chaplain, Father Conway, died from exhaustion the day before, Quint thought, what power does God have over their fate now? The traditional sailor's stubbornness inside would not allow him to let go. A funeral should have some words spoken. No matter how angry and begrudging he felt towards God, he would give his friend a burial at sea deserving of all who sailed. And if he should die on this day, Quint hoped someone else would do the same for him.

A whispered 'Our Father' prayer, then he released the inanimate cold and pruned soft hand in a gentle motion. Herbie's peaceful face fell forward, and his body stayed with Quint for a minute. It comforted Quint that his friend didn't want to leave him just yet. He watched the body get swallowed by the surface.

Quint reached into his tied life jacket and pulled out an empty liquor bottle made of clear glass. In the first night's scramble to collect anything that was floating nearby, he found an empty crate of straw and one half-full bottle of rum. With all his bad luck, he found some storekeeper's stash he couldn't even drink because the alcohol would speed up the dehydration. He emptied its contents into the ocean four nights ago but kept the bottle—it would now be his underwater eyes.

Quint unscrewed the cap and held the bottle by the neck, placed the glass body into the water, and peered into the finish. Through the undersea window, Quint watched his friend, once larger than life, now shrink away on a slow-motion descent. In an eternal minute, Herbie Robinson from Cleveland, a baseball player, boatswain's mate and friend, fell out of the ambient ocean light and disappeared into the darkness below.

2   OCEANIC WHITETIP

Five fathoms down, in the vast cerulean blue of the eternal waters stretching from the shadows of the Marianas, the oceanic whitetip shark studied its prey. Instincts, honed over one million years of hunting in bleak wastelands of prehistoric empty abyssal waters, have led it to this moment in history. The oceanic whitetip is the dominant predator here. Those shivering shapes at the surface are trespassing.

For over five millennia, the shark's direct ancestors learned to follow the large dark shapes of ancient explorer ships, Spanish galleons, merchant vessels, and ships of war. Its species tracked the massive shadows cutting across the surface for endless miles. They learned those shadows meant only one thing—food was coming.

In this domain of the open ocean, the oceanic whitetip knows it could swim for a week and never find prey. Within this vast blue nothingness of water, seven miles deep—life is scarce. When it finds a source of food, this shark takes the opportunity to its fullest. The dark hulls breaking the surface and blotting out the sunlight, always produced a source of sustenance. For a thousand generations, the oceanic learned to lock onto those slow-moving shadows and wait—wait for what could be the only opportunity to find food in weeks. They must keep moving. Precious energy must burn to push water over their gills and survive. A constant source of food needed.

The whitetips of yore learned to cruise and wait. It was only a matter of time. A few scraps of galley waste from the ship's cook tossed overboard and a juvenile whitetip can grow into a young adult by following the large moving host. It could feed off those bits of chicken bone and gristle mixed with rotting vegetables and spoiled gruel the ship's crew no longer had any use for. In the luckiest of moments, maybe a burial at sea. A gift delivered from the gargantuan dark escort above. Ever the present, a chance of an unfortunate sailor, whose iron grip didn't hold fast to the backstay of the upper topmast when his ship took a large wave broadside. An unfortunate soul sent on a death plunge into the depths and domain of the oceanic whitetip shark. Those moments are the payoff for days or weeks of waiting and stalking.

The instincts of a hunter's intellect and devious patience passed down through its lineage and encoded into the brain of this king of the requiem sharks. It became intelligent out of necessity. Nature created it for stalking and hunting.

Nature did not build the oceanic whitetip for combat like its cousins, the great white or tiger sharks. Those lumbering relatives, with their size and strength, can afford to attack at will. The large sharks overpower their prey while absorbing collateral damage from the thrashing and defending the victim has before succumbing to death. Hit first and think later. This is the creed of the larger sharks. But out here, in this part of the ocean, such tactics must change, for a shark to feed. Prey in this realm is faster, scarcer, and harder to surprise.

The elder oceanic whitetip shark circled its eleven-foot sleek body back around and watched the shapes above. Listening and learning—feeling their breathing. Electrical impulses from hundreds of rhythmic heartbeats, echoing through the water and striking across its lateral line of sensory nerves. The stalker felt their motion when they struggled to stay afloat. It heard their voices, and the splashing sounds they made. The shark couldn't just smell their fear, it tasted it.

The predator swayed its shovel-like nose back and forth, navigating itself just deep enough to stay out of sight from the groups of thrashing bodies that remained on the surface. Long and wide pectoral fins, each tipped with a dull white smear of opaqueness, caught a strong undercurrent. The ocean pulled the fish along the length of its food source.

It surveyed them with careful eyes. The shark glowed bronze, passing through orange beams of sunrise that penetrated deep through the clear saltwater. Cruising in a euphoric trance, its stomach digesting all it devoured after taking part in the latest wave of attacks on those dark figures above. Any other shark would have taken its fair share and moved on. Not the oceanic—it was here to stay until there would be no more.

The oceanic whitetip swam with the confidence of the deadliest shark in the world next to the great white. The great white developed its reputation as a killer of opportunity while the oceanic is a killer of necessity. Here is its home, and it will do whatever it takes to continue its dominance over this domain.

Most hunting sharks will travel to where the food is. They cruise from one food source to another, just passing through on their way to a coastal reef or seal inhabited shoreline. Maybe sampling whatever is found along travels to where life is more abundant. But not the oceanic whitetip. The oceanic is stubborn and will not leave to search for food. It stays, waits, then kills.

The unusual and alluring taste of human flesh plagues this animal. This taste; sampled over the last thousand years of finding cadavers from maritime burial ceremonies, shipwrecked sailors, or downed pilots adrift with their parachutes.

It will not leave—this fish of nautical nightmares.

The elder oceanic continued its prowl. A robust male of an ample size that sired countless pups in its lifetime of twenty-six years. The large shark seemed to swim at will and the other oceanic whitetips moved out of his way. It swam, knowing there are many of his species spread out under the tired and slowing victims collected above.

He was the first to pick up the deep drone of the four propellers pushing the USS Indianapolis through the water from the island of Tinian towards Leyte. In its lifetime, the oceanic learned the deeper the noise, the bigger the ship, the more chance for food. It tracked that noise from thirty-five miles away until it caught sight of the dark shadow the steel hull cast across the depths. The large familiar shape cruised ahead, blocking the intense equatorial sun rays. The whitetip took refuge within the six-hundred-foot shadow and swam with it. It kept a smart distance from the violent chop of the propellers, but close enough to observe anything dropped or left behind.

Before long, it was not alone. One turned to three, and then soon, six whitetips tracked the ship. Each keeping a respectful distance from the other. They moved in an eerie synchronized unison—communicating only by instinctual intuition. They knew their strength lies in numbers. No matter what drops into the water from this shadow, no matter how big and strong, it may survive and defend itself against one oceanic but not six.

By the time the midnight moon hung overhead on that Sunday night of July 29, 1945, they were a shiver of twenty-nine oceanic whitetip sharks. With the largest one, the first to track the ship, taking a position just aft of the prop wash, fifty feet below the surface.

It didn't swim very far when the two explosions of sound and light sent a violent shock wave of water from the front of the ship's keel, hitting the oceanic across its sensory organs. The shark, along with the others, dispersed and created distance from the sounds of violence above. But it did not go very far. The last five years have taught it; loud sounds above only meant food will come soon. For this shark, the two sounds of the Japanese torpedoes slamming into the steel hull were the ringing of the dinner bell, and it stayed close.

The oceanic went deep and watched. A foul taste and smell of fuel oil covered the surface and churned with the Pacific Ocean waters as the hulking ship limped forward and rolled onto its starboard side. The massive hull made terrible screeching noises of tearing metal and breaking rivets. The ship suffered, becoming a dying great sperm whale of steel in the throes of death—knowing it took a mortal injury from the whaler's harpoon but still fighting to stay alive. In twelve minutes, the gray iron-clad giant made its last sounds of life, rolled on its side, then pointed down to the deepest parts of the ocean and sank.

The oceanic watched as the great shadow now became part of its world. Moonlight and the fire-burning oil slick across the surface illuminated the large stern when it fell below the surface. The shark turned at the long amplified prehistoric sound of the ship's death, heard six-hundred feet below. The iron-plated hull, crumpling and giving way to the immense pressure of the sea, bellowed a deep percussive roar. Distant rumbling sounds of implosions reverberated through the water. Air pockets and trapped sailors' last breaths escaped the crushing hull in a barrage of bubbles which found their way to the surface along with debris and pieces of ship, ripped from the superstructure on its way down. The last of the gray giant fell out of the moonlit blue and disappeared—swallowed by the black waters of the abyss.

That's when it hit the oceanic whitetip.

The shark lived a long life and never experienced a rush of sensory overload like this before. Within the twelve minutes it took for the USS Indianapolis to sink, especially those final few minutes, bodies hit the water by the hundreds. The shark shook its head and swayed in erratic, quick movements. Its mouth hung open and swallowed large gulps of the delicious, sweet seawater to taste what made it so drunk—human blood. Eyes once closed in knife-like slits surrounded by yellow, dilated wide within the moonlit water.

It heard their screams of pain and felt their panicked thrashing when the survivors of the sinking ship of war entered the sea. It watched their silhouetted motions against the thick fuel oil-covered surface. The struggling bodies were aglow with the bright blue phosphorescent light from the plankton, churned up in the tremendous disturbance of bio-luminescent life. The more the bodies kicked, the brighter they glowed.

The shark's first bite—a motionless body, already dead. Killed by a secondary explosion of one of the ship's boilers, the sailor never saw it coming. Volatile fuel lines, ignited by the raging fire on board, caused a detonation that ripped through the steel deck plating. The concussion of the shock wave broke the sailor's neck on impact. His ribs reduced to fragmented shards of bone when his body went overboard in a blast of fire and black carbon. The ship was now gone, but the motionless body drifted on the surface. It sank.

Twenty feet below, after circling and observing the listless corpse, the first whitetip savored in the dark red cloud of a blood trail and fed. With triangular, serrated-edged teeth, the shark seized the back of the thigh and convulsed its head until a mouthful of flesh and muscle tore away. The other whitetips closed in with long, rounded pectoral fins dropped. Their backs hunched, swimming in erratic strokes, and minds no longer thinking nor analyzing—they became a feeding frenzy. The zombie predators converged and ripped the body to pieces.

And so, it began—one hundred hours of feeding-frenzied ecstasy for the sharks and a living nightmare of aquatic hell for the survivors. The sharks watched the ocean separate the groups of men. The surface swells and powerful undercurrents proved too much for some, and tight-knit clusters of defenses broke apart. Injured and weakened, when a sailor pulled away—the sharks were waiting.

Those on the surface fought the sharks and the ocean, doing everything they could to stay together. The tragedy dispersed the survivors over the one mile of water where their ship met its doom. This distance between the groups of survivors spread to fifty miles over the next four days. The Pacific winds took the lucky few who found life rafts, or something to float on during the sinking, in a southwesterly direction. The ocean currents pulled those floating in the water due south.

Eleven hundred souls went into the water. Whoever survived the sinking now found themselves at the mercy of the ocean and those who lived there. A shark could reach its fill on the survivors and cadavers at one end of the flotilla, swim to the other end, and be hungry for more. Regardless of what sounds and sights attracted the oceanic whitetip over the fifty miles of human debris and detritus, it always returned to its primary source of victims—the largest group of six-hundred and fifty men. They struggled to hold on and did battle to stay alive.

The oceanic whitetip numbers grew. Sweet smell of human blood calling in more of their kind. Aside from the occasional tiger shark, doing as it pleased because of its size, the oceanic whitetips drove away all the other requiem sharks. Blue sharks, silky sharks, and a few blacktips found themselves attacked if they dared to trespass into the area. This was their table, and the oceanic whitetips would not leave until they depleted the food supply.

The struggling bodies of the survivors on the surface made formidable opponents. The large oceanic whitetip only needed two encounters to learn and change tactics. On its first move to pull a potential victim, the fish took a kick to the head. Knocked back and thrashing its tail, the shark raced to create distance and regain its senses. The next encounter, one of those shapes reached down and stabbed it near the large dorsal fin. It felt the sting of the knife, and once again, retreated to a safe distance—waiting for the right time.

Their numbers grew to a thousand. A layer of sharks in perfect synchronization underneath this largest group of survivors. The sharks attacked together in unison every twelve hours—dusk and dawn. When the dim light lulled their prey into a defenseless trance. In the time between the coordinated attacks on the huddled masses of shivering and kicking sailors on the surface, the whitetips continued their patrols. They scavenged and consumed the many pieces of fed-on corpses that scattered their ocean. They turned the sea into an aquatic morgue of horrors. A living nightmare for those survivors above, while a paradise for the circling sharks below.

No matter how many pieces of flesh they discovered drifting in the oily mix of bloody Philippine Sea, no matter how full their stomachs, the sharks could not ignore it. The instinctual attraction to the noise and panic made by the living remained and grew by the day.

Thursday morning. The second day of August in the year of our Lord, 1945. The large oceanic whitetip, along with one thousand of its species, circled five fathoms below the surface and waited for the light to tell it the time was right. This fifth day of murder and feeding on the survivors of the USS Indianapolis.

3   FLOATER NET

They started out with six-hundred fifty men on the night the torpedoes hit. Their group was the largest and carried the unfortunate weight of being the last to leave the Indianapolis after the captain's abandon ship order reached them. Communication lines failed in the explosions, causing many to think they could still save the ship. The ship's speakers remained silent, so they stayed. It wasn't until the final few minutes, when the words 'abandon ship' found them at the stern.

With the Indianapolis dying at a full ninety-degree list to starboard, these men fell, slid, or walked, down the port side of the ship's hull with whatever they had on and leapt into the black sheen of oil on the Philippine Sea. Others who left from starboard, hearing the order to jump several minutes earlier, found life rafts, survival materials, floater nets and extra life preservers. They were the lucky ones.

During the sinking, the ship continued to plow ahead through the water, depositing survivors over a one-mile-long strip of Pacific Ocean. The port side sailors went overboard together in the last minute. Some with life jackets and some without. Some wore clothes while others, woke by the rush of fire and flood consuming their berthing compartments, only wore a pair of shorts and a t-shirt.

They entered the water on Sunday night as six-hundred-fifty powerful spirits—optimistic of a rescue ship steaming just over the horizon. Word spread fast throughout the group to stay together and maybe get spotted from the air. By Thursday morning, they were now only two-hundred depleted souls waiting to die. Some still had hope. While others decided it was over. The horrors of the sharks taking their shipmates one at a time proved too much to bear.

The outstretched arms of the other men grabbed hold of Quint and pulled him closer. His lungs ached and his throat, already swelled up with extreme thirst, now agape and gulping air from the swim back to his group. Quint reached up and held on to the eight-foot-long piece of floater net that served as their anchor—their home.

The floater net, a series of black-painted cork cylinders threaded together with rope and tied in a grid of squares, rested on the water's surface. Not a full-sized net—only a small corner section of one. They salvaged it from the debris that surfaced with the giant bubbles of air from the ship's last breaths. The rest of the net, tangled and torn between a starboard anti-aircraft gun and the severed railing of the navigation bridge, hung up in the darkness four miles below.

"I thought you were gone for good, Quint," said Jack.

"So did I."

Quint coughed the salty oil from his mouth before taking another draw of air and wincing at the burning pain in his shoulders.

"Who was that out there?" asked Boyd, holding onto Quint's life jacket to keep him close as a swell picked them all up.

Quint pulled the extra life jacket up from the water.

"It was Herbie Robinson. The BM1."

Quint paused after verbalizing the death of his friend while looking at Herbie's stenciled initials on the inside collar of the life preserver.

"We gotta get this on him."

Quint gestured up to Seaman 2nd Class Harold Shearer, who laid out across the floater net.

Harold Shearer laid on his back, still and unconscious, wearing only a torn white undershirt and dungarees. His arms suffered extreme burns while he ran down the passageway next to Boiler Room number two when it exploded. The blast threw him against the bulkhead and the burning fuel oil soaked his shirt while catching fire. Harold climbed the next two ladders to the main deck after he shed his shirt and jumped. He relished in the immediate relief of the cool water on the burning skin of his arms when he took the plunge off the slimy wet steel hull, but he never found a life jacket. Two other seamen, Jack Cassidy and Chester Eastman, both dressed in life preservers, grabbed Harold as he lay in the water, struggling to stay afloat. After a few minutes of exhaustion, the piece of floater net rose next to them as if the sea gave them a gift. They hoisted a screaming Harold onto the small collection of cork cylinders to keep him from drowning.

Harold laid on his back in the same position ever since. The long net kept Harold from the sea, while a victim of the sun. His hair and eyebrows singed off from the fire and now sporting a face of dried black oil and burns from days of severe sun exposure. His arms, firing the brain with a constant pain, held out straight up in the air from the elbows. The burned skin of his forearms melted and sagged away from the muscle below. The relentless sun had baked the burns into a crispy brown and black.

Quint, trying to blink and clear his stinging eyes, squinted as he focused on Harold's arms. The way Harold held them out reminded Quint of Bela Lugosi, hamming it up as the monster in *Frankenstein Meets the Wolf Man*. The movie he saw on port call at Pearl Harbor two years earlier. Herbie convinced him to take the two girls they met at the bar to the cinema. They all left that night laughing with arms locked and held out, doing their best Frankenstein imitation. Now, here was poor Harold doing the same imitation. Quint wanted to laugh at the insanity of it all. Part of him still didn't believe all of this was real.

The sun continued its creep over the horizon. The sailors shivered off the dawn breeze and welcomed the heat from the orange light touching their faces.

Chester, holding on to the floater net down by Harold's left leg, looked at the extra life jacket floating in front of Quint.

"I liked Herbie. I worked in his deck department. He always looked the other way when I was late for muster."

Howard Hodge chimed in from the other side of Harold.

"Mr. Dowdy is gone, Quint."

Hodge was a radioman second class and felt useless in the water. Never a strong swimmer and growing up in a St. Louis suburb, he earlier realized his nautical survival skills were next to nothing. However, he felt strong when following a chain of command and wanted to keep it going in their little group. Hodge recognized somebody should play the role and contribute to some sort of order.

"You are the senior guy now," Hodge said to Quint.

Hodge referred to Chief Warrant Officer Lowell Dowdy. The lone officer of the small group. Upon finding his place at the end of the floater net during the first night, he welcomed anyone that wanted to join. The last few mornings, Mr. Dowdy conducted a roll call of the group to make sure they stayed together.

By Wednesday night, they accounted for twelve men in his little flotilla. The group: three deck crewmen—Seamen Jack Cassidy, Chester Eastman, in the water and holding on, with Harold Shearer, burned and laying on the net. The two gunner's mates, Quint and Troy Boyd, holding on by the left side of Harold's body. Water Tender 2nd Class Clarence Machado shouldered up to the floating cork cylinders under Harold's head. On the other side of Harold, Hodge held on tight with both hands next to two third-class petty officers. Radarman 3rd Class Earl Wallace, held onto the tattered mess of rope lines and floaters next to Harold's right arm. Tied off to Earl's water sodden vest, Machinist's Mate 3rd Class Leonard Fritz, who faced the open ocean and nodded off from the sleep deprivation. Down by Harold's right leg were two US Marines. Private 1st Class Raymond Rich and PFC Frank Spino, watched the commotion and kept to themselves.

The space by Harold's feet that Mr. Dowdy had occupied the night before now drifted empty.

Quint gathered his strength and kicked to get higher in the water, seeing for himself over the body of Harold. The space at Harold's feet between Eastman and Rich was indeed empty. Quint didn't have to say anything. He already knew what happened—the same that happened to him. The ocean never sleeps and is always working to pull them apart. The old man never woke up. Quint burned with the thought of him adrift a half mile away.

Quint shot an angry glance over towards Hodge.

"Did anyone try looking for him?"

"Yeah, of course. At first light, we saw you both were gone, so we all looked around as best we could."

Quint scanned the dark water horizon of swells with random deceiving white caps breaking against the sunrise. Even if he saw a sign of Mr. Dowdy floating out there alone, he lacked the strength inside him for a rescue. He respected the Chief Warrant Officer—a Chief Electrician's Mate before he went to the officer's side of things. The captain insisted on having one of these thankless jobs on board, so somebody had to step up. Onboard, Mr. Dowdy dealt with the labeling of 'traitor' by the lower ranks for leaving the enlisted side, and the dismissal of being 'inconsequential' by inexperienced upper ranks. However, he knew the position played a vital role in the crew's cohesion and the order of things. A warrant officer is the political bridge between the enlisted and officer ranks. He volunteered for the job and performed it well.

All those Navy games finished once they hit the water. The ocean became the great equalizer. In the water, only their heads showed above the surface. Tall men became even with short men. Officers faced eye-to-eye with enlisted. To avoid panic and insanity, the survivors needed structure—an order forged out of the chaos. To keep an order of things meant stability. Even without a ship underneath them, the survivors found it natural and calming to recognize naval traditions and rank. To the men of the small floater net, having their own warrant officer served them by keeping the sanity. They felt lucky to have Mr. Dowdy, yet never acknowledged it.

Positive and steady, even though his health waned, and his forty-two years of smoking caught up to him by Wednesday, he calmed them. 'That's the one. They are radioing for help now,' became a repeated mantra by Mr. Dowdy with every blinking light of a plane that passed in the night sky overhead. The optimism is why the men enjoyed having him around.

Quint gritted his teeth and slapped at the water. Mr. Dowdy was gone.

"You take the lead. I don't want it." Quint said to Hodge.

"Can't do that, Petty Officer Quint. You are the only first class here. I'm still second class."

"Like any of that matters now. We all taste the same to the sharks."

From the other side of Harold's laying body, Hodge looked towards Quint. "Maybe so, but it's what Mr. Dowdy would've wanted. To go on being proper in the order of things."

Quint understood what Hodge meant. He was now the highest ranked and longest serving member of the group. Quint found himself in charge. At twenty-eight years old, Quint became the 'Old Man' of the group. The younger guys would respect that for what it's worth.

4 FRITZ

Seaman 2nd Class Harold Shearer screamed in agonizing pain as the two Marines, Rich and Spino, did all they could to hold his right leg down. Eastman pleaded as he held the left leg from kicking him in the face.

"Just put your arm in right quick, Shearer. You gotta."

Quint and Cassidy fought to get Harold into the extra life preserver, starting with the left arm as Hodge held down Harold's right shoulder. All the men were beyond the point of exhaustion—voices hoarse and shaking. Just reaching from the water took all their effort and concentration. Emotions broke into frustration and anger.

Quint squeezed Harold's left hand and pulled his arm towards the soggy life jacket, while trying to be careful with the charred remains of forearm and exposed muscle.

"Quit your hollering and just put this on, dammit."

The dried burns cracked open at the slightest movement, and Harold screamed as if he was being murdered.

"Don't kill me! Don't kill me! I can make it! I promise I can make it! Don't put me in the water!"

Harold cried out in terror at the hands holding him down. His eyes were empty. His mind was irrational and on the edge of unconsciousness.

Harold lurched, and it took all their strength to keep him from falling off the floater net. Quint lost his last remnant of patience.

"We're not trying to kill you, you damn sonova—"

In the struggle of wet, salt-corroded fingers, Harold's left hand slipped. His arm lurched forward, and a hanging piece of melted skin caught on the seam of the life vest and pulled away from his forearm down to the elbow. The nerve endings caught the cool morning air and sent a shock of terror into his brain. Harold let out a bloodcurdling scream of agony and then passed out into silence. His arms held up in the air by atrophied tendons and indescribable pain.

Quint and Cassidy fell back in a splash of failure. Their life jacket collars kept their chins just above the waterline as their bodies hung limp. Quint slapped the water and cursed. His first order as leader, to get the life jacket on Harold, ended in a resounding defeat.

A voice called out from another group of survivors ten yards away.

"Hey, leave him alone over there. What are you trying to do?"

One of the two Marines was quick to respond.

"Mind your own business. We are trying to help him."

Frustrated and weary, Quint rolled the life jacket under the water in front of him and tied it closed with the strapping. He lifted Harold's head and placed the rolled soaking gray bundle underneath as a pillow. This kept Harold's head out of the sloshing water from the spaces between the cork floaters. With the extra strap, Quint weaved it around Harold's neck and knotted it with a running bowline.

The remaining two-hundred survivors all floated together in a one-hundred-yard radius just north of Quint's group and their tattered piece of floater net.

They all fought the sharks and the sea to stay together. The survivors held together in close groups and worked to keep a ring formation for safety, with the injured, weakest, and most vulnerable at the center. The sharks struck the outside of the ring first. Those on the outside had to fight the hardest to stay clustered together in tight formations.

In the previous days, Mr. Dowdy urged his small floater net group to keep close to the main floater net drifting on the inside of the vast crowd of survivors. The full-sized floater net was the same as theirs, only larger and could hold more weight—rope and painted cork floaters woven together in a square that measured ten feet on all sides. This net held sixty sailors, on top or holding on around the edges, and many without life jackets or survival gear. The ones on top were the injured, clinging to life. This main floater net served as the only landmark in the open sea by which everyone in the water could keep their bearings. And right now, it drifted a distance away from them. Without Mr. Dowdy's instructions throughout the night, their little group drifted outside the large ring of survivors by twenty yards.

Quint lifted his chin from the waterline and saw the tangerine light of the morning sunrise paint the sky. The silhouetted group of men huddled together on the large floater net became an island of human despair rising above the distant waterline. An ocean swell picked them up, and Quint saw the other lone survivors drifting in the surrounding water. The men spread out even more. Everyone lost their hope and fight to survive. The last four days reduced the men to hollow shells of humanity, too weak to hold together. Across the survivors, doubts and a sense of dread emerged. They thought about their shipmates, who had already disappeared. The ship pulled the lucky ones down to the depths—their suffering minimal.

"Fritz is dead."

Quint looked up. On the other side of Harold's unconscious body, Earl reached back and held the head of Leonard Fritz—the young machinist's mate who only transferred to the Indianapolis two weeks ago. His seabag still unpacked, and the captain's orders to set sail from Mare Island shipyard in California on a last-minute secret mission announced across the ship's speakers.

Four nights ago, Fritz considered himself lucky. While trying to keep engine room number one from going under, the rush of ocean overwhelmed his damage control team. They rode the rising water up past the injection ports and exhaust manifolds of the massive two-story diesel engines. The water brought them to the top hatch of the engine room. They all escaped to the main deck to abandon ship while the others, caught inside the bilge, drowned in a mess of salt water and leaking engine oil.

Over the next few days, Fritz's throat had swelled from unrelenting thirst. Falling face first from the port side, Fritz met the darkness below with a face full of fuel oil and salt water. The oil he swallowed that first night and the constant vomiting of black stomach bile dehydrated him more than the others. He wanted to drink the salt water but saw what happened to the men who did. They all watched those who drank from the poison sea lose their minds and die in the first two days. No two went the same. Some became maniacs and tried to kill their friends in delusional, frenzied attacks while others turned into zombies of the undead and drifted in silence—their brain cells ruptured from the overload of salt. The sharks took them first. Vomiting brown ooze from their nostrils, these victims of the saltwater nourishment swam out on their own and the sharks took them, sometimes without a hint of retaliation or scream of objection.

Fritz didn't want to die that way, and never partook in the deathly temptation of one little sip. Before last night's sunset, his neck, bulging with infection and sores, swelled to a diameter larger than his head. It scared the others to look at him. His tongue, too swollen to stay in his mouth, caused the few words he tried to communicate to become sounds of painful pleas for mercy.

Earl tied off Fritz's life jacket to his own to keep him from floating away. With the light of the sun, Earl could see Fritz wasn't just sleeping.

"Fritz is dead, fellas," Earl said. "I thought he was sleeping."

Quint's strength had left him, rendering the swim to the net's other side impossible. He saw the confirmation in Hodge's eyes and gave a nod. Hodge reached out and untied the life jacket.

"What are we going to do with him?" asked Earl.

"The same that Doc does with everyone else, collect his tags and send him off," replied Quint.

"With a prayer," said Hodge while looking back towards Quint.

Quint turned back to the horizon.

"Yeah, with a prayer."

The ocean grew quiet, and the men watched Hodge take the identification tags off Fritz. The silver chain slipped over the swollen neck that nobody wanted to look at. Some in the group saw themselves suffering the same fate and turned away. Hodge handed the chain of shiny metal tags over Harold's unconscious body and Quint collected them. He could hear them clink against Herbie Robinson's tags when he dropped them in his shirt pocket and fastened the button.

Earl slipped the life jacket off and placed it under his own arms for extra buoyancy. Hodge took a small piece of metal out of his mouth. He drew the sign of the cross on Fritz's forehead, then put it back into his mouth.

Clarence was watching.

"You got something to eat there?"

"No, this is just a Saint Anthony medal. My mother gave it to me when I left for boot camp. Never thought I would use it like this. Helps me not want to drink, keeps the pain away."

Hodge, no matter how much death they experienced, was still uncomfortable around the dead. He hesitated and looked back at the guys watching him.

"I saw Father Conway do it like this with those burned up guys on the first night."

Hodge put his hand on Fritz's forehead and held his body while whispering some prayers under his breath in a quiet tone.

Quint stared at the sky, and the splash of orange light broke into streaks of blue. He saw countless sunrises at sea over his life. He remembered the first fishing advice from his father to him at five years old, when the old man was shaking him awake to get his boots on. *C'mon, boy. The big fish bite at first light.*

Quint smiled at the thought of his father. He was with him for every sunrise thereafter, out at sea. Then the guilt washed over him like the warm light of the sun on his face when he remembered hiding from his father as a sixteen-year-old teenager that dreadful morning. The night before, they got into an argument and heated words passed. Quint remembers sneaking out and hiding around back, next to the seawall, waiting for first light. He laid low behind the eel grass and slept there. That morning, he watched the lights flicker on inside the house and heard his father calling and looking for him. The victorious feeling when the old 1930 Ford Model A pickup truck rumbled away. He heard the distant creak of those old salt-air corroded leaf springs when the truck's lights disappeared around the bend. The teenager hoped the old man felt guilty and needed to work harder to land the catch.

He never saw his father alive after that morning.

Twelve years later, floating near death, under a tangerine sky. This sunrise mirrored the morning they found the old man. Quint closed his eyes and looked away from the light. He remembered the all-night search for the boat, the Coast Guard patrol, and the community beach lookouts. He watched Hodge let the body of Leonard Fritz go and thought of the body of his father. They found him laying across the transom with one hand still on a boat hook buried in the remains of the dead giant marlin. The largest marlin any of them had ever seen.

The old man tried to land the giant fish before the sharks could close in. The strain broke him, and the heart gave out. Quint remembered staring at the torn remains of the giant marlin—caught by the hands of his father and eaten by the sharks. That's when he first learned to hate them.

The hate hid the guilt. He failed to help his father bring that giant marlin over the gunwale and into the well. Together, they would've landed a catch that size with ease. They did it a hundred times. It was the sharks that made his father rush to haul it on board all on his own. The old man could have secured the great fish to the stern cleats and towed the massive catch back to town, but the sharks wouldn't allow it. The other fishermen jumped over, tending to the old man's body. Young Quint stood in silence, looking down into the cloudy, lifeless eye of the giant marlin, staring back at him. That eye and remnants of torn bony vertebrae were the only souvenirs left. The sea took his father. Naturally, the sea should now take him to a watery grave. Quint closed his stinging eyes and wished for it.

The men watched the body of Fritz float away from them on the surface. Each resigned that this would be their fate—a lifeless body floating, rocked to a steady motion by surface currents. This may be their last sunrise. If they had any water left in their bodies, tears would have touched the eyes of some.

5 FAREWELL

Fritz had yet to leave their view and continued to stay with the group, as many bodies did. In the distance, they heard singing voices.

"I knew they wouldn't disappoint me," Jack Cassidy said with a smile. "Doctor Haynes is a true sailor. Keeps everything the same... got them boys singing at sunrise again."

Jack pulled out the homemade knife he fashioned from the handle of a floating oil can he found on the second day. He had wrapped a torn piece of shirt around the handle and tied it tight for a grip. He looked over at the gunner's mate next to him. Boyd nodded to him and held up his US Navy-issued shark fighting knife. He won the weapon off a pilot over a hand of poker during their brief stay on Tinian Island the week before. The officer was out of cash, and Boyd agreed to the bowie knife as a bet. He won it with a dead man's hand, aces and eights, and the spectators all sat back and laughed when Boyd insisted, he would not be a dead man with that thing holstered to his belt.

Boyd spoke while holding the knife part way out of the water and staring into the sunrise glow on the six-inch blade. "That sounds like the Navy Hymn."

He checked the knots that tied an eight-foot length of survival line from the handle to his wrist. He wound the excess line around the handle and tried to look down through the black oil slick on top of the water. Whatever happens, he didn't want to lose his trophy, and he gripped it tight. He decided to go find that officer and buy him a drink when they get back.

Hodge shifted the Saint Anthony medal in his mouth from one side to the other and glanced over to Quint.

"Well, Mr. Dowdy isn't here, so one of us has to start it. Who's it going to be?"

Quint shook his head.

"Does it matter?"

"It did to him," said Hodge.

Jack chimed in, "I'll take the helm, Captain."

Jack annoyed Quint for being positive. However, his voice was weak, and his eyes were just as infected and red as Quint's from the oil seeping from his hair. Quint appreciated the tradition and respected the sailor. Jack looked back at Fritz, who was still floating face-up five yards away, then sang in a weak voice.

JACK
We will rant and we'll roar like true US sailors
We'll rant and we'll roar all on the salt seas
Until we strike soundings in the channel of old Plymouth
From Ushant to Portland in thirty-five leagues

Jack turned in the water to face the horizon and glanced over his shoulder to Boyd, who also turned from Harold's floater net to face south. They looked down at the sunlit-sky colors reflecting off the blackened water's surface.

BOYD
We hove our ship to with the wind from sou'west, boys
We hove our ship to, deep soundings to take;
'Twas forty-five fathoms, with a white sandy bottom
So we squared our main yard, and up channel did make

All the men shifted in the water, holding on to the floater net with one hand. The group drifted into a thick patch of fuel oil that extended a few feet below the surface. They each pulled their legs up high into the black oil and tried to hold them from dangling down into the blue vastness below.

Quint stayed silent and reached into his life jacket to pull out the empty glass bottle. He looked across the surface of the water, which flattened out. They were now on the outside edge of the group of survivors without the strength to push themselves back inside. Quint parted the oily blackness to find a space of blue water and unscrewed the cap off the bottle. The glass body dipped halfway in. He peered through the bottle into the deep. Quint saw his bare feet dangling against the blue backdrop—a stretch of eternity underneath him lit with the rising sun. He smelled the oil and salt when he pushed the bottle further into the sea to get a better look but kept his face just far enough from the water. There was nothing.

The two Marines held on in silence at the far end of Harold's floater net while the Navy guys joined in…

SAILORS

We will rant and we'll roar like true US sailors
We'll rant and we'll roar all on the salt seas
Until we strike soundings in the channel of old Plymouth
From Ushant to Portland in thirty-five leagues

EASTMAN

Now let ev'ry man drink off his full bumper
And let ev'ry man drink off his full glass;
We'll drink and be jolly and drown melancholy
And here's to the health of each true-hearted lass

Hodge looked to the sky and prayed but couldn't keep his eyes from coming back to the drifting body of Fritz. He wondered if he said the right prayers, and if they were good enough to bury someone at sea. Thoughts pierced his mind of Fritz's wife back home, who wouldn't have a body of her husband to grieve over and say goodbye. He thought of his own wife crying at the news of him lost at sea forever. Hodge pulled his legs up even higher and tighter to his chest. He prayed.

The other weak, shivering voices carried on…

THE BOOK OF QUINT

SAILORS
We will rant and we'll roar like true US sailors
We'll rant and we'll roar all on the salt seas
Until we strike soundings in the channel of old Plymouth
From Ushant to Portland in thirty-five leagues

There was a pause in the cadence and the others glanced over at Quint, who had his head down, looking through his sight glass into the water.

"Quint, it's your line. C'mon, you gotta say it. Don't jinx us now."

Quint ignored Eastman for a moment, then looked up at the waterline. He saw the body of Fritz and thought of Mr. Dowdy, their leader, who was always good to him. He thought of his friend, Herbie.

QUINT
Farewell and adieu to you, fair Spanish ladies
Farewell and adieu to you, ladies of Spain
For we've received orders for to sail back to Boston
And so nevermore shall we see you again

Quint finished his verse and looked over at the men. The others started their chorus. Quint looked back and held his breath—Fritz was gone. The men didn't notice, and they sang louder.

SAILORS
We will rant and we'll roar like true US Sailors
We'll rant and we'll roar all on the salt seas
Until we strike—

Clarence Machado screamed out and hit the water with his fist when the first shark bumped him. The water churned. The oceanic whitetip attacked from below with lighting fast precision. Its jaws clamped down on the front of his life jacket and pulled. Machado screamed and pounded at the fish as he dropped below the water, his fist still clenched on the floater net. Quint grabbed hold of the floater net with both hands and reared his legs back. He kicked the fish with all the strength he could find. The ten-foot oceanic let go of Machado and retreated as fast as it had appeared. The shark thrashed its tail on the surface, which kicked a wave of water into Quint's eyes. Quint shouted out in pain as the sandpaper feeling on the inside of his eyelids flared back up and scratched across the corneas of his eyes. He used the back of his hand that held the bottle to rub them clear.

In the distance, they heard another scream. And then another. The men looked over towards the edge of the large group of survivors. At random, sailors started disappearing from the surface. They started shouting and pounding at the shapes circling below them. The sixty weakened and defeated men huddled on top of the large floater net tightened their grips and shrank away from the edges in fear. Their struggling caused the already-taxed floater net to sink a few inches in the water and the sharks hit inside the circle of safety—probing for a way in. Some in the water attempted to climb on top of the space at the edges of the floater net, but their weakened arms could not pull themselves up. Other survivors kicked at them and shouted that any more weight would scuttle the entire group.

Quint peered through the bottle and tracked the now visible collection of sharks beneath them.

"They are everywhere! Most we've seen yet!"

The sharks moved in erratic, strategic motions, changing directions and darting back and forth. Quint watched them looking above for targets to attack.

"Damn white-tipped bastards... all of them."

"What about Oscar?" Jack looked over at Quint. "I'm gonna get him this time, I promise you all that!"

Jack clenched his homemade knife even harder, his left hand brushing the water to part the sheen of oil so he could peer down through.

Boyd reversed his grip on the knife in his hand and held the blade, pointing downward, ready to strike at anything that might rise from below. He looked over at Quint, who was the eyes of the group watching through the glass bottle, and then turned back towards Jack.

"Not if I don't get him first."

Boyd breathed out with an exhausted smile.

Quint reported back. "No, I don't see him... just the whitetips."

Hodge looked over at Machado, who was still in shock from the initial attack.

"Macho, you okay? How bad were you hit?" Hodge pulled himself along the edge of the floater net to get closer to Machado.

Hands shaking and still in shock, Machado didn't answer. He stared down at the tattered remains to the front of his life jacket.

In the distance, random screams of terror cried out. Quint's group looked over to see the thrashing and splashing red ocean as the sharks claimed another victim in one of the other small groups.

The sharks continued to grab the legs of the men and drag them deep. Those who became separated from their groups, or not looking down and kicking at anything they saw, found themselves pulled under. Their heads disappeared from the surface one at a time. With a feeble rescue attempt by the other sailors around them, an empty torn life jacket surfaced with bubbles from below. Lives taken and never seen again.

Each man handled witnessing and surviving the attacks differently, but they all ended with the same conclusion. Cries of despair, terror and helplessness would give way to anger then pure hatred. The patch of fuel oil that drifted with them since the sinking had served as their cover of protection from the terror below. The sharks didn't come into the black water and if they kept their legs high into the three-foot thick layer of oil, they could be invisible. But now, the oil broke apart—the sheen was thinning out, and the sailors drifted more exposed than ever before. The sharks grew bolder and attacked with an added ferocity.

Quint saw the familiar dark shape in a slow ascent out of the blue towards them.

"Here he comes, boys. He's back."

Thirty feet below them, it rose. Parting the endless layer of oceanic whitetip sharks of various sizes, a thirteen-foot-long tiger shark swam. The massive girth and dark spotted stripes of its body glistened in the rays of sunlight that punched through the dispersing oil and highlighted the predator against the blue ocean.

Jack could only speak by yelling—his heart rate increased in a steady panic. "Well, I'm not waiting to die Quint, let me know when that damn fish is close enough and I'll go down there!"

Hodge slapped at the water in front of him.

"You'll stay right where you are, sailor. You are no good on your own. If we stay together, we can survive this!"

42

Jack ignored Hodge and undid the front ties to his life jacket. While looking down at the water, he whispered to the sea.

"C'mon on in, Oscar, I got somethin' for you right here."

Watching the giant tiger shark circle below them, getting closer and closer with each pass, Quint saw the handle of his knife still sticking out of its side. That was back on the second day, right before sunset. Quint was always good at knifing fish as a boy and now in the water he fought them hard. He counted six other sharks he believed met their demise at his hand. The massive tiger took his best shot and ripped away from him, taking Quint's knife and leaving him defenseless. He wished he had that knife back.

"Ten feet! Jack wait for—"

With the tug on the last tie, the life jacket opened, and Jack Cassidy dropped below the surface before those closest to him, Eastman and Boyd, could reach out and grab him.

Jack's veins swelled with a dump of adrenaline when he saw the dark mass below him. His eyes stung in a salty blur, but the clarity of the water under the oil enabled him to see the tiger shark. He kicked his feet and dropped onto the back of the fish. With both hands, he plunged his homemade knife into the hulking breadth of the head. The knife buried two inches deep, and the shark reared back, swinging its powerful body to the side. A snap of the blade and the knife ripped away from Jack's hand. The shark's tail hit him on the side, turning him over.

The tiger thrashed and kicked its tail, disappearing in a cloud of bubbles and blue.

Jack erupted through the surface of the water, gasping for air. His eyes raged with the sting of the salt and all-too-familiar oil running down from the once-dried patches of black on his forehead and scalp. He didn't care about the pain as he lurched for his group of survivors. Quint let go of the net to reach for him just as Jack's flailing arms gave out and he sank. Boyd tossed Jack's life jacket to them as Quint, holding onto the weakened sailor's shirt collar, pulled the water with his free hand to crawl them back to the safety of the net.

"That took some... ah, forget it." Quint exhaled and clutched the side of the net next to Harold's head. He was too tired to breathe, let alone give a lecture. Thoughts raced through Quint's mind: *Who the hell are you to tell a man how to survive and live? Get over yourself.*

Boyd held the heavy water-logged life jacket and Jack used his last bit of strength to reach back and slip his arms into it. He fumbled to secure it in the oily water with the front tie strings.

"Don't think we'll see much of Oscar anymore, fellas." Jack wore the slightest of smiles under his trembling blue and chapped lips.

"Where did they all go? You think they are done?" asked Earl from the other side of the net.

"I can't tell. The oil layer is too thick for the bottle to get through to see anything now. Just keep your legs up." Quint called out the instructions while looking over at the large group of survivors nearby. They were fewer in numbers now.

Chester Eastman chimed in from down by Harold's right leg, "Hey, I have an idea. Why don't we send one of the two Marines down to have a look and report back? Halls of Montezuma, right boys?"

Rich was quick to dismiss. "Not funny, sailor boy."

Spino glared towards Eastman, "You first."

"C'mon, I thought it was a bit—"

With a wicked strength of speed and violence, the terrifying noise of shock and pain let loose from Earl as his body broke through the water. The strength of the attack surprised them all. Earl's already-weakened grip let loose from the side of the floater net and his body pulled backwards. The men couldn't believe their eyes and watched Earl lift from the water. Below the surface, a freight train caught his waist at full-steam—his body went from zero to twenty knots before the splashing water of the initial impact landed on their shocked faces.

Earl felt the squeeze of his intestines and the stomach bile compress into his esophagus. Out of a survivor's instinct, he tried calling for help but all that came out were deep guttural sounds of air and blood rushing over his vocal cords. He watched the group of men get further away and then felt the pressure of the teeth cut into him even harder.

The last they saw were the outstretched arms and terrified eyes, reaching out to them from the wake of water and thrashing tail, carrying him away. After twenty feet and sounds of death they never imagined hearing from any man, Radarman 3rd Class Earl Wallace pulled under the surface.

6   THE CRATE

As suddenly as they had begun, the attacks stopped. Those still alive whispered prayers of thanks, which then turned to mournful sorrow at the loss of friends taken from the surface. Their minds strewn, broken and defeated by the repeated waves of carnage and death. A curse to endure after the sinking.

This latest attack was the worst. The sharks outnumbered them more than ever. The sounds of terror and pain pierced their souls. Many still covered their ears tight, trying to block out the horrific screams and last-minute pleas of mercy their shipmates made from the swelled collars of the failing life preservers, while the ocean erupted red around them. The attacks ceased, but the screams still echoed in their minds. No matter how hard they pressed their ears, the sounds remained and wouldn't go away.

The scattered survivors moved to each other and tried to close in ranks. Some gave up and just floated—helpless and surrendered to the fates. Thoughts about their families, who they would never see again, filled their minds.

The sun hung full in the sky, and the warm light illuminated the surrounding water. The black oil slick, continuing to thin out, turned a fresh shade of dark crimson with the blood of the dead mixed against the pure blue backdrop of the depths underneath them. Rolling swells presented each of them with a reminder that death was an inevitability. Wherever they looked, severed limbs and half eaten torsos drifted alongside. The oily salt taste of the water that splashed their faces broke to a coppery bitterness of blood and toxins emitted from decomposing bodies—some five days old. Their mouths breathed in a layer of air mixed with the stench of rotting flesh that bubbled from the liquid tomb below.

Quint resented the gluttony of the sharks. They had done enough killing to feed themselves fat for months, and yet they ignored the dead corpses just to take someone struggling to stay alive. Only pure evil would conduct itself in such a way. Every breath of rotten decomposition he drew into his lungs lead to the smell of death that burned the inside of his sinuses. His hatred grew.

Boyd held onto the side of the floater net and perked up at the sight of a wooden crate floating just off to the south, about twenty feet away. The wooden crate seemed to bounce to its own rhythm with the ocean swells rolling underneath it.

"Say fellas, I got an idea here... we gotta get that crate."

Under the water line, Boyd unraveled the length of survival line he had wrapped around his knife's handle.

Chester Eastman looked out at the wooden crate that Boyd was staring at.

"Forget it. That's too far, Boyd. Those rat bastard sharks will take you before you get out there."

"It's only twenty-five feet. I can make it. There might be food in it." Boyd shifted his life jacket down from his face. "Besides, it's the wooden crate I want. We are only down to one knife and Oscar will be back."

Boyd took the length of line and handed one end to Jack, who clutched the floater net to his right. Turning to his left, Boyd held up his knife to Quint. Even though he never verbalized it, Quint felt an older brother's sense of protection over Boyd. They were both gunner's mates and only met a year ago when Boyd first reported to the ship. Two ranks below and five years younger than Quint, Boyd kept to a different group of sailors. During port calls, they both went their separate ways, but underway, Quint was in charge of Boyd.

During general quarters, they manned the port-side aft quad 40mm Bofors—an anti-aircraft gun station. Boyd was the fastest loader Quint had ever worked with, and Quint was the most confident operator Boyd had ever seen. Together they handled six kamikaze planes shot down off Iwo Jima and another three during the battle of Okinawa. It was during that early morning towards the end of the Navy's Okinawan invasion when Quint jolted awake at the controls of his gun turret to Boyd screaming 'Oscar Oscar port side!' as the morning twilight broke through the sky. The kamikaze fighter sneaked up on them in just twelve seconds under cover of darkness but, at the last minute, a hint of light off the horizon betrayed him. Quint leaned into the controls and the mechanized motor swung the four barrels of the anti-aircraft weapon around and straight up at the diving Japanese plane. The movement was so quick and fast that Quint's hearing protection fell off his head. He didn't hesitate to press the trigger and fire off the 40mm rounds with a perfect aim at the target. Boyd looked up to see the rounds from their gun station being the first to meet the plane, followed by the tracers from the other port side weapons that equipped the USS Indianapolis. The covering fire laid out across the sky and caused the kamikaze fighter to veer off course away from the bridge of the Indianapolis and head straight down at them. Concussive blasts of the guns pounded on their bodies. A storm of hot brass casings rained down against their legs. Boyd pressed his headset closer to his head to further muffle the sounds and looked up to see the blood coming from Quint's ear as his ear drum ruptured.

Quint didn't flinch as he kept the trigger squeezed and fired off the last rounds, trying to sway the aim of the heavy guns into the diving plane. Those precious last second rounds caused the kamikaze to bank hard from its original target of the bridge where the captain stood. The plane exploded in a fiery crash against the port side of the ship's stern, but not before the doomed enemy pilot released a bomb at a height of twenty-five feet above their heads. Quint dove to the side, grabbed Boyd and held him down as the bomb broke through the deck right next to their station, sending shrapnel and metal exploding across their backs. Eyes squeezed shut, they waited for the flames to consume them, but to their surprise, the bomb never exploded on impact—instead dropping through the decks below and out through the keel, detonating beneath the ship on the sea floor. They picked themselves up, dusted off, reloaded, and watched for more enemy planes while the damage control crews secured the flooded compartments and kept the Indianapolis alive.

Boyd never forgot what Quint did at the end of those twelve seconds it took for the kamikaze and its bomb to reach them. As the damaged Indianapolis sailed back across the Pacific to get repairs back home, Boyd felt as though Quint was his big brother watching over him. He never mentioned it to Quint but wanted to return the favor if ever the opportunity arose. This was his chance.

Boyd looked at Quint and handed him the bowie knife. "You were always good to me, Quint. If I don't get back, use this to kill Oscar. Give it to him for me." Boyd pushed the knife over with a half-smile.

Quint shook his head. "I can't let you go."

"You can and you will. We gotta try something." Boyd held the handle to Quint's life jacket.

Quint reached from the water and took the knife, then nodded his head. They were all too weak to resist each other. There was no holding anyone back at this point. Boyd was right.

Boyd looked out at the crate, drifting further away.

"You boys hold on tight to this line and pull me back in when I say so."

Eastman and Jack both acknowledged the order by clenching onto the end of the line with their free hands, and Boyd let go of the floater net. He sucked in a few quick breaths, looked around the water for signs of fins and movement below, then leaned forward and struck out at the sea with his tired arms.

The men watched Boyd press on through the water. His swimming form broke down into a desperate crawl forward with his head and face being held out of the water. The taxed life jacket did everything it could to hold Boyd's torso towards the surface.

"Hey Quint, are you married?"

Quint heard the voice behind him at the other end of the floater net. He turned to Machado, who was by himself, hanging onto the stray ropes of the net by Harold's head. Machado's face turned ghost white, and his lips shook. Quint pulled himself along the floater net away from the other men, who had all gathered around the opposite end to watch Boyd on his quest for the floating crate.

As Quint pulled himself closer, Machado asked again, "You married Quint? You gotta wife back home?"

The question took Quint aback, and he wanted to ignore it while glancing back at Boyd, who now struggled against a swell in a continued swim off in the distance. Quint turned to Machado.

"Not anymore. Was married twice. This last one didn't last very long. When we got back to port on the last go around, she was gone." Quint leaned in and looked at Machado.

Machado's eyes became glassy and unfocused. His movements all carried a slight tremor of frailty to them. Quint pulled himself closer to listen.

"Then you and I are alike. I don't have anybody waiting for me, except maybe my mom... she's back in Cape May. I was supposed to write her back in dry-dock, but this led to that, and you know how it is, we were back on the water headed out to sea."

Machado reversed his hand, gripping the edge of the floater net and pulled himself closer to Quint. His voice dropped lower.

"Do you know what my mom said to me before I left for boot camp?"

Quint shook his head.

"She said 'Clarence… you should've joined the Air Corps.'"

Machado let out a laugh and then winced with pain. Quint smiled but stayed silent in response. He felt something was wrong. Quint looked back to check on Boyd.

Twenty feet away, Boyd ran out of line ten feet from the crate. He turned to look at the floater net off in the distance. It seemed a mile away. It took so much out of him to get this far. Boyd looked down at the end of the line in his hand and released it, letting the knotted end float on the surface of the water. He turned and continued for the crate.

Hodge, huddled with the two Marines down by Harold's feet, yelled out while watching Boyd.

"He let go of the line, dammit. You crazy kid. Forget it and get back here!"

Quint heard the shouting and went to turn away, but Machado reached for the collar of Quint's life jacket.

"Listen, I didn't want the other guys to know… didn't want to scare them."

Machado stammered his words as he looked down and held up the tattered remains of the front of his life jacket. The water in between him and Quint turned a shocking red. Through the surface, Quint saw Machado holding his stomach closed with his free hand. The lower jaw of the attacking shark had taken a part of his abdomen along with the front side of his life jacket. Machado felt no pain through the attack. He still couldn't believe his eyes when he looked down to see shreds of muscle and skin leaking blood from the missing piece of his body.

Quint looked around for anything to patch up the sailor, or maybe get him to the main floater net back at the center of the group just to the north. Machado pulled him closer to whisper.

"No, don't tell anyone. I don't want them to know. I'm so thirsty, Quint. Just want to drink something before I die. So, I'm going down there to have a drink. It will feel so damn good. Better than the finest whiskey in town. And I don't want you to stop me. Just do this one favor. For me. Just this one thing…"

Machado took his identification tags up from his collar and over his head. With his bloody shaking fingers, he placed them in Quint's hand. The shiny metal tags and chain felt cold when they gathered in his palm.

"Make sure these get to my mother. I have nothing else left. These are it. If you could do that, I would be very grateful."

Quint just nodded his head, for he had no words.

Ten yards away, Boyd reached the crate and grabbed it. Up close, it was a lot larger than it looked from back at the floater net, and to his surprise, it held him up when he pulled on it. He floated with the crate for a few seconds and looked down. He thought he saw movement beneath the gleaming knives of white sunlight streaks reflecting off the ocean's surface. With all the strength left in his body, he held the crate in front of him and kicked with his feet, pushing it back toward his floater net group.

Boyd saw the end of the survival line floating in the water just ahead of him and stretched for it. He called to the men while raising his hand, holding the line. The line went taut and pulled. He wrapped it around his forearm twice, then hung in the water and felt the tug.

Back at the floater net, the two Marines joined with Eastman and Jack in pulling Boyd's lifeline hand over hand.

Quint heard the commotion but didn't look away from Machado.

"Look, there is a better way than this. Maybe we can get you to Dr. Haynes."

"This is the end of the line." Machado shook his head and grew calm with his explanation.

"Them sharks will smell this blood and come for me first and take the rest of you with me. Might just happen this very minute... and I don't wanna die thirsty. This is the only way, and I'm not mad. I'm really not, Quint. This thirst. I heard the further down you go, the less salty it is... tastes like a fresh waterfall. I'm so tired, so thirsty. It will feel great, Quint. I promise you; this is what I want."

Machado leaned back from Quint and pulled on the front tie string of the torn life jacket. Quint looked back but hesitated to call for help from the others. Machado closed his eyes and slipped out of the destroyed life jacket in silence. His oil covered face sank below the surface. Quint froze at the sight of the translucent arm reaching up from the water—the hand paused and held tight to the floater net. In the morning sun, the salt-water acid bathed skin of Machado's forearm glowed. The dark lettering of the black tattoo ink stood out in a stark contrast. 'USS INDIANAPOLIS—USN' over a detailed bald eagle, with its powerful wings extended, stared back at Quint and burned into his mind. Quint watched the hand release its grip. The tattooed ghost-white forearm of Water Tender 2nd Class Clarence Machado, without further hesitation, dropped from the sunlight.

The four men pulled on the survival line with weakened and fatigued shoulders. An exhausted Boyd, kicking and holding onto the wooden crate, arrived at the net. The mission was a success. Boyd swore the sharks bumped him twice, and they joked about him being the 'largest damn worm on a hook them fish had ever seen'. Even Harold Shearer, who laid in pain atop the floater net, jostled back to consciousness by the unusual laughter and anticipation of the crate Boyd had salvaged.

The crate measured three feet and rose two feet from the water's edge. Made of solid Southern Georgia pine, the crate sat right on top of the water. The wood carried such a robust buoyancy, Boyd could hang from it and the crate only dropped six inches. Boyd found a few weakened boards at the upper corner and reached in. The smell of rotten vegetables caused his stinging eyes to widen.

"Alright boys, dinner is served!"

Boyd yelled and whooped in a hoarse voice when he pulled out black rotten potatoes. Days of salt-water soaking rotted the potatoes' exteriors into a putrid black jelly of foulness, but upon further inspection, a desperate and starving Boyd scraped off the black slime to find a gray solid inner core. He took a bite and chewed as if he just bit into a prize-winning slab of Texas beef back home.

With no hint of self-preservation, Boyd reached in to the crate, exclaiming the fact that these were the best potatoes he had ever eaten. He pulled out the black and brown balls of rotten slime and toss them to the men who all ate something for the first time in over one-hundred hours. Boyd pitched a potato over to Hodge who moved down on Harold's right side. He broke pieces off to feed to Harold, who laid still while relaxing his fire damaged arms.

Quint was relieved to hear Boyd's voice but couldn't look away from the torn life jacket that drifted in the cloud of blood Machado left behind. Boyd, using the crate as a floating support, pulled himself along the edge of Harold up to Quint.

He held out the least rotten black potato reserved for his superior.

"Machado?" Boyd asked, looking at the space along the net where Machado once was.

"No," Quint said while shaking his head.

Quint accepted the offered potato from Boyd. He ate while staring at the gray clump of torn life jacket. It drifted away to join the other floating mementos of lost lives littering the surrounding ocean.

7 LOCKHEED VENTURA

What little breeze the Philippine Sea offered died away, and the water became a pane of glass. The ever-present oil slick continued to thin out. Patches of clear blue water changed shapes around the men and became temporary windows into the undersea world that held them.

Quint held his free hand in the water in front of him. He watched a small tropical scavenger fish drift towards him. It nibbled on the loose dead bits of skin hanging from his fingers. The saltwater was a corrosive on the men. It ate away the weakened skin with every minute they spent submerged. Their arms and bodies formed white patches of dying flesh. Quint took his index finger and scraped the edge of his nail down the side of his thumb, tearing away a strip of dead skin. He felt nothing and flicked the skin to the little scavenger fish. The fish didn't hesitate to kick its tail and with a flutter of fin, sucked the offering into its mouth. Quint let out the faintest of snickers—the morbid amusement of witnessing himself being eaten by a fish before he died.

His mind wondered what would happen to his body. He never gave it much thought until that very moment when he watched the small scavenger fish consume part of his flesh without hesitation. It moved backwards and continued to watch him—waiting for its next meal. Quint didn't blame the fish; it was just doing what it had to do to survive. He reached out to touch the fish, and it moved back further but never took its gaze off the ghostly white dead flesh of Quint's hand. Like the sharks, it had all the time in the world, and it waited.

At that moment, Quint first felt the fear of death and he became angry. His whole life, the only reaction he knew as a response to fear, was anger. The kamikaze attack plane that flew straight down on his anti-aircraft gun station in twelve seconds scared him. It was the extreme rage he felt devour him which kept his hands on the firing controls despite feeling his ear drums rupturing and the rapid, intense pounding on his rib cage by the sound concussions of ammunition shells detonating. The anger and rage became so intense he never felt the sting of pain. Quint stared at the little scavenger fish and became afraid of dying. He didn't want to see his father and explain to him what he had done. With a fist, Quint lashed out at the fish and struck the water.

The water splash hit Boyd on the side and startled him. He tightened his grip on his wooden crate.

"What the hell you doing, boss? You see a shark?"

Quint ignored the question and just stared ahead into the water.

With shivering hands, Boyd finished weaving the survival line around a few pine slats at the end of his crate and secured it with a hefty collection of amateur knots that would make a boatswain's mate blush. He held his display of seamanship out for a final examination and then turned it to Quint.

"Can't tie a knot, then tie a lot. Right, boss?" Boyd said with a chuckle.

Quint looked back at him. "My fingers are so destroyed, I don't think I could open a bottle of beer without losing a knuckle. Damned saltwater got us all soft and falling apart. You did just fine, Troy."

Boyd was tired. His movements slow. But hearing Quint's compliment made him perk up and show some life.

"Never gonna lose this now."

Boyd held his shark fighting knife up out of the water with the other end of the survival line wrapped around the grip and secured in another motley collection of knots.

Eastman and Jack listened off to the side as Boyd explained his plan to keep the knife around should it get knocked from his hand in a struggle with the massive tiger shark. His plan was complete—now all anyone would have to do was find the crate and the knife would be right there, dangling from the handmade tag line. The rotten potatoes were a welcomed bonus.

Quint floated alongside the net and listened to Boyd and saw Harold looking over at him with glassy blue eyes.

"What day is it, sir?"

Quint had never met the young seaman before and this would be the first time he heard his voice, other than the screaming from earlier.

"I'm not a 'sir', son. No need to call me that."

Harold gave a weakened grin and leaned over towards Quint, still holding his burned arms up and away from the water that sloshed through the spaces between the net's cork floaters.

Quint didn't want the kid to fall off into the water, so he motioned for him to stay still.

"It's Thursday, Harold." Quint spit out a splash of wave that touched his face and raised his hands to push Harold back on the net if he rolled off.

Harold stared at Quint, almost losing consciousnesses, but then back to reality.

"Tomorrow is my birthday... I'll be twenty-four. That's kind of old, ain't it?"

"Not really, boy. I'll be twenty-nine soon."

Harold pondered the age difference in a weakened voice.

"Too young to die then? Don't let me die, okay? I was kinda hoping to get back to the farm. You know, all those chores and work I used to complain about? They seem awfully nice right about now."

Quint didn't have the strength to tell him what he had been thinking. They were all going to die. It was just a matter of time. Instead, Quint just shook his head and summoned up a lie.

"You aren't going anywhere today. I'll get you to twenty-four."

Harold breathed relief and took an exhaustive roll back to his right. He readjusted his motionless, charred arms, which continued to bake in the late morning sun. He became numb to the pain. As long as he didn't get wet, he could take it. Quint reached up and pushed the rolled-up life jacket into the space under Harold's neck. He was never good at caring for anyone, but he felt that's how he would have wanted it if he was laying down on the floater net.

On the other side of Harold, Hodge tried to swallow but felt his throat close. The hoarseness of his voice earlier told him the infection started, and now he felt the back of his tongue swell with pain and scratch at the roof of his mouth. He shifted the Saint Anthony medal with his tongue from one cheek to the other and tried to generate some saliva. The strain on his salivary glands led to a stinging pain in the roof of his mouth—he was dying of thirst. Hodge looked up to the blue sky to pray, and that's when he saw it.

The smallest black spot, hanging in the sky miles away. Hodge looked over to the two silent Marines, who floated down at the other end of the net. One of the Marines, Frank Spino, couldn't speak and his neck swelled already. He just hung low and lifeless in his life jacket; the water lapped at his chin in a gentle touch. The other Marine, Raymond Rich, looked to Hodge who didn't have enough strength to raise his hands out of the water. Hodge just motioned with his head to look out west.

Rich turned in the water and looked southwest, scanning the sky. He saw it as well.

The weak Marine yelled with all the strength he had left. "Plane!"

The men of the floater net looked over to the Marine and then out in the direction he was staring.

"That's a bird, too small to be a plane."

"It's a Jap coming back to finish us off!"

Their eyes strained and stung from the light of the afternoon sun. They dared not look away as the black silhouette took a dive and then evened out above the horizon. The calm seas allowed them to see further out from their surface vantage point more than any other day. Quint gripped the floater net with both hands and watched. If this was a Japanese fighter, he was ready to pull Harold right into the water and hold him under while they took fire. He remembered his Chief telling him he saw men survive off France by swimming down and letting the water take the bullets. All you need is a few feet, and they bounce off you like rocks.

All the men grew silent and listened to the sound of the twin engines on the tiny object off the horizon. They held their breath in unison and strained to hear the faint buzz grow into a distant rumble. The sound of the plane and the gentle lapping of the water against the floater net were all they could hear.

A voice yelled from another group of survivors.

"It's a Betty Bomber! Incoming!"

Boyd turned to Quint. "He can't be right. How could a G4M get out this far?"

Quint relaxed his grip on the floater net, "He's wrong, that's too small to be a Japanese bomber. Wingspan isn't wide enough. And the pitch is too high."

The gunner's mates of the Indianapolis prided themselves at identifying aircraft, both friendly and enemy. After being at war for a few years, those with the most battle experience had the sights and sounds of the enemy committed to memory. Quint had a talent for estimating sizes and sounds at a distance. The plane was a few miles away and then it dipped again, and leveled off, getting a closer look at something far out from them.

Quint reacted as the approaching sound became familiar. "That's a PV-1. They found us."

None of them wanted to look away, and they all prayed Quint was right. The aircraft, growing larger than ever, banked left then right, and the men saw the white star and blue circle on the side. A streak of white sunlight gleamed across its aluminum skin.

Boyd couldn't contain himself. "Lockheed Ventura! You gorgeous girl, right here! Right here!"

The men came alive with adrenaline, and they screamed declarations of joy. They slapped the water, trying to make as much of a visual disturbance as possible. Throughout the large group of survivors, those who still had a voice strained to use it. Those who could not speak just raised one hand in the air in a feeble last-minute attempt to will the pilot to see them. The injured, burned, and near-dead men on the full-sized floater net towards the center of the survivor group each struggled to sit and wave their arms for help.

The beautiful shiny silver bomber became a roaring reality when it skimmed over their heads, only three-hundred feet above. Quint saw the Ventura's crew staring down through the open bomb bay doors. One of them waving his hand in acknowledgment to the two-hundred helpless souls that screamed, laughed, cried, and prayed their thanks to God for saving them.

Hodge went to shout as the plane passed over and the St. Anthony medal flipped out of his mouth. His swollen tongue couldn't keep it inside his cheek. His heart skipped when he saw the medal hit the water with the tiniest of splashes. Hodge let go of the net in a panic and reached for the shiny medal just out in front of him below the surface. He missed, and the medal flipped from one side to the other and began its descent. With panic and urgency as if he lost a member of his family, Hodge pushed into the water with eyes open. He fought against the buoyancy of his life jacket and reached for the tiny piece of metal. The water, pushed by his outstretched fingers, took the medal and carried it further away. It swirled from him in the ocean current. His vision blurred and eyes stinging, he watched the shiny haze of St. Anthony fall away from him in slow motion, making his moment of loss even more painful. His only possession and connection to his life back home was now part of the Pacific forever. In his mind, he was sure he'd soon follow.

The PV-1 pulled up to the sky and rocked back and forth. Sailors cheered at the pilot's flying maneuver, dipping one wing, then the other, to signal they were found. The twin engines roared, and the sunlight bounced off the polished metal wings when the fast-maneuvering US bomber banked hard to the right, drawing an arc to come back around for a second pass.

"Ah! You son of a bitch! He just hit me!"

Jack shouted and looked down below to see the enormous mass of a dark gray striped body. He kicked at the gigantic tiger shark and landed a blow to its body, right behind the gills. The shark flinched and swung its tail to the side—gliding back down into the deep.

The men all froze and looked over at Jack. Quint looked down and he could see the swarm of sharks building below them. Mid-sized and large oceanic whitetips circled and darted back and forth. In the center of them, the dark shape and broad head of the tiger lurked.

"It's Oscar, isn't it?" asked Boyd, holding his knife out in front of him.

Jack confirmed with a nod of his head.

The cheering around their group halted. They no longer cared to watch the Ventura circle back around. Their silence amplified the continued cheers and hollers of joy from the other groups of survivors.

Eastman only had time to release the very first hint of a scream before the massive force of nature pulled him under. His grip held tight to the tether of the floater net and the back of the net dropped below the surface, starting at Harold's feet. Boyd didn't hesitate and lunged for the churning water of the vacant space where Eastman once was. Quint reached for Boyd's life jacket but missed. Boyd pushed the wooden crate and dove headfirst. Kicking his feet, he disappeared below the oily blue surface. The end of the floater net released and rose from the water.

Quint watched the wooden crate as the tag-line Boyd tied to it from the end of his knife went taut. The crate pulled from one side, then to the other, and bounced along the water's surface. Quint searched for his glass bottle when the entire wooden crate disappeared under the surface in a geyser of white water.

The grip hands of the remaining five men all tightened on the floater net at the sight of the churning water with bubbles that rose from below and dispersed along the surface. The twin engines of the Ventura grew louder as the plane circled around and began another approach over the outstretched and cheering arms of the other survivors.

It took the sea only half a minute to regurgitate Eastman and Boyd, but it felt an eternity. Quint let go of the floater net and pushed out to where the two men settled back in the water, gasping for air.

"I got him! I got him good, and that bastard took off with my knife buried in his head." Boyd smacked the water in triumph. "You should've seen him swimming away, pulling that crate along with him!"

"You okay? Chester, you got bit?" asked Jack.

"It grabbed my boot and took me down. I thought my whole foot had come off when Boyd got down there. Sonofabitch was strong!" Eastman felt all over his body in frantic hand movements to see if he still had all his parts. "The laces gave way, and the shark took off with my boot in its mouth. I can't believe I still got toes!"

Quint pulled on Boyd's life jacket collar and stroked back towards the net.

"Get back here, both of you."

Eastman leaned back in the water and lifted his left leg up, wiggling pruned toes in the air. "Bastard fish got my sock too!" Happy to be alive, he leaned into his life jacket and laughed.

The Lockheed Ventura dug in low overhead, and they looked up to see the different shapes of objects start dropping from the plane. Its bomber crew pushed out anything they thought could help. Survivors watched the crates and canisters of water fall and explode on the water. The plane was right over the large group of survivors when it released a life raft, which rocked and tumbled three-hundred feet and landed in the water, sixty yards outside the circle of safety they had fought to maintain.

Rich yelled at the sight of the raft. "Let's go for it! C'mon!"

Boyd surmised after having swum for a third of that distance to get the wooden crate. He knew how much it took out of him after getting pulled back by the others.

"No way any of us will make it. It's too far."

Eastman agreed with the Marine that they should make a swim for it. "It's not that far. I could swim that easily back home."

Hodge called over from the other side of the floater net. "What about Seaman Shearer? You just gonna leave him?"

Harold heard his name and looked over to Quint in a panicked voice. "You promised, sir. You promised."

Quint looked out at the lone life raft. It was a good size and could hold ten or fifteen men. He saw a few sailors break off from the other groups and swim towards it. The Ventura roared overhead and climbed higher into the sky.

"Look fellas, this aint back home. You don't know how weak you are until you are out there and it's too late," said Boyd. "That PV-1 is calling in our position right now. All we have to do is wait it out and—"

The sound of water and air interrupted Boyd's argument when the wooden crate broke through the surface five feet behind him. Boyd looked at Quint's reaction to what was behind him and turned around in the water. Quint reached for Boyd to pull him back from the crate, but as soon as he touched the soggy life jacket, the gaping maw of the tiger shark emerged from the blue depths and clamped down onto Boyd's hip. The impact of the hit launched Boyd from the ocean. The force of the water and the wide head of the tiger shark rocked Quint back. Boyd's knife handle that jutted out from the side of the shark's head hit Quint's shoulder and cut into his shirt. Quint watched the black, lifeless eye of the shark stare back at him and then roll over white. The shark and a screaming Boyd both flopped forward and slammed into the water, sending the floater net off to the side and causing all the men to lose their grips. Without hesitation, Quint dove into the water and grabbed hold of the survival line tied from Boyd's knife to the crate. Quint strained his stinging red eyes through the ultra-clear blue water to see Boyd caught in the shark's jaws. Its bite latched on with an unbreakable strength. Boyd pounded with closed fists on the shark's head and clawed at the white eyes, but the shark swung its powerful tail from side to side and re-seated its grip on the muscle and bone of the hip. Quint kicked and stretched with all his might, fighting his life jacket that struggled to pull him back to the surface. His fingers wrapped around the survival line, and he felt the pull of the shark on his body. They went deep and Quint's eardrums pressed with the water pressure.

A ten-foot oceanic whitetip shark attacked from the side and struck Quint in the head. It went to take a bite, but the commotion and Quint's movement caused it to miss. Instead, the fast torpedo-like body of the shark changed instant direction and the sandpaper skin of its side struck Quint's forehead, taking some burned oil-stained skin with it. The impact knocked Quint over and caused him to lose his grip on the line. With all the rage buried deep in his soul, Quint released a muffled scream of bubbles and terror while his life jacket pulled him to the surface. He watched Boyd's body let out the last bit of fight and air.

The wooden crate brushed along Quint's back. Its tether line strained, and the crate followed the tiger shark into the depths. His arms and legs locked and the atrophied muscles in his body collapsed. All Quint could do was drift back to the surface and watch Troy Boyd and the shark fall into oblivion.

Quint broke through the surface, screaming. The men of the floater net thought he was being eaten alive, for the screams of wrath and rage were of an intensity they had not yet witnessed. Quint pounded the water and looked up. The twin engines spun the propellers of the Lockheed Ventura and drowned his screams as it flew over for another pass.

8   FEEDING FRENZY

Deep below the surface, the large oceanic whitetip shark continued to stalk them. Over the last four days, the mass of black oil was a blanket of darkness that coated the waters above while casting the sharks in permanent shadow. The oceanic could feel them struggling. It felt their panicked and erratic movements within the oil. It could not see them, but it knew they were up there hiding—concealed and surviving inside a layer of murk that stretched for miles.

The numbers of its species swelled to the thousands in this area of the Philippine Sea. The late arrivals still hunted in traditional ways and fed off the pieces of human cadavers that fell to them from above. This large oceanic was the first to follow the USS Indianapolis. It learned how to hunt those who survived inside the black surface.

The largest of the oceanic whitetip sharks no longer hunted for necessity. They fed so much their bellies swelled. Their girth doubled in size. Even the pilot fish, those black-and-white striped tag-a-longs that swim alongside the whitetips and scavenge off their meals—even they had grown and struggled to swim from the constant access to food. This faction of the crowded layer of oceanic whitetip sharks which swam below the survivors at a depth of fifty feet, no longer needed to kill to survive.

Now, they killed for sport.

Over the last few days, the large oceanic led the way as the whitetips changed their tactics. They rifled into the blackness, grabbed whatever they could, and swam hard with whatever they locked their jaws around. The predators dragged their catch back down to depth and had their way with it. It became a guessing game. The shark swam and scanned the dark cloud above.

Senses feeling. The breathing, the pulses, the voices. It homed in on the dead giveaways, struggling and kicking in the water above. At dawn or dusk, when the light dimmed enough to hide its presence, the shark chose an area of sound or activity and locked on its target.

The oceanic whitetips, with their undying hunger quenched by the bodies of dead sailors, resorted to playing this game with the helpless ones living on the surface. In the same way a cat toys with an injured and desperate mouse, the sharks played with the survivors.

Until today.

The sun hung high and the large oceanic cruised through a forest of sunlight. Dark oil broke apart on the surface and dispersed. Spaces formed, allowing rays of light to beam down into the endless blue. The ocean became a moving collection of white illumination. Its bronze skin glistened as the massive body swayed side-to-side, swimming in and out of the light columns.

Through the swarm of oceanic whitetip sharks, the large one looked up and finally saw them. Hundreds of bodies hanging in the water, moving and kicking—arguing and fighting.

Upon seeing them, a tidal wave of sensory overload rocked the shark and paralyzed it with surprise. The droning rumble of the plane passed over and echoed against the water's surface, sending a wave of vibration into the semicircular canals of its inner ear. A sensation it never felt before followed. All at once, those bodies hanging on the surface exploded in unison with cheers and screams. They slapped and pounded the water, sending vibrations to jab the tiny sensory hairs lining its ear and telling its brain that prey was struggling and calling.

This sent the shark, and the thousands of its species that swam alongside it, into a deadly trance. It was no longer about food, or games, or hunting. The sounds of voices and cheering, the thrashing and splashing, and the rumble of machinery above, speared the most primitive parts of its brain. They needed to be silenced.

Coalesced by this massive wave of epic censorial overload, the sharks swarmed. Without the grace or eerie stalking prowess they once had, the oceanic whitetips became raging, frantic wraiths. The hunters darted through the shafts of light and swam without a cognitive purpose, only operating on an instinctual guttural desire to silence and kill the sounds above.

Blood and bodies littered the surface by the hundreds. The smell of death made them react to the commotions with more aggression.

The massive crowd of oceanic whitetip sharks became a feeding frenzy of colossal proportions. Together, the sharks were a dark mass of writhing and circling bronze bodies, rising from the depths toward the surface.

The last of the USS Indianapolis survivors didn't know their cheers and shouts of joyful salvation were invitations for death—the conjuring of unimaginable terrors.

9   THE RAFT

Last night, as the moon hung overhead, they were twelve. Fifteen hours later, only seven remained. They heard others in the distance cheering and talking with newfound vigor over the glorious Lockheed Ventura bomber. The plane continued to circle the sky above them. The men of the small floater net drifted in silence. No laughing or stories of a rescue—just the stillness of defeat.

With the loss of Boyd, they all knew they were as good as dead. Unless they got out of the water, they would be next. In the backs of their minds, if anyone was to survive, it would've been the brash young Gunner's Mate 3rd Class Troy Boyd. They could not shake the sight of Boyd caught in the powerful jaws of the tiger shark. The image of the animal lifting him out of the water burned into their minds. The sounds he made before going under stabbed deep inside their souls.

Quint drifted in silence. His head bleeding and eyes stinging from the salt water and oil after the dive to save Boyd. He looked up to the sky and saw the Ventura circling and raged inside. His fear of dying became wrath. The fire burned inside. He didn't blame the Navy for what happened—he blamed the sharks.

No prayers for salvation and forgiveness for his sins. No prayers for God to save him. Quint prayed to find that tiger shark one more time. He envisioned himself letting the shark get close enough. Maybe even put a leg out so he could get taken, and when he did, then he would get his chance. With his dying breaths locked in the shark's jaws, he would go for the eyes to gouge and claw at them. Yes, that would satisfy his rage. With the last fight of his soul, he would dig his fingers in, wrap his fists around the eyes of that bastard shark and squeeze. He envisioned himself ripping those rolled back black eyes from its skull and crushing them with all the strength he had left. The shark may have had a belly full of him, but it would have to live the rest of its days without sight— condemned to suffer a slow death of starvation, unable to find prey. Better yet, he'd render the blinded tiger shark a helpless prey, and a victim itself, to a larger shark. Without a weapon, Quint resolved to kill that tiger shark with his bare hands.

These thoughts made him smile, and he hummed the melody that played in his mind. The sea shanty their group sung over the last four days in the water played over and over in his subconscious. The others looked over to Quint as they heard the haunting *Farewell and Adieu* melody seep out in a gravelly tone. Quint dropped his gaze from the plane in the sky to the blue water beneath him. The others became even more unsettled, for their leader seethed with a fearful anger. They dared not speak to him. Quint took out the bottle from his life jacket and spun the cap off with his thumb. The cap dropped into the water and Quint let it sink away. He continued his melody while looking into the water through the glass.

He never saw such a blanket of sharks that covered the ocean just twenty feet below their legs. Quint grinned and searched back and forth for the tiger. It would have to come back. It must come back.

The others drifted and stared at the water, each losing hope and going mad in their own way. The death of Boyd was the crack that opened the dam of dread inside them. Until they heard it—a new sound on the horizon.

To the west, the noise grew against the backdrop of the Ventura that continued to circle the blue sky. They saw the shape grow larger, along with the sound of twin Pratt and Whitney radial engines—their propellers cutting the air in a deep drone.

The entire group of survivors looked up and watched until it was recognizable. A PBY Catalina amphibious aircraft dropped lower from its cruising altitude and the men erupted in cheers. The sight of the flying boat's gray-painted hull and those massive wide wings, stretching one-hundred feet across, brought greater tears of joy and shouts of triumph than when the Ventura arrived. The survivors slapped the water and raised their hands in glory—throwing water as far as they had the strength to.

Quint raised his stinging eyes up from the looking glass and wiped the blood from his face when he watched the PBY buzz over their heads. He looked around. Those in his own group tossed water in the air and hugged each other.

This was the last energy they had left. Someone would rescue them soon enough and being in the water another day was unimaginable with further help just overhead.

Up in the sky, the PBY climbed high and fell in behind the Ventura. The two aircraft circled the area, making a wide sweep off to the distance and then heading back towards the survivors. They appeared to survey other areas of the ocean far away.

Quint felt a large body brush against his leg, and he looked down. He didn't need the looking glass to see the hundreds of silhouetted shapes that swam in all directions just below his feet. They were closer than ever before.

The latest eruption of cheers and vibrations is all the oceanic whitetip needed to continue the final stages of a feeding frenzy. Fifty feet below the surface, they started together in a tight and chaotic formation. A monumental cloud of twisting bronze bodies with no thought or purpose. Their eyes pinched down into small black slits over yellow, and they became soulless. The cognitive skills shrank to raw instinctual aggression with only one desire—to kill the sounds and vibrations of the struggling prey above.

They swam together, backs arched, and long pectoral fins dropped. The sight of other whitetips in a state of aggression pulled each of them further into a madness of murder. The sharks no longer cared about surviving, safety, waiting for the best time, or the best light, to begin their hunt—all overruled by the wanting desire to turn the sounds off. Kill the noise into silence, as nature designed them to do.

With the smell and taste of blood in their mouths, the cloud of sharks moved as one. It rose from the bleak blue wasteland of nothing to the silhouetted, struggling, and shouting victims above. The consummate aggression and hunt culminated from ten-thousand years tracking and feeding off humanity crossing these waters.

With the low rumbling of engines in the sky bouncing off the water surface and those rapid electrical heartbeat signals in the two hundred chest cavities only a short distance away, the oceanic whitetips locked onto the noise and began their most aggressive of attacks.

Quint saw the broad, white-tipped brown dorsal fin cut through the surface of the water a mere ten feet away when the sharks hit the main group of survivors around the edges and stormed within their circle of safety. Sailors left the surface at random selection. Blasts of white sea-foam muffled screams and terrifying horror.

A sailor felt the tug and stinging pinch. He kicked away from the commotion and realized he wasn't moving. The boy panicked and kicked harder, but still couldn't get any further. Around him, the ocean turned red, and his vision clouded. He reached down to feel for his legs. His fingers searched through the streams of tendons and torn muscle from his thighs—his legs torn away at the knees.

The survivors floating on their own became desperate. They attempted to swim to other groups or the large floater net. The sixty men that remained on the net pulled their legs away from the sides. A survivor looked through the space between the cork floaters and watched the swarm of sharks rising. Before he could scream, the large oceanic whitetip shark fired into the floater net with its jaws extended and the mini triangular serrated teeth exposed. The shark bit down on the section of cork floaters right below the survivor's head and caught the collar of his shirt that hung through the net. It thrashed and pulled with its five-hundred-pound body.

Injured and weakened survivors on the main floater net backed away and watched an open space tear through. The sailor's shirt, caught in the shark's teeth, stretched tight around the man's neck, then cinched down to choke the sound from his voice. His shoulder and head pulled to the opening by the large oceanic whitetip. In a deadly coordination of terror, another whitetip rose from the opening and clamped down on the sailor's skull, taking him into the sloshing sea. With his head below the water and locked in the jaws of the shark, the sailor struggled to pull himself free—his frantic dying hands grabbed for the others. The men of the crowded floater net fell from sanity when they watched the net open and swallow the doomed sailor.

They all felt the strikes of thirty sharks attacking in unison. Cork floaters broke and failed. The net exploded from underneath. The powerful force was too much, causing the rope bindings to tear and drop into the ocean. Their floating platform disappeared below the surface and the ocean rushed over them.

Quint turned away from the sight and repulsive sounds of death. The high-pitched screaming reached a terrible crescendo as the men struggled to keep their heads above water while being eaten alive underneath. No two sailors went the same. Some called for God and Jesus, while others called for their mothers. Some remained silent—just releasing sounds of aggression and strain from deep inside while pounding and kicking at whatever had bit into them from below. Regardless of what or to whom the pleas of mercy and salvation were for, they all ended the same; abrupt and immediate silence after the last bit of living drowned away, and the salt water rushed in to snuff out the sounds of terror. The sharks pulled, chewed, and reset their jaws while dragging the bodies down. A victim's last sight—watching his muffled shrieks of bubbles rise away through a red cloud of water.

The men each tried to survive and fight the sharks in their own way. Some pounded with closed fists on the shark in front of them, while another whitetip swam in from behind for the kill. The ones that kept their heads above the water prayed the next wouldn't be himself. Through the tearing of sinew and bones pulling from cartilage, some men tried clawing and crawling on top of others to get themselves higher out of the water. The panicked sailors held down and drowned those too weak to fend for themselves while trying to climb to safety. Those who climbed on top only lived long enough to feel the powerful bite and pull from many sharks in many directions.

Within fifteen minutes, the churning red water of dorsal fins and thrashing tails consumed the entire large floater net and all sixty men who lived on it for the past five days. The survivors in the water had pushed themselves away and thanked heaven they were not on that net.

The oil dispersed enough to show red hanging clouds of blood refusing to leave the area around the remaining survivors. The PBY's engines roared and the massive plane dove from the air to make repeated passes over their group. Side doors of the PBY stayed open, and the crew tossed survival gear across the wide area of survivors. Tin canisters of fresh water exploded on the surface, breaking open and breaking the hearts of those sailors close enough to watch the pure liquid drain into the salt sea. The PBY Catalina crew ejected whatever items they had on board their plane that could help, fresh and dry kapok life jackets, rubberized inflatable belts, survival packs of canned food, and medical supplies.

The items rained down and hit the water all around the panicked group of remaining survivors. The ones in the water that hadn't found a raft or something to float on dropped earlier by the Ventura, all grouped tighter together and watched water cans explode around them. Paralyzed by the fear of watching their closest of friends taken by the sharks, the men kept to their groups.

After the PBY ran out of items to drop, it made one last pass and they saw it fall. The large rectangular shape took hold of the air two-hundred feet above their heads. They squinted from the sun and watched the shape toss and sway—tumbling through the white light in a random dance of twists and turns before hitting the ocean with a dead thud. A slight splash of water displaced by its landing.

The large Navy life raft touched down only fifty yards from Quint and the other six sailors in his group. With other screams of attacks in the water back towards the large circle of survivors, and the massacre of the sixty men on the main floater net only thirty yards away, panic stood fresh in their fatigued and frantic minds. There wasn't a word of discussion or moment of hesitation. Once the life raft hit the water, closer to them than anything dropped before, the two Marines let go of the floater net and struck out for the raft.

"It's so close, boys. They got the right idea. Let's go!"

Jack pulled himself down to the base of the floater net by Harold's feet and let go while watching the splashing Marines swim further away.

Hodge looked on from the other side of the net. "What about Harold?"

Chester Eastman looked over to Quint, who ignored them all, and just stared into his bottle, watching the sharks below.

"Looks like Quint is going to stay with him, Hodge. I'm ready to get out of the water!"

"It's too far, gentlemen." Quint called out while not looking up from the water. "Better to stay together here."

"I'll take my chances out there instead of waiting for that tiger shark to come back. C'mon, Hodge!"

Eastman pushed away from the net and started clawing at the water to follow Jack and the Marines.

Hodge hesitated and looked up at Harold, who rolled to his side and saw the men swimming away.

"You better watch over them, Hodge. They are going to need help, too."

Hodge nodded in the affirmative to Harold and pushed away from the net, starting his overhand strokes towards the life raft.

Halfway to the raft, Private 1st Class Raymond Rich and Private 1st Class Frank Spino felt the stinging and burning sensation of their skin pulling away from the emaciated muscles of their shoulders. The life jackets had become solid weights, and they realized they fought them as much as they fought the water to stay afloat. Rich paused and started tearing at the front tie strings on his life jacket, pulling them open. Without missing a beat, he ditched his waterlogged life jacket and lurched forward, heaving his arms over his head. He saw the life raft only ten yards away.

Just behind him, Spino did the same. The life jacket pulled him under. His weakened arms strained to reach for the surface. He broke through and took a gasp of air. The thirty-yard swim seemed an eternity, and the twenty yards to go an impossibility. He grabbed at the front strings and pulled, but his frantic movements only tightened the knots. The jacket wouldn't keep his face above water and pulled him back down. Just underneath the surface, Spino saw the aggressive bodies of oceanic whitetip sharks swimming all around. One came closer to him, and he kicked his legs to keep it away, while trying to pull at the jacket tie strings. He could feel the burn of his lungs yearning to breathe. When the last bits of adrenaline passed through his body, he summoned the strength to pull his right arm out from the life jacket and felt the sagging pruned skin tearing away from his shoulder under his olive drab Marine work shirt. Spino struggled and pulled the life jacket up over his head and kicked hard.

Spino broke through the surface, gulping air back into his exhausted lungs. Rich heard the commotion and turned back to his fellow Marine. Spino's thirst-infected throat closed, too swollen to call out any commands. He saw Rich stop swimming and waved to him to keep going—to get to the raft. Rich saw Spino swim towards him and he turned. The raft was only ten feet away now.

Spino slapped at the water and kicked his feet, but the strength was now gone. Without the weight of the saturated life jacket, he felt light as ever, but his muscles depleted. He couldn't move his arms fast enough. His body couldn't stay horizontal, and his legs lost the ability to kick. Spino's overhead arm strokes turned to an uncoordinated flopping of limbs. He was no longer grabbing the water to pull himself along, but only slapping the water, struggling to stay afloat. His mind fought to remember the earliest of swimming lessons he took as a boy back at his family's camp on Big Bear Lake. He knew how to swim, but his body didn't want to listen. His shoulders burned and cramped. He gulped one more breath and sank below the surface. Only the sharks that circled and closed in could hear his scream of frustration. The fight released from him in a steady stream of bubbles. Spino watched the sunlit surface fall away when his arms gave out and no longer wanted to move.

Rich reached the raft and took hold of the rope line that wove itself around the entire edge of the raft's rectangular canvas-covered outer shell. He pulled and kicked his body onto the edge of the raft and rolled over inside, landing on the wood slatted bottom resting in one foot of water. Out of breath and burning all over from the use of emaciated muscles, Rich wanted to just lay and be still, but he knew Spino was going to need help. He pulled himself back up to the edge of the raft and looked over for his friend, who wasn't there. He could only see the set of two life jackets floating twenty yards away.

Sapped of any strength to call for Spino, Rich rested his chest on the edge of the raft. He looked down into the blue water and imagined that his fellow Marine would emerge with a triumphant hand out for him to grab. For the rest of his life, Raymond Rich would repeat what he did over the next few minutes—look deep down in water and wait for the hand of his friend, Frank, that would never arrive.

The sun hung lower in the late afternoon sky and reflected off the increasing ocean swells. Jack saw the raft rising and falling just ahead. He heard commotion in the water behind him and turned to see Hodge and Eastman pulling themselves along as well as they could. Their arms flopping and slapping the water like limp rawhide saddle straps. Out of breath and gasping for air, he felt the bump against his thigh and looked down upon the shovel-shaped head of the oceanic whitetip shark emerging from his blind side. Jack spun around and kicked at the shark, landing a foot on the top of its head. The rabid fish flinched and scurried away. Only ten yards from the raft. Jack untied his life jacket and slipped out but held it to his chest, using one arm to sidestroke his way forward.

Ten yards behind, Hodge felt he was pulling away from Eastman and he stopped and turned.

Eastman gasped—his breaths heaving and labored.

"This jacket is too heavy. Feels like a lead blanket. I need to get out of it."

Hodge adjusted his life jacket and kicked himself higher in the water.

"We're almost there, Chester. We are too weak to go without them."

Before Hodge could get the words out, Eastman slipped from the over-sized cumbersome life jacket. He never had time to get his issued jacket before the ship went down and could only grab one that was sized for a gorilla. Eastman took the jacket and rolled it up, then pulled it under the water and placed it between his legs. The little buoyancy steadied him, and he called to Hodge, who he could see was about to swim back for him.

"I got it. It still works! Just keep going." Eastman felt a swell pick him up, pushing him in the right direction. He pulled with his arms and felt the seas were with him. Hodge turned, kicking his feet for the raft.

Jack reached the raft and slapped the side with an outstretched hand, grabbing the safety line. Rich reached down, searching for Jack's arm. Their skin was slimy and impossible to hold. The strength in the bodies had been exhausted, and they struggled to just hold on to each other. Jack tried kicking one leg up and could not get it high enough to break the surface. The eighteen-inch-tall sidewall of the raft became an impossible cliff to climb. Every repeated attempt became more panicked and more desperate, with Rich trying to pull and Jack trying to climb.

Jack saw the dorsal fins break through the surface, leaving a trail of disturbed water all around them. He shouted in terror upon feeling the water rush from behind and a heavy push on his back. Jack swirled around expecting to see the shark with its jaws coming down on him but found an exhausted Hodge reaching out to help.

"C'mon, get your leg up there sailor, let's go!"

Hodge reached down under the water to grab Jack's leg and lifted.

With Rich pulling from above, and Hodge pushing hard, Jack's right leg swung up and landed on the raft. His momentum carried his body up, rolling over the edge. Jack collapsed into the belly of the raft with aching lungs—every muscle weakened and trembling. The dehydration rendered their limbs useless.

"C'mon Jack, we gotta help Hodge!"

Rich leaned over and reached down to grab Hodge's life jacket. The weight of the jacket proved too much, and Hodge dropped back into the water.

"You gotta get it off! Come on!"

Jack struggled to lean over the edge and reach down. Above the water from the raft's edge, he saw the sharks all around them—only a few feet below.

Hodge's finger nails tore back and the dead skin on the fingertips split while he fumbled to untie the life jacket tie strings. Rich looked down at the large bronze bodies of the oceanic whitetips stalking the deep blue beneath them.

"C'mon fella, get those knots untied. Move!"

Hodge's bleeding fingers pulled the remaining tie, and the life jacket fell away, just as his grip slipped from Rich's hands. Hodge dropped below the water faster than any of them expected. Without the life jacket buoyancy, he panicked while kicking in a frantic mess and tried to breathe before he broke the surface. The poisoned salt water sucked into his lungs. He emerged along the side of the raft, heaving and retching the salt water up from his system. He felt his brittle ribs crack as his body lurched forward from the diaphragm and stomach muscles convulsing.

Jack looked up to see the broad rounded edge of the white-tipped dorsal fin emerge a short distance away, closing in on Hodge and the raft.

"No time, gotta get in here now!"

Rich looked at Jack and saw what he was staring at. The fin grew larger and rose further up from the surface. The usual kicking and pounding would not ward off this size of a shark. They both leaned over and grabbed Hodge by the arms. Hodge saw them looking out while they pulled on him. He turned his fatigued gaze to see the dorsal fin of the shark rocking back and forth at great speed. The exhausted men pulled from above while Hodge kicked with desperation. He went to swing his leg up on the side for one last attempt when the wet, waterlogged skin of his forearms broke free and tore, causing Jack and Rich to lose their grips and Hodge plunged back into the sea.

With a grip on the raft's rescue line, Hodge turned towards the shark and closed his eyes.

The shark stroked its powerful tail three quick beats and launched forward. Jaws agape and extended, it bit down on the dead life jacket that floated next to Hodge. A great splash and hissing sound of compressed kapok material and the life jacket disappeared from the surface. The shark hurled itself forward and scraped along the waistline of Hodge tearing away shirt and skin with its sandpaper gritted hide. The shark struck the raft with its powerful tail and the men fell backwards after receiving a face full of warm sea water.

Hodge kept his white-knuckle hold on the raft's survival line and looked back towards the approaching splashing sounds.

An exhausted Eastman closed in on the raft. He had a tired smile and wanted to speak, but not enough breath for words. He threw his arm out for one last stroke and Hodge reached. The enormous head of the oceanic whitetip broke the surface to grab Eastman by the chest. A flash of glistening brown skin, a clap of a dozen rows of shark teeth meeting rib cage and sternum—a quick disturbance of water and Seaman 2nd Class Chester Eastman disappeared forever.

Hodge closed his eyes, too tired to call out or attempt to swim for Eastman. He held the raft and cursed its existence.

Why did it have to fall so close? Tempting them.

Why didn't they stay with Quint and Harold back at the floater net? The others might still be alive.

Why did it take him and not me?

Hodge clutched the side of the raft while Jack and Rich collapsed. Neither of them spoke. They each pondered these questions in their own way for the rest of their lives.

10   PBY CATALINA

The PBY Catalina and Lockheed Ventura bombers both continued to circle the skies. Quint readjusted his grip on the space between the cork floaters of the net by Harold's right side. He moved over to the opposite side to see what happened to the men who abandoned their small group. With his chin constantly in the water, his swamped kapok life jacket teetered on the edge of complete failure. When the sea flattened, Quint couldn't see more than a dozen yards out. The horizon broke apart by the increasing swells. He couldn't see those who made a swim for the life raft. He wanted to think they made it out of the water, but the darkest thoughts swelled from deep inside.

Quint's mind settled into darkness, and he thought of them all dead. It serves them right—they should've listened to him and stuck together.

What do you know about survival, anyway? You couldn't even keep the kid alive when it was all said and done. You just let him get pulled away. The others would be all the same if they had listened to you.

Harold moaned prayers and begged for mercy while drifting in and out of his semi-conscious state. His words just spit out into a garbled mess. Quint looked up at Harold from the water's edge. Disdain and contempt overwhelmed him.

You want to survive? Just pull him off and let him go. No way could he stay up in the water with those charred arms of his. You could pull yourself up... be out of the water in two minutes... no one would ever know.

Quint turned away from the sight of Harold.

His family would know, and so would you. You ready to live the rest of your tomorrows knowing you killed this kid on the day before his twenty-fourth birthday? For what? What are you going to do with life? We are all gonna die today. Just make sure you take the tiger out with you before you go.

Quint's head snapped at a distant shriek of terror and thrashing water—another victim taken by the sharks. The sounds of murder consumed by the roaring plane passing overhead.

The wide gray hull of the PBY Catalina banked hard against the blue sky, cutting across the sun's orange glow—its one-hundred-foot wingspan casting a shadow across Quint's face. After righting itself, the plane dropped altitude. Hydraulic pumps whined while lowering the pontoon floaters from the tips of its wings in a landing approach just off to the north. Quint's hands bit hard into the manila rope of the floater net—the hard fibers now cutting the weakened soft white skin of his salt-water eaten palms. A large twelve-foot swell picked him and Harold up. Quint saw further out as the wave crested.

The plane hit the surface hard on its wide steel belly and bounced off a large moving ridge of water. Its engines went into a stall and the three-bladed propellers chopped the air over the sound of rapid-fire exhaust—the two fourteen-cylinder engines fighting against the wind. The powerful plane caught air on the rebound from the initial impact. It steadied itself and dropped again, detonating the sea. White water crashed high over its sixty-three feet of metallic length.

The rivets along the bottom, not designed for open sea landings, rang out like gunshots as they failed and popped. Seams broke and opened in the hull. The plane bounced once more, then settled in hard. As the large rolling swell set them back down, Quint's last view of the PBY Catalina was the vertical stabilizers of the tail digging into the erupting ocean.

Back down to the water's edge, Quint, along with the rest of the survivors of the large group, could see the wings and propellers of PBY stretched across the top of the plane. The aircraft towered twenty feet above the surface. With its engines droning, and the propellers still chopping away, the amphibious plane moved through the water. The men watched and couldn't believe the sight of it turning towards them.

The nose of the PBY crashed against the ocean when the slow-moving boat-like hull of the aircraft plowed through the crest of an approaching wave. Quint watched the sea spray blanket the windshield of the cockpit. Faces of the plane's crew filled the windows of the nose turret and gunner's hatch back on the tail. They watched in awe at the sight of ocean-tortured survivors waving for help from the oily water, littered with blood, bodies, and remnants.

Once numbering six-hundred and fifty, now only less than one hundred faces of this large group of survivors stared back at the winged rescue sent from the heavens. The plane taxied across the outer edge of the group of survivors and stumbled its way into the first set of men, who all thrashed their way towards it.

Quint saw the plane fifty yards to the northeast. The starboard side hatch just behind the cockpit opened and a rope ladder tossed out. The massive wings tilted with the turmoil of the open sea cutting across and rocking the hull of the Catalina.

"C'mon, boy. We're going to that plane!"

Quint's commandment startled Harold. He shoved the glass bottle into his life jacket and took hold of the floater net with his left hand. Right arm reaching out, Quint grabbed for the water and kicked his legs.

With all the strength he could find, Quint moved the floater net, with Harold on top, a few inches at a time. He decided. Get Harold as close to the plane as fate would allow him. The tags clinked together in his shirt pocket and reminded him of his duty to those men. When he got close enough, he'll throw the three sets of identification tags from Herbie, Fritz, and Machado around Harold's neck. If it was his turn to die, at least the tags that were trusted with him will get to the families where they belong.

Quint had a purpose, and he felt that momentary strength of a conviction fight back the dark thoughts of death and hopelessness—at least for now. His right arm pulled harder. Quint's eyes stung again from the sweat and oil seeping into them.

He didn't dare switch hands. His right arm was always the strongest.

Back home, Quint won many arm wrestling contests on the docks during payday with his right. During the drunken brawls—liquored-up gladiator matches with barroom heroes on cold winter nights, his right hand always settled the score and ended the night in victory. Quint remembered wearing a smile while stumbling his way through the brown dust clouds of broken glass and pushing aside the other drunks. He ignored the crashing bottles against breaking chairs with his right arm bent and waiting—fist cocked and loaded against his chest. With a target found, two decades of rolled-up aggression from hauling and heaving fish, nets, lobster pots, or whatever paid the bills at the time—all loaded into that right arm. Quint's right fist was famous in some establishments for delivering what felt like a strike from the hammer of Thor himself to whoever was unlucky enough to be on the receiving end.

Quint strained and grabbed at the water with that right arm and pulled. His teeth remained gritted and face clenched. The pain and fatigue served as proof he still lived. If he was going to see his father on this day, he will tell him how he saved one man before he went. Quint became a methodical machine, issuing rapid pulls toward the rumbling engines of the PBY.

Harold rolled to his side and looked ahead. His blackened and oozing arms flinched from the splashing water made by Quint's thrashing. Harold saw the water spray from the waves catching the hull of the PBY. Around them, other survivors flailed away at the sea with their heavy arms as they all tried to claim the next chance to get out of the water. The closer the men swam towards the PBY, the more they panicked. Their movements became more erratic. Some men pulled others out of the way or pushed floating dead bodies aside and into the path of another. The exhaustion set in, allowing fear and dread to take over.

Quint fired his right arm into the water with the mechanical repetition of a piston's connecting rod. Off to his left, he watched an oceanic whitetip rise out of the blue water and black oil. The shark snatched a lone sailor with its lethal bite. Only a chirp of a scream released before the sailor and the shark both disappeared from the surface. The quickness of the attack startled Quint, and he felt that now-familiar sensation of fear wash over while he pulled another stroke of ocean towards him. The fear translated to anger. Quint gnashed his teeth and released a guttural war cry so loud the others in the water turned to see if someone else was being attacked.

The back of his neck bled as the heavy life jacket collar dug into the skin on every stroke. Quint kicked and pulled. His left hand of white knuckles bled and squeezed the rope of the floater net under Harold's rolled-up life jacket pillow. The net continued its crawl forward in the water.

An aircrew member reached down and pulled another limp body from the water. He shoved the survivor into the belly of the PBY, which roared to life. Through the windshield of the plane's cockpit, the pilot's eyes contacted Quint's bloodshot, enraged gaze. The propellers chopped at the air and the floating plane took another swell across its nose. It pushed forward into the sea towards the small crowd of survivors, who slapped at the water with leaden arms trying to get closer to the plane. Far to the back of the swimming survivors, Quint pulled the floater net with the near-death Harold. The PBY closed in to only a distance of twenty yards. Out of fear of running over a survivor in the choppy water and crushing them, it couldn't get any closer and the engine's roar settled—the steel hull set into a drift. The men would have to close the rest of the distance themselves.

Harold shouted out in fear and the strength of the shark jerked Quint backwards. An aggressive ten-foot oceanic whitetip shot from below the floater net, biting down hard on a section of cork floaters under Harold's feet. Its brown head glistened in the failing sunlight and shook in a violent back-and-forth. Cork floaters fell apart and sections of rope frayed and split. The shark rolled and contorted its body, throwing all the weight of its trunk against the tattered end of the floater net.

Quint screamed in pain. The net caught his left hand and pulled him backwards—his legs kicking out from underneath him to the surface. He released his bloody grip and righted himself, spinning around in the water to see the thrashing of white-tipped fins, with Harold pushing himself back towards the head of the floater net. Surface water swallowed the end of the net as the shark tangled itself in the destruction of ropes and floaters. The trapped predator crashed to the side, pulling the end of the net further into the water with it.

With arms extended towards the net next to a terrified Harold, Quint met a shock wave of water as an even larger whitetip lurched from the deep and landed its upper half on the net—its jaws snapping away at Harold. The net pulled down even further by the weight of the second shark and Harold, laying on his back, slid towards the monster's yellow eyes. Rows of triangular teeth stared back at him. The net convulsed and jerked in the water from the continued thrashing of the first shark wrapped in the ropes. Harold screamed, holding his charred and useless arms out to the side and kicking his feet at the searching mouth of death, now only a mere three feet from him. He felt his body slide towards the shark, which locked its eyes on Harold. The frenzied fish kicked its tail and pushed itself further up on the net. The shark's jaws opened and closed in a rapid-fire repeat motion. Harold pulled his legs further back, but the shark was too heavy, and the net's buoyancy gave way. It dropped further into the water, causing Harold to slide almost on top of the shark's head.

From out of the side of the net, a burst of white water and the oceanic whitetip heaved to the side. With hands held fast to the right side of the net for leverage, Quint tucked his legs and generated all the force he could, kicking both feet into the side of the attacking fish. Stunned, the shark rolled to its side and slid back into the sea. Quint saw the stubborn shark in the water at the base of the net, with most of its large twelve-foot body submerged. He reared both legs back a second time. Both of Quint's feet landed a blow against the shark's gill slits along its left side. The monster fish snapped out of its frenzied state and into a survival reaction. The fish dropped, surprised and in pain. It swung its tail in two quick beats and retreated into the crowd of frantic oceanic whitetips only ten feet below.

Harold lowered his legs when the lower half of the net surfaced. The net shook from the first oceanic whitetip shark, tangled in the shreds of manila rope and cork floaters. Quint, hand over hand, pulled himself to the end of the net towards the trapped shark. The fear of death produced rage. Both emotions combined, allowing him to ignore the pain. Every movement caused more of his skin to be pulled from his body by the coarse and hard material of his life jacket and clothes. A strength emerged from inside his being, overriding all feelings of exhaustion and fatigue. For the next precious minutes of his life, Quint became superhuman—no longer feeling or reacting in a conscious state. Like the frenzied oceanic whitetips attacking from below, he lost his soul.

He pulled himself to the thrashing shark and held his clenched fist into the air, bringing it down hard on the shark's head. Again, raising his right hand to the heavens, he brought it down in a thunderous thud and he felt the shark's cartilaginous skull crack just behind its left eye when the hammer-like fist landed.

The voices of survivors calling for the PBY crew to rescue them, the terrified shrieks of pain and death from other victims, and the intense heavy roar of the plane's engines dissolved to a muffled silence. All Quint heard was the deadened thuds of his repeated strikes against the head of the fish. With every dull impact his fist made against the brown sandpaper skin of the shark, he felt its hard interior reduce to soft jelly. Quint had visions of despair and rage. He watched Herbie's face sinking away from him. Machado's hand disappearing into the water. He saw the kid, Troy Boyd, deep under the water, pounding at the head of the giant tiger shark that took him. His father's dead hand holding on to the boathook, buried into the giant marlin. Quint threw all his weight down into his hand and felt the metacarpal bones fracture with every strike. He didn't care. He slipped from reality when all the thoughts of life suppressed—vanquished by his unmitigated hatred for the sharks.

A minute later, the shark lay still. Quint laid across it, out of breath and shaking. He couldn't tell what was his blood or the shark's blood covering his hand. Quint pulled hard against the pain to open the fingers from the iron-clad ball of fist his right hand had become. He now felt the sting of pain from his right wrist and broken bones in the base of his hand fire back through his forearm.

With shaking hands, Quint reached over the dead shark's body and pulled at the rope wrappings. Harold, soaked and trembling, lay on his side to catch his breath. Burned arms held out in front, Harold shifted back onto his life jacket pillow and looked at the crowd of men scrambling to get pulled into the open hatch of the PBY just twenty yards away.

Quint's bloody and pruned flesh-shredded fingertips pulled on a piece of rope that was caught across the dead whitetip's mouth. The shark moved. He held his breath and flinched at the thought of its reanimation back to life. Below him, another shark reset its hold on the lifeless tail and started shaking it back and forth. Quint pulled hard and the last wrapping of the manila line frayed apart against the dead shark's teeth. Its body slipped into the water. Three other sharks came in and hit the sinking carcass at full speed. A cloud of shredded shark skin and blood expanded below the floater net. Quint watched through the empty surface as the crowd of marauders swarmed and devoured the dead shark. The feeding frenzy showing no allegiance or mercy to even its own.

11 RESCUE

More planes arrived in the area to conduct low sweeps over the large patch of survivors. Most remained too far from the PBY Catalina and too weak to make a swim for the salvation offered by the landed amphibious plane. Survival gear rained down from above. Inflatable rubber life rafts hit the sea around the helpless men. Canisters of food rations and fresh water exploded on the surface. Many broke on impact and lost their contents to the ocean.

The last ten yards to the PBY were the deadliest. All the men in the water underestimated the distance and their own strength in making the swim. The weight of taxed life jackets pulled them down below the waterline. Their skin abraded to a bleeding mess by the heavy seams. Some struggled to break free from the Navy-issued survival gear that devolved into a vested sack of lead. Life jackets ditched and back on the surface, they pushed forward, only to discover they couldn't tread water to stay afloat on their own. One-hundred hours of trauma, starvation, and dehydration took a devastating toll. Bodies failed in the panic. For some, the last view of the world was the aircrew of the PBY trying to throw life rings and lines to pull them in. Last breaths spent with desperate fingers searching for lifelines. Emaciated muscles of the legs and shoulders locked, and they fell below the surface, never to be seen again.

Quint pulled the small floater net closer to the PBY and saw a struggling sailor without a life jacket go under only a few feet away. He released his grip on the net and lunged for the sailor, but felt his own body go under the surface—his life jacket now waterlogged and past the point of failure. Quint opened his eyes. Through the saltwater sting, he saw the desperate young boy clawing for the beams of setting sunlight that broke through the surface. With only one leg able to move, the boy sank lower and lower. Quint struggled back to the surface, fighting against the weight of the life jacket. He watched the last air bubbles of terrified failure leaving the young sailor's mouth. The boy dropped into the layer of swarming sharks that waited further down in the bottomless blue.

At the surface, a struggling collection of thirty sailors gathered in a small group ten feet from the PBY Catalina. The ones who were closest reached for the ladder and needed to be pulled in by the two airmen at the open hatch. With the engines at idle and the propellers silent, another airman climbed out on top of the plane's fuselage. He tossed a coiled line to panicked sailors on the outside of the group, trying to pull them closer if they could reach the lifeline.

Quint broke through and gasped for air while struggling with the front ties on his life jacket. He held on to Harold's small section of tattered floater net. The life jacket released, and he tossed it on the net next to Harold. Quint saw the shimmer of orange light bounce off the glass bottle sticking out of the sopping inside pocket and remembered the dog tag collection in his shirt pocket. He tapped his chest underwater and heard the clinking metal, confirming that they were still with him.

The large wings and starboard side of the PBY Catalina cast a shadow from the setting sun across the group of sailors in the water. A massive silhouette of safety crested with the swells of the ocean in front of them. Quint looked up to the weathered, salt-stained glass of the cockpit windshield and saw the pilot lording over the chaos of fins and bodies. The pilot barked orders into the radio equipment and shouted commands to his crew. Another ocean swell rolled the plane close to the floating survivors. The time was now—get on the plane or die.

Quint pulled the net a little closer to shout over the idling engines.

"We got an injured man here! Make room!"

The airmen pointed towards Harold, holding his fire-damaged arms above the floater net. Quint made a few more strokes. The net moved closer to the hatch when a shark grabbed one of the waiting sailors and pulled him away from the group. None of those who were there in that moment ever forgot the noise of the unfortunate sailor being carried off without warning. An unforgettable scream—the sound of death arriving only feet from salvation.

Panic flared and all the men made a crazed lunge for the plane. Six sailors climbed on top of Harold's floater net and sank it in mere seconds as they did anything possible to get their legs out of the water. Harold dropped into the water and took a kick in the face by another sailor who crawled over him to get to the open hatch of the PBY.

Overwhelmed, the surge of swimmers pushed Quint back. He saw Harold treading water with his legs and screaming. Harold's blackened arms, bathed in the acidic saltwater, held above his head in sheer agonizing pain.

One airman reached down from the open hatch and grabbed Harold's arm. He gripped and pulled as he did with all the others. Only this time, he pulled on the forearm and all that came up was the charred, dead loose skin that tore away from Harold's arm. Harold dropped back into the water with a shriek of terror—his skinless right arm wore a glazed color of dark red. Quint lunged for him, but it was too late. Harold, paralyzed by the shock, dropped into the blue.

The strap tied from the roll of Herbie Robinson's life jacket cinched tight around Harold's neck. The life jacket, having dried long enough out of the water on the floater net, regained its buoyancy. Enough to catch and suspend Harold's body just under the waterline. Quint pushed two panicked sailors out of his way and dove into the water. He reached for the unconscious Harold, whose body hung by the neck from the surfaced life jacket. Three feet underwater, Quint grasped the strap and pulled Harold to the light. The airman climbed down the rope ladder from the open PBY hatch and waited with an outstretched arm when Quint and Harold surfaced.

With Quint pushing from below, the airman grabbed Harold's shirt and pulled him to the reaching hands of others. Quint saw Harold's feet disappear into the hatch when the fear of waiting for their turn at the ladder caused a wave of survivors to rush the PBY. Others shoved ahead and began climbing the ladder into the plane past the airman hanging off to the side. Quint felt his strength vacate his muscles. His body reached the max depletion of any stored fat and protein remnants. He felt life abandon him. After his tow of the floater net, the fight against the sharks, saving Harold; he didn't have the strength to overpower the others. He fought to keep himself afloat.

The tags. Remember the tags. You promised.

Quint reached into his shirt pocket under the water and captured the handful of dog tags.

"Make sure these get saved!"

Quint's hoarse voice still carried and alerted the airman hanging outside the plane. He raised his bleeding right hand with a fistful of metal identification tags and chains hanging between the fingers. While holding the ladder, the airman strained with his free hand to Quint's outstretched arm.

Two late-arriving sailors thrashed their way to the plane from behind Quint and hit him hard in their mad dash for safety. They struck Quint's elbow and, for the first time in his life, his right arm failed him. He lost his grip. He watched in the nightmarish second it took for the shiny collection of dog tags and chains to take flight and catch a gleam of the orange sun. They hit the water only a few feet back from the plane just beyond the struggling group of survivors waiting their turn to get aboard.

Quint shouted out in terror, as if he just lost the lives of his shipmates all over again. With little strength left inside, Quint charged out of the group, swimming towards the spot of disturbed water where the metal tags disappeared.

To that point, Quint was terrified of dying, but he now realized what scared him even more—failure. He failed his father, his two marriages, his friends during the sinking. He failed to protect Boyd. And now he failed at even the smallest of responsibilities. Machado's request—deliver the tags to a grieving mother. Herbie's tags were the only concrete memory left of his friend. And Fritz, the first casualty under his charge of the floater net as senior man.

Quint dove into the water, straining his already bloodshot eyes through the brine and debris. Before him and just out of reach—three sets of tags dropping in peace. They separated from the surface eddies created by the latest oceanic swell to roll past. Quint kicked, thrashed, and flailed his body to get closer to the metallic mementos of the fallen. They flew from him like angelic doves, each going their own way on an ascension to heaven.

Quint couldn't swim any deeper. His lungs burned for air. He reared back in an angry grief and surfaced, breathing in the air of defeat. Quint washed in his fear of failure and knew there was nothing he could do but wait for his turn to die.

"Grab the rope!"

The airman on top of the wing of the PBY yelled and tossed the lassoed end of the line towards Quint.

The line hit the water between Quint and another sailor. The other sailor looked at Quint, then lunged for the rope himself. Quint just watched and didn't try for it. The sailor opened the loop at the end to throw it over his head and around his chest. With a tug, the running bowline cinched, and the line became taut. The weakened sailor pulled towards the hatch, which only had three men waiting their turn.

Quint was numb. Sapped of emotion, he noticed the small section of floater net with his life jacket not too far away. He ignored the fins cutting the surface. The bodies of sharks circling below him meant nothing. He gripped the net and pulled himself up. Quint laid across the cork floaters and watched the other sailor get pulled towards the open hatch when he saw it.

One hundred feet from the shadow of the PBY, the wooden crate broke through the surface and moved through the water. It tracked through the floating dead bodies and around rubber life rafts filled with sailors lucky enough to find one and pull their legs out of the water.

The wooden crate surged forward. Life rafts of men watched it pull past— the shadow of the giant tiger shark below the surface, leading the way.

The line hit the water again next to Quint, but he didn't care. His eyes only saw the wooden crate, and with it, a new feeling. A feeling that quashed any emotion and psychological condition his human mind could create. A feeling of such magnitude that fears of death and rational decisions in pursuing safety dissolved. A new fuel for life from that moment forward. Quint saw Boyd's wooden crate swerve and cut through the water, and he tasted it for the first time in his life—revenge. Just the mere hint of it on the lips, on the edge of attainability, was all that it took. Quint would never be the same. He wanted revenge.

The airmen of the PBY all shouted for him to grab the line, but Quint ignored them and instead did the unimaginable. Quint took the glass bottle from his life jacket, pulled the sodden vest into the water, and slid his body off the net. He submerged the life jacket under his arm for a float and kicked away from the open hatch of stunned airmen.

The airmen shouted and ordered him to grab the line, which was pulled back in and recast. It landed in front of Quint, and he once again ignored it. His eyes locked on the moving wooden crate. Quint reached the pontoon floater at the end of the starboard wing of the Catalina.

"C'mon, you bastard sonofabitch. Come here and finish what you started!"

The crate slowed on its track away from the PBY and Quint stretched, clutching the bottle by the long neck. He shattered the glass on the plane's riveted sheet metal. The impact made a ping against the hollow pontoon and reverberated through the water.

The wooden crate crawled to a stop. Out in the water, it turned. The crate faced Quint and crept towards him.

Quint, holding the life jacket under his left arm and the knife-edge of broken glass in his right hand, steadied himself with his legs and smiled with gritted teeth at the sight of the approaching wooden crate.

"Farewell and adieu to you fair Spanish ladies."

The crate swerved and shifted and locked in on Quint's voice.

"Farewell and adieu to you ladies of Spain."

The sight of Boyd's crate enraptured him. The ultimate impending revenge on the tiger shark drained his senses. Quint ignored the screaming crew of the PBY and the airman who dove into the water, swimming up behind him to throw the rope over his head and left shoulder. He didn't feel the rope cinch down and pull, for all his soul locked on the approaching crate of wood. Only hours before, the crate was a sight of relief and hope—now a symbol of death and revenge.

"For we've received orders for to sail back to Boston!"

The crate increased in speed and honed its direction.

Quint, throwing his life jacket out towards the crate, grimaced and yelled. He leaned into the water, but the three airmen back at the hatch pulled hand over hand on the line.

Thirty feet and closing, the crate surged.

His body hung in the water and his legs kicked out from being dragged backwards. Quint held out his weapon of shattered glass.

"And so never more shall we see you again!"

Quint finished in a growl of angry resentment, layered with the sheer joy in knowing what he will do. The tiger will be blind and dead before this day is over. Already dead inside—the imminent taste of revenge made him feel alive.

The crate closed in. Twenty feet. The airmen pulled even harder.

Quint slapped the water and thrashed in wild yawps of primitive ancient mariner howls. Like the calls and taunts at their Poseidon by those who would climb the topsails and face a raging hurricane of doom. There was no tomorrow. It would end here and now.

The wooden crate left a small wake of water. It moved fast. The airmen watched the massive shadow below the surface get larger and closer. Quint hit the hull of the PBY. Arms reached down to seize him. The rope pulled up and took his limp body higher.

With his waistline still in the water, Quint saw the dark spots and greenish brown skin of the tiger just out ahead of him. He lurched forward and struck at the water with the broken bottle.

The tiger shark rose higher on a targeted track. Its maw of wild, angular teeth and jaw extended. Eyes rolled back and white.

The men pulled all at once and Quint's body hoisted up from the breached attack; the shark missing its target by a moment. They dragged Quint kicking and screaming into the hatch, fighting against his rescuers with whatever weakened strength he had left. He clawed and crawled to get back in the water with a mind lost to insanity. A thirst for revenge denied and unquenched. His body dropped to the dry floor of the crowded plane.

12   LIGHT

His heart raced and denied the brain its passage into the unconscious oblivion where many of the survivors already went. Instead, Quint tried to fight the two airmen that carried him. Famished muscles refused his instructions, resulting in a meager resistance to the hands that dragged him from the revenge he craved. The surreal feeling of floating for days, then carried through the cramped interior of the PBY Catalina patrol plane, captured him in a euphoric daze.

Quint saw flashes of imagery, with his stinging eyes pulling in and out of focus. Dehydrated bodies of survivors, covered in saltwater ulcers and bloody translucent skin. The deck of the aircraft strewn with writhing figures. The crew of the plane bailed water out with buckets and empty cans. They fought the steady stream of ocean flowing in between broken welds and busted rivets of aluminum seams on the plane's hull. Damage from the open sea landing, never allowed by military regulations, but overruled by the pilot on this day. In the corner, two shirtless marines, shrouded in black sticky oil, sharing their first drink in five days—warm green bean juice from a punctured steel can of rations.

The airmen carried Quint to an overhead hatch just behind the cockpit. Two other sets of hands were waiting. Through an engineer's crawlspace and then to the top of the plane's wings, they took him. Quint watched the orange glow of a late sunset stream across the sky and turn into the dim purple light of dusk. They carried him across the surface of the large one-hundred-foot wingspan.

His eyes closed, and he saw Herbie—his friend leaving him and dropping into the deep water below. He then saw the kid, Troy, in the tiger's mouth. Only this time, Troy was not fighting the tiger, but staring back at Quint without expression while being carried away into the dark blue thermocline below. The shimmering innocence of the dog tags fluttering and falling from the sea-shredded skin of his outstretched fingertips.

The imagery struck the fear of failure into Quint and his eyes fired open. He realized it wasn't a dream and his soul fell into despair. He rolled to his side, next to other tortured bodies of survivors on top of the starboard wing.

Out of space inside the belly of the PBY, the pilot, Lieutenant Adrian Marks, ordered the crew to take the influx of survivors topside. The aircrew lashed the dying weak bodies down to the vast wingspan with parachute cord to ensure none would roll back into the sea of oil and blood below. Quint felt the plane rolling and tossing from the ocean swells that held it.

"Hang in there, pal. You are home-free now," said one airman, whose hands worked to pull the line tight around Quint's chest, securing him to a still but breathing body of another survivor.

Quint closed his eyes to the insanity. His brain gave up and shutdown.

Nothing could have decimated the sweet pleasure of sleep and awaken him except for the quenching of the accursed thirst that plagued him for five days. Quint did not resist the startling consciousness when the cool fresh water touched his dried, sun-burned lips. He swallowed and the cold liquid life settled inside him.

"I can't give you too much. We pulled fifty-six of you fellas out of there and we don't have enough for everyone."

Quint felt another flow of water pour into his open mouth while he struggled to open his red eyes. The eyelids bulged and swelled with infection.

Laid on his left side, Quint's head rested on his biceps muscle. His first blurry sight was the USS Indianapolis tattoo on top of the left forearm, glowing in the moonlight. His arm's salt-corroded skin was a ghostly white transparent film—a translucent covering in which he could see the spider web of veins underneath. The bold tattoo lettering stood out, just as it did when the black ink was fresh in that Pearl Harbor parlor. The full moon and stars lit the sky over the plane that pitched and rolled with the sea. Quint felt the rise and fall.

Next to him knelt a man of slight stature. With a cigarette hanging under a trimmed mustache, he held a small stainless-steel kettle. Quint recognized the officer from the khaki uniform but did not move in the slightest—he didn't care to salute anymore.

"I saw you out there. Pulling that kid on the net like you did. The crew medic is patching him up with fresh bandages. You saved the kid's life."

Lieutenant Marks leaned in and poured Quint a third ration of water from the kettle.

"I'm going to put you in for the Navy Cross for that," said Marks.

"Not interested. But if you are the one that put this dumbo down today and picked us up, you put yourself in for one." Quint's voice improved after the third drink. "Tell them I said you can have two."

The pilot had an amused smile, impressed with Quint's candor. He looked down the wing at the bodies of two dozen men, laid out and tied to the dark metal. They reminded him of the cases he saw strapped to the roof of a traveling salesman's car once.

The moon hid behind dark clouds overhead, trying to illuminate the calm black seascape. A muffled sound popped off not too far away and a red signal flare fired into the sky from one of the many life rafts dropped in the rescue earlier. The red light lit up the sky, and Marks saw the shine of the bodies on the survivors.

"There's too much damage to the hull and we can't take off with this much weight, so we gotta sit here. They are coming for us."

Quint lost over forty pounds during the last five days, and he felt the protruding ribs of his torso grind into the rivets on the wing's steel sheathing. He steadied himself with his right hand to readjust his body and, upon applying the slightest pressure, a pain knifed through Quint's arm. He flinched and dropped back down to his left side.

"Easy does it. They'll have a doc look you over soon enough. I'm Lieutenant Marks, the pilot of this dumbo. What's your name, sailor?"

Quint ignored the question and held up his right hand. The broken bones caused it to swell. The fingers wouldn't close to make a fist. His arm, thin and shaking, lowered to his side.

Marks saw Quint didn't want to talk and understood.

"I was flying above you all, and I looked down. Saw one of you swimming. I believe we all have a special talent—a gift from God. Mine was always my eyes. That was an edge I had. Shooting back in Indiana, I could see the target hit two-hundred yards out. In flight school, they practically passed me on excellent vision alone. Today, I saw this kid swimming from nine-hundred feet up. I don't know where he thought he was going, but he was swimming. We dropped to three-hundred feet, and I could see his face. He wasn't angry or afraid—just swimming flat out. Like he was in a lake back home. Then I saw one of those things come up from below and grab that kid. He was gone. Right there, the choice was simple. I didn't care about rules and regulations. I knew I had to dump this thing in the drink and get you guys out of there. But that face, that kid's face—he was so at peace. Almost like he knew he was going to die, and he just wanted to go out doing something he loved. So, he swam. I don't know what horror show you fellas saw out there. I'm sure living with it won't be easy. But you are living. It's gotta count for something. I still see his face. That poor kid."

Quint shifted his eyes and peered over the edge of the wing, across the illuminated water. Floating bodies and debris of the rescue items dropped from planes throughout the day, mixed with inflatable life rafts filled with survivors who pulled themselves out of the water. The red signal flare drifted further down, and the sea snuffed its light out. The blackness of night returned except for the glow far out to the north.

On the horizon, a brilliant beam of white light fired straight into the dark sky. The illuminated shaft cut the darkness and caused many to question whether they were dead. Was this the bridge straight to heaven approaching them? The survivors who were conscious could not look away from the indescribable sight of beauty.

Marks saw Quint looking out at the tower of illumination in the distance.

"That's the USS Doyle, sailor. They are telling us help is on the way."

Marks turned to the rest of the starboard wing and the men laying across it. "You see that, gentlemen? That's a fine example of American courage. Making themselves a bright shining target for an enemy submarine in order to let you all know help is on the way. Just hold on a little longer."

Marks turned back towards Quint and leaned in.

"Now, you going to tell me your name, sailor?"

Quint shook his head no and just continued to stare out over the edge of the wing and into the water below.

Marks put his hand on Quint's shoulder, gave a friendly pat, then stood up to move to the next man with his kettle of water.

In the life rafts around the floating PBY-5A Catalina patrol plane, men cheered with relief upon noticing the approaching beam of light hailing from the twenty-four-inch searchlight on the bridge of the USS Doyle. Another flare fired off from the darkness and the sky, once again, lit up red.

Quint stared into the floating carnage that surrounded them. Right below him, empty kapok life vests clustered with empty canisters of fresh water and lifeless bodies. He watched it rest against the plane. The wooden crate, still and peaceful, tapped against the hull in a slight rhythmic pulse of ocean waves.

13 MAUREEN

Quint turned up the large, flared collar of his heavy Navy pea coat and watched the military chaplain walk away in silence. Only he and the lone groundskeeper remained. The stiff February breeze off San Francisco Bay bit harder with the sobering realization that she was gone.

The groundskeeper unfolded his hands, put his winter cap back on, and stepped to the formidable pile of dirt with two shovels. Quint raised his hand to ask him to wait, while pulling a small half-bottle of scotch whiskey from a pocket. He thumbed the peeled edge of the Whitehorse Cellar label twice and flattened it back to the glass to feign proper etiquette, unscrewed the cap, and offered it to his fellow gravedigger. The groundskeeper took a drink and returned it with an appreciative gesture. Quint took a turn and felt the warm numbing effects that erased the pain—not just from the cold air, but from the guilt as well.

The fog horns across the bay offered the only sounds that disrupted the duet of shovels biting into dirt and tossing their burdens onto the humble pine box. The coffin stared up at Quint. With every shovelful, he recalled her care for him when he returned to the states. The war was over, and they hailed victory, but his battle with demons had only begun. She never questioned him when he woke up at night from the visions. Never an objection over his constant needing of a drink and leaving half-empty glasses of water all over the townhouse on base, sometimes three to a room. Maureen watched her friends leave the military life with their husbands and settle down in those new homes built on the outside of the city. She never fell into envy watching them start families and welcome new babies. She never blamed him for delaying theirs.

Maureen lived as loyal a wife as any man could wish for—yet he failed her. Quint flipped another shovelful into the grave and watched his last view of the wooden coffin disappear forever. This was his third attempt at marriage, and one he was sure would last forever. He watched everyone around him move on from the war and hoped settling down with her would be the way to leave the guilt and shame of defeat behind—to move on and leave it all.

It was the opposite. With every hint of affection and stability she offered, he resisted and left. Maureen never complained when he disappeared for weeks at a time to hunt them. The ever-loyal wife, she refused to even hint where he might be when the military police made another routine visit on a manhunt for Quint. 'Absent without leave' was the repeated charge.

When Quint returned to the world, broken, battered and smelling of decayed shark blood, Maureen never had a crossed word. In the final year, she drank to escape the loneliness. To keep him around when he was home, she drank even more. While he escaped from base and worked to hunt and track them, she worked to hold the house and hide her broken heart.

Quint shoveled faster with the anger of resentment. She deserved better, and he failed her. He left her alone and wasn't strong enough to reach out and rescue her. She was now just another face staring back at him from the endless abyss below his feet. Dragged away by the sharks.

And here he stood, five and a half years after being plucked from the Philippine Sea in a screaming rage of denied revenge. He threw the last shovel of dirt on her grave and still felt ever the failure.

Quint tamped the earth with the back of his shovel and stood up straight. The familiar pain stabbed the base of his right hand and the fingers let loose. Quint dropped the shovel to his side. Embarrassed, he knelt and gripped the shovel. The doctors never gave him a conclusive answer why they couldn't fix the extensive nerve damage and bone restructuring that occurred on the last day in the water. Quint passed the shovel to the groundskeeper and remembered what the doctors told him—live with it.

With the two shovels propped over his shoulder, the groundskeeper turned with a nod of condolence and started down First Drive towards the main gates of the San Francisco National Cemetery. Quint could not afford a headstone, but maybe the Navy would make one for her. If they got around to it. For now, the stamped metal place holder would have to suffice.

THE BOOK OF QUINT

Maureen Margaret Quint
Born September 23, 1917
Died February 2, 1951

Quint massaged the feeling back into his right hand and then reached for the bottle in his pea coat pocket. After another pull of numbing whiskey, Quint tried to drown his disdain. He couldn't even get her a proper headstone in time. He had a pocket full of cash from the latest military pay; $106.56 but needed $186.51 to purchase the carved marble one with the angel statue. Maureen deserved better than becoming just another stone in the endless sea of white stones blanketing the hillside.

He failed her in life, and he wanted to die before he failed her in death.

Quint shoved his dirt-stained hands into his pockets and strode across the cemetery towards the Presidio Chapel from where they started. He looked across the bay to the red steel of the Golden Gate Bridge and decided he was going to make things right.

For a sailor to make an extra buck, they could do one of two things; get a side job working the docks while on liberty or find a bookie and gamble it all away. There wasn't any time for either. Quint walked with an intensity. His purposeful stride fueled by resentment and anger. Maureen did not have any family, and neither did he. The celebration of her life tonight was to be a solemn and lonely one. Quint would honor her and the loyalty she showed him, but first he needed to find the place to make it possible.

The winter sun never shines in San Francisco, and the bleak overcast sky grew dim while Quint found his way past the Crissy Field marsh and started down Marina Boulevard. The hour grew late for his long walk across the city waterfront to Pier 9. They would be there on this cold Thursday night.

Quint no longer felt a part of society. The world was different after coming back to the United States. The parades and revelers in the street throwing confetti on V Day pushed him away. Victory did not exist for them—those who survived the sinking and the sharks. Only questions remained. An endless stream of questions; why did the shark choose the guy next to me? But that guy had a family, a wife, kids. Why not me? Why didn't the planes come one day earlier?

For Quint, it was all those questions and more. With Maureen laid to rest, he expected this haunt of regret. He weaved his way through the night life of the Embarcadero and Fisherman's Wharf. He scoffed at the tourists and drunken sailors who spilled out of the nightclubs and bars. They did not understand. They would never know the pain.

That is why Quint only found solace among the darkest and most dangerous corners of the city. In these places, a man of troubled stature could find victory. Maybe looking to settle a score, purge his demons, or erase his memories in a haze of drunken brawls and emerge feeling like a triumphant gladiator from the arena. To find all of this, a man needed to step out of the safety of the city and its laws.

The real action was in the illegal bars and speakeasies that started back in the 1930s and never lost momentum. Two decades later, with the post-war economic boom, the number of workers in San Francisco increased by the hundreds of thousands. The various paydays released a cash tidal wave across the city. Those who established venues for illegal gambling and unlimited drinking binges soaked up as much of that cash as possible.

The best and most dangerous of these venues were the ones that moved around and set up on designated nights in a location out of the eye of the San Francisco police department and the nosy loudmouth sailor on a two-day port call from Los Angeles. Over the last few years, Quint learned the schedules and locations, memorizing where to go when he wanted to disappear.

On Monday nights, they were across the bay in Brickyard Cove. Tuesdays, one could find them in the anchored barge on the southeast docks of Treasure Island. Wednesdays, the lower level of 'Fisherman's Grotto', back storage room. With all the fine seafood dining upstairs, they were below with the fishermen who moored up to the docks on payday.

Tonight was Thursday and Quint knew the Baska Brothers were in their usual place. The far end of Pier 9, second to last door on the right.

Quint walked down the Embarcadero with the city lights cutting the night and casting shadows of all sizes across a scattering of palm trees lining the brick sidewalk. He no longer felt the cold and even broke into a light sweat while moving past all the piers of various numbers and sizes. The waterfront was an aged jungle of wood timbers that jutted from the waves at various angles and states of neglect. Each pier bustled with activity. Ships, both great and small, moored alongside. He knew by sight which one was number nine. The dilapidated, dark building that stretched hundreds of feet out into the water would be his destination. A large delivery truck sputtered out of Pier 9's wide front entryway and hung a right, disappearing behind a cloud of warm exhaust and a passing cable car.

He stared into the opening of darkness. This far down from the tourist traps and safer nightlife back on the north shore lived a danger only a few could live with. For those whose home is living and working on the edge of the sea, this darkness was tolerable.

It was here, in the shadow of the Bay Bridge carrying the twinkling red and white lights of society's traffic, that Quint stood, determined to honor Maureen. He looked up at the weathered concrete's crescent-shaped archway looming over him from twenty-feet above. Quint stepped forward into the shadow of Pier 9.

14 PIER 9

The ambient light seeped in from the monolithic stone entrance way, eight-hundred feet behind him after the long walk down Pier 9. Quint was sure to stay to the center of the wide tunnel to not trip on the random packaging crate or stacked shipments of goods. It was always safe to keep to the center. Miscreants might hide in the side doorways and shadowy outcroppings to ambush their prey. Above him, the stars shone through dried seagull droppings that painted the pier's glass roof. He approached the second to last door on the right and already heard the music.

With three solid raps on a door of bruised steel that saw its fair share of ejected drunken-sailor skulls, a towering Portuguese strongman of epic proportions greeted Quint. Not a word needed between the two, for the Portuguese strongman had seen Quint before. The Navy pea coat was authentic enough. Quint could pass.

Inside was a different world. The world of Billy and Balthazar Baska—two brothers brought by their family to San Francisco twenty years earlier. Driven out by the dust storms and drought, their family fled Cimarron County, Oklahoma and found refuge in 1930s San Francisco. The young brothers grew up on the streets and vowed never to see poverty again. They saw enough pain and suffering to know this world is unforgivable and no help is ever on the horizon. You must fend for yourself and become ruthless doing so.

After a few run-ins with the law, they rose to power during the fall of prohibition and seized on the opportunity of illegal trade, shipping, and gambling offered by the dangerous waters of San Francisco Bay and its endless miles of police-ignored coastline. It was in the shadows of passing battleships, the US military presence, and the specter of Alcatraz, where Billy and Balthazar found their enterprise. War delivered droves of sailors and soldiers shipping out to far-away lands but having to stay in the city, if only for a day. Their enterprise grew to proportions, never imagined. Whatever a sailor should want, before or after endless nights at sea, the Baska brothers provided.

Quint moved through the vast dark room of tables and walls lined with abandoned booths under dimmed light bulbs. Loud music and light radiated from the 1951 Seeburg jukebox in the corner. Crowds of worn fishermen laughed and drank their fill while women of the night worked the lonely. The illegal bar comprised the back two shipping bays of Pier 9. Instead of aligned pallets and shipping crates, lounge chairs, card dealers and billiards tables took their place. Windows facing the bay swung open to allow the thick layer of smoke and loud conversation to ventilate. The openings offered a glimpse of the Bay Bridge and its sea of red and green lights, providing navigation aides to ships passing underneath.

Tonight, the crowd was larger than normal, for a contest was brewing—a tournament.

To the back of the cavernous space, in the very far corner under the large thirty-foot ceilings, a raucous crowd of fifty men yelled and bantered. Under a lone hanging shop lamp, a table stood four and a half feet off the ground—much higher than any of the other tables in the establishment. The table shook from the pounding and shouting of the tall and aggressive Balthazar Baska.

"C'mon, all you apes. Aren't there any more willing to pony up and take the plunge? The top two places payout. You can triple your money if you're man enough. Don't let these Chinamen come down here and dominate."

The elbows and bodies seemed to part for him when Quint stepped up to the bar on the other side of the room.

"Any games going tonight, Billy? I gotta get some winnings fast," Quint said to the bartender, the other half of the brothers.

Billy Baska walked over to Quint with a smile and poured him a shot glass.

"The only game we got going on tonight is the arm-wrestling tournament. Take it or leave it."

Billy motioned with his head to the noise and cheering while studying Quint. He knew Quint had a right arm that was strong as an ox. For a man standing only six feet, Quint held one of those physiques that many underestimated. Billy saw Quint around during recent years but noted with special attention the times he watched him arm wrestle twice during the war, when the Indianapolis dry-docked for repairs across the bay at Mare Island.

These sailors couldn't afford to get in fights and duels of conflict in order to prove the strongest and most dominant of the species. Winners and losers still needed to pull in the lines and turn to for ship's work the next day. This required less-damaging ways to find out who was the better man. If one was worth their weight onboard a ship; fishing, trawling, tugboats, crabbers, ships of war, any ship—strength of the arm carried the most value. No better way to test your worth as a sailor than to challenge another adversary to an arm-wrestling contest.

To win at arm wrestling, the muscles of the forearm, wrist, biceps, and shoulder work in tune, along with the grip strength of the hand. To those that could do it well, their arms operated in a symphony of developed muscle fibers and well-coordinated timing. Quint's God-given talent was the natural strength of his arm. Although not as chiseled as the herculean opponents he squared off with, Quint still won many a contest over larger unassuming sailors who challenged him to a duel of arms. Billy Baska knew this the first time he saw Quint back in 1944, at one of their other illegal dive bars. And a good entrepreneur on the docks never forgets a talent or a face.

Quint turned to the crowd and studied the group of colossal figures standing around, each sizing the other up and pondering their chances. He raised his voice to compete with the raucous drinkers.

"What's the buy-in?"

"Hundred dollar buy-in, winner pays out five-hundred, second pays three."

"And third?"

"Third, you get a free t-shirt."

Billy wore a slick smile and stared at Quint, who turned back to him. An obvious rip-off for the risk of one hundred dollars.

Quint knew he had been AWOL for over two weeks, and the two reporters were there when he docked his boat to take photos. It was dumb luck they were there. Someone had made a call to the San Francisco Examiner and the Chronicle on a tip-off for a warehouse fire across the street from the docks of the new Mission Rock terminal construction project. It was a slow news day, and the photographers arrived on site as the fire was under control. Nothing much to see until they turned around and saw Quint tying up the stern line with his catch laying across the aft deck and hanging over the gunwale. The camera bulbs started popping. The story made the papers, and they were looking for him. He would get time in the brig, and Maureen needed that stone. For her to go one day longer without it was a sacrilege to him.

Billy Baska cast the bait out further. "There's just one thing, friend."

Quint tossed back the drink. It was Kentucky bourbon—the Baska brothers always had the best bourbon.

"The Chinese fishermen brought two of their heavies here from Chinatown. And I'm not talking about our Chinatown, but the one across the bay, in Oakland. Never seen these two before. They look big. The Chinese came to win. Just a fair warning to you."

Quint turned back to the crowded corner. Against the window stood six short Chinese sailors, surrounding two massive bodies. Two brothers; Chang Fu-Sheng and Chang Zheng-Sheng. Both grew up on freighters shipping out of Hong Kong. Over twenty years, the Chang's heaved and hauled the heavy hawser mooring lines of these ships under dictator captains who refused to get the capstans fixed. This forced Fu-Sheng and Zheng-Sheng to pull by hand—creating their legend as being able to moor up a coastal tanker all by themselves. Not a word of English spoken, but their value was the size of their shoulders, and the swollen forearms that tapered down to hands of iron. They each stood a foot taller than the older Chinese men who yelled while waving fanned out fistfuls of cash at Balthazar. The Chinese contingent taunted him to get on with the tournament.

Billy knew what he was doing. He had his fish in Quint. He set the hook, and now all he had to do was wait for the right time and reel him in. As Quint turned to the crowd, he didn't notice Billy raising his hand to catch the attention of his brother. The two brothers made eye contact from across the space. No words needed to be said. They knew the scam and conducted it many times before.

Another pour of liquid bravery hit the glass in front of Quint, and he turned back to the bar. She was watching from above. He felt her gaze and couldn't say no. He was going to win this tournament or lose an arm. This was no longer a choice. The light reflected off the bourbon in the glass in front of him. He watched the light reflect in the same way when he came home and found her in the bath, asleep under the water. The smell of bourbon touched his nose while he held her unconscious body—the memory vivid as ever.

Quint slapped five twenty-dollar bills on the bar and took down the bourbon in one forceful motion.

"I'm in."

Billy waved his hand. Upon seeing his brother, Balthazar bellowed an uproar.

"Well, look at that! We have one more just coming in. More of a man than any of you. That makes sixteen."

Quint wrote his name on the small piece of paper Billy slid over to him. A young runner grabbed it from the bar and ran it over to Balthazar.

"We have the man called Quint going into the hat. The window is now closed and let's draw."

Quint shook out of his heavy Navy pea coat and tightened the belt on his black canvas carpenter dungarees, still soiled with dirt from the grave. He rolled the sleeves of his dingy white wool Navy-issued thermal shirt, making sure the right side was a few rolls higher over the biceps muscle.

The air in the vast space carried a damp chill, and the crowd grew as those who were sitting at tables, or at the far end, migrated towards the noise of the combatants and their handlers. Balthazar drew the names from the wrinkled hat and announced them to the errand boy who stood on a chair and scratched them down on a large green chalkboard—the different sides of a lined tournament bracket filled. Quint looked around to study the unique collection of races, cultures, and occupations that made up his opponents.

The Baska brothers and their hidden web of Okie bars, brothels, and gambling parlors supplied the yin to 1951 society's yang. There was no segregation or judgment in a man's color, choice of job, or even lack of a job and only boasting a prison record. None of that mattered. The only color that carried weight with the brothers was the color of cash—and how much of it one could generate. Because of this, every outcast, convict, drunkard, scam artist, thug, and those at the very end of their ropes sought them out. If one survived a night at one of their establishments, your life could be very different—prospects improved, pain eased, mistakes and memories forgotten. The allure of this attracted some of the meanest and motivated figures in the maritime underworld for the last twenty years.

Quint continued to look around and study the sizes and faces of the men he would have to wrestle. The Nigerian steamship stoker, tired from a trans-Pacific trek with money to burn. Two drunk army buddies on leave. A formidable Ukrainian tuna fisherman standing next to his captain and crew. There were some Quint had seen before; the three extra-large crab fishermen from Bodega Bay always counted on to start strong but flail away in the end. Next to the chalkboard was a familiar face. Quint didn't know his name, but remembered he was a guard from Alcatraz, known to rough up inmates three at a time. The sight of the guard made Quint suspicious. If he was here, the brothers were up to something.

The two Chinese heavies would be the greatest obstacles. Quint had never seen them before, but their size, strength, and youth were apparent. His right arm felt strong. If Quint had to face one, he hoped it would be at the beginning.

"We set the brackets, gentlemen."

The chalkboard turned, revealing the placement of names on the sixteen-man tournament bracket. Eight combatants on each side. The crowd cheered and side-action flowed—money passed; markers exchanged.

Quint saw the con right away. One side of the bracket listed all the names of the unknowns. There was his name, rested between some of the largest men in the room, including the Chinese brothers. On the other side were the usual local tough guys and too drunk to be serious military men, along with the guard from Alcatraz. The brothers, having a side deal set-up, gave the guard a smooth paved road to the finals with little competition. No matter who reached the finals from the other side, the battle fatigue would keep them at a disadvantage.

"Random picks, my ass," said Quint.

"Another one on the house, Quint?"

Billy slid the bottle down to the edge of Quint's glass. Quint looked at him and wanted to wipe the grin off his dapper face. Maybe even strangle him with one of those shirt sleeve garters Billy wore like a bartender from the wild west. Quint despised able-bodied people like Billy and Balthazar, who stayed home and took advantage of those who signed up to fight in the war. He knew he'd been had, but there was no turning back now. It was time to pull harder than ever before. A celebration for her. For Maureen.

Quint continued to drink, and the tournament started.

With only two folded liquor-stained towels to rest their elbows, the men were called to the tall table, two at a time, locking right hands and gripping the opposite sides of the table with their lefts. As Balthazar called for the start, the crowd erupted in cheers. Calls and taunts goaded the men to not give up and pull as hard as ever. To see if, for one night in their lives, they could taste the victory and glory of a gladiator left standing over a fallen warrior in the arena.

Ten years ago, Quint would have torn through these men with ease, but tonight doubt crept in. He felt older. He hadn't eaten a full meal in over a week. Then there was his hand—his right hand.

Why did you let go of those dog tags?

The doubt was a demon resting in plain sight on the back of his mind. He lied to the medics to clear him for active duty, refusing to tell them about the loss of feeling in his hand that seems to come and go. He felt strong tonight, and that's all that mattered now. Quint took another drink to numb the adrenaline pumped nerves of his teeth and jaw. A familiar feeling from his waiting for incoming planes behind the controls of the 40mm anti-aircraft guns on the Indianapolis.

A crash of the table and another competitor's hand pinned. Another man moves on to the next round. Arm wrestling tournaments move fast, and the energy of the room grew with every new set of names called.

Quint didn't hesitate when Balthazar called his name. He turned from the bar and walked with confidence across the room to the table. His mind was steadfast. No holding back. Treat every match as if it were the last one. And that's just what he did.

The crowd gasped when Quint dispatched his opponent with a speed and strength none of them had seen up to that point. The well-built arm of the Nigerian sailor, who spent many years hurling shovels of coal into boilers below decks, appeared larger than Quint's. However, the intense thick webbing of muscle fibers backed by years of hurt and pain made Quint's arm into a pillar of stone, with the force of a titan pushing behind it. In less than a second, the back of the Nigerian sailor's hand hit the table. The man walked away, shocked by a newfound respect for this smaller rival, accompanied by fresh doubts in his own strength and abilities.

Quint found himself back at the bar. He worked the bottle and didn't watch the next few matches and the start of the next round. He heard the screams and Mandarin shouts from the Chinese sailors and fishermen who came to watch their secret weapons dominate. And dominate they did. The two brothers crushed their opponents and moved on to the quarterfinal round of eight men left standing.

The guard from Alcatraz defeated one crabber from Bodega Bay in an easy first match of the quarterfinals and moved on to cheers from the local gamblers who were in on the fix. Their horse would be fresh and ready for the finals, while the others broke each other on the opposite side of the bracket. The Ukrainian strongman from the large tuna fishing vessel moored up to Pier 15 was the next winner to advance into the semifinal round.

Under the lone swinging light illuminating the haze of excited spectator breaths exhaled into the damp cold air, the first of the Chang brothers, Fu-

Sheng, advanced by almost throwing his opponent off the table. The force of his arm pinning the opposing hand to the marred wood table landed an impressive thud. A resounding roar of adulation from the Chinese contingent followed. Fellow gamblers doubled their money and laughed with glee.

The next Chang brother, Zheng-Sheng, was called to the table to square off against the unknown late entry—the man they called Quint.

Quint turned to the crowd, pausing at the sight of two military police in uniform entering the establishment. Escorted by the large Portuguese gatekeeper, both men, muscular and tall themselves, stepped forward. The white MP letters emblazoned on their green military helmets cut through the darkness, causing Quint to turn away and ignore the inevitable. He strolled to the table, looking at the large Balthazar, who smiled from under his thick handlebar mustache.

15 SEMIFINALS

Zheng-Sheng wouldn't take his eyes off the man before him, who looked tired and aged. Quint stared back and studied his much larger opponent. Brute force would not produce a victory. The Chinese sailor was stronger and younger.

Quint stepped to the table and looked over his shoulder. Back at the bar, Billy Baska was talking to the MP officers. He motioned to Quint's direction while working out a deal—they could have him after the tournament was over. The officers agreed and removed their military helmets. They stood back against the bar while refusing a bottle and two glasses Billy tried to push onto them.

"Lock hands, gentlemen."

Balthazar motioned for the men to get into position.

Quint turned back to Zheng-Sheng. The crowd raged and frantic hands passed money for side bets. Massive odds waged against the smaller man. Quint didn't care. He didn't pay attention to the noise. His mind cleared. The opponent was strong but young. He knew his experience and tactics would win him this match if his body held up.

Just give me that one chance. One mistake is all he needs to make. Lord, give me the strength. Who are you kidding? He left you a long time ago. You are on your own.

The men gripped hands and settled their elbows into the towels. Quint shoved his right leg forward and squeezed the side of the table with his left hand, locking his arm for support. Zheng-Sheng looked over Quint's shoulder at the calls and screams from his shipmates, who yelled instructions in Mandarin. While he was nodding, Quint was quick to adjust his grip and moved higher on the thumb of Zheng-Sheng by an inch.

There it is you dumb bastard. Now I got you.

At that moment, Quint knew he had the match won. Now, all he had to do was finish the job.

Balthazar raised his hands.

"Ready—"

Quint's gripped hard. In that instant, he pulled his body closer and drew himself in against the strength of the inexperienced opponent.

"Begin!"

The opposing forces of each arm locked, and either side gave no ground. The crowd screamed and cursed—the smaller man should've gone down. What they saw was unnatural.

Both men pushed and strained. Zheng-Sheng stared with bewilderment. Nobody has resisted his arm other than his brother. Quint leaned in and made his move. He applied pressure to the thumb of Zheng-Sheng by hooking his wrist while leaning in with his shoulder. The Chinese sailor screamed and pushed back, his giant biceps straining and pumping.

The crowd gasped and watched with stunned amazement. Zheng-Sheng's arm faded and shook. Quint's arm moved forward, pressing at a slow, methodical pace. Zheng-Sheng panicked and moved to adjust his left-hand grip on the table, but it was no use. Quint stepped forward and leaned over the table, now pushing with his back and shoulder—the right hand closed over, curling forward with the high grip on the adversary's thumb.

Zheng-Sheng screamed again as his wrist bent backwards, now reduced to just the strength of the biceps muscle as his only weapon. Quint's technique took his opponent's grip, shoulder, and wrist strength away. No man can win an arm-wrestling match on the biceps alone.

Checkmate, friend.

The back of Zheng-Sheng's hand, now inches away from the sweat covered wood, trembled, and turned ghost white. Quint leaned in further and saw defeat in the eyes of Zheng-Sheng.

A powerful pump of his shoulder and Quint dropped his upper body weight down on top of his locked arm, taking the opposing hand to the table. The sound on the table sent a shock wave through the room. Many lost money, some lost pride, while the Baska brothers won business.

Quint helped Zheng-Sheng up and shook his hand, then headed back to the bar. The blustering and chaos of the crowd didn't notice Quint when he threw his Navy pea coat over his shoulders to stay warm, but also to hide that he was massaging his hand. Quint's right hand had gone numb. He squeezed it, trying to get the sensation back to his wrist and the last three fingers.

Not now, please. Don't fail me now.

Quint glanced over at the two military police, who stared at him from the opposite corner of the bar. Billy was talking and trying to distract them. The brothers knew they had to keep Quint in the tournament to take out the final Chang brother and pave the road for their horse from Alcatraz. Maybe the MPs could then take Quint and they wouldn't have to pay out the second-place prize. The Alcatraz guard would win by default, and the brother's walk away with the entry fees and side action.

Close to seventy spectators cheered, with the noise filtering outside and attracting the usual street hustlers and lost souls. The four men were called to start the semifinal round, peaking the suspense of the moment. The gamblers became delirious from the amount of action, with some men betting money they didn't have—their next paycheck. Even the Portuguese heavy abandoned his post by the front door to watch.

Quint took another swig of bourbon, this time ignoring the glass and pulling right from the almost empty bottle. His arm felt strong, but the fingers—still no feeling in the fingers. The demon of doubt crept back up from the far corner of his mind. Quint tried to shake it off and ignore it, but there it was, and there it would stay.

Another thud of the table and roar from the crowd, as the guard from Alcatraz bested the Ukrainian fisherman in the first semifinal match. The young kid in the back leapt to the chalkboard, scratched off the name, and pointed to the other side of the bracket.

Quint had to face the second Chang brother, Fu-Sheng.

Both men were called to the table.

Quint tossed his coat across the bar and moved forward. The jeering crowd parted as he stepped through them. Hands patted his back and money changed for last-minute bets. His right hand held by his left; Quint shook the last of the feeling back into his fingertips.

With the panache of a carnival barker, Balthazar stepped forward to the table and raised his hands to the two men, while calling out in a showman's voice.

"Let's see who will reach the finals. I guarantee the winner is three-hundred richer. And the loser? Well, he'll go home as just that. Lock hands, gentlemen, and prepare for battle."

The crowd thrived with louder voices.

Quint stared at Fu-Sheng when he stepped to the table. He was bigger than his brother, with larger hands, too. Also, unlike his brother, Fu-Sheng's eyes stayed on Quint, ignoring the Mandarin directions and strategies yelled by his crew.

This one isn't so easily rattled. Just give me the opening. C'mon, all I need is one.

The two men locked hands. Quint went to adjust and take the higher line of Fu-Sheng's hand. The Chinese sailor was wider than his brother, and his fingers latched down tight. Quint pulled the hand of Fu-Sheng forward, and met a return tug, which pulled him into the table.

"Whoa now. Easy, gentlemen. Let's wait for my call," said Balthazar, reaching forward to place his hands on the wrists of the two opponents. "Ready—"

Quint shifted his fingers and took the precious real estate on the grip of Fu-Sheng—just a half-an-inch higher on the thumb.

"Begin!"

Balthazar pulled his hands away and the wooden legs of the table groaned from the opposing forces locked together on its surface. Fu-Sheng and Quint both pulled and moved to gain an advantage. Quint used his technique and pulled Fu-Sheng's hand closer to his chest. Fu-Sheng felt his elbow open and resisted in a violent tug. He pulled back, but Quint already had his upper body over the table. Quint pushed his right leg forward and held his elbow down on the table, not allowing Fu-Sheng to pull back.

The crowd screamed as the two men shifted and strained, neither conceding ground. Their fists locked with forearms rising towards the hanging light above.

Quint's fingers shifted and climbed higher on the thumb of Fu-Sheng's sweaty hand. That was all the edge he needed. He went to curl his wrist forward and felt the blood rush out of his hand. Quint's eyes went into a blur. The noise of the crowd became a steady ring in his ear.

Fu-Sheng looked at Quint. He felt the opposing fingers go limp against his grip and pushed even harder, listening to the howls and cheers from his shipmates in the background.

Quint let out an exhale and shook the senses back into line. The ulnar nerve, damaged and torn in the abuse and impact stress from that cursed last day in the water, once again failed. There was no control or feeling from his right wrist to the lower fingers.

No! Dammit, not now. Not now.

He tried to will the wrist to close over Fu-Sheng's fingers, but there wouldn't be a response. Quint lost the leverage of the moment and instead had to rely on the muscle and bones of the forearm to take the stress. The hulking strength and massive arm of the Chinese sailor proved relentless. Quint's hand faded.

The crowd thundered its excitement. The Chinese sailors raised their hands and shouted down Quint.

Fu-Sheng strained and pushed harder. His hand took Quint's another few degrees over towards the table.

Upon realizing what was happening, Quint shifted tactics and moved to gain an offensive edge. He kicked his right leg to the side, pulled his hand closer and dropped his shoulder to get under the angle of the arms. He pushed up with his back and leaned in, the right deltoid muscle of the shoulder pushed forward, regaining the much-needed leverage.

Gasps of shock and surprise leaked from those who witnessed Quint, the impossibly smaller combatant, move the hand of the taller giant that stood across the table from him. Fu-Sheng shook and strained with the sweat of stress pouring from his brow. Quint pushed and focused all his might on his shoulder and back—his hand was useless. Technique was all he had left.

The interlocked hands shook and pushed back to ninety degrees from where they started.

The spectators, now a relentless mob, cheered and yelled—one warrior would have to break. Not a soul in the room could ignore what was on display. Even the military police officers moved in closer to get a better view.

Fu-Sheng shook with tension, readjusted his stance, and leaned into the table. He felt the bone in Quint's upper arm break and looked into Quint's eyes. Quint never flinched, just stared right back and took the pain. Fu-Sheng pushed harder and felt the forearm of Quint give way. The Chinese sailor stood in disbelief as his opponent's arm failed, but the strength and resistance never faltered. He laid into Quint's arm with all he had, feeling the tearing and popping of a tendon.

Maureen. I'm sorry. Forgive me.

Quint watched his arm leave him and get pulled over by the towering man across the table. His hand turned white. The blood and any semblance of feeling abandoned it. Quint leaned to the left and pulled with his left hand. He vowed to win the tournament or lose an arm and that's just what he did.

Strands of sinew stretched and strained while muscle pulled from bone, and Quint's upper arm twisted in a gruesome slow-motion defeat. The final six inches, the large Chinese sailor dropped all his weight down and Quint's arm rifled into the table with a dead thud. Quint fell to his knees, and the crowd roared with revenge and victory.

Balthazar stepped forward in all his glory.

"Winner! Chang Fu-Sheng. Going to the finals."

Fu-Sheng never let go of Quint's hand, instead pushed the table out of the way, and stepped forward, letting Quint drop to the floor. His right arm flopped motionless and useless to his side. The crowd grew silent, and Quint stayed kneeling, looking down at the floor.

The two military police officers stepped through the crowd that closed in and gathered around Quint. They each moved to one side of the fallen sailor. The officers looked at the man kneeling before them in a somber gaze, for what they witnessed was the same as everyone else in the room. Nobody ever watched a fight against the impossible quite like that. What experience does a man have to live through to make him fight like that?

"It's time to go back to base, Chief. I'm sorry," said an MP.

The crowd backed away. Fu-Sheng stood and watched the two soldiers reach down and help Quint to his feet. One touched the right arm. Quint's strength faltered from the shocking pain that bit him, and he tumbled back down to one knee.

Fu-Sheng stepped forward to help Quint back to his feet. In his culture, a warrior like this should be honored, not arrested. The other military police officer placed the Navy pea coat over Quint's shoulders and Quint turned to Fu-Sheng. The giant sailor stood up straight and rendered a hold fist salute with a nod to his fallen opponent.

Quint returned a slight nod, raised his left hand, and pointed to the guard from Alcatraz standing next to Balthazar.

"Rip his arm off."

The crowd roared back to life as Fu-Sheng smiled at Quint and turned back to his next opponent—the once confident guard, now hesitant in stepping forward.

His left hand held his right arm across his stomach. Quint walked through the thick crowd and back towards the door. His breathing compressed into short, painful gasps.

Halfway up Pier 9, on his walk back to the world with the military escort by his side, the roar of the crowd reduced to a muffled clamor in the distance. As the noise faded away, so did the adrenaline in Quint's body and the right arm swelled above the elbow. The blood rushed from his head, causing the legs to buckle. Quint collapsed into the cool dampness of the dusty brick pier floor.

In his pocket was $6.56.

It was all he had left.

16   CAPTAIN AND CHIEF

The morning sunlight broke through the San Francisco Bay fog bank, throwing symmetrical shadows of the cell window bars across Quint's face. He woke from his sleep when the bright light touched his eyelids. For that moment, he didn't feel any pain, and the cool stone floor of the holding cell was just the right temperature. Moving to the bed would be more trouble than it's worth. To deal with the annoying sun beams, Quint opted to turn his head to the side only an inch, to where the bars pulled in front of the white light.

Quint found amusement in the perfect space between the bars. Two could cast their shadows over each of his eyes if he held still, and the sunlit warmth would touch the rest of his face. For the moment, he was the luckiest tenant of the US Army post's main guard house in the Presidio.

His damaged right arm draped across his stomach. The dusty Navy pea coat rested in a crumpled mess behind his head and shoulders. Quint smiled with the warmth on his face. It didn't take long for the pain to settle in.

Not the pain from his arm, which swelled to double the size above the elbow. He learned to ignore that. There was a pain he couldn't ignore.

The sting of regret drove into him with the force of a harpooner's spear, and it hurt. There were so many words he wanted to say to them—those he let down. None more so than Maureen. Her loss didn't seem real. Maybe it was all a dream, and he would hear the familiar heavy clunk of the lock thrown open on the distant hallway door, followed by footsteps. She would appear in front of the cell with a breath of relieved disappointment, ready to take him home. After five years of marriage, Quint struggled to think of any time he stayed home for more than a week or two, instead choosing the sea over her. And yet, he always counted on her to be standing at the door of the cell. Not this time, though. He laid across the floor, with the shadows of the bars resting on his eyes.

The latch pulled open, making a heavy clunk echo down the hallway of chipped beige paint and steel bars. Quint kept his eyes closed and just listened to the series of footsteps falling on the checkerboard green and white patterned asbestos tiles. He tried to guess how many were coming—sounds like three but could be two.

The three figures stopped in front of the cell and blocked the sunlight from the large, barred window behind them. Quint opened one eye and saw the three silhouettes. He was more interested in the little particles of dust that floated in the beams of light, cutting across the figures looking at him.

"How long has he been here?"

"I'm not sure, sir. We relieved the prior duty team at zero four hundred and he was already here. They must have gotten him last--"

"Open this cell door right now, before I make it so you are guarding a Korean latrine with the 91st on Monday."

"Yes, sir."

The nervous fumbling of keys rattled against the lock and the young military police officer pulled open the door to Quint's cage. Quint never moved.

A Navy captain stepped forward into the cell. His gleaming appearance and impeccable uniform, highlighted by the four gold bars on the sleeves and shoulder boards of his Navy pea coat. He stood a striking contrast to the broken man lying on the ground before him.

Captain Edward Woodyard knelt next to Quint. Already annoyed at the sight of his breath exhaled into the chilled and damp air of the guardhouse, he now boiled with a reserved anger while looking at Quint's enlarged upper right arm. The biceps muscle was now colored black with shades of purple from the internal bleeding.

The captain leaned in closer and spoke under his breath.

"Hang in there, Chief. I'm going to get you out of here."

Quint opened his eyes and looked at the captain. They didn't exchange a word but understood each other.

The captain pivoted to the two nervous MPs who stood outside the cell door and barked out. His words caused the two enlisted men to lock up and stand at attention.

"Sergeant."

"Yes, sir."

"Get on the phone with the infirmary. Get an ambulance down here right now."

One of the military police officers took off in a sprint down the hallway, keeping his MP helmet from falling off with one hand and leaving the other standing next to the open cell door. Captain Woodyard stood up and walked over to him.

"You see that tattoo on this man's forearm, Corporal?"

The shaking young man looked down to Quint and the sleeve of his shirt half pulled up on his good arm. The 'USS Indianapolis' title resting over an eagle's wings—faded ink pigments now shining in the sunlight.

"That means this man has seen enough pain to last three of your lifetimes and doesn't need one more minute in your drunk tank with an injury like this. If anything—I repeat, anything happens to this man, I will be back here to blame somebody."

"Sir. Yes, sir."

The corporal snapped to attention when the high-ranking officer pushed his way past and stormed down the hallway. Once again, the sun warmed Quint's face.

"The captain is here. Waiting for you outside with a car, Chief," said the nurse with a slight knock on the door frame to Quint's white-walled room of the hospital.

Quint knew it was time to face the music. He had been absent without leave now for over twenty days. This was, even by his admittance, quite the stint and repercussions were a certainty.

He sat on the edge of the bed and gathered himself for one more minute. No use rushing. Whatever was going to happen was likely already decided.

Quint stepped out into the cool air for the first time since the ambulance drivers collected him from the guardhouse three days ago. His right arm hung in a sling and tucked against his abdomen. He pulled his coat over his shoulders a little tighter and held it closed with his left hand. Quint still found it amusing to see palm trees while feeling the cold air bite at his skin. So goes the giant fraud that is San Francisco to a New Englander. He once thought, upon hearing orders to be stationed out of California, that life would be nothing but sun and warmth. A naive kid, not knowing what the future had for him.

The black 1951 Ford custom deluxe sedan with government plates idled at the curb. As soon as Quint hit the steps of the Presidio hospital, the high-gloss metallic doors opened.

Quint tried to spruce himself up with his free hand and looked down at his sullen dungarees and scuffed up work boots.

"I'm gonna have to apologize, Captain Woodyard. I haven't got a cover, or I would render a salute."

The captain stepped up to Quint and looked him over.

"When I heard they found you alive, I was relieved. I heard about Maureen. I went to the house, and you were gone. Chief, I am sorry for your loss."

"Thank you for your concern, Captain. I wish things were different. It is what it is."

The captain paused and looked into Quint's eyes. Quint wore a steel facade and looked away to the idling car. A Navy driver waited by the opened back door. The captain was never great at expressing his condolences to the families and spouses of those who died under his command. Even with plenty of practice over the years, he felt frustrated that his words failed him once again while standing in front of another broken man.

"It's a little warmer inside the car, Chief. We need to talk. It's out of my hands this time."

The Ford engine bellowed out a cloud of exhaust, and the government vehicle rumbled away from the curb.

Captain Woodyard settled into his seat and reached forward towards an open briefcase full of files. While thumbing through the papers, he tapped the driver's seat.

"Take us down Mason Street and stop at the Coast Guard station. We'll walk from there."

"Yes, sir."

Quint knew this was bad. When they want to walk with you, that means there's a problem. Before the captain would just offer him a cup of coffee and drop him off at his little shop on Mare Island. They had an understanding, and Quint always kept it quiet. But this time he pushed the limits, and it went public. For the last five years, Quint reached the rank of chief and settled into a job created just for him. A one-man repair shop of M1 Garand rifles that came back from the war. Five days a week of changing out spare parts. The odd forging and experimentation with custom stocks and various barrel lengths was just a cover for what drove him. It allowed him to sink further into the madness. Further into the failures and losses. All the time in the world to dwell on them while resisting the need to move on.

"Those sideburns are getting a little past regulation, Chief."

"Yes, Captain, I concur. I was looking forward to a shave back on base."

The captain, amused with the answer, looked over to Quint while pulling a folder from the briefcase.

"You expect me to buy that one, sailor?"

"That I do, sir."

They both exchanged a sly smile. The captain appreciated the traditional Naval back and forth between a superior and his subordinate.

"The report says spiral fracture of the upper humerus. Partial tear and stretching to the radial nerve. What happened out there?"

"Nothing too serious, sir. Got into a bit of a shoving match is all and—"

"Honestly, Chief, you and I are both tired. We're out of time. This has the Admiral, and all those shiny pants who sit around him, in a huff."

Quint knew what was coming as the captain reached forward and pulled out the newspaper. Captain Woodyard handed the front page from last week's San Francisco Chronicle Sunday evening edition over to Quint. The headline, in bold black letters, screamed from the page:

NAVY MAN KILLS 3 MONSTERS OFF ALCATRAZ

Below the headline was a black-and-white photo of Quint, in the well of a small fishing boat, standing over three dead great white sharks. Quint's old navy work hat, with the yellow lettering—USS Indianapolis CA-35 visible. The brim obscuring part of his face.

"Now if that wasn't bad enough for the Admiral to get it delivered to his house on Sunday evening, this falls onto his desk Monday morning…"

Quint wore a half smile when the captain tossed the San Francisco Examiner front page on top of the other paper. The same bold black lettering splashed across the page:

NAVY FISHERMAN SNAGS 3 SHARKS IN 1 DAY

Another photo of Quint unloading his massive fishing rod and reel, with three white sharks of ten to twelve feet, stacked in the boat's well.

"I have to say, I'm impressed at the size of the catch, but the Admiral wasn't."

"Yes, sir. I'm sure of that."

Quint looked up from the papers. He had already seen them earlier in the week and didn't care. There was a funeral to arrange. He tried to push off and tell those photographers to clear out, even threatened to throw one of them right into the water, with the fancy bulbs and camera equipment included.

"Those pushy bastards got off two flashes before I could chase them away. I never intended for this to make the papers, Captain."

"I'm sure of that, Chief. I'm sure of that."

The rows of palm trees changed to sand and a parade field of rich green grass when the car took a turn and started down Mason Street. Quint looked out at San Francisco Bay. The slight chop peppered the water with little white caps.

"They want to know what you are doing on the front page of the papers and not on a ship somewhere. One of those academy pencil-necks trying to make a name for himself checked your records and found you AWOL, then sounded the alarm. I tried all my tricks, but they want you brought in for a captain's mast."

The car slowed and drifted to the side of the road, brought to a halt in a slight squeaking of drum brakes.

"Coast Guard Station number three ten, Presidio, Captain."

"Very well, driver."

Quint folded the newspapers and handed them back to the captain.

"You don't want to keep those? It's not every day a man lands on the front page of the Chronicle."

"I gotta feeling this won't be the last time I'll be on a newspaper headline, sir."

The captain took the papers back and looked at them before filing them into his briefcase.

"Well, my kid will like them. He's fascinated with sharks."

Quint scoffed to himself at the thought of sharks bringing fascination to anyone but bit his tongue. He respected Captain Woodyard, and all he did for him after returning from Guam with the rest of the survivors back in '45. The good captain bailed him out of many altercations and mini-AWOL trips that Quint liked to call his 'little escapes'. If anyone was going to deliver the bad news, he would rather it be Woodyard.

"Let's take a walk, Chief. I have a patrol boat waiting at Torpedo Wharf to take me back to the island. Let's see if you are going to board it with me."

The driver opened the door for the captain and Quint reached over with his left hand to open his own door. As he stepped out of the car, he bumped his right shoulder on the door frame and winced at the pain. They gave him enough codeine tablets to last him for a while. It felt like he needed another round already.

The slight head wind whipped off the bay and met both men with a push as they started their walk across Crissy Field. Quint looked ahead towards the white coast guard station and its weathered red roof. Maybe he should've joined that outfit instead of the Navy. Quint pondered how life would be different had that been the decision.

"I had lunch with Admiral Nimitz two weeks ago and he still asks about you. Every time I see him, 'How's my boy doing?' he asks. He's getting older and forgets how often he tells the same stories, so as an exemplary officer, my job is to sit and act like I never heard it before. There he goes, telling me all about how Admiral Spruance went to the Base 18 hospital in Guam to pin purple hearts on the Indy survivors and when he got to the end of the line, he had one extra— you skipped the entire show business. They found you wading in hip-deep water on the north island, spear fishing. He laughs himself silly at the thought of Spruance calling your name and standing there looking around."

Quint watched the seagulls dip and dive over the water. He listened to the captain with a patient ear.

"It's been over five years, Chief. Since you boys arrived back home, every one of your crew has left the Navy, except you. You stayed, and Admiral Nimitz respected that. 'That's my boy, Captain. See to it he's taken care of.' My standing order from Nimitz. Well, I tried, Chief, and I'm still trying. I got you set up at that little shop rebuilding M1's and tried to keep you off the radar, but this time they left me with little to maneuver with."

"Captain, this isn't your fault. The admiral always treated me well, and he stuck his neck out for Captain McVay. I always respected that."

"We all looked at the Navy different after what they did to McVay."

The men reached the sandy paved path in front of the Coast Guard station and turned left. The red steel of the Golden Gate Bridge glowed in the noon sun.

Some of the last remnants of a thick morning fog bank had yet to burn off and clung to the hillside while cutting across the bridge support cables. Quint watched the cars and trucks stream across the bridge in the distance.

The captain and the chief continued their walk. Torpedo Wharf stretched into the blue waters of the bay. A few local fishermen sat in the shadows of the wooden pylons, waiting with their lines cast.

"The war is in Korea, Chief. The USS Rochester is just about finished with repairs, and I'm taking her out there. Just say the word, and you'll be on her with me. I could use the best gunner's mate in the Navy. You are a legend on the Bofors and I wouldn't want anyone else protecting my bridge more so than you, Chief Quint."

Quint remained silent and shifted the strap of his arm sling that pulled on his neck.

"With Admiral Nimitz retired, we lost our pull at the top. Aboard my ship, I can cover for you. Either that, or I process your paperwork and get you a medical discharge effective immediately. They are going to take you to captain's mast, and I can't control what happens there. Under my command, you will make Senior Chief within the month."

Their footfalls echoed on the ancient timbers of the wharf. In the distance, the engines of the seventy-eight-foot Higgins PT Boat lit off in a loud rumble. The crew spotted the four gold stripes of the captain's shoulder bars and the khaki fabric of the navy officer's hat approaching.

Quint looked underneath the Golden Gate's shadow, to the open Pacific Ocean horizon and beyond.

"You are a good man, Captain Woodyard, and I want to thank you for the help. My fight is not out there anymore."

"The Lord only knows what you men went through. I can't even imagine. But you have to move on. There are eight-hundred and seventy-nine men that would love to be standing where you are right now."

Quint nodded and appreciated what the captain was trying to do.

"Aye aye, Captain."

A junior petty officer climbed up from the ladder and hurried over, locking into a perfect position of attention and snapping a hand salute.

"Engines are up to temperature, Captain. Awaiting your departure, may I take your briefcase?"

Captain Woodyard returned his salute and handed over the briefcase. The petty officer collected it and hustled back to the waiting PT boat.

130

"You want a ride back to Mare Island? I can put you on a plane, train…anywhere you want to go."

"No, sir. I think I'll walk from here and take my time."

"You do that, Chief. It's been a pleasure serving with you. Consider yourself discharged and you can pick up any personal items from your shop when you are ready. I wish things were different, Chief. I really do."

"Respectfully request one more favor, sir?"

"Anything. It's the least we owe you."

"I'd like to keep my rifle."

The captain paused and looked out at the chopped surface of the bay.

"You can't kill them all, Chief."

Quint returned a nod of approval.

"Yeah."

The captain fastened the top button of his Navy pea coat and turned the collar up to shelter his neck from the impending boat ride's headwind.

"Take anything you want, sailor. I'll sign it out, personally."

"Thank you, sir."

"Be safe out there, wherever 'there' may be," the captain said while reaching out to Quint.

Quint didn't care about the pain and extended his right hand from the arm sling. The two men shook hands and parted ways. Quint stayed at the end of the wharf and watched the crew cast off the mooring lines. The PT boat rumbled away. The captain, removing his officer's hat, stood tall and proud while the boat cut the water then banked its way towards Mare Island Navy Shipyard across the bay.

Quint turned to head back into town. For the first time in his life, he found himself homeless.

17 THE OFFER

His strides grew wider and faster. The traffic and pedestrian bodies seemed to drift in slow motion. That palpable sting of failure and guilt, hammering his mind to a steady beat. The waterfront streets took forever to navigate. The people couldn't get out of the way fast enough. Only one way to push back the sting. To suppress the pain. He had to get back to his boat.

Quint tossed back another two codeine tablets, but the pain was not physical. They would have no effect. The boat contained the only solace available.

He made his way past the endless rows of shipping piers, trucks full of cargo, and the laughing sailors mooring up their ships. The thought of Maureen waiting for him all those nights turned to images of Herbie Robinson reaching out from below. The collection of dog tags falling away became his arm breaking across the wooden arm-wrestling table. Under the shadow of the Bay Bridge, Quint continued ahead and saw Troy punching at the large tiger shark. That sting turned to images of his father. The gaff hook. The head of the marlin.

By the time he reached Mission Bay, and the half-built piers of new construction, Quint was sweating and stumbling. It had been too long since his last taste of sweet ignorance. His hands shook. His thighs numbed and weak.

Quint stumbled down the gangplank of the small pier off Berry Street and onto a dilapidated twenty five-foot wooden boat. The stain and stench of dried shark blood painted the cracked decking. Quint stepped down into the vessel and lost his balance, catching himself on the fighting chair bolted to the center of the deck. The chair swiveled with his momentum, allowing him to maintain his balance and push into the wheelhouse.

Inside the abused cabin, one lone table of tools and dirty engine rags stood across from a simplified steering wheel and throttle control. His blurred vision found the small collection of glass bottles in the corner, each half empty of liquid relief.

Quint took a bottle and raised it to his lips. He pulled the alcohol into his body and felt the immediate effects. The burn of the throat, the warmth on his brain, the calming of the mind—most important, the fading of memories. The broken man leaned against the open door of the wheelhouse and shifted his right arm in the sling. Raising the bottle with his left hand, he took in another drink.

"Mr. Quint?"

Quint looked over his right shoulder at the voice behind him. A man stood on the small pier, looking down at him.

"I'm looking for a Captain Quint. I was told I could find him here?"

The man, dressed in a slick gray suit and thin navy-blue tie, shifted his tan overcoat and put his hands in his pockets.

Quint placed the bottle on the table in the pilothouse and turned to step out into the open.

"Yeah, I'm Quint. What do you want?"

"You are a hard man to find, Mr. Quint. I suppose this is my lucky day. The harbor master said this was your boat, so I've been by here off and on for the last few days, and what do you know? I finally found you."

The polished eastern accent isn't what made Quint uncomfortable at first, nor was it the fancy clothes and city slicker shoes. The man was the same age as Quint, early thirties, well combed black hair and a rehearsed smile. Quint paused at the confidence the man carried. Nobody on the up-and-up should be that confident in life.

"Are you FBI? Police? What did I do now?" Quint said with a wry smile. The effects of the alcohol already loosening him up.

The man laughed and took out a pack of cigarettes from his pocket.

"I'm about as far from that as you could imagine."

He gestured to Quint with the pack of cigarettes, and Quint responded with a silent shake of the head. The man shrugged and stuffed them back into his pocket while lighting a cigarette in his mouth with a fluid motion and the click of a Zippo lighter.

Quint pulled himself up the small three-step ladder with his good hand. He stepped back on the pier to approach the stranger, who breathed a cloud of smoke and looked at the right arm in the sling.

"I see you got banged up, Mr. Quint."

"A little."

"You still going to fish?"

"Who wants to know?"

The man let out a polished laugh and took another drag of his cigarette. Every mannerism, movement, and stance of the feet appeared rehearsed and purposeful.

"I forgot to introduce myself. How could I? My name is Larry Vaughn. I traveled from a little island back east called Amity."

Larry Vaughn reached out with his right hand, and Quint raised his left. Vaughn smiled, snatched the right back and reached out with his left hand to execute a firm, opposite handshake.

"Amity is a dump. Nothing but skells and campers there," said Quint.

"Not anymore. We established a township, refurbished the old town hall, even built a full-service gas station."

"There's not even electricity on that island."

"You've been out of the loop. The last section of submarine cable got laid back in November from Nantucket to a cable junction. They are working on the line to Amity now. Should have electricity by summer."

"Sounds like you folks been busy then, Mr. Vaughn."

Vaughn nodded his head in another exhale of smoke.

"It's the right time to build. Brand new decade. The country's never been better. My investors and I are looking to make Amity into a summer resort."

Quint laughed at the absurd idea.

"You are wasting your money. Nobody is going to want to get all the way out there—"

"If all things go as scheduled, utilities, roads, motels, we'll even have our own ferry terminal built. Ferries to and from the mainland in about ten years, maybe fifteen tops. When that happens, tourists will be there. I can guarantee you that."

Quint stood back and looked Vaughn over once again.

"So, what makes you leave all that fancy business to fly across the country?"

"The census registry had you last listed in Barnstable County before the war, Mr. Quint. So, I imagine you are familiar with the area?"

"Yeah. Lots of people are."

Vaughn took a long drag on the last few centimeters of tobacco. He flicked the cigarette butt into the water and stepped forward through the final cloud of warm smoke. Vaughn reached into his overcoat and pulled out a folded newspaper.

"I have come here to hire you, Mr. Quint. I could use a man of your talents."

Quint looked down at the wrinkled San Francisco Chronicle front page being handed to him. In the description under the large photo of himself standing over the three dead great white sharks, the name 'Captain Quint' had been circled in red ink.

PART II

18   HERSHEL

My name is Hershel Salvatore. I was born on Amity Island and I'm gonna die on Amity Island. I've never set foot on the mainland of this country in all my eighty-one years. Of course, I've made stops over on the Vineyard, Nantucket, the Cape, and that one time in Boston back in '66. I'll get to that later.

I suppose what I'm trying to tell you is that I don't know a hell of a lot about the big cities. New York is a mystery, as are trains, highways, airplanes, cornfields, sports stadiums. I've never seen them. Been nowhere but here. Amity Island is what I know.

I'm one of the last people who can tell you—there were always big sharks off Amity. Until he arrived.

I don't know how to tell you this story. Never considered myself much of a storyteller. My father used to take me down to the whaler's wharf when I was a kid. The old sailors sat us kids up on the lobster traps and told us sailor ghost stories—tales of horror on the seas. I remember the lantern light would hit their ancient cheekbones and black out their eyes. Make us lose a few hours of sleep for the next week with the way they spun those yarns. I don't think I have that type of talent to do this story justice. But I've told it enough and I know it well. The constant waves of curious tourists, the cars and out-of-state plates driven by morbid thrill seekers, they all ask about him. He has become somewhat of a legend. Everyone wants to know who he was. What was he like? I know what I know. He was my captain and every bit the legend you heard—and then some.

In order to tell you his story, I'll have to start with Amity. I was born on this island around 1931, in this very house. It sits above the small cluster of houses, fishing shacks, and docked boats around a harbor on the far west end of the island. Seven houses up Harbor Hill Road on the left. This is the only house I've ever known. I stared at this tiny harbor from on top of this hill every morning of my life, unless I was at sea. My mother rocked me to sleep out on this back deck under the starlight. In her arms, the warm ocean breeze whistled through the beach heather and knocked me right out. Even today, on those special warm summer nights when I sit out here on this deck, I can still smell her lavender perfume.

This deck is like Amity: old, portions rebuilt a few times over, with little pieces of its history still strewn about for people to ponder and wonder. A few rusty nails, tired and misshapen, with some shiny new neighbors added in later on. Over there, under the far railing, you will find three gouges where my grandmother left me at two and a half with a bottle of milk and a horseshoe crab tail. I got bored and tried drawing myself a sailboat. A deck from fresh cedar lumber salvaged off a prospector didn't come cheap back then. My mother hid the marks with a tweed mat, fearing my father's wrath upon discovery. She's long gone. So is that mat. I'll be gone soon as well, but those marks will still be there for the next tenants to ponder over.

Amity is not a very large island. If you look on the map, it is near half the length of Nantucket. Ten miles long and thin. About half a mile between the north shore and South Beach at the center of the island. It juts out two and a half miles wide in the far eastern end where the Town of Amity and Amity Harbor is located. The rest of the island all falls under Amity Township. My little harbor is on the far west end where the island tappers down. Amity Point is what we always called it, but I never thought they made it official.

Did I mention it's not very large? It isn't. If you felt up to the task, a walk the full length of Amity would cost you four hours and you'd not even break a sweat. By boat, if equipped with a decent-sized engine and opened to full throttle, you can leave Amity Point and moor up to the fuel pumps of Amity Harbor in a little over an hour.

Amity Island sits less than ten miles southwest of Nantucket. It is the last island before the open ocean. Off to our south, there is a shelf on the sea floor, and it drops off to the deepest parts of the north Atlantic. This shallow shelf makes for turbulent waters and rough seas, so if you want to sail the length of Amity, my advice is to take the north shore route and save your back.

Because Amity is the smallest island and furthest from the mainland, we were the last with electricity. After I was born, they threw the switch on Nantucket. On clear nights, if you were high on the bluffs overlooking the northeast corner of Amity, you could see the twinkling and shimmer of lights along their shores. We didn't mind. Nantucket was always the fancier island. They had light bulbs while we were still burning oil lanterns.

A religious colony settled Amity in the 1800s. The oldest parts in town, main street, the town hall, those large white houses you might've seen—all built by people looking to be apart from society. It was hard work just getting out to Amity, and even harder work living here. Whoever lived here wanted nothing to do with the modern world. Amity was always an outcast island. Only natural that it attracted the outcasts of society as well. We avoided the world, while the world avoided us—it's just the way it was.

I am an islander. Many people like to brag about that title. They try to give rules on who is and who isn't an 'islander,' but they don't know what they are talking about. It's easy to be born on Amity these days. We have a hospital, schools, roads, supermarkets, gas stations, ferries to and from the other islands and the mainland. There are jobs, tourism, and a booming fishing industry. This all came about in the last fifty years. Before that, Amity was a life of desolation and isolation.

In the 1940s and some 50s, we still didn't have electricity. The first power lines didn't reach my end of the island until 1953. The roads outside of town lacked paving, and the sand was everywhere. During the winter months, the postman air dropped mail once a week because of the ice pack and rough seas. It was a hard life to live on Amity. It was primitive and only made for the toughest of citizens. If you weren't here when there was no electricity—you aren't an islander. You are a transplant. You all showed up and prospered on the backs of us who settled this place on hardship and hard times.

That's okay. Most of the island is transplants and tourists these days. Real 'islanders' were always scarce. The population of this island wasn't much over five hundred back in 1951. All remnants of families that started here in the early 1900s. Most of them lived in town, and the rest scattered about the island in beach shacks and cottages found at the ends of winding sandy roads.

The Amity fishing industry was small time because the larger harbors of the other islands, and their stone-throw distance to the mainland, made it easier and cheaper to process your catch. All the serious fishermen lived over there. If you were a fisherman on Amity, you were just fine with the usual rod and reel business. Blue fish, Atlantic tomcod, a yellow fin tuna here and there if you were lucky. Maybe set a few lobster traps and hope to sell a couple at the market in town. It was enough to survive. All those serious crews, with their fancy nets and long lines, stayed far away from Amity. And good riddance—nothing but trouble, anyways.

19 LOSS

Yes, I understand you want to hear about the sharks. My captain's tale isn't only about his war with them. It just isn't that simple. This did not take a few years. This wasn't just a few days on a boat. Many people sensationalize and focus on the great one from 1974. His legend began long before that. Before him, the sharks of Amity were just that—legends. Myths. He made them real.

Those old fishermen and the ghost stories on the wharf—that was all part of it. They had you so scared to swim out past your belly with those tales of gigantic monsters lurking where the water turns black.

Before the war, there weren't many kids on Amity. The schools were back on the mainland. If you were a kid on Amity, you only got there from misfortune. Depression era made folks do a lot of stuff to survive. My folks built this cottage on a hill of the farthest island from civilization they could find. And Amity was the last stop until the open Atlantic.

The few of us squirts that found each other, ran the beaches and talked of local stories. Amity mythology—the kid whose father caught him stealing from another man's lobster traps, then took him out past the shallows and made him swim back, never to be seen again. The washed-up sea creatures with giant holes gouged out or entire halves of them missing. It was the sharks, always the sharks.

Of course, none of us had ever seen any of them. But that didn't matter. After you hear enough tales a few times over, you believe in them.

I'm here to tell you they are all true. Every last one.

After the depression and throughout the war, we saw more recluses and scoundrels move in to set up shop. The respectable folks stuck closer to town and build homes around Amity Harbor and the eastern shore. Those who wanted to be left alone drifted up-island, settling around our little harbor in the far west end.

By the end of the 1930s, I sat around this deck and watched more small cottages get built. It looked like a cluster of ants fell on our little harbor. I may have been seven or eight. My family never told me my birth date, so I can only guess it was early '30s. I remember my father's small fishing boat moored up on a lone wooden dock at the end of the harbor and the stretch of this shore laid bare. All the rest of the folks who staked their claim on this harbor gave me dates of 1934, or '36. Mr. Stanton built his shack in '35. I'm assuming us Salvatores built our shack on the hill in 1930 and I was born right here on this deck either the same year or after.

With the added population, came added competition for fishing grounds. Areas to set your traps, if you were into that sort of thing, were now challenged. The men started pushing to the outer limits to get a better catch. Sailing further out.

They started coming back with the panic of giant fish attacking their hulls. Fishing rods pulled from the hands of fishermen, and some strapped into those rods got pulled right in. All ended like that kid who got caught with the lobsters, never to be seen again. Fishing nets ripped to pieces. Marlin on the line one minute, then only the great fish's severed head pulled up moments later.

We all knew what it was, but never talked about it. The fishermen adjusted and kept closer to shore. Some just stayed in the estuary and saltwater ponds, living off the smaller fish caught there.

The praying type would close their eyes and wish it all to go away. My mother used to say a prayer when she held me while waving to Papa as he cast off his bow line and started out to sea. To get out of the harbor, the boat needed to cruise right by our little shack on the hill. He would look off the starboard side and see us up here waving. He'd return three waves of his hand before facing his console and throttling up.

When he was gone, no matter how hard the weather; driving salt-sea rain, savage winds, or a calm autumn breeze—my mother stood watch on the deck. She paced these gray cedar planks and prayed as a lonely Civil War wife in her widow's watch, waiting for the cavalry to come over a distant seafaring oceanic hill and bring her husband home.

Autumn of 1938, we waved to Papa, and he turned away as usual. The throttle of his little single engine pushed down, with white water churning behind the stern. He passed the rock jetty and turned towards the white caps of the rough seas like he had a thousand times. Only this time, he never returned. Those three waves he gave back to us were the last time I ever saw him alive.

The sharks got him. Nobody will ever convince me otherwise. My mother stood on that deck for hours and hours and then days. He was gone—boat and all.

There were no authorities on the island. Not even a telephone line. All men made the choice of the hard life on Amity. So, when the hardness took its toll, nobody ever complained. The missing were just given a prayer service dedication over at the small seamen's chapel across the harbor. A few sailors and fishermen gathered around the wharf and tipped a bottle to his memory. Then life went on. That's just the way it was.

I lost my granddad to the sea. And then the sea took Papa. It would only be natural for the sea to take me. Therefore, my mother forbid me to go on any boats and work on the water.

To make a few dollars and survive the following years, she worked the window at Mr. McQuitty's small coffee and breakfast shack on the other side of the harbor. Mr. McQuitty was one of the few with a working truck. He'd buy the catch from the boats as they returned to Amity Point, then run it all back down-island to town. The few restaurants there could buy it back from him at a small mark-up.

Over the next many years, while my mother served coffee and crackers to the fishermen, I spent the time walking around the small fishing shack my father built at the end of the harbor. The other kids made fun of me because I lacked the sea legs which they developed from working with their fathers on the boats. Still, despite my pleading and protesting, my mother insisted I stay ashore. I took refuge from the ridicule in Papa's fishing shack. I made repairs, explored, and just spent time there. His tools and gear hanging along the walls. It was my private chapel to him. It was my grade school. If I held my breath and listened, I believed he was there with me. Every day, I paid a visit to the dock to make sure the bow and stern lines he last cast off laid coiled and prepared—waiting for him to return. Those pieces of hemp rope were the last things he touched. I held them as if I was holding his hand.

I miss him so. Even now, at eighty-one years old, I miss him like I was eight.

My mother died when I was fourteen. During the winter of 1945. She came down with some sort of sickness. I was sure the fireplace was going when I left to go find the doctor back in town. During the winter, this island is a ghost town. It's soulless—empty. My legs ran the entire length of the island. I remember the running. Every step ending in a crunch of snow was the only sound I heard across the island. Even the ocean iced over and laid silent. I didn't want to leave her, but she told me to go. Maybe she knew death was near, and she didn't want me to see her leaving this world. Maybe she didn't think I was strong enough to handle it. I'll never know.

By the time I reached town, and Dr. Nevin took me in his little truck back across the island, we hustled up the snow and cobble road to our little shack. She had turned on her side, facing the wall—already passed. I'll always wonder what made her turn to her side before dying. Was it she didn't want me to see her face? Did she see my father lying next to her? Maybe turned for one last kiss? I'll find out soon enough when I see them again.

I spent my teenage years living in this little shack on the hill by myself. To take odd jobs around the harbor for a few cents or a dollar became the norm. With my mother gone, I was free to be a deckhand and tried to go out with a few of the boats to work on the water. It never ended well. I would get the worst pains of sea sickness and spend the time getting laughed at while hanging over the side of the boat, dry heaving an empty stomach into the saltwater. I'm not the tallest of sailors either. My height of five feet kept me from even standing up for myself. Those deployments never ended well.

You could say I was a ship that lost its rudder. I had no steerage. No direction in life. Until he arrived.

20 ARRIVAL

The wood of this deck is tired and gray. Warped and curled, the constant assault from the north Atlantic has taken its toll. The first and last time I ever saw him was from up here. The last time, the Orca sailed right by as she always had. Like my captain, the boat was menacing and calculating. He took her out to sea with the policeman and the scientist.

Funny thing, when someone leaves, it's not memorable. You don't even think about it because you just know they'll be coming right back. The routine of life is easy to get used to. I wish I stood and watched just a little longer that afternoon in 1974.

But when you see someone for the first time, especially a significant figure such as him, you never forget it. When I first saw him, I fell off this bench and jumped out of my skin.

The icy winds of late February in 1951 delivered a dusting of snow to Amity Point. Everything sat covered in a gray haze. I finished cleaning the coffee pots for Mr. McQuitty and he let me take a small pot back to my house with whatever was left at the bottom of the big percolating urns. The fishermen had all shoved off, and the harbor sat silent, awaiting their return.

After making my way to the other side of the harbor, and up the snowy cobble of Harbor Hill Road, I didn't hesitate to come out to my deck. The cold never bothered me, and I didn't have any firewood—used the last during the deep freeze we just suffered one month prior. It was almost March, and you can always feel spring moving in from up here.

My little tin cup was warm from my inside coat pocket. I tried to pour what little liquid I could from the mess of ground coffee sludge. Whatever I salvaged was still hot, so it would do.

And that's when I looked up.

Just over the gray wood deck railing, I looked down at my father's fishing shack, and a figure in black was standing on the dock. At nineteen years of age, one still has an imagination, and I swore it was a ghost. I dropped my coffee cup and fell out of my chair—most definitely making a noise, but how loud? I ducked my head low enough to keep out of sight and crawled to the edge of the deck with caution.

The water of the harbor glassed over while the morning mist hung in stagnation. Not even a reed whistled. I was certain the figure in black heard me. I rose my head high enough to peer over the dwarf shrub and broom crowberry. There he still stood. Broad shoulders of a black coat, with the collar propped up and hiding his face. A black wool sailor's watch cap covering his hair. He shouldered a green sea bag. The same kind I've seen some sailors carry when they get off the big boats back in town.

I thought he was a ghost. It was something with the way he moved—or didn't move. He stood and studied the harbor. The figure looked down at my father's coiled mooring lines, then glanced up and down the small wooden dock. He looked up in my direction and I ducked, pulling my head down to my chest. My breath held, I tried to think of what the ghost of a sailor lost at sea would want with my father's fishing shack. I shook the thoughts of nonsense and supernatural from my head and mustered up the courage to stand. The decision to act like I just finished repairing a plank of wood on the deck seemed like an excellent strategy. I rose to my feet and dusted the snow from my knees, then attempted a casual glance down to the dock. He vanished.

By 1951, Amity was crawling with unfamiliar faces. After the war, those who fell into money started looking around for places to settle down and build businesses. If you were an islander, you could recognize when someone was new to the island. Most of the new arrivals stayed down-island, but we would see a few up here. When someone new arrived at this part of the island, everyone noticed. It wasn't difficult to stand out in the small cluster of fishing shacks and cottages inside our little horseshoe harbor of sixty or seventy residents.

I knew he wasn't from Amity, even though I hadn't seen his face. If I didn't imagine him and he was real, I tried to think of reasons for him being on this side of the island.

I didn't see him again for the next few hours and believe me; I tried. Even went back inside the house and watched with the binoculars. By early afternoon, I threw my coat on and hustled back to the docks on the other side of the harbor. The fishing and lobster boats returned for the day, each moving ahead down the center of the thin waterway. The weary watercrafts meandered toward their docks and fishing shacks to moor up.

If I was quick enough, whoever had the most successful day out on the water would sometimes hire me to help offload their catch and clean the boat. When small time sailors have a big day, the menial work of hosing off salt from the windows, fish scales and blood from the deck, or pumping out the bilge— it all impedes the good time. That's where I fit in. If in the vicinity, I could pick up a dollar and square away the boat while they went to drink away the extra spending money.

"Hey, Hershel. Looks like we got a little work for you over here."

Of all the boats to have a good day, why did it have to be them? I never liked the Papov boys. Their father, Yuri, was an angry man who, if not on his fishing boat, was down on the docks with a bottle of vodka in his hand. His two sons, Stefan and Andros never passed up an opportunity to give me a hard time.

Their fishing shack sat five spots up the west side of the harbor from my father's place. A small little one-room shack with a double door in the middle, and two smaller windows of chipped paint and broken glass. They had the biggest dock on the harbor, and it stretched out into the water past the others. Like their personalities, the dock imposed itself and crowded the other docks and fishermen on either side. Those fishermen said nothing. It was best to let the Papov's just be. Without the interaction, your day was better.

But I needed my dollar, so with a sigh I stepped down from the planks and made my way to their small white lobster boat.

Andros and Stefan were struggling with the lines which had fallen into the water.

"Hershel, get the lead out of your ass and give us a hand here."

With their father barking at them in a slurred Russian and English hybrid that only they could understand, I knelt and pulled up the lines so the stern could come alongside. A line in the water can be dangerous. With a rope fouled around a propeller, you paralyze the boat. This was one of the first things my father told me. I smiled as I tossed their lines to them.

Andros didn't like me being able to hear them getting the business from their old man.

"Hey Stef, Hershel here thinks we are a funny bunch."

"No, not me. I'm just here to give you fellas a hand. Don't want any trouble." I raised my hands in a surrendering fashion.

Stefan threw a few figure-eight wraps around the cleat and jumped over to the dock. "Then why was you laughing?"

"I wasn't laughing. Just smiling at thoughts of my dad. He told me not to leave lines in the water like that."

Andros took a wrap on the bow's cleat and pulled in the slack, tied it off, and jumped to the dock.

"That's funny. If your father was any good of a sailor, maybe he would've been able to find his way back to the island."

"C'mon, fellas. What work do you have for me?"

"That's not what I heard, Andros. His father took off and found some broad in Plymouth to shack up with. He took one look at his runt son and said 'Dasvidaniya'."

The Papov's always hit below the belt. I was used to it. We grew up together on this island and they were like this since I could remember. Just today, for the first time in my life, I didn't want to deal with the insults.

"Keep your dollar, Mr. Papov. I don't need it," I said to the father while turning to walk up the dock and leave.

The two brothers argued with their father, barking back and forth in that language I couldn't understand. They ran after me, realizing they would have to clean the boat off themselves in my absence.

I was passing the wall of stacked lobster traps, six high and five deep, when Andros and Stefan both ran up behind me. Stefan stepped in front of me with a quick step.

"Where the hell are you going, little guy? You have work to do."

They were both over a year older than me, at twenty and twenty-one, and each of them a foot taller. I was never good at confrontation. My whole life I had to look up at folks. It isn't a problem, but when two taller and aggressive men are closing in, I hold my breath and my hands shake. My reaction is always the same: look down and forget about speaking.

"We left the deck an extra mess for you today, and it would be a shame for you to leave. Now, maybe we got carried away back there—you know, talking about your dad and all, but you can't leave."

As Stefan spoke his false words of reason, I didn't feel Andros clip a sink line from a lobster trap to the back belt loop of my dungarees.

That strange feeling of braveness came over me. In the last few years, I would have turned around and shuffled down to the boat, but today, I felt different. I just didn't want to deal with it.

"Sorry, fellas. You are on your own today." I stepped to the side and went to move forward.

"Well, go on and get. Who needs a sawed-off runt anyways?" Andros grabbed a fistful of my plaid wool overcoat and gave me a shove.

I fell forward onto the sandy path next to the fishing shack, and in doing so, brought an entire stack of lobster traps down with me. My chest met the sand in a crash of wood and mesh netting. The top trap fell the hardest and broke into pieces right at his feet.

Andros and Stefan's laughter stopped as they stared straight ahead.

I pushed a lobster trap and buoy float off my side and looked up. There he was.

A black US Navy issued pea coat with the collar turned up. His broad shoulders and chest fanned out, and he kept his hands in the coat pockets. Sideburns extending from his wool navy watch cap. A slight mustache over a chiseled chin. He was unlike anyone I ever saw on this tiny island.

Mr. Papov came running up the planks of the dock towards the commotion.

"Hey, what the hell is going on with all this nonsense? We gotta catch to sell and you are up here breaking traps?"

While Mr. Papov barked out his broken English, we continued to stare at the man in black. I can tell you with the greatest sincerity, the Papov boys would've blamed the lobster trap crash on me and cooked up a story to tell their father any other time. This time was different. The stranger just stared back at them, almost daring them to tell a lie. They stumbled through a partial explanation, as the man in black just kicked a piece of the broken trap back into the pile. Mr. Papov didn't even wait for the entire explanation and threw a hand across the back of Stefan's head, and a back-hand swing to the shoulder of Andros, sending the boys running back to the boat to get to work.

I stood to my feet and brushed the snow and sand off my clothes.

When I looked up, he was gone.

The street down the west side of our little harbor came alive with several fishermen and trucks from town. I stepped forward and looked down the street. The man in black moved through the hustle of island life. The villagers seemed to part and step aside as he approached. This man had a different purpose on this island. I could tell that from the first day I saw him.

21   HIRED

Three months passed before I spoke to him. During that time, he was the ghost of Amity. Everyone on Amity Point whispered rumors of who he was or what he was doing there, but nobody ever approached him.

He was never around long enough. Throughout the day, you would see him one minute and the next he was gone. A week might pass and when you least expect it, there he would be. The anonymous figure—standing, observing, moving around the island with a purposeful mystery that none of us could explain.

I would wake up at nights and look down from this shack on the hill, to see a lantern lit in my father's fishing shack. The small window on the west side aglow. I saw the smoke trail from the short tin chimney. It was him.

I didn't want to approach him, because I wanted to imagine it was my father who came back from his long voyage at sea. Just seeing that light on in the window made me miss Papa. It comforted me to see the fishing shack have a sign of life again.

Every few days, I gathered enough courage to walk down to the fishing shack and approach the stranger, but when I did, the place was empty— vanished without a trace once again. Like I said, it would be three months before I spoke to him, and when I did, it changed my life forever.

Now you gotta remember who I was on this island. I was a nobody. A five-foot tall orphan that couldn't even find work as a day sailor. Of all the islanders in 1951, I was at the bottom of the barrel in importance. So, when I was the one he hired, I found myself at the center of some of the biggest moments in

Amity Island history. I believe it was more than just a chance when I saw him leave the shack that warm May afternoon.

"That'll be all for today, Hershel. Maybe I'll be seeing you tomorrow."

Mr. Mishkin handed me a dollar, but I didn't answer. I was done with the morning's work after he brought in a few lobster traps, and I struggled to get them stacked off to the side and hosed off with fresh water. Over the top of the highest trap, I balanced on a small ladder with the hose when I saw the stranger step out of the side door of our fishing shack. Down the steps he walked and emerged from underneath the shack's overhang. The shack, resting on the wooden pylons my father set back in 1930, cast a shadow over him. He stepped out into the sunlight and made his way to the end of the harbor. Paused and looking around, he headed down to the bay on the other side of the road.

This was my chance to do some investigating. And maybe it was about time I approached the figure that had been staying on and off in what was my property by rights—although I'm not even sure there was ever a formal deed issued. I'm telling you; the frontier mentality of 1950s Amity was the last in the nation.

With cautious steps, I approached the top wood plank of the stairway. On my toes, I reached the first window and brushed away the dried salt from the glass. My eyes widened and peered into the dark shack.

The lantern hung dark, and the wood-burning stove appeared cold. The setting sun out on the ocean cast an orange light through the windows of the loft and illuminated the gray wood interior.

I opened the door and stepped in.

The air was still, and I could smell the remnants of last night's fire in the stove. The hammock hung with a gray wool blanket crumpled up at the center. In the corner was the green Navy seabag I saw him carrying on that first sighting. Along the side, stenciled in black paint:

QUINT

Along the wall, my father's tools and tackle with one hook cleared. On that hook, an olive drab military jacket. The kind I saw some soldiers wearing in the newspapers and *Life* magazines down at Mr. McQuitty's. That also had the same name stenciled on the patch above the right breast pocket.

In the corner is where I saw it. Propped up and leaned back against the wall next to the hammock. A rifle. I only saw it in pictures until that moment. The M-1 Garand which all the men carried to war. It was larger in life that I ever imagined.

I was so taken by the sight; I didn't think twice about stepping to it and picking the rifle up into my hands. The weight was unexpected—it had a sledgehammer feel to it. The wood grain and stock had scars of abuse and history one could only imagine. In all my nineteen years, this was a moment where I felt the outside world become real and into my hands. I only heard stories of the war and seen the photos—never imagined holding a weapon such as this.

I shouldered the rifle and peered down the sights, aiming it towards the setting sun.

"Do you know if it's loaded, boy?"

The rough voice from behind me made my heart drop. I remember the feeling in my teeth—the tingling numbness in my gums. It's the same feeling I always get when I'm nervous or excited or scared, or all three put together. I went to lower the rifle and turn around.

"Don't move. Stay there."

I did just what he said, froze while holding the rifle to the window. The sunbeam shone through the little round rear sight, and I remember its shadow sitting on the webbing of my right hand. My arms shook with the rifle's weight bearing down.

He stepped up to my side and studied me.

"Get your finger out of the trigger guard, boy."

I gave a slight nod and eased my finger off the rifle's cold steel trigger, then out of the metal guard.

"How old are you? Thirty? Thirty-five?"

"I'm nineteen, sir."

The man let out a slight laugh of disbelief and moved in closer.

"What the hell do they feed you kids on this island? You look like you got one foot in the grave, as does every other crazy nut who lives out here?"

"I suppose we are born old on Amity, sir."

My hands shook and forearms burned, so I went to lower the gun.

"I said don't move, didn't I? Now get that rifle back up there. You were man enough to pick it up, now be man enough to hold it steady."

I snapped the rifle back to my shoulder and continued to peer through the sights.

"What's your name, boy?"

"Hershel Salvatore, Mr. Quint, and this here is my father's fishing shack. I was watching—"

"How do you know my name?"

"It's written on your bag... and your jacket, sir."

Mr. Quint looked me up and down and nodded his head in approval.

"Observant. Not much in height though, just assumed you would be good at digging ditches. How does one get on an island looking like you?"

"I was born here, sir. I'm an islander. This was my father's fishing shack. My house is up on the hill, south side of the harbor. Seventh house on the left."

My arms trembled. This rifle might as well have been a six-foot cross arm.

"Mr. Quint, I can't hold this much longer."

"Shut up and first check to see if it's loaded, Hershel."

"I'm not sure I know how. This is the first time I've ever held a rifle, sir."

"Lower the weapon with your left hand. With your right, take the operating rod and pull the bolt back."

My breath held. The sweat beads ran down my face. I did what he asked and lowered the rifle to my chest. I tried to pull the bolt back, and it wouldn't budge. The damn thing was so stiff, I don't even know how them boys went off to storm those beaches with such a stubborn piece of armament. I went to pull even harder, and the damn thing racked back and locked in a click of metal.

"Now look down into the receiver. You see anything?"

"No, sir. Just some piece of metal."

"What about the barrel? Anything up in the barrel?"

I saw the orange light shine through the barrel and rest its glow on the oiled steel of the receiver.

"No, sir. Looks empty."

"Then it's empty. What are you standing around so nervous for?"

I dropped the rifle and felt the blood rush back to my hands while Mr. Quint laughed with amusement. He walked back to the wood-burning stove and opened the front door. The cast-iron hinges sang out in a creak. Mr. Quint moved to a small pile of chopped wood.

"Back in town, they think this place is abandoned. And you are saying your father built this?"

"Yes, sir. I've been seeing you in here with the lantern lit from time to time, so that's all I was doing was seeing who you were."

"Where's your father now?"

"Lost at sea. He left to go fishing back in 1938 and never came back to port."

Mr. Quint paused and stood there gripping a small block of wood. I figured hearing about my father and dying at sea meant something to him.

"He was a good man then," said Mr. Quint and tossed the block of wood into the belly of the stove. "All the tackle and tools hanging around here his?"

"Yes, sir. I never took them down, because I always kinda wished he'd come back."

"Where's your mother?"

"She died six years ago, sir. She's buried up on Cemetery Road."

Another wood block hit the back wall of the stove and Mr. Quint slammed the black iron door shut. He turned and moved towards me, and this time I got a good look at him. The direct stare of his blue eyes had me frightened and weary. He approached as a predator on the attack—direct and methodical.

"I've seen you around, boy. How much they pay you to scrub fish guts for small time pikers on this island? Or hand out coffee and donuts?"

"A dollar on a good day. Fifty cents on the regular ones."

"How about you come work for me, and we put your father's equipment here to good use? He was ten times the sailor than these bums will ever be. He gave his life to the sea. Where I come from, that is an honor."

Words can't describe what I felt when he said that to me. Never heard one person talk about my father like that before. I couldn't reach out my hand quick enough. Mr. Quint's giant hand gripped my palm and squeezed. I thought of my hand getting swallowed by a fish. It disappeared in his grip.

"You have rough hands, Hershel. You'll do just fine," Mr. Quint said while studying my handshake.

"What line of work are you in, sir?"

"Sharkin'."

At the time, I had no idea what that even meant.

22   THE DEAL

"Mr. Quint, I'd like to have a word, please. Sir?"

That summer of 1951 was the longest summer I could remember, and I had run out of patience.

It had been a few months since he hired me as his first mate. I imagined we would be on the high seas every day. Maybe I would be the most experienced of sailors on the island—hauling in giant sea monsters with my right hand while backing down a boat in rough seas with the left. I wish I could tell you it was mariner glamor and adventure from the get-go. But I can't. I never even saw the water, except from standing on the dock.

The August heat was oppressive. The humidity and stagnant air settled in over our little harbor by June. Like a stubborn drunken sailor clutching on the bar the night before getting underway, the heat would not leave.

I didn't complain. He paid me three dollars a day, and it was the most money I ever made in my life. However, I wanted people to see me on a boat. I wanted all those who said I was useless to see they were wrong. When I pulled into port with Mr. Quint, I'm sure everyone would wish they were me. There were a lot of good talkers on Amity. It seemed the island was full of them; those who talked about being fishermen and liked to look as if they knew what they were doing, but they didn't have a clue. And when someone arrived on the island with experience, all the day-players would scurry and hide—their hidden ignorance threatened with exposure.

There was no greater a figure of salty sea experience on that island than Mr. Quint. It was obvious from the first day he arrived. Every man, woman, and child who saw him wanted nothing to do with him. The women felt insulted;

the men became intimidated, and the children were plain scared of him. But I was walking and working by his side. He had a way of making you feel taller just by stepping into a room with him. Eyes stared, then averted. People changed directions and walked to the other side of the road if they saw us coming.

I wanted so much for them to see us on a professional fishing trawler or lobster boat. In reality, there wasn't a boat in sight for the entire first summer. I buried my delusions of sailing grandeur and swashbuckling adventure in a face full of sawdust and a rusty bucket of carpenter nails.

Mr. Quint put me to work in the fishing shack. We built an entire two floor addition onto the shack. This section required extra pylons to be sunk into the harbor and other large pieces of framing wood. His plan was for a bath and shower on the first floor, with a sleeping quarters just above. Sounds simple, but on an island with no electricity, and the mainland an impossible distance away, if you didn't have cash to import a supply ship and a crew of men, this was a job that would require half a year.

The work became routine. I'd walk down from the shack on the hill and start where we left off the night before. Mr. Quint was always gone at first light. I would finish what he left in the coffeepot on the stove and get ready for the heat as the sun rose higher. Around noon, Mr. Quint would arrive in a rumble of exhaust and a cloud of dust. He drove a 1943, or was it a 44? It doesn't matter. It was a black Chevy AK pickup. Rusted out running boards towards the front and a missing starboard headlight, but it handled the sandy paths and roads just fine. I'd hear that distinctive squeak of the salt-corroded drum brakes and knew he was out front with a fresh load of lumber.

Lumber was scarce back then. He never told me where he got it, and I didn't ask. I just kept my mouth shut and head down. It was salvaged lumber. I could tell from the rusty nails pulled through and some weathered paint lacquered across one side.

His routine included drinking. Aside from the boards of wood and building material, Mr. Quint would unveil some fresh bottle of mystery liquid he also salvaged. I knew it would be an interesting day when he did. There were two versions of my captain—the one he showed the world, and a second that only came about with a bottle in his hand. Mr. Quint always drank alone. Before I worked for him, I couldn't afford to drink. So, the attraction to the bottle never seduced me as much as it did him.

"What?"

"I said I like to have a word with you—"

"I heard you the first time, Hershel. What is it you want? And don't call me 'sir'."

Mr. Quint balanced on the third rung from the top of a twenty-foot ladder. He stretched out to the side, straining to hammer in a few nails to the exterior board of the second floor. I approached the ladder and put my foot on the bottom rung to hold it steady.

"It's been three months, sir, and I was kinda thinking that you and I were going to be doing some fishing and all. And it's just that…"

"C'mon and spit it out, boy. I don't got all day."

I looked over at the Papov brothers mooring up to their dock. They didn't hesitate to do their daily gawking at me and our work on the shack. They laughed and turned away to another good day's catch weighing down their boat.

"Well, you said we were going to go fishing, but I haven't seen a boat yet and…"

Mr. Quint paused and cut me off in mid-sentence. "You smell that?"

"Smell what, sir?" Breathing through my nose, the stagnant air smelled of the usual low tide black sand sulfur and dead crab legs the gulls left behind.

"You lived here so long, you must be used to it."

"It always smells like this at low tide, sir."

"No, Mr. Salvatore, this isn't what low tide is supposed to smell like."

He leaned back out with his long arms and held a nail up to hammer in.

"Do you have a boat, sir?"

"Yeah. Sort of."

"Are we going to take it out?"

"When the parts arrive."

I moved in closer to look up and saw him straining. His right arm hammering home the final nail. The sounds of the hammer reverberated down the harbor and came back in a faint echo.

"Well, it's already August and the season for fishing is—"

"Watch it!"

The breeze of the three-pound mallet rushed across my ear when the heavy object dropped and exploded the aged wood of the deck next to my feet. I never saw the hammer that just missed my head, but the noise it made caused me to jump back.

"Dammit, boy! I told you to never get underneath me when I'm working aloft. What are we gonna do with a hammer buried in your skull while on this piece of garbage island way out in the middle of the ocean?"

Mr. Quint came stomping down the ladder. His right arm hung at his side. Something wasn't right with him, but I was too afraid to ask. When he yelled at you, your only reaction was to stand there and take it.

We both dripped with sweat. Mr. Quint pulled his light blue navy work shirt out from his belt line and snatched the ladder with his left hand. Fighting the pain, he used his right hand to steady the ladder so I could get in there and grab the rope release to lower it a few feet. We both rested it back against the half-finished addition of the fishing shack.

Quint turned to me, out of breath and wincing in pain. "And I told you. No need to call me 'sir'."

"Looks like you settled in nicely here, Mr. Quint."

Mr. Quint and I both looked up. There he stood, as out of place as I would be in Nebraska. A man in one of those slick gray suits, business shoes, and fancy combed-back hair. He stared at us with a smile from the shoreline between the neighboring fishing shack and ours. Quint let go of the ladder and stepped out onto the dock from under that shadow of the addition.

"Mr. Mayor, I was thinking you might never show up."

The man raised his hand and smiled. "No, no. Not the mayor, yet. Selectman Vaughn. Or Larry, whatever you prefer."

Remember when I told you that after the war there were a bunch of unfamiliar faces on the island? I had seen this guy before, but he didn't speak to anyone. He was part of the wave of businessmen that came about a few years back. They had entire crews of workers with measuring tapes and steel rods crawling all over the island. Easements, property lines, partitions, setbacks, zoning codes, and a whole slew of high-end city terms tossed around Amity Island after they arrived. The five businessmen even gave themselves a fancy term—selectmen. They talked about starting a township of Amity and how there was potential to grow the island. I know that some of them were from the mainland. Only two were islanders. This man was an islander. He grew up in town, left a while back, only to return with money and ambition. Nobody up-island liked his kind. I'm sure he didn't like us much either. At least, the selectmen got us a water main line installed out here at Amity Point. They won over many of the up-islanders with that.

"Listen, I have little time. A charter is leaving later today to take me back to New London." Vaughn walked under the addition, stepped out onto the dock, and turned around to look up at the structure. The two-story addition rose to the sky in a triangle peak and appeared as a tower of a castle looming over the water.

"I can't say this is approved by the building codes here. They have a one-story height limit for structures set within thirty feet of the water line."

Vaughn paused and looked over at Mr. Quint, who didn't even break his gaze from the smooth-talking businessman.

"Looks like the arm's back to normal. I was kind of thinking you were almost ready to get to work," said Vaughn while slipping out a shiny metal cigarette case from the inside pocket of his jacket.

Frustrated and not in the mood to talk, Mr. Quint was more direct. "You gonna make this island into a summer town when it stinks to high-heaven around here?"

Vaughn never broke the act. He pulled out a cigarette and lit it with the flip of a fancy lighter. Matches were too up-island for men like him.

"That's just seasonal tide stuff, Mr. Quint. Plus, this here is up-island. The ocean winds keep it from town. It comes and goes. You know how it is."

Mr. Quint didn't acknowledge as Vaughn delivered his answer in an exhale of smoke and a smile. Vaughn held out the case to offer a cigarette, but then took it back.

"Oh, that's right, I almost forgot. You don't smoke," said Vaughn while taking a step closer and closing the distance between him and Mr. Quint. "Now, I didn't come all the way up-island to talk about the air quality, Mr. Quint. I thought we could discuss the rest of our terms before I leave. Might be months before I'm back."

Mr. Quint nodded and looked back towards me. I was still holding onto the ladder.

"Hersh, why don't you go in and clean up those window frames for install?"

I already didn't like Larry Vaughn. Folks from down-island were always high society types, but Vaughn was different—he moved and talked with a purpose. I could tell Mr. Quint was on guard with his words. I stepped back under the overhang and went up the steps to go inside the shack, stopping under the open window to see what I could hear.

Vaughn turned to the harbor and watched the saltwater minnows dart below the surface.

"Your cargo arrived in town. The harbor master will tell you where the crates are. I assume your starting funds have been adequate."

Mr. Quint nodded his head. "It would be a lot easier if you could get me a boat to start with."

"This must look organic, Mr. Quint. You can't just show up with everything brand new. People will start asking questions. I'm sure the one you found will do."

"Then I won't be getting underway just yet. There's a lot of work to do."

"That's alright. We have time. They just threw the switch last night in town. Lighting ceremony. They completed the underwater power line from Cable Junction, and now it's going to take another one or two summers to get the overhead wires and poles installed on the island. I don't see the infrastructure ready for a ferry service and tourist season until a long while after that. Things take forever to get done on Amity. You have time."

"How much time?"

"As much as it takes to change people's opinions on the matter. These people around here are kind of stupid. Don't get me wrong. They are simple and mean well, but they aren't getting off the island much. So, the stories are just stories. When someone sees one, they might as well be seeing Bigfoot. Nobody cares because there is no proof."

Vaughn started walking down the dock, and Mr. Quint walked with him. I had to move to the next window, but their voices carried so I didn't have a problem listening.

"But when my investors and I spend money, and the hotels, motels, restaurants all start getting built, we want these summers to turn into summer dollars. We need beaches that are safe and tourists to choose us over Cape Cod, the Hamptons, Long Island. All it takes is one of these locals to start a rumor, generate a photo, or lose their ass in an 'accident' and it's a national headline. That could affect us financially."

Vaughn stopped and turned to Mr. Quint. He reached into his suit coat, pulling out a folded piece of newspaper.

"I came here to do two things. I wanted to remind you that when you go out there and start working. Your work stays out there. I don't want to see any of this..."

Vaughn unfolded a gray piece of paper and handed it over to Quint. I may have been one of the shortest men on Amity, but my one gift was always my eyes. Born with impeccable eyesight, seeing objects in the water or under the water was a gift from above. When Vaughn unfolded the paper and handed it over to Quint, I leaned in and strained my eyes to see every detail from back at the shack window.

It was newsprint—a newspaper clipping. I saw 'San Francisco' in bold black letters. There was a photo of a figure standing over a few large sharks.

Vaughn pointed at the paper in Quint's hand.

"I don't want to see one photo. Not one fish strung up. No poses for trophies. No celebrations. If I do, then the deal is off. You catch 'em, you kill 'em and leave them out there." Vaughn pointed towards the inlet to the harbor and the open ocean that churned beyond.

"Fair enough, Mr. Vaughn. I don't think that will be a problem."

"And now for the second part. You quoted me five hundred dollars a fish. Sounds fair, but I'm a politician, Mr. Quint—trust but verify. I'm not gonna take you for just your word. How will you be able to prove you are doing the work?"

Mr. Quint paused and looked back at the shack.

"I'll bring back only the jaws. You can come out here and count them."

"And if anybody comes around asking where they came from?"

"I'll tell them I collected 'em from the waters down south. I may not be a politician, but I can bullshit just as good as you can, Mr. Mayor."

Vaughn laughed to himself while finishing his cigarette. With a steady hand, he flicked the butt into the green water of low tide.

"Well, that should about do it, Mr. Quint. But I'm not Mayor… yet."

I watched Vaughn take the newspaper clipping from Mr. Quint, ball it up in his hand, and toss it into the water.

23   WARLOCK

He tasked me with painting the addition of the shack in a red. I think this was a way for Mr. Quint to further grate on the locals of Amity Point. Now, every fisherman who piloted his boat back to port after a long day's work, there at the end of the harbor, a giant red two-story tower glared back at him. Without even being there, my captain intimidated them.

I don't know where he got the red paint from. At the time, the rumors flowed about a United States Coast Guard station slated for construction once we established electricity on the island. Those Coast Guard stations are white with red roofs and there was a government stockpile of building material back in town. They listed many cans of white and red paint on the building material records. It just so happened that a few cans of red went missing right around the time I got to painting our fresh addition. I can't say for sure, but Mr. Quint had great luck in finding enough of the red paint. We even had a few extra cans sitting in the corner.

"Hershel, get in the truck. I need your help."

I dropped the paintbrush from the shock. Until that moment, I worked for Mr. Quint for well over half a year and he never once asked me for help. He had an uncanny ability to work. The man could saw a wood plank with ease and work that lumber like the best carpenter you had ever seen. His strength was something to behold. Where it took me six or seven strikes with a hammer to get a nail flush, Mr. Quint drove them home with three.

He was so efficient; I had a strange feeling he could've built that addition and taken on this island all by himself. Maybe he just kept me around because he liked the idea of having a crew. I know for a fact I held him back, but my short stature helped

169

him out. When it came time to dig a ditch and tap into the Amity Point septic system, it was me who could fit into the hole and make the connection.

This was the first time he needed my help outside of that septic pipe hookup and I was more than happy to drop the paint brush and jump in the truck.

I know the island pretty well and I walked most of the roads around here. I knew where most of the sand traps and dead ends hid around which corners and assumed he would need my help with that. Not a chance. He knew where he was going.

We drove with the AM radio on, picking up the static station from Cape Cod. I even remember the song. That lovely voice of Mary Ford singing *How High the Moon* while the twang guitar of Les Paul plucked away at the single speaker inside the dashboard. I never experienced cars and music. The drive-ins and diners of the teenagers over on the mainland were foreign to me. I heard about it all, but my life on this island never offered it. This was my first time experiencing such freedom.

The early October air hit my open window, and I could have been the coolest guy in town. The music cracked with the static of a waning signal as the truck turned off the main road and hit a sandy trail. I didn't ask where we were going, nor did I care. At that moment, I held my hand out the window, catching the wind. It reminded me of the terns and gulls I watched all my life, with their wings catching an updraft from the sea. I felt alive. Something big arrived on our little island, and I was in the passenger seat at the forefront of it all. I had never been so important, and it felt great.

Mr. Quint pulled a hard left and the truck's worn leaf springs rang out when we hit the edge of a dune. I launched clear out of my seat and landed with a thud. I looked into the back and saw great big metal cans tied off to the corner. A pile of coiled ropes and lines laid to the side. Empty bottles rolled around and bounced off each other. We headed towards the water.

I knew he was taking me to our new boat. He didn't have to tell me. I felt it. This was the day we were going to put to sea. I envisioned a shiny hulled vessel of impeccable stature. Something fitting the likes of Mr. Quint. Intimidating. Strong. Unconquerable.

This was going to be the day all of Amity Point would see me with the captain at the helm of our new vessel. We were going to conquer the seven seas. I couldn't breathe from the nervous anticipation of excitement.

My excitement turned to dread when we veered onto the beach from the end of the path. There wasn't a road to where we were going. The years of smugglers, pirates, looters and poachers, making their own secret runs and hauls, cut a path through the thin layer of trees.

Our aged pickup truck turned to the north to reveal the graveyard cove. I had only been to this place once before, maybe ten years prior. And to a group of ten-year-old's, raised with the ghost stories and tales of despair coming from such a place, it was an eerie thrill to hike out here. None of us ever dared to stay and snoop around.

We called this the graveyard because it was where boats came to die. A small cove sheltered by an out-cropping of bluffs to the west and east, with a man-made path straight into the small beach that stretched in a crescent around a calm inlet of seawater.

All around laid the carcasses of dead vessels. Decaying skeletons of metal leaking their rusty burnt umber colored blood into the sea. As far as you could see, boats abandoned by fishermen and merchants from decades ago. Memories and lives scuttled and resting as corpses in their tombs. Some boats sat in the water and stared back out at sea, longing for the days of their youth. Others had decayed and rolled to their side, broken and tossed from their moorings by hurricane-delivered high seas. On the beach, a maze of wooden vessels, dragged to high ground and left for dead in various states of rotting decay.

Mr. Quint brought the truck to a stop and cut the engine at a row of three shattered wooden schooners.

"We walk from here."

I grumbled to myself because if we were in a place like this; the future looked grim.

He gave me a heavy truck battery to carry and some cables, while Mr. Quint carried two large metal drums filled with liquid. On the sand was a length of rope that stretched out in front of us. We walked in the rope's direction.

I followed Mr. Quint across the sand, and we wove our way through the maze of dead boats. As kids, we didn't dare go this far because of stories; holdouts, fugitives, and society's refuse living within these hulls, just waiting for innocent prey to stumble in. Mr. Quint was here before many times. The rope stretched down the center of the well-worn path every step of the way. I struggled to keep up with Mr. Quint's longer strides while carrying the truck battery the size of my chest.

"What are we going to find here, Mr. Quint? Where does this rope lead?"

Mr. Quint ignored me and just kept walking, so I kept talking.

"The old men used to tell us ghost stories about this place when we were kids, sir. They used to say all these boats were cursed. They'd been left for dead because their captains broke the code, or whatever their reasoning was. When a boat was found adrift, red over red, the captain is dead—you know, that kinda thing. Well, they would tow them here and leave 'em. They said it was only a matter of time. The ghosts would come back to claim what was theirs."

"And you believed them?" Mr. Quint never broke his stride and forged ahead.

"Well, at the time, I didn't see it as too unreasonable, so I figured to just avoid this place and not press my luck."

An ancient merchant ship, three stories high of rotting metal, blocked our path. The rope extended into the black steel cave in front of us. We stepped through the massive opening in the hull, entering a dark cavern of dried sea slime and steel ribs. The midday Autumn sun disappeared when the body of the ship swallowed us whole.

Mr. Quint called back to me over his shoulder.

"Watch your step in here. Many things buried that will catch your foot."

I shifted the battery in my arms, which both shook from the strain.

A few more steps, and we emerged from a smaller opening on the other side of the steel tomb. That's when I first saw her.

Down by the water's edge, half propped up on some large rocks under her port side. A stack of crossed wood beams held up the starboard side. The wood boat, about forty feet long, pointed out to the waters of the cove. The bow listed to port with uneven footings under the surface of the rising tide. While we approached the vessel, I looked around and observed the gigantic track of a trench dug in the sand that stretched all the way back, about one-hundred feet up the beach. The entire patch of sand below the stern had been dug out to show the propeller and rudder attached. Still, the vessel looked abused beyond comprehension. It was old, but not that old. It looked as if it had been in a fight with another boat and lost.

The closer we walked, the uglier it looked. Its windows on the sides and up front were just frames of smashed-out glass. The door in the back of the pilothouse kicked in and hung by one hinge. An entire piece of gunwale was missing along the port-side aft. The flying bridge rotted away with collapsed bulkheads.

Distinctive metal letters nailed across the wood of the stern to form the name:

WARLOCK

"What a piece of junk."

Mr. Quint ignored me and made it to the edge of the vessel to set the metal drums down. He took two steps up on the rocks and then up to a rope ladder. With a swift motion, he boarded the Warlock and looked back at me.

"Hand me the battery."

I stepped over to him to reach up and press the battery over my head. He snatched it from me as if it were a box of crackerjacks. I wished I had his strength.

"You gonna sail this back to Amity Point, sir? It doesn't look like it will float."

"She'll do."

"I don't want to question your judgment, sir, but have you ever been on a boat before?"

"A few."

Mr. Quint reached down and took the battery cables from me, and I knew he would ask for the steel drums next. I picked one up and almost fell over from the weight. The diesel fumes hit my nostrils and already my head spun.

"She's a diesel, huh?"

"Yes, she is."

"Is this where you been working every day?"

Mr. Quint ignored my question as I looked around. There was a lot of work done to get this boat down here to the water's edge. That rope we followed in wove through a running block, chained to the top edge of another boat's steel bow, which emerged from the sand further up the beach. The rope came off the block and down towards us. It tied off to two separate lengths of rope that each headed out into the water on either side of the Warlock.

"Hey, this is my father's block and tackle from the shack, isn't it?"

"He's doesn't need it anymore, does he?"

"Well, no. It's just that I never seen it used like this. What exactly are we gonna do here, Mr. Quint?"

Mr. Quint took the second drum of diesel fuel from my hands and lifted it to the deck.

"Hershel, we haven't got much time. I'll explain it all to you later. Right now, we have about one hour to high tide and this hull will be wet. If everything works out right, this will be our boat and we'll have her back at the dock before sundown. Here..."

Mr. Quint reached into his pocket and tossed down the set of truck keys.

"You know how to drive?"

"Yes, sir."

I lied. I had never been behind the wheel of anything.

After dumping the diesel into the fuel tank back at the stern of the Warlock, I handed Mr. Quint various tools while he hooked up the truck battery down inside the engine compartment. It was close to the hour of peak high tide. The water surrounded us now.

I'm sitting here, talking to you with nothing to hide. There is no need to exaggerate or embellish. I can tell you I never met a master of rigging like Captain Quint. What he did on the beach, just to get the Warlock down to the water's edge by himself in the months prior to our attempt at an October launch of the vessel, was a feat unto itself. Most people pull on a wooden hull of a boat that sat on the beach for years, only to watch the entire hull explode into a thousand pieces. Using various running blocks, snatch blocks, chains, shackles, two steel-hulled vessels abandoned fifty-feet further out in the cove, all connected with lines and master seamanship, Mr. Quint made it possible. He made it so all I had to do was drive the truck forward, and the Warlock would push, not pull, into the water. I can't explain in words how he rigged it all, but I can draw you a picture:

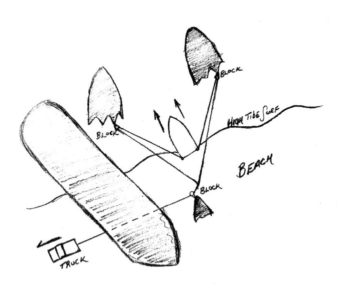

It served as a lesson in leverages and rigging that stayed with me for life.

Mr. Quint went inside the wheelhouse of the boat and emerged with a machete. He then went to the four corners of the boat and struck down on the ropes tied off to the port and starboard cleats. First up at the bow, then back to the stern. After he cut the last of the ropes loose, the Warlock floated, and Mr. Quint turned to me.

"Go."

That was the first official order my captain gave to me. I sprang into action. Before I bailed out over the side, I saw Mr. Quint tying off the set of push lines that extended to the two derelict vessels further out. After I fumbled down the rope ladder and into the waist-deep water, I waded myself back onto shore and ran with soggy shoes. My heart raced with adrenaline when I heard the engine of the Warlock fire and roar to life. I looked back and saw the boat coughing out a black cloud of diesel exhaust. I started my count, while following the rope back through the dead merchant ship cavern and to the pickup truck.

Earlier, Mr. Quint had turned the truck around and tied off the end of the long rope to the trailer hitch below the bumper. I watched how he started it, holding in the clutch and all. He told me to count to sixty after I saw the black smoke, and then step on the gas and pull ahead.

"Twenty-four, twenty-five, twenty-six…"

I ran to the truck, while reaching into my pocket. The keys pulled from my pocket, and I dropped them in the sand. My hands shook. I don't know why I was so nervous. I didn't want to fail in front of him.

"Thirty-two, thirty-three…"

I reached down and grabbed the keys from the sand, shaking them off before climbing into the truck. The key jammed into the ignition, and I turned it. Nothing.

"Forty-four, forty-five, C'mon!"

Turning the key for a second time. Nothing. I hollered at myself with the realization.

"The clutch, Hershel!"

I jammed down the clutch with my left foot so hard, it's possible I sprained my ankle. I turned the key for a third time and the truck fired up. A shout of relief and I looked back at the rope extending out into the maze of dead vessels. The engine of the truck idled, and I put a little pressure on the accelerator.

"Fifty-eight, fifty-nine, sixty."

I pushed the gas in and stepped off the clutch. The pickup lurched forward and died.

"No!"

I stepped on the clutch in a panic and keyed the engine. The truck screamed and shook. In the distance, I thought I could hear the echo of my name bouncing off the rocks and bluffs of the cove. He was shouting at me. I was sure of it. Already panicked, I stepped on the gas, revving the engine to a violent roar. The clutch spring was too strong and backed off. The truck's tires caught the solid sand and pulled forward. I looked back, while still feeding the gas into the engine. Through the plumes of exhaust, I saw the rope now taught and straining. A giant spray of sand showered into the air from the spinning tires, and I did just what he told me—don't let off the gas.

As quickly as it all started, the truck broke free. The rope snapped to slack, and I barreled down the beach, hitting every bump and rock in my path. I jammed on the brakes, and the truck stalled to a sudden stop.

My heart pounded in my chest when I ran a full sprint back towards the Warlock. I followed the rope line back to the looming merchant ship, jumped over the jagged metal edge of the rusted hull and emerged from the other side.

It was a sight to behold. Mr. Quint, working the stern cleats. The Warlock was afloat, launched and put to sea. I never in a million years thought we could do it when I first walked towards her. He cut the last of the rigging from the stern, gave me a wave, then went back into the pilothouse.

The engine groaned, and the water on her backside churned white. Captain Quint had his boat.

24   THRESHER'S TAIL

The next morning, I stood on the deck of my shack on the hill and looked down below. The October chill of early dawn held the sea fog low to the water of the harbor for a while longer than usual. Down at the dock of the fishing shack, I saw the Warlock moored. There was something about the boat that made me uncomfortable from the start. When I stared down at her, I felt as if it just sat there, staring back at me. And when it did, it filled me with a sense of darkness. Dread.

The Warlock's stature wasn't too far out from the ordinary Nova Scotia lobster fishing boat. I've seen a few of them around the harbor over the years. A snub bow at the front of a forty-foot wooden hull. A pilot house that rises amidships. Nothing fancy. No mast or out-rigging. They designed this boat to ride high on the water and get over the heavy seas off Nova Scotia, instead of plowing through the waves like the heavier steel trawlers do. The aft deck has very low gunwales, to make it easier to pull the traps over the side and into the boat.

The boat itself is not what rubbed me the wrong way. I still, to this day, can't put my finger on it. A feeling just came over me when I saw it tied to the dock on that morning. Maybe it was the mystique of where he found it. Those abandoned hulls and wrecked boats were all stories of loss. Not one of them hailed from triumph. Our trip to the cove the day before left me unsettled. While looking at the Warlock, with its dilapidated wood of the collapsed flying bridge, the bow sitting low in the water—the rot of neglect looked back and made me think of failure.

I walked down to the dock and stepped closer to the Warlock. The hull of the boat, painted in a chipped and scarred black, sat in the water on a slight list to starboard. Her pilothouse of broken glass and rotted wood wore a painted coat of dull gray. The damage to the wood of the rub rails down the sides of the hull was apparent. This boat had been worked and worked hard it was. What happened to its former captain? I had never seen it in Amity Island waters before, and it never pulled into port at Amity Point from my knowledge. So, it must have hailed from somewhere else? But what would a Nova Scotia lobster boat be doing this far away from a home port only to get abandoned like that? These are not unusual questions to have when pondering a relic from the graveyard cove. Amity Island always was and always will be the outcast island. The last stop for those looking to run away from life.

Mr. Quint emerged from below the fishing shack and stepped out into the early morning light wearing his olive drab military jacket and carrying the biggest two fishing rods and reels I had ever seen.

"Let's go, Mr. Salvatore. Stop standing around and posing for a photograph. No photographers from Field and Stream around here. Get in there, grab them buckets, and help load up. I ain't paying you to paint today."

My stomach dropped, and I turned back to the Warlock.

"You plan to get underway with that, sir? It doesn't look seaworthy if you ask me, sir."

"I'm not asking you, Hersh. She floats and spins the prop. The wheel turns port and starboard and that's good enough to get started. It's late in the season, but it was a hot summer—water's still warm. We gotta day or two still."

"A day or two for what?"

"To get to sharkin'."

When Mr. Quint got to talking a mile a minute, I knew he hit the bottle, and I learned it's best to snap to and do what he says. When he reached high-gear like this, I learned all one could do was just try to keep up. In these moments, he had a way of making you feel super-powered and ready to take on the world. I watched him step off the dock and down into the Warlock with those fishing rods. All my doubts and worries about the feelings I had looking at our new boat erased from my mind. And the sharks? Well, I still thought they were ghost stories, so I paid them no mind. We'd be lucky to catch a tuna or marlin this time of year. Working a boat in this condition, catching nothing was a reasonable outcome.

Over the next hour, my job was to chop up two buckets of Atlantic tomcod and herring while Mr. Quint went back-and-forth stowing more gear and rigging the boat for sea. A chance to hold still offered a quick look at the aft deck of the Warlock to study the working platform. The night before, while the stove fires of the houses along the harbor snuffed out, I looked down from my window and saw two lantern lights aglow on the aft deck. Mr. Quint never slept. He spent the entire night working on the boat. It wasn't until this moment, while hacking away at the slimy scales and quivering bodies of our bait fish, that I realized what he was doing.

The aft deck was the main working part of the vessel—about ten feet wide and extending from the back of the pilothouse eleven feet to the transom. It sat very low to the water, intending to collect and stack lobster traps. Mr. Quint made it very apparent that our operation on this boat had no intentions of hunting lobsters.

Mounted to the center of the aft deck would be the largest nautical fighting chair I had ever seen in my life. He anchored it right to the deck through a series of bolts and metal modifications that I can't even describe with accuracy. The chair, with its over-sized fishing rod holders and large kick plate extending from the base, resembled my captain in some ways; strong, larger than life, with a heavy history of scars and wounds that could fill a few books. A throne of heavy teak and bronze framing fit for a mythological sea warrior.

I looked around the deck and saw various engine parts and tools lying about. He put an excessive amount of time into this vessel in all the mornings I worked here on the shack.

"C'mon, boy. Pick up that knife and get to chopping. We haven't got all day."

Mr. Quint strode by carrying two short-handled baseball bats—more like clubs than bats. Slung over his shoulder was the M1 Garand rifle. His loud voice carried down the harbor. I saw the other fishermen at the neighboring shacks craning their necks and staring. They watched Mr. Quint as a village commoner watches an invading army stroll down main street, unabated and victorious. This was unlike any fishing expedition this little island had ever seen. We must have appeared to be getting ready to hunt elephants.

I smiled when I looked up to see the Papov brothers. Both bewildered and not daring to crack a smile or point from their dock across the narrow harbor. For that small moment, I filled with more pride than I ever felt in my life. I was ready to sail to the ends of the Earth for my captain from that point on.

With the engine lit off and resting idle, Mr. Quint and I made last-minute preparations for the boat before getting underway. My captain was unlike anyone this island had ever seen in more ways than one. One such way is how he moved. For work, he moved with a purpose. A forceful stride that didn't have any time for nonsense.

The two buckets of fish guts prepped and loaded. I had to fetch three more buckets of cow's blood from the back of the truck. I assumed he got those from the farm down-island on the north shore. There's only one farm on the island that had cows for meat processing. Mr. Quint made some connections there.

"C'mon and pick that step up, Mr. Salvatore. You have a lazy man's walk. Just like every palooka that lives on this island. All of you walk the same, move the same, talk the same... even perform the same. You are gonna be a proper seaman by the time I get done with you."

My captain brushed past me with shoulders full of coiled lines and two sets of wooden two-sheave blocks. My father collected a variety of line and rope. The shack had an entire wall of tackle—heavy hawser mooring lines to small quarter-inch hemp lines. The wall also boasted a collection of worn blocks, snatch blocks, pulleys, sheaves, and shackles in an assortment of sizes not used in two or three decades. Mr. Quint said my father must have wanted to start a tow company or tug operation with all the rigging that laid around collecting dust. He had other uses for it. After yesterday and seeing how he took a boat from shore to sea with the mechanical advantage the block and tackle offered, I had no reason to doubt my captain.

I struggled to get the last heavy bucket of blood down into the Warlock and lost my grip a bit. The bucket hit the deck hard and some of the red, putrid liquid sloshed up against the loose lid and spilled over the side. The crisp air couldn't hide the smell.

Mr. Quint had made a dozen trips back and forth to my four. I saw no one move like that before. If this was the way everyone had to move back on the mainland, I wanted nothing to do with it. Mr. Quint jumped down into the boat behind me carrying a set of nuts, bolts and square washers.

"Don't worry about the blood on the deck, boy. There will be a lot more of it on the deck before long."

"You think we are going to see one today, sir?"

"From what I'm told, we will find a few."

"Everyone says they don't exist. And if they did, they'd be in larger places. There's not enough food for them here. Wildlife is scarce."

"Do you believe them?"

Mr. Quint moved to a large metal pole that he heated in a coal forge and bent in a hook shape last month. The pole was now standing up, attached to the port side of the aft wheelhouse, between the exhaust muffler and the ladder that led to the flying bridge. The pole hooked and reached a foot and a half over the side of the boat, like a poor-man's jib arm. On the end, a shackle pinned through a makeshift hole in the steel. He used the bolts to mount another bracket on the pole and secure it tight to the wheelhouse bulkhead.

"I don't know who to believe anymore, sir. I heard stories about people that went missing. Fishermen that never come home."

"Like your dad?"

"Yeah, he wasn't the only one."

Mr. Quint stopped in mid-turn on a crescent wrench and looked back at me.

"Just do as I say, Hersh. You all seem to be worried about a few fish that keep you pinned to the shoreline. That Vaughn, with his shiny pants and wingtip shoes, he knows there's something else going on here and he's not telling us. We are going to take care of it."

I sat down in the large fighting chair and swiveled it around to my captain.

"If you got a special chair, can I bring a special chair of mine aboard too?"

Mr. Quint went back to tightening down on the bolts of the pole bracket.

"We are getting underway in five minutes. Bring whatever you want."

A quick trip up the hill and back. I walked down the dock carrying a small wooden rocking chair from my deck. I stepped down into the Warlock to place it in the aft port corner, against the transom next to the buckets of blood and fish. Mr. Quint stood at the doorway to the wheelhouse and watched me.

"Never in all my years, Mr. Salvatore."

"It helps with the motion sickness, sir."

"Whatever, boy. Get to releasing the spring lines."

Within minutes, the Warlock was underway, and we shoved off the dock. The other boats rocked and swayed in our wake. I stood on the aft deck and looked forward. In my peripheral, I could see all the other fishermen staring and watching without emotion. I'm sure there were a few calling claim to the fishing shack should we never return.

The open ocean kicked up at the mouth of the harbor. To be honest, I felt scared and nervous—hard to breathe. My captain didn't even flinch. He pushed down on the throttle and brought the vessel up to speed.

At this point in my life, this was the farthest I had ever been away from Amity Island. The calm sea carried rolling swells steady from the northeast. I sat in my rocking chair near the transom, facing the port side. My foot up on the gunwale, I rocked back and forth against the motion of the sea and kept my head steady. Not a hint of dizziness. Mr. Quint stuffed a small stack of saltine crackers in my jacket pocket and instructed me to chew on them. He told me the crackers will calm my stomach acids. Advice from his father a long time ago.

It was on this first trip out to sea that I felt Mr. Quint was family. The crackers were his way of looking out for me. He looked out for me in ways nobody ever had. I wanted so much to not fail him.

I sat next to the fish and blood. The smell never bothered me. Maybe he was right. Growing up on Amity, my sense of smell wasn't right, and I got used to it. Mr. Quint stood over the table inside the cabin and studied a set of large nautical charts. Looking around, turning the wheel a bit, then pushing on a few more minutes only to recalculate his navigation and charting.

To be part of a crew—to be accepted and counted on. There is no greater feeling in the world. The Warlock rocked back to starboard, and I rocked to port. For the first time in my young life, I was free from Amity. My captain broke the chains that bound me to the island and set me free. If I think about it hard enough, I'll have tears in my eyes.

"Hershel, get the chum line started. Get the scoop and start tossin' them fish guts."

"Sir, aye aye, sir."

"And knock it off with the buccaneer talk. This aint no TV show."

"Aye, sir."

The engine of the Warlock throttled down into an idle and we drifted with the tide. I stood up to notice the water change color. It became dark—almost black. We sailed out over the deep-sea canyon. We left the green shallow shelf waters off Amity's south and moved into something I've never seen before. The sea didn't just look sinister—it felt it as well.

I scooped fish parts and tossed them over the starboard side while sitting in my wooden rocking chair. Mr. Quint emerged with the two large fishing rods.

Fishing rods aren't the best description. To me, they were fishing trees. The thick wood of the handles, each boasting reels the size of paint cans, intimidated me. The reels spooled with the thickest heavy-duty fishing line on the market. Mr. Quint dropped them into the rod holders on either side of his fighting chair. The end of the fishing rods dangled steel leader lines. Secured to the end of each steel line was a hook sized for hanging slabs of beef in a butcher's shop. I watched him with the large tackle and got nervous. The sea crept into my head. I shook off the dizziness and kept scooping the fish into the water.

"C'mon, boy. Get those scoops closer together. Faster."

Mr. Quint stepped up next to me and flipped the lids off the three red-stained wooden buckets. He picked one up and dumped the entire bucket of blood into the water.

"Come on in, you bastards. I'm here."

He took the second bucket and did the same. The thick cascade of dark blood hit the water in a plop of soupy foulness. The ocean turned a cloud of red that extended out from the stern of the Warlock. I looked over and noticed the red water splashed up on the steel letters of the Warlock name nailed across the stern. The **W** appeared to be bleeding.

With the sleeves of his olive-green military jacket and light blue Navy work shirt pushed up to the elbows, Mr. Quint reached inside the third bucket of blood and pulled out the gelatinous mound of flesh that was once a cow's liver. He baited one of the over-sized hooks with the liver and then repeated the same with a second liver from the bottom of the bucket.

With a knife, Mr. Quint took an old orange life jacket out from a hatch in the lower transom and cut it in half.

"Shouldn't we be keeping life jackets around, sir? For safety and such?"

"No."

"Why not?"

"I don't believe in them."

Mr. Quint rigged the two halves of life jackets to the steel leader wire of each fishing pole, where it attached to the fishing line. While he was doing this, I saw on his left forearm a tattoo of an eagle and some writing.

"Are you from Indiana, sir?"

"No."

"You got a tattoo that says Indianapolis."

Mr. Quint pulled his left sleeve down and covered his arm.

"Just keep scoopin' those fish, boy. We got business to tend to."

Two cow livers hit the water with a flop and the red ocean swirled around the sinking hunks of bloody organ. The baited hooks sank to the pieces of life jacket, which stopped their descent. Mr. Quint moved to the chair and payed out fishing line from each reel. From underneath the chair, he pulled a leather harness and tossed it over his shoulders, then sat back into the dark red seat cushion.

I stared at the two pieces of orange life jacket that carried along the ocean rollers and sweat beaded on my forehead. The sickness. The damned sea sickness that cursed my very existence had sneaked into my brain. I felt the warmth of my chest and the blood left my face. My shaking hands scrambled to pull out another cracker from my pocket. I chewed on it and prayed to not get sick.

"Hey, boy. Slow down on those crackers. You gotta make them last. We'll be drifting here with the tide for a while. It might be two or three hours until we get—"

The port-side rod of the fighting chair snapped forward. The reel screamed in an awful high-pitched whine.

"Get behind me, Hershel. Get behind me!"

Mr. Quint grabbed the rod from the armrest and placed it in the center holder of the chair and clipped the leather straps of the harness onto the reel. He leaned forward and lurched back, setting the hook deep in whatever powerful animal took the bait. The reel stopped screaming and Mr. Quint leaned forward, working the crank of the reel and pulling in the taut line. Out in the distance, it pulled the orange floater under.

"I never seen one so quick to hit. You all are hungry out here, aren't you? Where do you think you're going, you fish? Where are you going?"

The large fishing rod was bent in a slight arc. The fighting chair shifted to port as the line pulled hard, but Mr. Quint leaned forward again and cranked away, then pulling back in a steady rhythm.

"Let's go, Mr. Salvatore. Get the top block of that tackle on the deck and lean out there. Rig it up to the shackle on the metal bar. He'll be up on us soon. This one is a good size."

I swayed and stumbled to the side of the boat. The heat of the muffler radiated across my face, and I tugged the collar of my shirt open. The blasted ocean winds turned and kicked a cloud of diesel exhaust over me while I leaned out and gasped for air.

"Get your gloves on, Hershel. This steel wire will cut your hand in two when he gets violent."

I struggled to get the gloves over my clammy hands. The leather stuck to the sweaty skin, and I shoved my fingers inside. I heard the cranking click of each turn on the reel when I leaned over the side. The boat took a deep roll and pitched to starboard. I lost my balance and grabbed the gunwale, falling to one knee. I looked over at Mr. Quint. His jaw locked tight under a slight smile while he fought whatever it was on the other end of the line.

"Let's go, boy. Get that block rigged up to the jib arm now. That's an order."

My vision didn't match with what I felt. I saw the boat rock one way, but my head rocked the other. The stomach acid filled my esophagus, and I gulped deep breaths to force it back down. It took all I had to reach down and grab the wooden housing of the two-sheave block and pick it up. The weight of the rope line that weaved in and out of the sheaves made me lose my balance again, when I pulled myself up on the gunwale and leaned out. I stretched as far as I could and clipped the hook of the block onto the crown of the clevis.

"Here he comes, boy. Here he comes. He's running right at us."

Mr. Quint cranked on the handle of the reel with a ferocious intensity as the line went slack.

I lost my strength when the diesel fumes hit me once more. I dropped to my knees under the steel pole and held onto the lines of the block I just clipped in. That's when I felt the blood rush to my gut. My face went cold and white. I leaned over the side and vomited green stomach acid and clumps of cracker into the black water.

My captain, seeing me lose control and dropping to my knees with my head over the side, stood up from the fighting chair and held the curved fishing rod with his left hand. My face hung over the side, only three feet above the water, and I watched my reflection mix with another round of green bile and stomach acid.

The water detonated in a splash of white and I saw the giant head of a monster lurch towards me. The back of my jacket cinched and pulled against my chest. Mr. Quint grabbed a handful of me with his right hand and jerked me back from the open mouth and rows of teeth.

Remember; we didn't have television sets on Amity, and the only photos I saw of sharks were from books and the National Geographic. When that silver pointed snout came at me, the image was what nightmares are made of. The largest, blackest eye looked right at me. I'll never forget how small that shark made me feel at that moment. Upon seeing it hang part ways out of the water, the hook stuck in the corner of its mouth. The white teeth, gleaming and grinning—I knew the stories from the old fishermen on the docks were all true.

The giant thresher shark landed back in the water and Mr. Quint stood at the side of the boat cranking in the extra slack of line. His body jerked forward with the weight of the shark pulling on the leather fighting harness, clipped into the giant fishing rod. The leather stretched against the thousand pounds of fish. My captain stood in full hand-to-hand combat.

"There's the wire. The wire and the clevis are showing. He's ours now, Hershel."

The water surged and the longest tail I'd ever seen kicked up a wave into the aft deck, soaking the both of us. My body tried to heave another round of vomit, and nothing came out. I felt locked in the seasickness. My legs shook and trembled. However, I saw my captain standing there fighting that thing on his own and I reached over to grab the other wooden two-sheave block. I was going to be as strong as him. I would rather have died than failed him at that moment.

"That's it, boy. Clip it on there. Right into the eye of that clevis."

With the last bit of strength, I leaned over and held the heavy block in both hands. The large thresher shark hit the hull of the boat. I saw the wide body thrashing just below the surface when I reached out and set the hook of the block into the steel leader line's clevis. My legs gave out, and I fell backwards while calling out to him.

"I got it!"

Mr. Quint reached down and grabbed the working end of the line coming off the top block and pulled out the slack. He now had the mechanical advantage over the weight of the fish. With strained fingers, he unclipped the reel from his harness, and Mr. Quint dropped the fishing rod to the deck. He hauled in the working line of the block hand over hand.

"I got you now. Thresher sharks grow big out here. But I'm bigger."

"You did it, sir."

Almost as if orchestrated by the darkest spirits of the ocean, the reel of the starboard rod shrieked. We both looked off to the distance to see the second orange piece of life jacket rocket across the water and head further out to sea with great speed.

His eyes wide with shock, he watched the entire rod almost leave the armrest holder of the fighting chair. Without hesitation, Mr. Quint pushed the strained line of the block down and took two figure-eight turns on a side cleat, locking the thresher shark close to the boat. The thresher shark breached the surface and whipped its giant tail against the hull in a loud smacking sound.

"Watch that thresher's tail, boy. Don't put your head over the side."

Mr. Quint jammed himself back into the fighting chair and took control of the other rod and reel. He clipped in and hit the brake on the reel, while pulling back. The hook set. I saw the giant shark jump clear out of the water fifty yards out. The steel leader line shimmered in the sunlight and the piece of orange life jacket floated with it through the air. The great fish landed back in the water with an impressive display of strength and agility.

"It's a damn mako. A big one too," Mr. Quint said, while straining and fighting the weight of the beast.

"Hershel, you gotta put a gaff in that Thresher before he breaks free."

The thresher breached again. Its large black eye looked right at me. The entire set of blocks and rope shook. The metal pole flexed and bent from the weight of the fish, causing the two brackets mounted on the wooden bulkhead to tear away from the rotted wood. We were losing it.

I pulled myself up and took the large pole on the deck into my hands. The antique fishing gaff tapered to a steel collection of six pronged spearheads. I looked at it and thought of the mythology book I had back at the shack. The metal stabbing weapon looked like something stolen from Poseidon's collection. I shook the nonsense out of my head and fought to concentrate.

The cranking of the reel buzzed away behind me. My captain fought the second shark and again, yelled for me to get to stabbing. My back tightened, and I leaned over to dry heave out saliva. I struggled to wield the large pole and hold it over my head while looking over the side. That's when the thresher's tail whipped another wave of cold seawater and doused me. The cold shock across my face made me lose my balance, and the boat took another roll. I went over on my back. The gaff fell onto the deck with a loud thud.

The monster mako exploded from the sea not ten yards off the starboard side and took to the air. Massive leaps were its only offense in trying to release the hook caught in the fleshy corner of its jaws.

The thresher's onslaught ripped the top bracket from the wheelhouse exterior. A discharge of weathered wood with gray paint chips and the entire pole bent over the port side of the Warlock. The lower block of the rigging went to the water's edge. The working end of the line snapped and held fast to the cleat while the thresher shark shook and created more violence along the hull.

"We're losing it, dammit."

Mr. Quint stood up from the fighting chair. He never moved in a panic, always in a steady, deliberate strength.

He hit the release on the reel and the line took off—the mako went deep. I pulled myself out of the way, to the other side of the fighting chair. Seated on the deck, I watched my captain move over to the port side and the noise of the thresher shark. He grasped the eight-foot pole and stepped up, balancing himself atop the gunwale. Mr. Quint towered over the caught thresher and raised the spear in the air with one hand. With the sun behind him, his silhouette became that of Hercules over the Hydra. The ancient spearheads of the rusty gaff aimed to kill.

Upon his downward thrust, the last bracket broke free from the rotted wood of the Warlock and the thresher shark heaved its massive tail in a sweep while rushing the surface. The long tail of sandpaper skin and muscle hooked across Mr. Quint's right leg, slicing him open. Our rigging blocks and tackle went crashing into the sea along with the pole and Mr. Quint fell backwards into the aft deck of the Warlock. The right leg of his work dungarees tore apart, with blood pouring from the wound just above the calf muscle.

The thresher shark broke free from the hook and disappeared into the depths below when the giant mako, as if in a choreographed dance of aquatic terror, breached a few feet behind me and soared high into the air. I'll never forget the sound the giant ten-foot mako made when it landed two feet from me, clear inside the aft deck. The shark didn't seem the least bit surprised.

If the first shark made me feel small, the giant mako on the aft deck only an arm's length from me was an image I never forgot for the rest of my life. This monster was twice the size of me, and the teeth—longer and sharper than the last one. Its snarled jaws of death opened to a cavernous gullet. I froze solid, with my back up against the gunwale near the cabin door. My first reaction was to pull my legs back and hope it didn't come any closer.

The body of the hyper fish moved and shook with speed and aggression, knocking over the last bucket of cow's blood and facing Mr. Quint. The entire shark, measuring the width of the deck, snapped its jaws of elongated teeth. Its blue upper body color stood out against the gleaming white of its underbelly in the light of the low-hanging autumn sun. The mouth of menacing calcium razors snapped at anything it is path.

Mr. Quint, on his back, kicked with his bloody leg at the nose of the shark. It turned and caught my wooden rocking chair in its mouth. The jaws clamped down, and the chair disintegrated into a dozen splinters of wood. Mr. Quint pulled himself back away and reached over to one of the short-handle baseball bats tucked under the gunwale.

He grabbed the baseball bat and swung the piece of wood around, catching the mako across the skull. The shark knocked backwards, giving him space to pull himself up to his feet.

The mako turned towards me and shook its head back and forth. I moved to the other side of the fighting chair and the shark slammed into the rig. The chair shook, and the shark bit down on the kick plate, sinking its teeth into the brown teak wood.

Like cracks of thunder, the noise of the M1 Garand hit my chest and rattled my skull. The loudest sound I ever heard. Mr. Quint, standing in a pool of his blood at the doorway to the wheelhouse, stepped in to aim his rifle. The muzzle flash ignited the cold air, and the cloud of gun smoke consumed him. The bullets ripped into the mako shark. It turned towards the captain and more shots rang out. I held my ears and watched the rounds rip into the head of the mako. Blood and meat stuck to the transom behind it. It's possible one bullet went clean through and buried itself in the white oak of the boat's hull.

The mako held still and died. It took four shots to kill the massive animal.

Mr. Quint, out of breath, bleeding and beaten, lowered the rifle to his side and leaned against the doorframe of the wheelhouse. There was a moment of silence, broken only by our breathing and the sounds of water lapping against the hull. He moved back in towards the cabin and, like a sprinter out of the starting blocks, he spun around and limped two steps toward the dead mako. Mr. Quint raised his rifle and fired. The head of the dead mako flinched with the impact of the bullet. An empty clip left the top of the M1 in a ping of hot steel and smoke. The captain had the look on him as if he had seen a ghost.

I never learned what that last bullet was for. Maybe I didn't want to know. Some questions never should be asked.

25 THE JAWS

The Warlock's engine lit off below, interrupting the sounds of the water pushing against her hull. I sat with my back against the starboard gunwale of the aft deck, just out of reach from the cabin door. Earlier, I tied the door open, but not tight. The little slack left in the line allowed the door to tap away against the chipped wood of the gunwale with the oceanic rhythm.

My vision cleared, but my head was a spinning mess. I didn't make a sound—too embarrassed to even look at him when he emerged from the cabin holding an old dirty shirt found in the forward berthing compartment. Mr. Quint limped over to the dead mako and sat back on the transom. He tore the shirt into two halves. One he folded over four times and pressed it hard against the gash on his right leg to stop the bleeding. The other, he wrapped around his leg twice and tied it on top of the patch. His knot cinched down and Mr. Quint winced at the pressure his emergency first aid applied.

Instead of looking at him, I stared at his blood on the deck of the Warlock. Mr. Quint's blood pooled with the blood from the mako around the broken pieces of what was my rocking chair. I watched the blood seep into the seams of the wood slats of the decking and channel along in straight lines. Under the fighting chair was the left armrest of that rocking chair. That was the rocking chair my grandmother sat in outside on our deck, and I remembered sitting in her lap, covered in a blanket and looking at the stars over Amity Point.

A funny thing about that moment. Minutes earlier was the first time in my life that I ever felt adrenaline. A sense of fear and the thought that I was about to die caused my heart to take right off. Despite the seasickness during the fight, the adrenaline made me feel alive. Right now, with the shark dead, the engine vibrating the deck beneath me, and the wordless aftermath of it all; I now experienced depression for the first time in my life. The adrenaline left my body, and I felt terrible. I wanted to be back in my grandmother's arms. Sitting under the stars on that rocking chair. I looked at the left armrest of the broken chair laying in the pool of blood and could still see the tender skin of her gentle hand holding it in the starlight. Life was so simple back then. It did not prepare me to deal with the swings of emotion this new life beseeched of me. Part of me wanted to jump into the water and disappear.

If it wasn't for the captain—seeing him in battle, and then dealing with the aftermath—I don't know if I would've survived that moment of guilt I felt while watching him stop the bleeding from his leg.

With his back to me, and somewhat obstructed by the fighting chair, Mr. Quint pulled out a long butcher's knife and knelt next to the mako. A small wave hit the Warlock broadside from port and kicked water up into the aft deck. The water washed the gruesome sight of blood puddles and carnage across the wood slats and onto my legs. I didn't dare move or say anything when he rolled the mako over onto its back. I just sat and watched Mr. Quint work the knife under the lower jaw of the shark.

I couldn't see much over his wide shoulders and the fighting chair obstructing my vantage point. After a few minutes, the raw set of shark jaws landed with a wet thud in the starboard corner against the transom. The long white teeth glistened in the waning sunlight. Bloody flesh and strips of white skin adhered to the jawbone itself, making for an unsightly mess. I stared at the inanimate pile of slime and gristle and thought of how, only moments earlier, they had their sights set on me. I've only heard stories of them, but never saw one this size. What other monsters could these waters conjure up if given the chance?

Next, Mr. Quint took a length of rope and slipped it around the midsection of the mako. Once around and then back over itself, he secured the rope with a timber hitch and cinched it down on the body of the great fish. I struggled to my feet when I saw him straining to pull the first half of the body up onto the transom. I moved over to him and reached down to lift what I could. The skin of the shark gripped my wet hands. It reminded me of the sandpaper I used back on the railing of the shack addition we built together. With some struggle and effort, we lifted the heavy shark in sections while fighting to keep our balance against the pitch and rolls of the vessel. I pulled the large tail onto the flat space of wood that extends to the stern while Mr. Quint untied the timber hitch.

With a shove, the deceased fish rolled off and landed in the sea. We watched the white belly and fins disappear below the surface. The black waters of the deep swallowed it right up. I didn't dare stick my head out to watch the mako drop from sight. I don't think I ever stuck my head over the side of a boat again after what happened.

A splash of water four feet away followed by a flash of brown. Mr. Quint and I both saw it.

"Was that a shark fin with white on it, sir?"

Mr. Quint paused and scanned the water around the stern. He saw something below the surface and stood up straight.

"As a matter of fact, Mr. Salvatore… it was."

The captain turned and hobbled his way over the aft deck battlefield of fishing line, steel leader wire, rods, pieces of shattered rocking chair, and blood. He disappeared into the door of the wheelhouse. I sat down in the fighting chair and held my head. It was to be the longest boat ride home in my life. We never spoke a word.

Any visions of triumphant returns to port by my captain's side disappeared in the darkness of Amity Point harbor. The Warlock moored to the dock and her engine fell silent a little after eight o'clock. I only know this because I heard the voices and singing from the pub on the wharf across the harbor. They always got to singing an hour before closing. Everything closes early when there is no electricity. Oil for lanterns and fuel for fireplaces become scarce, especially with winter approaching.

I lit two lanterns in the shack and carried one out to Mr. Quint, who stayed aboard the Warlock. He handed me a small stack of cash and a piece of paper with instructions to drive the truck into town, find Mr. Sullivan at Amity Grocery, and do what he says.

An hour later, I returned to the shack with five cases of King's Ransom scotch whiskey and two hundred cans of Campbell's tomato soup.

October was drawing the warm nights to a close. My breath exhaled into the chilled air coming off the ocean and I fastened the top button of my flannel shirt. After loading the cases of glass bottles and wooden crates of soup cans into the shack through the doors facing the road, I went to find him.

Out back next to the dock, I found Mr. Quint at the waterline with a fire built. He stood there, watching the embers flare off and spark into the night air. His large shoulders blocked out the firelight when I approached him in the shadow he cast across me and the shack.

"Everything delivered and loaded up, Mr. Quint."

He didn't move. Just stared and looked down at the large steel drum resting in the center of the fire pit he dug in the sand. The water in the drum boiled. A thick plume of steam bellowed out from under the metal lid placed atop.

I stepped up next to Mr. Quint and looked at him. His eyes focused and clear, but the mind was somewhere else. I wish I knew what he was thinking about. I didn't know his history. What did the sharks mean to him? Were these Amity sharks different from what he had seen before?

Mr. Quint stepped forward and flipped the lid off the barrel. The steam filled the sky, and the smell hit my nostrils. That awful smell of boiled fish oil and putrefied flesh made me recall the dry heaves from earlier. With a set of rusted metal tongs, Mr. Quint reached into the boiling water and raised the jaws up into the firelight.

The set of mako jaws glistened. Boiled clean, they seemed to glow against the black of night. I remember the shine of the elongated teeth—gleaming white and just as menacing as when they were alive. My captain looked them over and set them back into the boiling water of the barrel. Not quite done yet.

"How much do you have left over from Mr. Sullivan?"

I already knew but pretended to look down at the leftover cash in my hand to count it.

"A hundred and seventeen dollars, sir."

"We are shutting down for the winter, Hersh. Keep that as pay for the next four months. You don't need to be scrubbing up decks on these Amity Point boats for a few cents. You are better than that."

Upon hearing his words to me, I broke. For the last many hours, I felt so weak and embarrassed that I let my captain down. I even refrained from making eye contact with him while we sailed back to port and tied up the spring lines. The fire glistened through a layer of tears building up in my eyes.

"I'm sorry, sir. I understand I'm not a good sailor. There are others around here that can help you much better and they won't let you down. You don't have to give me this money."

Mr. Quint broke his gaze on the fire and looked over at me.

"Listen to me. We all have to fight the ocean in our own way. Our bodies are different, but spirits are strong. Every man's body lets him down. It's only a matter of time. Some sooner, others later. Knowing that it may happen tomorrow but still standing at the helm and taking to the sea—that's bravery, Hershel. What you did today was fight. You did everything your body allowed, and that's all I can ask for."

"But sir. Your leg."

"That's nothing. Would you go out with me tomorrow if I asked?"

"Yes, Captain."

"That's why I hired you over these other day-players around here. You have a fight in you, Hershel. Your father did too. He built this place and collected these tools for a purpose. Now I need to figure out what to do with them."

There wasn't an adequate response to communicate how I felt at that moment. Words failed me.

"I need to be alone for a while, Mr. Salvatore. I'll be wintering over here for the next few months and don't want to be bothered. See to it, the boat is cleared of snow and shoveled off."

"Yes, sir."

Mr. Quint turned back to the fire and reached inside the boiling water with the tongs of cast iron. I turned to walk away and placed the cash in my pocket. Before I passed the far side of the shack, I looked back. In the dwindling glow of the fire, he held the large white jaws of the mako in the cold air and studied them up close.

26 1952

People think living on Amity Island is a dream. Only the ones who visit in the summer months think that. They only know the Amity of today. They'll never know what Amity was to the islanders of 1952. It was a prison. This place held on until you succumbed to its life of forging and surviving. Once you got used to the hard life here, trying to leave or move to the mainland was impossible. Life became too busy and moved far too fast on the mainland. The spoils of mainland life seemed alluring. The luxurious heat of a furnace, a hot water heater, TVs, bank accounts and freezers—all nonexistent back then on Amity Island. We knew those came at a price. The hustle and fight to live on the mainland intimidated us islanders. After a while, building a fire every night for heat seemed far easier than balancing a checkbook or punching a time clock. Those who lived and stayed on the island embraced that lack of luxury. We made our prison without walls a home. We all had our reasons.

Mr. Quint stayed. The loneliness here was his penance. The winter welcoming 1952, and every winter which followed, became an act of contrition for the life he had before Amity. Something inside would not let him leave after our first run-in with the big sharks over the deep water. October turned to November, and my captain isolated himself on the last New England island to be isolated from the world. The fishing shack—his prison within a prison.

Northern winds pulled the final rustic leaves off the beech trees and the snow fell. There wasn't a day that went by where I didn't think of him. In the mornings, I awoke in my shack on the hill and looked for it. In the evenings, before laying my head down, I would check again—the tin chimney of the fishing shack. A slight trail of smoke meant he was still alive.

197

I did what he asked and left him alone.

Before Christmas, a foot of snow blanketed Amity Island. I pulled my rubber boots on and trudged my way down to the dock. This was the first real snowfall that year, and I wanted to make sure I followed his orders and shoveled off the boat. After starting under the shack, I worked the shovel towards the Warlock and felt it again.

It's hard to describe, but that feeling of dread came over me the closer I shoveled and stepped towards it. I didn't even want to look at it—just stared right down at the wood planks of the dock and shoveled the snow into the water of the harbor. After clearing the entire dock, I moved towards the Warlock. It stared back at me.

I stepped down into the aft deck. This was my first time there since the run-in with the mako shark. I remember shoveling fast to get the snow off the deck as quick as possible. A shovel full of snow and I saw the dried blood of Mr. Quint on the deck near the cabin door. The deep red mixed with the snow and stuck to the end of my aluminum shovel. I didn't trust the boat. Was it the sharks that drew first blood or the Warlock? It was the wood of the bulkhead that failed first when it spit the brackets out and set the thresher shark free.

With my shovel, I scraped a layer of snow off the gunwale and covered up the patch of blood on the deck. I buried it out of my mind, hoping a spring thaw would come and wash it away.

On New Year's Eve when the calendar rolled over to 1952, I looked out and saw the many windows lit across the harbor. I celebrated by visiting Mr. McQuitty for a cup of coffee and helped him serve the few revelers who wandered Amity Harbor looking for their way home from the pub.

On my way home, I passed the fishing shack. Mr. Quint's aged pickup truck sat in silence alongside the shack. Shoveled off and driven—the hood radiated warmth. It shined wet from the melted snow sliding off the metal.

This was my chance to visit and check on him.

I stepped to the back door but remembered his standing order; *I need to be alone for a while, Mr. Salvatore. Don't want to be bothered.*

My hand paused before the knock. In my hesitation, I stepped to the side where the window cast a light onto the snow-dusted sand. A quick brushing of frost off the glass pane. I saw him inside. Hunched over a table next to the cast-iron stove, a lantern hung above his head. Mr. Quint locked in concentration, studying a sprawl of nautical charts. A stack of books barricaded the right side of the table. Some opened and turned over to keep the page.

I turned to walk up the hill and remembered my breath of words drift into the night air.

"Happy new year, Captain."

27 ORCA

Three months passed. All you have is time on Amity Island. Time to ponder what should've, could've, and would've been in your life:

I should've stayed with my mom the night she died.

I could've been a skilled sailor; had I not been born in this weak body.

I would've killed that shark had I been stronger.

Time for so many damn questions. Second guessing it all. Replaying your mistakes for hours upon hours. Enough to drive yourself insane. We all go a little insane on this island. Some just show it more than others. By the time spring rolls in to warm the sands, you are begging to be released from the solitary confinement.

The hammering echoes pounded through my open window. When I saw Mr. Quint laying across the transom of the boat and working on the stern, I had a spark of life that morning. No time for coffee and a sit outside on the deck—my captain was working, and I needed to be by his side. I threw on my coat, pulled on my boots, and dashed from the screen door of my shack on the hill. The March air felt warm and clean in my lungs while running down Harbor Hill Road. I ran so fast; I nearly lost my footing on the corner of cobble and rocks made by the stream of thawing ice. Of course, I slowed to a walk when I reached the space between fishing shacks and stepped towards our dock. I didn't want him to see me as the eager boy I was.

"Hershel, come here and give me a hand. This wood is a stubborn breed."

I jumped down into the aft deck and laid across the transom next to Mr. Quint. He had removed all the metal letters of the Warlock name.

"Here, boy. Reach down and hold this here like so. Don't move it."

201

I leaned over and held the **A** with both hands. Mr. Quint, working upside down, reached out and hammered in the nails to fasten the brass letter to the transom. While he was working, I looked over the other letters. With the last nail driven home, the boat had a new name:

ORCA

"You renamed her?"

I sat up on the transom and picked up one letter he removed from the old name. The heavy **W** was made of solid brass and showed its age. It wore a patina coat of green from years of abuse by the sea. Mr. Quint dropped his hammer back into the tool bag by his feet.

"I should've done this earlier. Time to reset this vessel and remake her into something different."

"The old fellas used to say it was bad luck to rename a boat."

"It's got nothing to do with luck, Hershel."

"What are we going to remake her into, sir?"

"Something they will fear."

Mr. Quint took the **W** from my hand, and gathered it up with the **L** and **R**. Without hesitation, he tossed the stack of brass letters over the side of the boat. They met the water with a heavier splash than expected.

"There. It's settled. Gotta get to work."

The second longest summer of my life. For the next five months, Mr. Quint and I worked on the Orca and never left port. We tore down the collapsed wood of the flying bridge, then removed the small windows on the side of the wheelhouse. The wood that was worth saving, we left alone. The rest we took a sledgehammer to. Days turned to weeks, and we kept chipping away at the boat. Scraping paint chips under the summer sun. Sanding the decks.

Mr. Quint spent many hours below decks in the engine compartment. He overhauled the engine and rebuilt the entire steering system. The man sure knew his way around boats.

When something didn't fit, or a piece of metal just wasn't the right size or shape, Mr. Quint fired up a coal forge outside at his burn pit. You could hear him pounding away at some glowing shard of metal clear across the harbor. We made so much noise; the locals stopped staring after a while and got used to it.

While I worked at whatever task he assigned me on the Orca, Mr. Quint disappeared in his truck only to emerge with more material. Large glass windows, gauges, sheets of metal, an entire collection of reclaimed hard wood; all salvaged from the graveyard cove that born this boat.

By late May, Mr. Quint had a brand-new flying bridge framed out of fresh lumber he 'found' at the site of the new US Coast Guard station. The government workers set pylons into the water for an extension of the pier on the harbor's west side. Amity Point had limited space to begin with, so they brought in barges loaded with building material stacked and accounted for and anchored them in the bay. If a local was savvy to the location, a quick midnight row under a full moon would fetch you all the lumber and nails you needed for a boat rebuild such as ours.

The three walls of the flying bridge extended up from the Orca's wheelhouse. They were taller than the usual bulkheads of flying bridges on other boats. Mr. Quint made everything larger than life. He rebuilt the upper console and controls so when you stood at the wheel on the flying bridge; you were behind a giant shield. Protected from whatever he was building this boat to hunt.

I sat on the flying bridge, painting the insides with a primer, when I heard the voices from the water.

"Never seen anything like it, Harv."

"Look at those windows. They're bigger than the ones on my truck. One big wave broadside and the boat is gonna be full of shattered glass."

"That flying bridge is so tall, it's gonna ride like a pig."

"Top-heavy, she is."

I stood to see who was there. Two fishermen who I've seen from way down at the other end of the harbor sat in their little metal boat. The trolling motor puttered them alongside the Orca.

"Can I help you, fellas?"

"Hershel, what the hell he's got you working on down here?"

"We're getting her ready."

"Ready for what? There's so much wrong on this boat, I don't know where to begin. What's with all the glass windows?"

"Captain told me those are for seeing the barrels."

"Barrels? Barrels of what?"

"I don't know. That's what he said."

The other fisherman killed the trolling motor and cut in.

"And that flying bridge. There's so much lumber up there, she'll be a top-heavy sonovagun. Rough riding in anything over a two-foot chop. Might even capsize in heavy seas."

"You gonna get yourself killed with this guy, Hershel?"

I looked the Orca up and down and realized in the time I spent onboard; I didn't feel that sense of dread anymore. Maybe the name change was the cause? But when listening to the two fishermen and their warnings, I thought maybe the boat captured me like it did Mr. Quint. Maybe others felt what I did earlier. The closer you got to it, the darker you felt on the inside. I climbed down the ladder from the flying bridge and leaned on the exhaust muffler to get closer to the two inquisitors.

"You fellas really don't think this boat will get the job done?"

"Get what done?"

"We are going sharkin' to the south."

The two fishermen heard me and darn near fell out of their boat with laughter.

"Son, there aint no money in sharks. The meat is worthless. They are too much trouble to haul in. And besides, all you gonna find out in the shallows is dogfish."

"Or maybe a sand shark."

I leaned in over the gunwale.

"I never said we were going to the shallows. He's going out to where it's deep. Where the water turns black."

Both of the fishermen fell silent and exchanged a serious look with each other. The older one turned back towards me.

"Hershel, you don't want to mess with those things out there."

"Especially during the summer months," said the other.

Before I could engage the men further, Mr. Quint's voice barked from the second-floor window of the fishing shack tower.

"Hershel! Quit wasting time with those flubby bastards and get in the truck. We got work to do."

I thanked the men for their time, set my paint brush and can of primer down, then ran to the truck. When I looked back, the fishermen already had their boat halfway down the harbor.

He backed the empty boat trailer down the sandy beach of the graveyard cove. The dead relics grew larger in the rear window of the pickup. We needed a mast for the Orca. Something large enough to climb. Mr. Quint wanted a lookout platform—a 'crow's nest' if you want to use the pirate terminology.

The pickup bounced and pushed the boat trailer along the sand and rocks, coming to a stop next to the three derelict wood schooners. Mr. Quint already dropped one of the center masts from the boats and it laid in the sand, waiting for its new purpose in life. He chose the one in the best condition, with all the climbing steps still bolted through. The mast, made of wood, measured about thirty-five feet and had a slight taper from the base to the top. It was an odd shape—not a perfect cylinder like you would see on the utility poles along the side of the road. More of a flattened cylinder shape, which made it impossible to roll even with the steps removed.

With the trailer backed up to the mast, we got to rigging the blocks and tackle to load it.

"You going to put this on the Orca, sir?"

"We aren't loading it up for a souvenir collection, Hersh."

"Those fishermen said you are building the Orca too top-heavy, and she's gonna roll over and capsize."

"Those aren't fishermen. They are pretenders who don't have the slightest idea what work is. That's why they'll just get by catching a few stripers and thinking they are hot stuff."

I uncoiled a section of rope and handed it to Mr. Quint, who secured it to the mast.

"They seemed scared when I said we were going sharkin' in the deep water out to the south."

Mr. Quint pulled the running bowline tight and cinched it to the mast, then turned to me.

"If all the sharks out there are like the last two, we'll have a fight on our hands. The sharks here are different. Not like the ones on the west coast, but they are still just sharks. We can kill them. We got to tire them out first."

"You've caught sharks before, sir?"

"Yeah."

Mr. Quint moved to the pickup truck and rigged up his running block.

"Was that on the paper that Mr. Vaughn showed you back at the dock last summer?"

"Hershel, I pay you for your hands, not your mouth. Let's get this loaded up. Those things out there are just fish. I'm smarter than they are. You do what I say and don't listen to anyone else. Everyone on this island, from Vaughn down to the squawkers and pretenders—they don't know what danger is. They are soft. Nobody wants to risk anything around here. That's what life is all about—risk."

Mr. Quint pulled the slack out of the working end of the block and heaved his weight against the rope. The top of the mast lifted from the sand and slid up onto the end of the trailer. I moved behind him to help. Hand over hand, we pulled the rope and inched the mast further onto the boat trailer.

I looked out into the cove of dead ships. Beyond the inlet, it caught my eye. Out on the ocean, a ship of black steel sat adrift. A single plume of black smoke rose from the stack behind its pilothouse.

"What kind of ship is that, sir?"

Mr. Quint looked up and saw it. I watched him study the shape.

"C'mon, boy. Let's get this loaded up."

28   A CHANGE

The summer was long and drawn out. Another hot one. We were getting impatient. The minor setbacks of rebuilding the Orca grated on our nerves. For every nail that missed its mark and dropped into the drink, another curse was called out to the world.

I became him; ornery, stubborn, and determined. The boat was changing me. I no longer felt like a boy of optimism. I hadn't seen the ocean in almost a year and was ready to kill anything I saw under the water. No longer caring about what others thought of me, I did what I pleased. The July heat made me work harder and faster.

Everything we did became louder and heavier. We threw tools. Slammed boards. Stomped down the dock at all hours of the night. The longer it took to get the Orca finished, the angrier we became. There were no visitors. No more curious onlookers piloting their boats to see what the fuss was all about. Everyone avoided the two maniacs at the end of the harbor. The noisy ones in the shack of red painted wood, with a nautical Frankenstein's monster—pieces of cadaver vessels stitched, welded, and hammered together. We were creating a boat unlike any other. A boat with a single purpose—to hunt the large fish that lurk beneath the waves.

At the same time, we built her, the Orca created me. She forged me into hardened metal. I felt her molding me into someone unrecognizable. Someone who couldn't give a damn.

With the mast installed and bolted straight to the deck, I felt the Orca rock from a slight breeze. The weight of the thirty-five-foot spire rising from the back of the pilothouse made the boat top-heavy. Remember how I told you the

207

Nova Scotia design made the boat sit high on top of the water? With a shallow draft below the surface, adding a superstructure higher above the waterline made it a certainty to roll over and capsize after a little nudge from the sea. Mr. Quint figured out.

According to his calculations, we needed to load three thousand pounds of ballast—dead weight installed into the lowest part of the vessel to hold her down into the water.

Again, it was not a coincidence that the government construction project on the other side of the harbor needed to be placed on hold during late July 1952. The foremen and Navy engineers stood around scratching their heads when the foundation for the new Coast Guard station wound up a pallet and a half short of five-pound class B red engineering bricks. They dispatched an emergency order for six-hundred bricks from Cape Cod to Amity Island. Someone figured an assistant back at the office in Washington forgot to carry a zero or something trivial.

That wasn't the case.

Mr. Quint had nary a scruple about taking from the US government in order to gain an advantage. He confided in me while planning our nighttime operations to capture the six-hundred bricks from the government supply barge anchored in the bay. I learned he spent some time in the Navy. He said the Navy took advantage of many lives during the war and a few bricks, or some cans of paint, wouldn't come close to settling the score. I prodded with questions, but the conversation always shut down. We were a crew, and we had a boat to build. That was our priority.

With electricity reaching Amity Island last year, illumination had arrived on our shores back east. However, on Amity Point at the far west of the island, nights were still very dark. Power lines and poles hadn't reached us yet, so we stayed at the mercy of lanterns and fire pits. At night, you could look off to the sky and see the glow of the streetlights from town reach to the eastern sky in a yellow haze.

Mr. Quint timed it just right during a new moon, and with the help of some overcast, we had a complete cover of darkness to 'find' our ballast. It took us six trips over two nights to row out to the supply barge and capture the bricks, get them back to shore, and loaded onto the pickup.

We just about sunk three times. Only able to float one-hundred bricks at a time, each trip we took on water over the sides with our small rowboat overloaded, riding low to the water's edge. I bailed out the water while the captain rowed us back to shore, laughing all the way. A rare sight of laughter from him during those early years. He filled with glee while pulling another fast one on the Navy.

My size and short stature once again came in of use to the captain. With the hatches pulled up to the Orca's engine compartment, he sent me down to the bilge to stack the bricks amidship. Two bricks at a time, I crawled them forward and stacked them along the keel—the deepest part of the hull. Working in close quarters, hunched over, covered in sweat and grime from the wooden hull, with only a lone lantern to guide each brick.

My body started a change that summer. I saw veins bulge from my arms and hands. With every day of hard labor, my body collapsed in a whirlwind of aches and pain back in the shack on the hill. Only the next day, I felt reborn with a strength I never knew. By the end of July, my forearms sported chiseled angles. My shoulders rounded—carrying, hauling, gripping, reaching, and stacking those five-pound bricks.

Within the bilge of the Orca, she took hold of me. The boat had a way of making you feel fearless. I laid on my stomach and pulled myself forward with two more bricks to stack them in place. Inside her, she received me a boy and made me a man. The wood of the hull looked aged and abused, both inside and out. I sat between two frames and studied her with my lantern. What other men had been this deep below her decks? Did their souls fall victim to her? What happened to the former crew to make them abandon this vessel? Those marks along the hull. What put them there? I placed brick after brick. With every weight stacked, I felt myself drawing further into her—walling up my mausoleum and burying the person I once was.

We loaded five hundred bricks into the depths of the Orca, most of them under the pilothouse. The remaining hundred placed under the floorboards of the forward berthing compartment to keep her bow heavy in the water. With the government construction workers and cranes stalled across the way, and the small-time fishing boats going about their daily work—the Orca crouched lower into the water at the back of the harbor, waiting to hunt.

"Hershel! Get along with those fuel canisters and top off the tanks. We leave at dawn."

I squinted my eyes and looked up to see his silhouette. Mr. Quint stood atop the mast of the Orca, reaching over his head to tighten the last few turns on the mounting bracket. Welded and fashioned from salvaged steel, he fitted the topmast with a set of cross arms and two hoops. Together, they worked as a crow's nest to stand a look-out. The mounting bracket at the very top held six support cables which extended down and anchored to various parts of the Orca—ensuring the mast held fast to the deck while undergoing momentum swings of rough north Atlantic seas.

My weary eyes watched the setting sun sparkle through the diesel fuel pouring into the fill tube on the transom. Mr. Quint climbed down the steps of the mast with a sure hand and stepped onto the rebuilt flying bridge of solid wood. He looked over the working console of gauges and controls, giving half a turn to starboard on the steering wheel.

"She's getting there, Mr. Salvatore. She's getting there. Not quite done, but she'll have to do. We are almost outta time."

"It's almost September, sir. Still a few warm days ahead, and snow's gotta be months away."

"I'm not looking to go swimming, boy. These things are only here for a season. If what I think is going on, then we have a few weeks left until they head south."

Mr. Quint climbed down the ladder and onto the aft deck. He leaned over the side to examine the rebuilt rails and patches along the hull.

"Needs some paint, but no time. Never enough time."

29   THE BARREL

The Orca cruised along an ocean of glass. The air remained calm. I was no longer afraid of getting the sea sickness. In fact, I was ready and willing to toss my guts out if it meant helping the captain. A belly full of saltine crackers and not a wave in sight. I didn't care—just sat back in the big fighting chair and watched the white-water prop wash trail into the distance behind us.

My captain studied the nautical charts scattered about the wheelhouse. He looked off towards Amity Island for reference, then corrected his bearing.

The boat broke me. I existed as a seafaring warrior should. Still alive, but without feelings. I had no remorse or fear for what I was about to see. My time with the boat dissolved the myth and mystery of it all. Last summer, I saw their worst and lived to talk about it. This time, the boat felt stronger. I felt stronger. The Orca even sounded more determined and aggressive. She took to the water with a purpose, unlike last year, when there was only uncertainty.

The same goes for the captain. He was on a different quest. It wasn't a question of *if* he could find the sharks; it was how many he could kill before they left the area.

The aft deck was now an unfamiliar landscape from what I saw before. Tucked against the starboard aft gunwale were the three buckets of cow's blood, and I guessed a few large organs inside as well. Two sets of two-sheave blocks and tackle faked out along the port side decking. Gone missing were the two large rigs—the rods and reel, with fishing line now stowed below. In their stead was a large barrel made of oak wood. It stood upright, three feet tall, and shoved into the aft port corner where the transom meets the gunwale.

The barrel was heavy. Maybe sixty pounds empty. I know this because I was the one who had to roll it down the dock back in port and muscle it over the side of the Orca. I don't know where he got the barrel. It's possible he traded it back in town from a ship that stopped over from Martha's Vineyard. I understand there are a few wineries over on that island.

Constructed of aged wood staves, the barrel narrowed at both ends with a wide center—all held together and sealed by rusted steel hoops. Over the top quarter of the barrel, Mr. Quint fashioned a grid of rope around its girth with four leaders that met at the top and secured to a single metal shackle. He added an extra steel hoop over the top of the rope grid to secure it to the barrel. In my mind, this was to be the largest buoy marker the waters of Amity Island would ever see. Maybe the captain knew the whereabouts of an ancient pirate treasure ship and he wanted to mark the claim? Then why the long poles, spears, and harpoons lying next to the barrel?

We sailed over the edge of the undersea shelf and the seafloor dropped off. The water turned black. The color still makes my skin crawl. It isn't a color as much as it's a window into the netherworld. The edge between death and living right here in front of me. One wrong move, and we would cross over to the other side on this day. I looked over the edge into the dark waters of the abyss and understood it all. After twenty years on this earth, my initiation into this realm of the ancient mariner began here—this borderland of the living, where just on the other side is death. It takes a special breed of man to prefer living and working so close to this realm. I am alive and breathing while three feet away exists an entire ocean that wants me dead. Water wanting to fill my lungs and drown the life from my body. Creatures lusting to devour me. The ocean was the color of death and my reflection gazed back at me from it.

I looked over at my captain. He stood tall inside the pilothouse of the Orca. He steered the boat with determination. His resolve was undaunted. Mr. Quint seemed most comfortable right here—where the dangers were at their highest. Too far out to be rescued. No way to call for help. Nothing but the boat and seamanship keeping us from death. I think he wanted to be here and would do it for free if he could. The money and Vaughn were just an excuse. This man could make better money anywhere else up and down the coast. What drives a man to not only seek the most dangerous of waters to work but also find comfort among the nightmares?

The engine dropped back into neutral, then revved up. The entire Orca shook with a tremor. I felt my momentum shift and braced myself with a wider stance, placing a hand on the fighting chair. The Orca made a series of growls. Black diesel smoke coughed from the exhaust stack on the port side. The cavitation of water rushing the opposite direction shook everything on the aft deck.

"What's happening, sir?"

Mr. Quint looked back at me with a smile while cranking the throttle back and forth. I had to shout over the roaring engine below my feet.

"What's happening?!"

"I'm calling them!"

The Orca lurched back in reverse, and the propeller forced water under the hull. The boat continued to shake and made a distinct guttural groan. After a series of engine bursts, Mr. Quint cut the engine. We drifted in silence.

"Let's go, Hershel. Get the tops off them blood buckets. They'll be on us in minutes." The captain stormed out of the cabin door and gathered the block and tackle.

"Who's gonna be on us, sir?"

"Whitetips, boy. Oceanic whitetips—true devils. And God knows what else will come knocking after they arrive."

I pulled off the tops of the buckets to reveal the coagulated red liquid.

"How do you know they'll be showing up?"

"They are the only ones that listen and remember. First thing anyone does when hooking a marlin is reverse it, try to close the distance to the fish. Whitetips learned the sounds. They hear an engine in reverse, and they know a catch is on the line. Easy lunch for the shark. So, the fishermen stopped fishing here because they pull up half a fish, they go home and complain about monsters. You just gotta be smarter than them."

"So, the whitetips heard the Orca just now? When you were backing down?"

Mr. Quint nodded his head and took out a large clump of gelatinous liver from the bucket. "From miles away, they are coming in to see what catch we have on the line. Wouldn't be surprised if one was down there right now."

The ocean off the starboard turned a brilliant red when I poured the first bucket. Mr. Quint slipped a hook through the liver and tossed it by the tether over the side. The liver landed in the water with a clop, and he tied it off to the starboard side cleat. He reached down and washed his hands off in the water, slapping at the surface.

"Come on in, you bastards. I'm back."

Mr. Quint rose to his feet and gathered up a wooden handled harpoon.

"Hey, boy. Roll that barrel over to the starboard side here. Right to the edge."

"You've seen these whitetips before, sir?"

"Yes, I have. They will murder you and not think twice before doing it."

"How do you know that?"

The captain took the end of a coiled line off the deck and clipped it onto a ring at the butt of the harpoon. "Dispense with the questions, Hershel, and clip the other end of that line to the shackle on top of the barrel."

I did just what he asked and turned to see the captain standing tall with the harpoon raised over his head by his right arm. He waited with the patience of a tiger ready to pounce. His eyes scanning the glassy black surface, looking for the shapes.

"You stay clear of that coil on the deck. When the shark runs, you don't want your foot getting fouled in there."

I looked down and backed away from the rope coil. I wanted so much to look over the side to see what was happening.

There was a loud sound below. The hull of the Orca echoed a second hallow thud. The bait line twitched.

"What do you see, Mr. Quint? Are they there?"

"Yeah, they are. I see them. They are staying deep. Staying in the Orca's shadow. Smart fish."

His right arm fired, and the harpoon sliced into the water.

"Damn. Missed him."

Mr. Quint hauled in the line and gathered the harpoon from the deep. The boat shook again. I heard another bump and thud. The rope on the starboard cleat shook.

"Another one's hitting the bait, boy. Get that other bucket over here. They are too deep, gotta trick them to the surface."

I scrambled down the starboard side and took another bucket into my hands. My veins pumped adrenaline all over my body, pushing me in rapid, erratic motions. I set the bucket down by Mr. Quint's feet and some blood sloshed over to the deck of the Orca. The blood pooled in the decking seams and reminded me of the mako attack.

Mr. Quint, with the sleeves of his Navy-issued blue work shirt rolled up, reached into the bucket and pulled up another cow's liver. He baited another hook and handed the rope over to me. I watched the sweat bead on his forehead.

"Listen up. You hold this over the side at the surface—just bounce it on the water. When he hits, you let go. I don't want you to lose your hand."

He dumped the next bucket of crimson flesh soup into the sea. The surface churned. Careful not to step on the harpoon line, I leaned over the edge and dangled the hooked liver into the water. Another bump of noise. Were they trying to attack the boat? Mr. Quint stepped up and stood at the ready, balancing himself on the gunwale's edge with the harpoon raised.

A large brown fin tipped in white flashed along the surface and disappeared.

"That's it, boy. Just keep bouncing it on the water like that. Noise will bring them out from—"

The red layer of bloody water erupted with the bronze body of an oceanic whitetip shark lunging forward. The head of the monster opened to a mouth of razor-edged triangular teeth and bit down. I pulled the bait up high, and the shark missed, biting into the hull of the Orca. Mr. Quint fired his right arm and the harpoon stuck the shark on top of the head.

"Take it, you devil! See how far it gets you."

The shark crashed back and forth, swinging its wide head around. It whipped its tail in a powerful stroke and the harpoon ripped out of the flesh. The shark disappeared into the deep.

"Sonovabitch."

Mr. Quint climbed down off his gunwale perch and stood on the deck. We heard them bumping along the hull. There must have been quite a few down there. My captain didn't hesitate to throw the harpoon down to the deck and pick up the long pole laying towards the cabin.

"We are getting nowhere fast, Mr. Salvatore. They are staying under the boat and too deep. Pull that bait up and wait for me."

My captain leaned the long eight-foot pole against the fighting chair. Out of his pocket, he pulled a harpoon head with two sharp barbs forged together to a spear tip. On the end of the head, a steel eyelet punched through and hardened. With hastened fingers, he unclipped the barrel line from the wooden-handled harpoon and attached it to the barbed harpoon head. Next, he placed the head on the tapered end of the eight-foot pole. Mr. Quint held the barrel line taught against the pole, and once again, stepped atop the gunwale to balance himself above the water. He raised the pole with both hands and held it over the side. The stabbing spear tip, held onto the pole by the barrel line in his hand. I squinted from the sunlight reflecting off the sharpened barbs.

"Put the bait over the side again, boy. This time make some noise with it. Like you are a dying seal on top of the water."

I still didn't understand what we were doing. The large wooden barrel stood next to me. The dangling of a liver over the water confused me. In all the sea stories and fishing tales of Amity, I never heard a story describing what he was trying to do on that day. Attach a barrel to a shark? For what?

The hooked liver hit the water with a heavy force, and I pulled the line back in quick steady beats. My heart beat even faster. What was about to emerge from the red ocean water of our chum line? I had visions of the frantic thresher shark and its gigantic black eye looking into my soul. The mako lunging for me—eating away at the rocking chair and tearing apart a piece of my history.

The liver shook on the surface, and the bumping along the hull stopped. They stopped their thrashing just below. The silence of the sea fell over us. I looked up at Mr. Quint. He didn't break his stare into the water. His eyes locked in a trance-like focus—willing it from the depths.

The giant tiger shark attacked from below the hull. Lurching and taking the bait in its massive jaws. Mr. Quint didn't flinch. When the shark reared back and rolled, exposing the white underbelly, the pole shot downward in a powerful thrust. The spear head and barbs disappeared into the white flesh just below the gills of the angry fish.

Mr. Quint pulled the pole back and released the embedded tip.

"A tiger right there, boy! Get back and watch that barrel line!"

The shark rolled and slammed its tail against the hull. Water crashed over the side and doused me head to toe. The rope payed out of the coil on deck and disappeared into the water when the large tiger shark ran. The end of the line snapped against the shackle on top of the barrel. Mr. Quint dropped the pole to the deck and watched the shark thrash on the surface.

"Go on and take it, you shark. Take it!"

With an inhuman force, the sixty-pound barrel took to the air, over the side of the Orca and pummeled into the sea. The barrel raced across the surface of the water, twisting and turning its way twenty feet behind the fleeing tiger shark.

Mr. Quint hollered with laughter and sprinted to the cabin, where he keyed the engine. The Orca gave a great roar. I grabbed the fighting chair for support when the boat banked hard to starboard. Captain pushed down on the throttle and steered the boat hard around, putting her on track to follow the wooden barrel—now thirty feet from us to the south.

The Orca raced through the water to catch up to the barrel. I climbed up to the flying bridge and watched the barrel through the bow spray.

The barrel twitched and jerked, then disappeared below calm seas. The captain came down on the throttle. A tense ten seconds, the barrel broke from the surface and darted across the shards of reflecting sunlight in a new direction.

It was at this moment that I realized what my captain was doing. He was tiring the fish out. The weight of that barrel I had to roll across the dock, now tied off to its belly and forcing it up to the surface. I smiled when that barrel broke the surface. He had the shark trapped. The Orca adjusted its course and tracked the fleeing animal. We now had a visual to hunt. The advantage shifted to our favor. It was only a matter of time before the shark was too exhausted.

The barrel disappeared from the surface for a second time. One last feeble attempt at fighting the weight of the inevitable. Mr. Quint would deliver death to the tiger shark on this day, and the fish knew it to be so.

The Orca kept its speed, and I looked around in all directions for the barrel.

An immediate ten yards away, the barrel resurfaced and raced towards the Orca. I saw it and yelled to the captain.

"Port side! Barrel is up off the port bow!"

Not enough time to maneuver with the Orca's momentum carrying it forward. Mr. Quint saw the barrel racing towards us from inside the cabin and steered hard to starboard, but it was too late. The barrel met the port side bow of the Orca in a crashing force. Wooden staves broke and exploded into pieces. The barrel disintegrated against the crushing weight of the bow. The last I saw of it was two of the steel hoops caught on the shackled barrel head pull down into the depths. They disappeared along with our tiger shark.

Mr. Quint shifted the Orca down into neutral and stepped outside of the cabin. He walked across the aft deck and sat back on the transom with his arms folded. His hand stained red from the cow's blood. His blue shirt, drenched in sweat and disheveled. In the water, a few pieces of broken barrel drifted— reminding him of the one that got away.

He took in a deep breath and paused. The captain turned around and looked out to the horizon.

"There it is, Mr. Salvatore. Do you smell it?"

I looked at Mr. Quint, who stood motionless, gazing off to the east. I sniffed the air but couldn't detect anything of significance. Nor could I see anything on the horizon.

"No, sir."

Mr. Quint climbed the ladder to the flying bridge and took to the upper controls of the boat. I stood next to him and watched.

He pulled the steering wheel to port and eased up on the throttle, to not blast the air with diesel fumes.

"It's there, Hershel. It's there." Mr. Quint looked up at the topmast and the piece of torn fabric's direction blowing in the head wind.

For another twelve minutes, the Orca pushed forward. I could smell it now. The odor of death and decay, but unlike anything I ever smelled before. I have seen piles of rotting fish. Even cleaned out two-week old dead fish bait from dried lobster traps. I thought I smelled every bit of foulness the ocean conjured up at one time or another. Nothing prepared me for the smell of the approaching white hummock of flesh.

The Orca dropped into neutral and steered against it. It was large, about fifty feet long. A magnificent pile of rotting flesh and blubber soup, held together by loose tendrils of skin and streams of blood-drained meat. The ocean and heat had taken its toll, accelerating the decomposition and rot. I held my nose and looked over the side of the flying bridge wall. The floating pile of waste was longer than our boat and took no proper shape.

"What was it, Mr. Quint?"

"It's a whale, boy. Sperm whale, from the looks of it."

30 THE RIFLE

Every fisherman loses a catch. It's the natural order of things. You lose one, you rig one. That's just the way it is. It's why we pack lots of bait, ample hooks, and plenty of line. Losing the tiger shark on that morning was different to him. It stuck in my captain's side like the dart he put in the shark's belly. The loss buried inside him. Or was it he lost another shark in the past and it reminded him of that? Something about that tiger shark bothered him. As always, I was too afraid to ask. That'll always be my greatest regret—I should've asked more questions.

By the time we pulled the Orca alongside the dock that afternoon, Mr. Quint already finished half of the King's Ransom bottle he stowed inside the wheelhouse. Not even worrying about a glass, he pulled his fill straight from the bottle.

"Throw them lines over, Troy. Let's get her tied up. We got work to do."

"Who's Troy, sir?"

Mr. Quint had a way with words, and he never misspoke. He climbed down from the flying bridge and ignored my question.

Inside the shack, Mr. Quint stomped over to the wood-burning stove and swung open the cast iron door. He tossed in a log from the large wood pile stacked in an organized mess along the wall. Some of the wood in that pile had been there since my father stacked it. That stove took little to heat the fishing shack, and Amity Point always ran hot in the summer. You could winter-over twice around with one healthy pile of wood. Mr. Quint added to this pile for the last two years, as if in preparation to hunker down in Antarctica.

He hoarded firewood. There were plenty of trees on Amity Island, especially along the forested north shore—where the cliffs and rocks are. Never a danger of running out. With the way he stacked fresh wood on top of ten-year-old logs, we caught more spiders and dust than sharks in the early years.

Another thing was fresh water. He had running water at the tap, and a hose connection for a shower, but Mr. Quint kept barrels of it around. Our fishing shack's first floor wasn't at sea level. My father's early construction on pylons raised the first floor seven feet off the ground—unlike any other fishing shack on Amity Point, we had a basement.

Through the double doors off the sandy main road, you entered the lower level. On this lower level, we had room to work the catch from that day, storage for used parts, tackle, and places to hang wet clothes and gear to dry in the fresh air. The front of this first level opened to the world. Any seagull could fly in to steal a piece of cod or take off with a shucked oyster shell. It was here where Mr. Quint kept old barrels of fresh water. The barrels—not as sturdy and solid as the one we just lost to the tiger shark, but large enough to hold two or three-hundred liters. Mr. Quint had four of them filled to the brim with fresh water. He hoarded water like we were going to run out of the stuff. With old age, I may forget a few details here and there. I'll never forget his fascination with fresh water.

Up the steps and onto the first floor, I turned to see the extensive set of teeth hanging from the main wood beam overhead. Suspended by two lengths of cotton chord, the teeth hovered in the air and snarled down at me.

"I see you hung the mako jaws, captain."

He didn't respond. Just grumbled to himself while trying to stoke a fire inside the stove. I went over to the hammock and sat back in it.

With a slam of the iron door, Mr. Quint grabbed another log and paced back and forth in deep thought. I'm telling you, losing that tiger bothered him a great deal. He concentrated hard, like a chess player two moves from being checkmated. His large hand gripped the log and swung it by his side. Heavy footfalls on the deck. Back and forth, he paced.

"Dammit, Vaughn, what the hell you got going on here? You want sharks? I'll give you sharks!"

Mr. Quint spun around and hurled the log into the woodpile. Pieces of bark and splinters flew into the air on impact, causing the front of the stack to cascade to the floor. I sat up in the hammock at the sound. After a pause, I went to tend to the woodpile, and he raised his hand to me.

"No, don't bother. I'll stack it. You've worked hard enough this week. You don't need to be picking up after my temper."

Mr. Quint slouched over the logs on the floor to stack them. He noticed a wood case at the back of the pile—in the far corner of the room. Made of cedar, the case stood out from the rest of the logs stacked on top of it. The top covered in dust and cobwebs, the fallen logs had blocked it from daylight for over a decade.

"What's this here, Hershel?"

"Not sure, sir. I don't remember seeing it before. Must have been there since my father left."

A push of loose logs off the top-heavy pile, and the case pulled into open. The light of the late afternoon sun beamed through the window. I remember watching the dust float through the air, showing an angelic cascade of light onto the shoulders of Mr. Quint and the long wooden case.

The top opened to reveal a rifle. A silver barrel reflected the sun's shine. A stock boasting a dark wood grain.

"What was your father going to do with this antique?"

"I never knew he had it, sir. I remember him telling stories about some guys getting into an argument out at sea over lobster traps set on claimed areas. They fired shots. I don't know if anyone got killed. Maybe he thought he would need it for protection?"

Mr. Quint held the rifle and pulled down the lever to open the chamber.

"It's a single shot. Not much protecting you can do with this," said Mr. Quint as he read the engraving on the side. "Greener... made in England."

He handed me the rifle, and I held it for the first time. It was heavy. A solid blend of wood and iron. If my father had it, there must have been a reason. I held it and thought of the last time I saw him waving from the boat on the way out. The memory was a little more faded now. After two summers working together, I looked to Mr. Quint as a father and handed the rifle back.

"Do you think it works?"

"Only one way to find out, Hersh."

Mr. Quint dusted off one of the two small cardboard boxes of 303 British ammunition from inside the cedar rifle case. He pulled out a brass cartridge and looked it over. After deciding it was safe to fire, he slipped the bullet into the chamber, then racked the lever closed to load the rifle.

We both stepped down to the lower level of the shack. Mr. Quint stood over a barrel of water and turned to me.

"Cover your ears, boy. This might be loud."

I did. The captain shouldered the rifle and took aim into the water. With a great sound of fury, the rifle fired. The air filled with the distinct odor of burning gunpowder. Mr. Quint handed me the rifle and reached down into the barrel. He scooped some water and took a drink while feeling around the bottom. Locating the bullet, he pulled his hand out of the water and inspected the small plug of lead.

"It's clean. The rifling on the barrel is perfect."

"So, water stops bullets, captain?"

"Yeah. After a few feet, a bullet is harmless in the water."

"Too bad we can't shoot the sharks down in the water," I said to him when I pulled the lever down and the brass casing dropped to the floor.

Mr. Quint bent down and picked up the casing and looked it over. A significant silence hung between us. The steel stare of his eyes was enough to tell me he figured it out.

"Hershel, get in the truck. We're going to get more blood."

I steered the old black Chevy pickup down the main island road on our way to the farm on the north shore. Mr. Quint said he was too drunk to drive, and he didn't have time to get caught in a sand trap. I was always nervous when I drove the truck, and now having him riding along made me concentrate on the road an extra bit.

"Stop grinding the gears, boy. Maybe you are the one who had too much to drink."

"I rarely touch the stuff, sir. It burns my throat."

Mr. Quint let out a laugh. "That's the whole point, Mr. Salvatore."

Just outside of Amity point, the main road runs along South Beach—the longest beach on the island. The entire island is ten miles wide, and South Beach takes up six miles of it. All along the north side of the road, on the opposite side from the beach, we saw the wood poles set. Crews of linemen climbed those timbers and worked on the very top. Brand new wire stretched from pole to pole. The linemen balanced themselves on gaffs strapped to their legs, hooked into the wood. Their leather straps belted around the pole, holding them from a fall. There must have been thirty or forty men on twenty poles.

Mr. Quint leaned forward and watched the linemen working in the air as we drove by.

"Look at these fellas. At least we can see the sharks and know what's coming for us. That electricity hits that wire and they are all dead. You'll never see what got you."

"They are almost to Amity Point, sir. I think we'll have light bulbs before long."

"I'd rather keep the lanterns instead of dealing with what's going to follow once they wire us up for power."

Our truck drove past a line of crew trucks and wagons. The groundmen carried extra sets of lines, blocks, tools, and wire from the trucks to the base of the poles. Mr. Quint sat up straight and looked back.

"Stop the truck, Hershel. Go back."

The truck let out a squeal of brake dust.

"What is it? What did you see?"

"Just put it in reverse and back up to that big line truck there."

I did, and Mr. Quint got out of the pickup. He flagged down one groundman when he reached the back of the large, canopied work truck.

"Hey, there. Who's the foreman on this job?"

A groundman pulled a large coil of rope from the back of the enclosed truck and tossed it over his shoulder.

"The Chief is up there." The groundman pointed to the pole across the road. "Hey, Chief! This fella here wants a word!"

The silhouetted figure at the top of the pole yelled back. "I'll be right down!"

I looked over to the back of the truck and Mr. Quint was eyeing a black barrel tied off to the inside. The dirty canvas canopy of the truck flapped open in the ocean breeze. They filled the inside with miles of rope—all coiled and lashed to the sides in proper order. Towards the front hung blocks for rigging and devices for working the wire up in the air that I had never seen before. Mr. Quint reached up and took out a metal gripping device that was inside the barrel.

The barrel—a whole story unto itself. I never saw a thing like it on Amity Island before. It wasn't metal or wood, but something else. A dull black finish and scrapes along its thick sides. Grooved ridges marked the top and bottom quarters. The sides bulged—filled to the brim with the heavy brass equipment.

I turned to my captain and whispered, "What kind of barrel is this, sir?"

"It's plastic."

"Plastic? I never heard of it. The stuff's gotta be strong to hold all these tools."

Across the street, the lineman at the top of the pole unhooked his belt while holding on with his hands. The man dropped along the pole like he was walking down a set of stairs. Hand over hand, the click of his gaffs biting into wood on every step. I've never been to the circus, but I hear they have circus monkeys that climb the tent poles right up to the top and back down. I'm positive this fella could give those primates a run for their money.

"What can I do you two for? You looking for a job? We could use a few hands," said the chief lineman while walking across the road towards us. His tool belt and pole strap dangling by his side. The leg irons with the sharp pointed gaffs strapped to his boots made a click on the aged asphalt with every step.

"Not today, Chief," said Mr. Quint. "Where did you get this barrel?"

"Oh, that? Those are what the government rigged the floating barges with when we installed the undersea cable to the island. Plastic barrels with nothing but air in them. They kept the barges afloat and let us make splices and such."

"Were there anymore?"

"Yeah, a few. We left them all over on Cable Junction."

"Cable Junction, huh?"

"It's the island they made with rocks and boulders, about one mile offshore. The primary transmission line from Nantucket dead-ends there to the switchgear for the line to Amity."

Mr. Quint looked at the barrel filled with gear. He held up the brass tool in his hand.

"Can you spare a few of these?"

"You need some grips? Help yourself. We got all sizes there. This is all going to be part of Amity Island Utility. You live here, so as far as I'm concerned, it's all yours. We gotta head out to Nevada after this. Building another line off the Hoover Dam through the desert. All this stuff stays here on the island."

Mr. Quint pawed through the barrel of grips and tools while talking to the lineman. "Going out to work in the desert next? This must be an island vacation for you fellas."

"A dream come true. Climbing poles next to the ocean. Can't beat it."

Mr. Quint handed me a few grips, a small set of blocks, and two coils of rope hanging off the back of the truck.

The chief lineman took a drink of water from his canteen and turned back to us.

"Say, you fellas heading out to Cable Junction in a boat?"

Mr. Quint nodded his head. "That's right. I'll be needing a few of these plastic barrels. You can't find anything like this on the island."

"Just be careful. There's thirty-four thousand five-hundred volts, three phase, headed in and off that island. Don't go dropping anchor and catching your hand on anything that's buzzing. We had one fella get burnt to a crisp over there. Thought the wire he was working was dead, and it wasn't. Some things over there don't react too well with saltwater."

31 CABLE JUNCTION

We left that late afternoon in the Orca and sailed east. With the setting sun behind us, we cruised across the north shore of Amity Island. Along the way, I cast out a couple of lines and trawled for dinner. Mr. Quint checked his charts and visual references along the coast. It takes about an hour to reach Amity's northeast cliffs by boat. We set anchor outside of the boating lanes and the captain decided an attempt for Cable Junction would be best in the morning.

I cooked us a striped bass on the butane grill that Mr. Quint traded a few military pins for back in town. We built life on Amity through trade. When items are scarce, and so is money, people will always get what they need. You must get used to losing stuff. I never grew too attached to tools and valuables in such an environment—once you did, something came up and you had to trade it for matches, fuel, or a new carburetor. That was life on Amity, and Mr. Quint adjusted to it well. Outside of a random sweater or extra pair of dungarees, he wore nothing they did not issue him in the Navy. He still wore the same shirts. The same green military jacket. He even equipped the upper floor of the fishing shack with a military issued cot to sleep on. His body may have left the Navy, but his mind never did. His entire life on Amity had a purpose—an extension of duty to the country.

Close to midnight on the Orca and I couldn't keep my eyes open. I finished the half a fish and rinsed the plates off in the ocean water from the side of the boat. Mr. Quint, with his cup of whiskey, sat at the table in the wheelhouse. Under the lone hanging light of the Orca, he studied a few of the old rifle cartridges found in the ammunition boxes. He used a knife and the pair of lineman pliers we got from the line foreman to separate the bullet from the brass casings. With a surgeon's touch, he pinched the end of the brass casings closed with the heavy blunt end of the pliers.

"What are you doing there, sir?"

"Just seeing if it's possible, Hershel."

"If what's possible, sir?"

"If we can shoot a shark."

A tough task to accomplish if one were to remove the bullet from the casing like he did. But by this time, I learned to not question the captain. I lost him to his thoughts, and he seemed to know what he was doing. He was some sort of gunsmith or expert with a weapon in the Navy. He just had a way about him when dealing with a weapon. A natural in the way he held, assembled, cleaned, and used a rifle. Mr. Quint knew how to work out any jam or misfire issues in all the time I sailed with him. I'm sure he came in handy during the war.

"If you don't need anything else. I'll be hitting the rack, sir."

He never looked up from the brass shell casing in his hands. "Good night, boy."

"Good night, sir."

I stepped down into the lower berthing compartment of the Orca and laid my head on a rolled section of fishing net.

"There it is, boy. That little spec of nothing off the port bow. About three-five-zero."

The captain called down to me from the flying bridge. I sat on the bow of the Orca with my back against the forward cabin windows. The waves picked up when we rounded the northeast corner of the island and cruised down the east shoreline.

I saw it on the horizon and thought it was a fishing vessel of some sort. Mr. Quint adjusted his course and pushed a little harder on the throttle. The Orca's diesel engine revved louder. Its bow pushed into the oncoming seas, and I felt the up-down pull of gravity on my head. The hint of dizziness made me reach for the small stack of saltine crackers in my shirt pocket. If I'm going to vomit, let it be something other than empty stomach acid and last night's fish.

The man-made island started thirty feet below on the sea floor. Cable Junction was the name they gave it. Large boulders the size of small cars, with giant rocks of all shapes and sizes, piled on top of each other. The tip of this disheveled pyramid rose above the water, making an island of rocks. A thin island, stretching over one-hundred feet. The sharp, jagged edges of the fractured boulders made up its small coastline. The captain circled the rock island with the Orca and studied it.

On the north end, a structure of solid cement served as a base for the large green metal enclosure—big enough for a man to walk in through the side door. Inside that enclosure, the electricity for our entire island, fed from the Nantucket power grid over ten miles of ocean away. A small steel tower sat on top of the metal building. That held a signal light, warning night boaters to stay away. Cable Junction only had two signs posted. On the barbed wire fence surrounding the junction enclosure, a sign read:

HIGH VOLTAGE KEEP OFF

About mid island, another larger sign held up by two pylons buried in the rock:

NO ANCHORING: CABLE CROSSING

"Hershel, get a few of the lines ready. We are going to pull up to the dock there. I don't want to be here too long. Who knows what these waves are going to do to us out here?"

I heard my captain's command and jumped to my feet. From inside one of the forward storage bins, I retrieved two twenty-foot sections of rope.

The overcast moved in on us and the skies opened. The rain started soft and steady—a fine mist. On the north end of the tiny island, a small dock protruded from the jagged rocks. Mr. Quint piloted the Orca over to the dock and we tied her up but left the engine running.

"There's a small structure over there on the other end. Head that way and be careful. Damn rocks get slippery in the rain."

Mr. Quint headed over first, and I followed. We used our hands to crawl over the large edges of rock. Extreme angles of the terrain, sea slime and algae covered stone facings, along with the rain in our faces, made a treacherous journey. I looked up at the green metal structure. The entire thing buzzed with an eerie humming. You could feel the electricity coursing through its insides. Electricity scared the hell out of me. I had no experience with the stuff until then, and all I ever heard of it was you get cooked alive when you touch it. They had electric chairs now to strap murderous convicts to for the death penalty.

This entire island was one over-sized electric chair. We crawled in the rain, making our way across it. I had a thought about jumping in the water and taking my chances with the sharks, but then I remembered the mako and shook it off.

"Stay off those rocks close to the steps. I don't want you to put a foot where it doesn't belong."

"Yes, sir. I never heard buzzing like that, sir. Is that what electricity is? All I ever seen was lights on boats. I do not know how it works, but I much rather leave all that stuff to the big cities."

"You don't have a choice anymore, boy. These power lines go from here along the sea floor all the way to Nantucket. Every light switch and washing machine on Amity will pull current through this place for the rest of your life. Everything is going to be different from now on."

We reached the other end of Cable Junction, where a second steel enclosure sat upon a base of concrete. Just below it, tied off and pulled up onto the rocks, were two short barges of broken wood. Lashed to the wood were the black plastic barrels. Mr. Quint lifted a knife from a holster on his belt and cut away at the rope lashings to free the barrels.

The barrels were smaller than the wooden one we lost the day before. Just as tall, about three feet, but not as round. They had tapered ends that made them easier to hold on to. Much lighter than the wood barrels, the thick black plastic containers only weighed thirty pounds.

"Here you go, Mr. Salvatore. Take this and get it back to the Orca. Come right back. We need five."

Mr. Quint wiped the rainwater from his face. We moved with soaked clothes and sloshing deck shoes. The rain chilled me to the bone. I felt my hands twitch with a slight shiver.

"And when you come back, bring me the bolt chops from the wheelhouse."

"What are you going to do with those?"

"Don't worry about it, just go."

Lightning flashed through the towers of dark clouds that built over our heads. The crack of thunder followed and made me lose my footing on one of the angular rocks. I bruised my hip but held onto the barrel.

When I returned with the bolt cutters, Mr. Quint had the other four plastic barrels lined up and waiting for me. He was working the mounting bolts that secured one-inch stainless steel tubing to the cement base of the small steel vault. With a pair of pliers, he spun the nuts off the brackets and released the tubing from the rock.

"Mr. Quint, here are the bolt cutters."

He took them from me and crawled up to the metal enclosure. The cutters snapped the lock on the large double doors, and he swung them open.

The rain poured heavy. We shielded our eyes and looked inside. A set of three large electrical devices stood next to each other, buzzing with the sound of energy. The top of the enclosure had already rusted through, and water cascaded inside. Mr. Quint hesitated and looked it over before stepping forward.

"Let's get back to the boat, sir. We got the barrels."

"Not without this steel pipe. Gonna need that too."

"What do you need that for, sir?"

"No time to explain. I just need it. All of it."

"What is this thing?"

Mr. Quint looked up at the dials and gauges, the large wires that connected the ceramic bushings on top, and of course the large wires disappearing into the cement base.

"I was no electrician's mate aboard the ship, but this is a regulator bank. We had them onboard some of the diesel electrics. They regulate the voltage going to Amity."

"You touch any of that, you'll get fried, sir."

"Not if I'm careful. C'mon and grab a keg."

The waves picked up, and we headed back to the Orca. We carried our barrels in front, looking down where to place our feet. An awkward trek—trying not to slip and fall into the waves crashing the rocks only a few feet below us.

Back to the dock and onto the Orca, Mr. Quint dropped his barrel into the aft deck. The wood of the deck glistened with the pooled rainwater. The drops danced across the small lake, collecting against the transom. I set my barrel next to the other two and followed him into the cabin door.

"Sir, let's go in. We can always come back for the other two barrels. And I'm sure some more metal will show up somewhere."

My captain laughed while rummaging through his toolbox.

"Don't worry about it, Hersh. I will not touch any live wires. It's just the ground wire I gotta jumper out. That steel pipe is just the size we need. Not much time in the season left. Gotta get it now."

He collected a small coil of wire, two crescent wrenches, and a pair of rubber deck gloves. A quick drink from the whiskey bottle and he stepped into the rain. I followed him.

Back at the far end of Cable Junction, Mr. Quint perched in front of the open enclosure and connected the small copper wire between a larger stranded copper wire that emerged from the thin steel pipe. Wires ran all over into a maze of electrical nonsense. The seven-foot-tall metal cylinders he called regulators lorded over us from their cement pedestal. The buzzing and clicking inside them seemed to grow louder. Our faces flowed with rivers of rain.

"Let me help you, sir."

"Get back and stay back, boy. I'm not wearing these rubber gloves for a fashion show. Grounded wire will still pop you if you touch it with your soggy hands and standing on that wet rock."

"So, the high voltage is up there at the top?" I asked while pointing to the ceramic bushing and connected wires running from them.

"Yeah, that's the stuff that'll kill you dead."

Mr. Quint would later explain to me that the entire island connected to copper rods sunk deep into the sea floor for a ground system. The steel piping he wanted was used to protect the wires from the saltwater spray. He further explained other ground wires make up the system and attaching a jumper over to another ground wire wouldn't harm anything. At least, in theory, it wasn't supposed to harm anything.

With the jumper wire installed from the copper ground to another on the other side of the enclosure, Mr. Quint took his bolt cutters and looked up. The rainwater was pouring in now, and the top bushings glowed with an electrical arc. A brilliant bright blue flash and a crack of sound. I flinched and dropped back. A second arc followed, and everything lit up. I could feel the heat on my face from the flash.

"Hershel, get the next barrel and get the hell outta here. This doesn't look good."

I scrambled across the rocks and picked up the next barrel. Mr. Quint looked up at the blue arcing flame that danced between two ceramic bushings on top of the regulators. He knew he had little time, but he went for it anyways.

With the quickest of reactions, the captain jammed the bolt cutters into the copper ground wire and cut it in the clear. He dropped the cutters and moved around to the outside of the enclosure. With two violent tugs, the steel tubing pulled out of the metal case. Mr. Quint fell backwards onto the rocks with the steel tubing in his hands. He pulled it clear from the ground wire, and with his free hand, grabbed the fifth barrel.

He hustled by me while shouting over the thunder above. "C'mon, you green horn piker! Let's get off this rock before we get our asses fried."

We scrambled ahead over the landscape of slippery rocks. The violent sound of arcing and popping grew larger behind us. I looked back and saw a light show more brilliant than any storm lightning I've ever seen.

Mr. Quint didn't even look back, just slid his way and stepped with light feet from one rock to the other, holding his barrel and length of metal pipe out in front.

I set foot on the Orca when the explosion rang out behind me. Another first for me. A tower of flame under great plumes of black smoke. The metal enclosure and those regulator things erupted in a fireball of blue light and flaming oil. We watched the pieces of sheet metal, and those cylinders take to the air like rockets headed to space.

"C'mon, boy! Release that stern line and let's get outta here. We aren't waiting around for an encore."

The Orca's engine released a resounding growl, and we shoved off that dock. Through the rain, I could still see the fire burning on the other side of the island. Mr. Quint steered the Orca from inside the wheelhouse, and I fell back into the cushioned seat behind the table. We both laughed and shook the water from our faces. Five plastic barrels and one length of steel pipe, courtesy of Cable Junction.

There would be other electrical disturbances on Amity Island over the years. I'm pretty sure this was the first. Still, to this day, every time I flip on a light switch, I think of that dark morning and have a quiet laugh to myself. The way my captain introduced me to the concept of electricity would make Tesla himself blush.

32 AMITY HARBOR

After leaving Cable Junction, the Orca headed back towards Amity Island's eastern coast. Experienced captains will always know the distinct eastern beaches of Amity. From the water, you will see white strips all along the shoreline. The sands there take a stark white appearance. The theory I heard from time to time is the strong currents between Amity and Nantucket, along with the salinity content of the water in those currents during specific times of the year, deposited sand of white powder all along the way. After a million years of this, you have a coastline resembling a ghostly apparition.

With those white sands on our starboard side, we sailed south and rounded Cape Scott. The storm clouds moved on, and the skies opened to a late afternoon sun when we arrived in Avril Bay.

In my earlier visits here, the only light seen from offshore was the flashing white glare of the Amity Harbor lighthouse. Things changed in such a short time. Even in the late sunlight, the town of Amity peppered with lights from houses and ornamental streetlights lining Main Street. Only a year with electricity on the island and people just couldn't wait to flip the switch—even in daylight.

The Orca cruised through Avril Bay, passing the lighthouse, then turned into Amity Harbor. The harbor had become a zoo. Many new boats of all sizes moored to brand new docks and piers of fresh construction. The usual derelicts and small-time seasonal fishing boats pushed away and forced to drop anchor further out in the harbor in order to make room. I was watching the island change before my eyes. Recluses and islanders that kept to themselves gave way to prospectors and businessmen looking to invest their earnings. The Larry

Vaughn effect was already in motion. From the Orca's aft deck, I studied the changes and wanted nothing to do with them. I hoped in secret it would stop at the town line and not come up-island—back home to Amity Point.

Mr. Quint brought the Orca in slow and steady alongside the fuel pumps on the main dock of the harbor. I worked with the captain for two summers by this time, and we didn't have to speak that much. I knew the right moment he wanted me to jump over to the dock and which lines to get to first. The bow line and take a turn, then back to the stern. Wait for him to take a pound on the bow, then take three turns on the stern cleat. Back up to the bow, take in the slack and lock her off on the cleat. We operated as a well-oiled machine.

"What will it be today, Cap?"

Mr. Quint stepped around the black plastic barrels on the aft deck of the Orca and looked to the harbor master, Frank Silva, walking down the small pier to meet us.

"Some of your best grade diesel fuel, if you will, Mr. Silva."

"All I got is watered-down ethyl, Mr. Quint."

"We'll take it. She runs on piss and vinegar so that won't hurt much."

Frank removed the pipe from his mouth and let out a great belly laugh. The part-time sea captain and summer harbormaster handed the nozzle from the faded red diesel fuel pump over to me. I took the heavy hose across the deck to the fill cap on the transom.

"What you guys got here? Giant kegs of something?" asked Silva.

Mr. Quint was always quick to not give out any details. "These are empty. Got a little flotation project to get to back at the point."

"We are getting barrels delivered all day by you fellas."

"We aren't working with anyone."

"Oh, I just saw the black barrels and thought you was with them other guys."

"Who's 'them'?"

Silva looked around and gestured towards a black metal boat sitting at the end of the dock across the way from the fuel pumps. The boat looked to be thirty feet long. It sported a small wheelhouse and an open aft deck—resembling a miniature Orca but without a flying bridge and covered in painted black sheet metal.

Mr. Quint sensed something upon seeing it. Still soaked from head to toe, we needed drying off, but he didn't care once he saw that boat.

"Hershel, mind the pump. I'll be back."

The captain stepped up onto the dock and slipped between the fuel pumps. I wanted to follow him and see what was going on. The diesel couldn't pump fast enough. I strained my neck to watch.

Mr. Quint walked down the creaking timber planks of the dock and studied the black boat. He stopped at its bow and looked it over. The horse flies buzzed around the shiny spots on the gunwales and puddles of stench collecting inside the small well deck towards the transom. The stern lacked any markings or a name. Around here, a boat with no name is bad news.

He turned to walk back up the pier to meet the harbormaster.

"Looks like she was a thirsty lady today, Cap. Ninety-seven gallons. That'll be $26.19."

Mr. Quint took a roll of soaked cash out of his pocket.

"You keep raising the price on this diesel, Frank, and you will have to fend off the pirates."

"The selectmen slapped a three-cent tax on each gallon last week. It's not my doing."

"They did, huh?"

"Yes, sir. Called it a 'town revitalization fee'. We tried to push back the other night at the town hall, but them clowns have everyone bamboozled. They got us electricity, so the people voted to give them free rein."

I stepped up behind the captain and stared at the black metal boat at the end of the dock.

"Tanks are topped off, sir."

"Well done, boy." He turned back to the harbormaster and peeled off three soggy ten-dollar bills. "Keep the change, Mr. Silva... if you can point me toward those other black barrels."

Mr. Silva's eyes lit up. A trip to the town tavern was a certainty tonight.

"Them fellas, they don't speak English—Portuguese, I think. They delivered black steel drums over there at the boat lift."

He pointed two docks down the waterline. A large steel boat lift stood over a ragged pier of stone and packed sand. Mr. Quint nodded his thanks to the harbormaster, and we both took a stroll towards the boat lift.

Two workers, struggling with a dolly cart that only had one good wheel, loaded a large black steel barrel into a delivery truck. I counted nine one-hundred-gallon steel drums on the pier, but who knows how many more they already loaded into the truck. The barrels were leaking fluid. The smell—the smell from the other day, but with a new fragrance. Mr. Quint looked at me and sniffed the air. I knew what he was thinking. The entire area smelled of a dead whale, only with a touch of sweetness, which left me confused.

Back on the Orca, we heard them first before we saw them. Mr. Quint looked over and watched them walk down the dock. Five men, dressed in disheveled fishing clothes of black and gray, laughed and talked in a foreign language. They all turned and climbed into their black-hulled boat of metal. The last one, before stepping down into the boat, paused and looked over towards us in the Orca. He had dark eyes and a slight grin from under his black mustache. He seemed like their captain from the way the others acquiesced to him. The crewmen stood out of his way when he turned to climb down into their boat. They moved around him to take off the mooring lines while he just stood and watched us.

Mr. Quint never broke his gaze with the other captain while their boat fired up and backed off the dock. The exhaust from their rich-running diesel engine flowed heavy and black. We watched the steel-clad boat move out to the harbor and come up on a plane with a roar of the engine. The other boats at anchor rocked from the wake they left when they raced away. Their boat appeared faster than the Orca, but not as strong.

"Hershel."

"Yes, Mr. Quint."

"Go to the hardware store. We need paint. The brightest color they have."

33   DEAD MEN'S HATS

Over the next two days, September continued its assault on a lingering summer. The chilled winds of fall closed in on Amity Point. He didn't sleep. Mr. Quint worked every hour. I tried to keep up with him, only to collapse from exhaustion in the hammock of the fishing shack at the end of each day.

Before the blue edge of dawn traced across the sky, I awoke to see my captain sitting by candlelight at the large table of oak. He removed all the bullets from a case of 303 British cartridges and lined all the brass casings filled with gunpowder along the table. One at a time, he crimped the ends closed with the lineman pliers, and sealed them with melted green wax from a small candle. I watched him for a few minutes and closed my eyes, falling back into a dark sleep.

Exhausted and pushed beyond limits—those final two days of that hunting season. There were no dreams in my sleep. I only remember the rest being dark moments of lost time. After we saw the other sailors in the black steel boat, Mr. Quint drew back into himself; resentful and dark.

During daylight hours, he spent time at the coal forge under the shack. Armed with an anvil and a mallet, he slammed away at the hot metal—the pipe salvaged from Cable Junction. He took a hacksaw to it. The pipe laid at his feet in pieces. Everyone down the harbor could hear the rapid metal hammer pings striking steel. They stopped and stared. I looked back from the Orca and saw him under the shack with orange sparks spraying from each strike.

I painted until the bristles of our only brush came off. The brightest color in the Amity hardware store was two cans of 1951 'Fleet Armour Yellow' from Chrysler. Automotive paint left over from a road painting project on the north shore. I bargained with the owner, Mr. Tashtego, because it was such an odd color. I knew they would sit there for years collecting dust. Bought them half off. Mr. Quint tasked me to slather the five black barrels from top to bottom with the yellow paint. It wasn't bright enough for him, so he had me mix in a half-can of white. We had plenty of white and a few cans of red leftover from those nightly raids on the government supply barge in the bay.

Each barrel received three coats. The plastic made it impossible for the paint to stay put. The slightest scrape or bump, the yellow paint tore away. Those barrels would need painting a few times over for many years to come.

While the barrels dried from each coat of yellow, Mr. Quint had me take the last cans of government red and get to work on the Orca. He wanted the boat painted red, but we only had enough to paint the top portion of the black hull—just above the rub rails, down the sides. I started at the bow and spent all day painting. Mr. Quint continued his immersion in blacksmithing under the shack, and the Orca became a striking beauty. I even had enough left over to paint the deck and trim of the flying bridge. By the second day, my hands looked like I had an accident with mustard and ketchup. I didn't have my first cheeseburger until many years later, when I turned thirty-seven years old. Beef was such an upper-class commodity on Amity for the first half of my life, I never could afford it. The waitress that served me said the burger tasted best with mustard and ketchup. I watched her mix the red and yellow and all I could think about was this time—September 1952 and the painting of the Orca for my captain.

"Hershel, cover your ears."

I woke up to see Mr. Quint, standing in the center of the shack and raising the antique Greener rifle to his shoulder. The coffee percolator on the stove settled down. Morning sunlight beamed in through the windows and I reacted while looking at him. He aimed the rifle at the woodpile next to the stove.

My hands slapped over my ears. The rifle let out a flash of smoke with a loud detonation of sound—nothing. I thought he would blast the wood pile right to hell, but it remained intact. A racking of the rifle and an empty brass casing dropped to the floor. The crimped end never had a bullet to fire. He slipped in a new cartridge and racked the rifle closed. Through the haze, Mr. Quint reached into his back pocket and pulled out a foot-long section of that steel pipe. The tip of the pipe now forge-welded into a harpoon dart with sharp barbs extending out the sides. He slipped the crude dart onto the end of the rifle barrel and aimed.

The rifle erupted in another flash of sound and smoke. The dart fired across the room and buried into a wood log at the center of the pile. I leaped from the hammock in surprise.

"You did it, sir. It worked."

It all made sense to me now. Mr. Quint figured out how to shoot a shark.

The Orca's engine lit off. The now-familiar rattle of lifters inside the diesel engine calmed down into an idle of low rumbling sounds.

I waited on the bow per my captain's orders. He went back inside to get a few more nails and a piece of lumber for a brace. I held the large twelve-foot board of southern pine on the bow and made sure it didn't move. Mr. Quint came back with some more nails and continued. He positioned the plank of wood so six feet of it extended over the bow of the Orca—straight off the front, like a tank's cannon reaching from its turret.

Mr. Quint laid on his stomach and looked at the wood of the boat's bow to make sure it could hold a few nails.

"Here, we gotta brace it from below. I think it will hold me for now if I can rig this block to the bow."

I wasn't sure if he was talking to me or the Orca.

"Let's go give a look in the chain locker down below and see what's doin'."

We made our way across the deck of the bow and shimmied along the ledge down the side of the wheelhouse. Through the cabin door, we stepped down into the berthing compartment by a hatch in the center of the Orca's helm. Past the bunks and small kitchenette sink with potable water storage, at the very front, a door to the forward most compartment of the boat. The chain locker, as he called it—an area designed to hold shots of anchor chain. With no access hatch in the overhead to the deck above, it settled on being a closet.

Mr. Quint opened the door to the chain locker and pulled out the rain slicker jackets and dry-rotted wet gear that someone hung inside there years ago.

"I've never even looked at the inside of the bow. Who knows what the condition of the wood is back here? Hersh, take these effects and get them off the boat."

"You think this was the stuff from the crew who took her to sea all them years ago, Captain?"

"Most likely, boy."

Three used yellow rain jackets, two lengths of heaving line, one landing hook of descent size came out of the chain locker and piled at my feet. The last article to drop was a small waterproof sea bag. Made of a waxed cotton and sealed by a pulled-tight drawstring, the small bag looked perfect to stow my crackers and coffee beans while underway.

"Can I have this bag, sir?"

Mr. Quint didn't even turn his head while leaning into the narrow space and testing the wooden bow's density with his hammer.

"Whatever you want. It's yours."

Anytime I found something new and useful on Amity was a special occasion, even if it looked twenty-years old. I picked up the bag and looked inside with excitement.

Two hats—fisherman hats. A small one and a larger one. The smaller hat was a dull and faded red. So faded, it appeared a slight orange. Its bill, made of heavy leather, bent and twisted. The waxed leather, for repelling the rain and sea spray, had a shine to it from the daylight leaking through the porthole. On the front of the hat, stitched a square patch of dark leather—different hide from what they made the hat of. I ran my finger over the patch. A leather artist's pressing of two crossed harpoons.

The larger hat, made of a tanned canvas, scratched and creased inside and out. It wasn't shiny, like the smaller faded red hat, but it changed hues when I held it up to the daylight. At certain angles it appeared gray, but out of the light it appeared tan or even a dark brown. I tried on the smaller hat, and it fit me just right. A small tear in the back stitching provided enough slack to fit around the back of my skull. I never had a fisherman's hat before. This was my first ever.

"What did you find there, boy?"

Mr. Quint, satisfied with the condition of the wood of the bow, turned to see me wearing the red hat.

"The Orca gave us some hats, sir. This one fits me just fine. This one here looks too big for me. Might just fit you."

I held out the hat of dark tanned canvas, and Mr. Quint took it. He looked it over, smiled, and flipped it onto his head. The hat seemed to belong to him already, as if it was made just for him. He pinched the bill and folded it in half.

"It's bad luck for a captain to turn down a gift from the first mate. This hat will do, boy."

The captain stepped forward, and I shifted to the starboard side of the berthing compartment to give way.

"Gotta get that gear off the boat and load up two barrels. We are wasting fuel idling this long. Let's go, boy. There is hunting to do—sharkin' and all the rest. Nobody gets paid sitting at the dock."

I smiled and felt at home when he accepted the hat that I found. While he stormed away barking his orders, I felt proud to be part of a crew, successful, and with a family. I looked down at the bag in my hands. The sea bag—on the inside scrawled the name:

Blake

That terrible feeling of dread washed over me once again while seeing the name. The last men to wear these hats were dead. I felt them. Gone and taken by whatever mystery the sea bewitched upon them years ago. I went to shift the hat on my head while thinking of this man, Blake, whose personal effects I rummaged through and claimed for my own.

The Orca. Would she do the same to us? Will we disappear and be forgotten, only to have our effects rummaged through and divvied up by finders-keepers?

I heard Mr. Quint calling for me outside and closed the sea bag in my hands.

For the first time in a while, I felt fear again. I feared for the future. We were about to get underway with dead men's hats on our heads. Was I being paranoid? Still an immature kid with an island-life imagination? I scampered out of the Orca's lower cabin. Mr. Quint wore his hat, and he wasn't afraid, so why should I be?

I kept the hat on and went to work. In the back of my mind, I was certain the spirits of the sea were watching and taking note.

34   TIGER FOR TROY

By the afternoon, we were back on the hunting grounds. South, then southwest at full throttle from Amity Point. Mr. Quint steered the vessel from the flying bridge while I sat in the fighting chair, holding the Greener rifle. I looked down at the rifle and thought of my father. If he could only see me now. Heading out to the deepest waters off Amity Island to hunt the monsters the old-timers told stories about. I held the rifle a little tighter and felt the bravery of the moment. Maybe the Papov brothers or the other fishermen couldn't see me, but my father could. I was sure of it.

The engine dropped into neutral and settled down. I swiveled the chair to port with one leg and looked up at the flying bridge. Mr. Quint pulled the canvas fishing hat down hard on his head and took to the steps on either side of the mast. He started his climb, hand over hand, never looking down. The mast pitched back and forth with the rolls of the sea. The motion never phased him. A tinge of dizziness hit my head while watching his silhouette make it to the look-out cross arms. Slipping his body inside one of the steel hoops bracketed to the mast, Mr. Quint stood tall above the ocean's chop and looked around. He already zeroed in on the scent, and all he needed was the visual.

"I see it, boy. Get up to the bow with that rifle and wait for me. It's just over there."

He pointed off the starboard bow, and I made my way into the cabin. There were two ways to get to the Orca's bow from the aft deck. The first way was to scurry yourself like a rat along the narrow walking ledge of the gunwales on both sides of the pilothouse. To go that way, I needed both hands to take hold of the rails alongside the cabin's overhead. I wasn't about to chance dropping this old rifle into the drink should we take a heavy roll from the opposite side. I'm certain Mr. Quint would've tossed me right in after it. So, I took a shortcut. The forward windows of the cabin had a secret—the ones you would look out when steering the boat from the helm. They flipped up and made an escape hatch for someone of my size; short and slight. With the use of a small wooden crate, I climbed out through the forward port window. I managed the tactful shimmy from the cabin and the window frame clapped shut behind me. With both hands holding that rifle as tight as possible, I crawled over the deck of the bow.

I sat next to the two yellow barrels I loaded before we left. Mr. Quint rigged each barrel just like the wooden one from a few days ago. A piece of line tied around the upper quarter, inside the molded plastic ridge, woven to a grid of rope secured by a brass clip at the top of the barrel.

The captain completed his descent from the crow's nest and pushed on the throttle control of the flying bridge. The Orca leapt forward, and a blast of sea spray hit the large plank that extended out over the bow.

"You see it, boy? Dead ahead. Three-hundred yards. We'll find some there."

Masked by the whitecaps over the dark water, the white mound of flesh came into view and then disappeared. Now that I knew what to look for, it was impossible to miss.

We had all the rigging and hooks, another three buckets of bovine blood and guts ready to chum the water, but he caught the scent and found it. No need to bait them in when you know where they collect.

The Orca dropped into a slow creep alongside the carcass.

"Another whale, sir?"

"Yeah. This one is fresher than the last. Maybe killed only a day or two ago."

The mountain of a body had begun the decomposition process. Already turning ghost white in patches amid the gray skin. The smell—repugnant but not as strong as the last one. I looked down from the bow when the Orca drifted close. The body didn't even budge as our hull rubbed across it. Mr. Quint climbed around the edge of the flying bridge and slipped down to the bow alongside me.

"Another sperm whale—with the head missing. See those marks there. Too straight to be ocean critters. Those are slices. This whale's been processed."

"I thought whaling went out of business ages ago?" I asked. "Illegal in most places and not enough money in it where it is legal."

"That's what I thought too, Hershel. That's what I thought too."

I pointed down to the very edge of the carcass where the waves met the blubber. A collection of large crescent-shaped bite marks decorated the hide.

"A pretty big shark made those, huh?"

"Those are a good size. If we wait a little, I'm sure one will pay us a visit."

The Orca's engine fell silent. Mr. Quint let the ocean current push us into the floating whale's body that doubled the length of the boat. We sat and waited. After twenty minutes, the splashing and shaking started below the bow.

Captain Quint heard the commotion and slowed his movement to crawl forward. He moved in a methodical, silent way. As a lion stalks its prey, he took the rifle from me and peered over the edge of the bow spray shield.

Sometimes, life comes full circle. In my experience, life has a way of bringing different people together—or even an animal and a person. Others may see it happening by chance or coincidence. That's fine, but when the laws of probability defy the statistical odds, is it still considered luck? There aren't enough mathematical equations on this Earth to prove to me that what was about to happen would be a mere coincidence. Lives have a way of intersecting because of how we choose to exist on this planet. Mr. Quint, from the time I knew him, had a way of putting himself into positions to cross the impossible. The man lived and died doing what everyone said couldn't be done. Only God knows what he survived during the war. I watched him turn a derelict wreck into a heavy-duty hunting machine. He turned me, a weak and timid nobody, into a sailor willing to sail right off the charts next to him. If anyone could build an empire on a mountain of boiled shark jaws, it would be him.

So, if you knew Captain Quint's story, you would understand how when he peered over the edge of the Orca's bow—below him a large tiger shark fed. I heard the spattering of water mixed with chomping gulps of flesh from the buffet. The side of the whale pushed and heaved. The wide head of the tiger shark took in hunks of blubber at the waterline.

Mr. Quint reached down and picked one of the silver steel darts off the deck. On the back end of the dart, an eyelet forged into the steel. Through the eyelet and secured to the end of the dart, a rope line made of quarter inch natural fibers.

The shark hunter pushed himself out above the water with his chest pressed to the plank of wood. The Orca bobbed up and down with the seas but held her position against the whale. Mr. Quint moved out three more feet, almost

247

directly over the feeding frenzy of the tiger shark. The nails holding the large plank of wood to the deck of the Orca creaked. The wood flexed. I shimmied myself over to the planking and sat on the nails to provide a counterweight.

Mr. Quint slipped the dart over the barrel of the rifle. It clicked into place, held by the grooves he carved into the barrel. He took some line and pulled in five feet of slack before propping himself up on his elbows.

I held my breath and expected the boat to take a roll. No way in hell he could hold on. He didn't care. For that moment, as Mr. Quint raised his harpoon loaded rifle and sighted in on the feeding tiger shark—no concern of money, safety, or future remained. He saw revenge. It bled from his eyes when he pulled the trigger.

A loud blast of gunpowder and the steel harpoon left the rifle. The dart hit the tiger shark towards the back of the head, just in front of the dorsal fin. The large fish flinched and dove. Its tail crashed against the surface, throwing water over the ragged edge of torn whale blubber.

The coiled line payed out fast and snapped taut against the first barrel. I moved out of the way just as the barrel dropped on its side and pulled over the edge of the Orca.

"Take this rifle below, Hershel. We got us a tiger on the run!"

Mr. Quint rose to his feet and took four large bounds towards the flying bridge. I took the rifle from him as he passed me. It still had a slight wisp of gun smoke trailing from the barrel.

Off to starboard, the yellow barrel raced away across the surface of the water.

The Orca growled to life and plunged forward, rubbing against the dead whale feeding grounds.

"Go ahead. Run! I will follow you as long as it takes!"

The captain yelled and cursed the tiger shark while he steered and held the throttle down hard.

A high-speed pursuit unlike anything I ever heard in all my years of tolerating the same tired tripe and recycled sea stories one lonely island could invoke. The yellow barrel danced and twisted its way against the waves. The Orca picked up speed. We pushed closer and gained on the barrel.

I set the rifle down on the bench seat inside the wheelhouse and stepped out onto the aft deck. The yellow barrel raced from the starboard bow. I leaned out to look in the captain's direction. He steered with a determined grit. An angry smile of a predator closing in on its prey.

The barrel dipped and pulled under the fractured surface of the water, only to erupt from below the next wave. Twenty feet below, the tiger shark was losing its strength. The barrel slowed. It pulled down into the water halfway, but not with the force it once had. Mr. Quint brought down the Orca's speed and kept our distance from the yellow keg.

As fast as the chase had begun, the barrel stopped dead in its tracks. The yellow cylinder twitched and pushed to the side by the wake of the Orca when we sailed past. Mr. Quint turned to starboard and watched his target. The Orca circled the stagnant barrel from ten feet away—waiting, watching, daring the barrel to run out once more.

After five minutes, the Orca moved in. The once-dominant predator gave up and succumbed to Mr. Quint.

"Hershel, get that landing hook stowed below and the two-sheave blocks. I'm bringing the barrel alongside."

I ran down below to the berthing compartment. One of the three racks we had down there served as our block and tackle locker. A disheveled pile of everything we might need in a situation like this. When I returned to the aft deck, Mr. Quint had the large eight-foot boat hook over the side. He grabbed the slack line floating around the barrel and scooped it up in one swift motion. He leaned over the edge and pulled in the slack with a methodical hand over hand motion. Once the line became taught, he held it and sensed the large body on the other end. The line extended into the deep. Its fibers, dripping with salt water, remained motionless.

"You're dead. I got you."

I stood next to the captain and watched while holding the large landing hook. He mumbled to himself and whispered words I could not understand. I leaned in closer and heard the name Troy again. My heart raced in my chest, watching him pull on the line to raise the animal from the depths. I recalled the last time I leaned over and stared into these waters. The familiar spike of fear fired across my brain.

From the darkness below, I made out the white underbelly and wings of pectoral fins. The captain pulled with slow delight, relishing every second. The large twelve-foot tiger shark broke the surface upside down. A belly full of whale was its downfall. Slowed and tired from the feast, the harpoon fired into its back and pierced a few major organs. The drag of the barrel served as the final nail in the coffin.

"Look at this, boy."

Mr. Quint reached down. With a wrenching twist, he pulled the forged harpoon head he buried into its belly only three days prior. Some of the wooden barrel rope still attached to the eyelet.

"He thought he got away, didn't he?"

"Yes, sir. I believe he did."

The captain tossed the spearhead onto the aft deck. Its heavy hit reverberated across the wooden planking. This was not by chance—one of those moments that are left unexplained. Years later, the young scientist told me there are three-hundred and fifty different species of sharks—over a billion of them swimming out there. Don't dismiss Mr. Quint happening across the same tiger shark a few days apart as a mere chance. This was fate. A purposeful interaction between man and beast, driven by an insatiable desire for revenge. A desire so great, it drives a man to risk everything to work the impossible.

I helped him sink the landing hook in the tiger's side and rig its body to the side cleat along the hull of the Orca. Not a word uttered between us. Mr. Quint had thoughts racing through his head about that shark that I'll never know. We removed the rifle's harpoon from its back. With the boat hook, he collected the barrel from the water. I gathered the line to coil it on deck.

While watching my captain get out his razor-edged hunting knife to process the fish and remove its jaws, he whispered to it. I wondered what this man had seen before Amity. What does one have to go through to become this way?

Before he cut into the white flesh under the mouth of the dead shark, Mr. Quint leaned over the side and looked deep into the black of its eye and whispered a few words.

"This tiger is for Troy."

I believe he found his revenge on that day.

35   ROUTINE

And so, it began. For thirteen years, my captain waged a great war with the sharks off Amity Island. Every year, the cycle continued. In late June, when the ocean currents warmed the waters and the sun shone higher in the sky—the killing season began. A routine as fixed and dependable as a calendar. An entire winter and spring preparing for the hunt. And for those three months of late summer, Mr. Quint became the dealer of death to all monsters that swam in the North Atlantic.

The sharks came at him in great waves. Drawn from the depths, their numbers were many. All species of ample size and strength—fought him to the death. He despised the water streaming through their gills. When he ran out of harpoons and barrels, he went to spears and bullets. No feeding frenzy was too great for my captain. He piloted his boat right into the middle of them. It was the hunt that made him feel alive.

I served as the only witness to his reign of aquatic terror. All the hunting and killing hidden offshore, under the cover of high seas and salt air.

The 1950s gave way to the 60s and the world outside changed. On the radio I heard of atomic age fears, wars and military conflicts, space exploration, a president assassinated—time carried on. Here in the fishing shack of Amity Point, time stood still—frozen in the routine. Unlike the rest of the planet, my captain's world stayed the course and never deviated. He didn't care about what was happening outside our island. In his world, he had his own war to fight.

The hunting became methodical and calculated. He studied the charts at night and listened to the reports of other sea captains visiting the island. The Portuguese crew in the boat of black steel—they had something to do with it. Illegal whaling in the waters off Amity—following the migration patterns of Sperm whales around the world. During these months, with the whalers somewhere in the area, the air changed. Drawn in by death's scent and offering of food, the sharks came calling. Mr. Quint was there to fight them. The cycle repeated year after year.

We never saw the whalers outside the one time at the Amity Harbor fuel pumps. They were wraiths, appearing and disappearing around town. Outside of the occasional stop in the tavern, they avoided the locals and kept to themselves. But we found their destruction. Every so often, during the summer months, another rotting carcass found at sea. A great body adrift and stinking up the air of Amity Point. The great sharks feeding below it, like pigs at the trough.

How long this was going on, nobody knew. Mr. Quint was too satisfied in the paid hunting of monster fish to tell Larry Vaughn about this attraction the big sharks had to the island. Instead, he told me to keep it quiet, and we'd make a tidy sum of money off the ignorance of them all.

His disdain for politicians and those who take advantage of working men was at an all-time high. Taxes, zoning laws, draft boards, interest rates—all terms used to take a man's life and push him into the ground. He laughed at the thought of having his hand in a politician's pocket and stealing their wallet for a change.

The Orca; let me tell you about the Orca. The years took the vessel through more changes and perfections. The hull and gunwales glazed with battle scars. It became the most feared boat on Amity. The locals wanted nothing to do with it. The superstitious felt the Orca to be cursed. Whispers and warnings to anyone who sailed aboard—anyone set a foot upon her decks was demanding the wrath of the sea to be wrought upon them.

Wherever she sailed, an aft deck full of blood, gristle, jaws, and teeth was the result. She doomed any shark that dared to feed within her shadow.

The crude planking off the bow turned into an eight-foot working platform, ascending its occupant over the water. A guard rail of piping, covered in the captain's best marlinespike ropework, created the ultimate hunting stage. He stood a sentinel, seven feet above the water in his pulpit. When he leaned into the guardrails, Mr. Quint preached his words of hatred towards the sharks with fired harpoons from a rifle. The five yellow barrels lined up behind him on the bow of the Orca—each a faithful soldier, ready to drag another shark from the deep to a surface of murder.

Mounted on the front of the Orca's flying bridge, above the yellow barrels of death—the menacing jaws of that first tiger shark. The one that almost got away. A trophy of teeth, mounted for all to see as the Orca approached. They served as warning to all the ocean that Mr. Quint was coming, and death followed close behind.

On the bow, Mr. Quint created a bracket for the barrels, complete with a retractable device of wire and rebar. Once the first barrel left the rack, the rest of them pulled forward and stood ready to launch. This was so he could hunt by himself. He didn't need a mate to hold the barrel steady or rig the next one. His hunting technique became autonomous. I tried to go on as many deployments with him, but my body didn't handle the abuse like his.

The sea takes a toll on everyone. Holding on through every pitch and roll. Legs swell from the ocean's relentless assault. Backs compress from fighting gravity all day long, sending me to shore hunched over in pain. If the waves grew too rough, I only slowed him down. He never slowed. He never gave in to the sea. I'm sure his body felt the pain of age, but he had a way of ignoring it. He laughed in the face of pain and asked for more. Almost tempting his body to die if it didn't want to deal with the demands.

As the years crept on, Mr. Quint took to the ocean for days at a time. His obsession led to life on the water, if it meant one more shark. I would stay back and tend to the fishing shack, boiling and drying the shark jaws from the previous hunt. A refill of the fuel tanks, two or three bottles of the alcohol, and a change of clothes, the diesel engine lit off and he headed back out to sea.

While he was gone, other boats came through the harbor with tales of a lone vessel further out. A vessel with no running lights drifting among five yellow barrels spread out in the water. His legend grew. The hunter of sharks which nobody ever saw. No tales of sharks strung up at the weighing scales on the docks. No monsters seen tied off to the hull of the red and black fighting boat moored in the back of the harbor. They thought he was crazy—a mad islander who would take you with him down to the depths below if you weren't careful.

They were all wrong. I watched it with my two eyes. Hammerheads, blue sharks, makos, tigers—no species of shark swam away from the Orca. And the oceanic whitetip? He hated them the most for reasons he did not confide.

At the end of every hunting season, Mr. Quint sailed out on his own for the last week. Hunting only whitetips in the black water before they could migrate south. This was his way of going to church. Sitting alone in his confessional of blood red chum lines across the sea. Each set of whitetip jaws collected—an act of contrition for sins only he knew.

We made money and plenty of it. Larry Vaughn paid the shack a visit in some fancy new car twice every summer for the first few years—at the end of July and again in September. He'd ask me to step outside, and Mr. Quint would show him the latest collection of jaws. Cash exchanged, and Vaughn would be on his way.

After a few years, Vaughn stopped dealing with us in person. Instead, he sent a representative to meet with Mr. Quint and pay the summer wages. Larry Vaughn had political aspirations and was building his own empire back in town, as well as around the island. He didn't want to be seen up-island, especially with the likes of Mr. Quint. We didn't care. As long as Vaughn sent his stooge—the lanky character with horn-rimmed glasses and a necktie to bring the cash.

Over the long winters, the fishing shack became the captain's prison—self incarcerated with months of supplies, hoarded liquor of whatever kind, and not a soul to talk to. He paid me well to watch over the Orca and the dock while the snow fell. Also, to make sure there were no visitors. The winters of Amity are long and dark. Before the dock iced over, he buried himself away in the shack—his coffin of wood. I served as the curator of his vampiric guilt.

If you didn't sail with him, you wouldn't understand. He locked himself away because he felt guilty for surviving another year. In the crisp spring air of the melting snow, my captain emerged with an even greater thirst for the hunt than before. He pushed his body and his boat to extreme limits. Forty-eight-hour hunts turned to seventy-two hour yellow-keg marathons. If he found one, he hunted during the day. He hunted at night if he felt the sharks were more aggressive. He didn't care about the next year—only what next fish he could draw his harpoon down upon and fire.

Mr. Quint always returned to port at night—careful to hide the bloody mountain of shark jaws stacked along the transom in the aft deck. I got to collecting and boiling the jaws while he squared away the deck, getting her ready for sea.

The routine made the time dissolve into one long memory. The routine became a jail unto itself. During the Amity winters, you were a prisoner to the island. Trapped by the isolation and desolation. During summer, the bars of the routine held us—impossible to break free.

It wasn't the sharks or Vaughn. It was the Orca. The Orca had us prisoner. She never broke down, never faltered, and never felt a trace of pity for her captain. She kept on pushing and feeding the demons inside him. And he never stopped.

36 CHRISTMAS EVE 1965

The quaint seamen's chapel of Amity Point switched off its lights when I stepped out into the snow. The priest, shipped in from Cape Cod, wrapped-up the night mass for the Catholics around eleven on Christmas Eve in 1965. Earlier in the evening, the minister from Nantucket took care of the Protestant service. I went to both because it's what I did on Christmas Eve. Over the years, I watched the old fishermen. The older they got; they started going to church more. Now feeling the aches and pains of age creeping up on my body, it seemed like the natural order of things. Never one to get confrontational over which denomination should take precedence, I looked at the intricacies. The Protestants had better singing; the Catholics had better coffee—so why not hedge my bet and go to both? It became my tradition.

Amity Point only had the small decrepit chapel nestled in the middle of fishing shacks and boat slips all the way on the other side of the harbor. Despite all the changes the island went through, one thing that didn't change—up-islanders were still outcasts. Our share of the new construction contracts awarded by the state to the island was a pittance. Never any room in the budget for fancy churches or stores on our end of the island. We still made do with what we had. The same little chapel still wears its gray cedar shake siding today. I can point out the piece I plucked off as a boy standing outside after a small prayer service for my father. The chapel still has the same oak pew, third row from the back on the starboard side, that I sat in since I can remember.

The linemen of Amity Utility never forgot about us. They wired our little fishing harbor for electricity. This was the ten-year anniversary of all the houses and shacks being lit up with bulbs and sockets for anything we ever needed.

Radios, television sets, refrigerators, power tools—all commonplace by the mid-60s in Amity Point.

I stepped out into a feathering of snow fall. It blurred the edges of the roof lines for the ten-minute walk home. Amity Point lit with the festive glint of a Christmas tree. The fishermen and their families decorated strings of colorful lights along their shacks and balconies of houses. I'm sure this was nothing new in towns across America, but it was a sight I had never seen before.

The dusting of snow left a layer of gray down the street cobble. I decided it was enough to give the Orca a quick sweeping. When the snow was this light, I ditched the shovel and swept the Orca clean with a broom. After the last few sweeps of snow from the pulpit, I noticed the window of the shack's upper level glowed. My captain was awake.

For the last fourteen years, between November to March, I never once bothered him. I always followed his standing order—to be left alone and not bothered by anyone. With 1966 fast approaching and now halfway through my thirties, I felt different about things. My captain's war with the sharks had taken its toll and hardened me. Most of the year, I didn't feel any emotion. I lived to work, and it's all I knew. On this Christmas Eve, however, my heart softened. I sat in the chapel and listened to the preachers and their sermons. It wasn't what they were saying, but how they were saying it—their cadence reminded me of how my father used to speak. He always had the answers to my questions as a boy. He spoke with such assurance; I felt protected from everything.

By this time in my life, I worked for my captain longer than I lived with my family before their deaths. He was my family. It was on that snowy walk home where I realized it. I walked up the fishing shack steps to knock on the door. Hearing no response, I stepped inside.

"Merry Christmas, sir. Just walking back from church… swept the Orca and saw the light on."

He sat with his back to me at the table in the center of the room. The wood-burning stove cracked. Its black iron seared from the fire's heat and carried a slight sizzle.

"Hershel, Amity Island's best first mate, is here. Indeed, this is now a merry Christmas."

Mr. Quint turned to me with a raised glass and tossed back the liquid left in it.

"You know, boy. I almost went through the roof last month when you said all Mr. Sullivan had left was five cases of this apricot brandy. I didn't know how

I was going to make it through the winter with such turpentine nastiness. But after a case and half, I'm kind of liking the stuff. Come on in and have some."

On the table, the disassembled M1 Garand, rags, cleaning oils, and one Bols Apricot Brandy liqueur bottle. I stepped into the shack. The light of the flame inside the stove flickered off the hundreds of shark jaws.

They adorned the walls and corners, from the load bearing beams to the door frames. More than a decade's worth of dulled shark remnants stared down at me. Their jaws, all dried wide open to flare their teeth at whoever walked inside.

"Here, boy. Have a seat."

Mr. Quint took his massive arm and slid the rifle and parts over to the side, clearing a place at the table for me. He moved the spare chair out with his foot and fell back into his. The brandy already left its fingerprints on his motor skills, but his mind held solid. He looked at me with welcoming eyes.

"I got here in 1951, Hersh. This is the first time you ever came for a visit on Christmas or any holiday."

"I thought you wanted to be left alone, Mr. Quint."

Mr. Quint let out a laugh and slid a little tin coffee cup over to where I sat. He flicked the metal cap off the bottle with one hand and poured. I smelled the strong apricot aroma from the liqueur and shuddered. I never liked alcohol. Not enough practice with it to have a preference, but I wasn't about to turn the captain down. We never sat at a table outside of work like this.

"I always wondered if you were just following orders, or maybe you had a sweetheart on the other side of town."

"No, not me, Captain. This island isn't right for women. Putting them through the waiting and watching for the boat to come back. My mother waited until she died."

"What about that girl you mentioned when you were younger? She lived here?"

"Delores Shaughnessy? One can't forget her. We'd meet in secret down by South Beach and take long walks. Must have been fourteen, the both of us. She told me if we got married, her initials wouldn't change, so no need to re-sew the labels on her handkerchiefs. Silly things like that. We had it planned out. Her father moved the family to Nantucket, and we never saw each other again. That's just the way it goes around here."

"You ever think to go over there and look her up?"

"Not really. I wouldn't want her to see me as the stunted half-pint I grew up into. I'd rather have her remember me when we were the same height."

Mr. Quint laughed and raised his glass.

"To Delores, wherever she may be."

I raised my cup to his and took back a sip of the brandy. It warmed my throat but left a sharp pain in my brain. He laughed at my reaction.

"Not too good. Is it, boy? Just live on it for another month... it will taste like a sweet nectar."

I watched the captain refill his glass with another round of brandy. He set the bottle back on the table and I noticed the labels—peeled and picked by idle hands. I wondered how long he had been sitting there staring at that bottle.

"How about you, sir? Ever had a wife?"

"Yes. Three of them."

"Three? The seafaring life gets in the way?"

"The first wife was just us kids being stupid. That was before the war. We spent the night in Atlantic City. After a month together, she took off back to her family. I enlisted. Got married again after the war started. It was a different time. Meet a girl, shipping out soon, emotions are high, took the vows. She wanted to start a family, so we had plans. I left for another deployment... fighting off Japan. After one battle, we had a mail call. The 'Dear John' letter said she was leaving for a new life. Had enough of the waiting and the war."

"Where did she go?"

"Didn't care. We took Iwo Jima Island and had more fighting to do."

I looked down at the tattooed eagle with 'USS Indianapolis' etched into his left forearm. Mr. Quint took the weathered canvas fisherman's cap off his head and set it on the table. He sweat from the alcohol and heat.

"It was the third wife that smacked me good. I knew her from back home in Massachusetts. It was after the war when I came back. She was working as a nurse in the hospital I transferred to. Just pure chance that we saw each other. We grew up in the same neighborhood even. She was going to go back home but stayed to take care of me back in San Francisco. We married there."

Mr. Quint took a small sip of brandy. He leaned forward on the table. His eyes fell to his right hand, which appeared to give him some trouble. He massaged the base of the hand with his left.

"Little did she know, she became a widow the day she signed that marriage certificate. We were married for a few years, and she maybe saw me for three months total—I might as well have been dead. She spent our time together waiting and watching the horizon for me to come home. I couldn't because I was at sea. Even when I was home, my mind was at sea. We drank together to forget. She wanted to forget the pain of solitude. The last time I saw her sober was Christmas Eve, 1950. I left her alone to go sharking. It wasn't too long after the new year's when I found her dead. Sleeping under the water of the bath. I should've been the one to die out there. Not her."

"Out where, sir."

"Out there on the Pacific with the rest of the men. She'd be living it up back here had we never met in that hospital. I'm sure of it."

I took another sip of brandy and held my breath. When the captain laid into a bottle, the conversation became loud. Words flew in rapid fire succession, and you had to work to keep up. Not tonight. I hung on his every word.

Mr. Quint looked around at the rows of shark trophies lining the wall. The jaws frozen open with rows of teeth to menace their victims. They all stared down at us, as if a hundred large sharks swam towards the both of us to attack and kill.

"No matter how many I kill, Hershel. It doesn't work. I can't do it. I can't get their faces out of my mind. Yet, every new year, I sit here in this shack and convince myself that this will be the year. I'll be able to forget about them. The terrible screams. The faces the men make when they realize they been bit and are being taken. Maybe this will be the year that it all fades to nothing. But I'll be back here, one year from now. Sitting at this table and thinking of them all over again."

Mr. Quint took a large gulp from his glass and looked right into me.

"It's all a lie, Hershel. Time heals nothing. It only makes it worse."

For the longest of moments, all I heard was the fire's crackling throughout the stove.

QUINT
Farewell and adieu to you, fair Spanish ladies
Farewell and adieu to you, ladies of Spain
For we've received orders for to sail back to Boston
And so nevermore shall we see you again

Only a handful of times had I heard my captain let the melody escape from under his breath while we hunted the sharks. This was the first time I heard him sing the words.

"C'mon, boy. Show me what you know here and assemble this rifle. Like I showed you."

I jumped up and Mr. Quint slid himself and his chair off to the side. After a minute of assembling the barrel receiver group, I slipped the wood stock over the metal. I pressed the trigger assembly into the stock and locked it in place. The rifle turned back over in my hands, and I checked the bolt action and trigger safety. Mr. Quint laughed and took another shot of brandy. I could smell the apricot sweating from his pores.

"Like a true US soldier, my boy. Well done."

He picked the M1 up and held it in his arms to examine it. I felt like a proud boy who just made the winning shot of the big game in front of his family. I don't remember ever experiencing this feeling.

"This rifle is a fine piece of engineering. What will become of it after I die, Hershel? A piece of me is in it. It seems lifeless. It's made of wood and metal, but I put enough sweat and desire into this thing... it might as well be part of me. Will it be around for an eternity to tell my story? How many more years do we have left in this life before we all must meet those we let down? If I die. I want you to make sure this rifle kills one more shark in my honor. And with it, a piece of me will do the killing."

"You can't die, Captain. Our work isn't done. What will I do?"

The rifle placed back onto the large table with a dense thud. Mr. Quint rose to his feet and caught his balance on the table to steady himself. With the alcohol taking control of his movements, he staggered to the wooden steps.

"We are all going to go at some point, Mr. Salvatore. It is what we build that will be around for everyone to decide on whether our work is done."

The captain walked up the steps with heavy footfalls. At the top of the steps, he turned and looked down at me past the rows of shark jaws along the wall.

"One thing I learned so far in my forty-nine years. I can't kill them all. Merry Christmas, boy."

The captain turned and collapsed onto his metal framed military-issued cot. I heard the springs under the pinstriped mattress squeak as his body sank into them. He passed out cold in the few minutes it took to finish my cup of brandy. I placed the cap back onto the bottle and looked up to the captain's quarters on the upper floor.

"Merry Christmas, Papa."

I buttoned up my coat and stepped out into the cold to walk home.

37   GOLIATH

The Orca had a way of making you feel your regrets. There was something about her which held your soul captive once you stepped down into the aft deck. You might not have felt it right away but spend enough time with her and you would know what I'm talking about. Maybe it was the realm she carried you to. She delivered us to the abyss and back. The Orca was our escort to where the water turns black. She was the only thing keeping them from killing us. That boat was our ferry across the river Styx.

The trip wasn't one way. She'd take you back to port, while leaving your mind out there to wander. In the long spaces between all the battling and killing, you think of your life and how much longer you have left. What follows are your regrets. What do you wish you had done differently? Could you have saved anyone that was close to you if you chose a different path?

My biggest regret was telling him the name of the ship. Every day of my life since, I wonder how things would've been if I kept my mouth shut and didn't tell him. Let me go back in time and change anything? First, I will stop my father from heading out to sea the last time I saw him. Next, I'll travel back to March 17, 1966. Saint Patrick's Day—to stop me from telling him. I believe he would still be alive.

The morning carried a crisp cold snap. Most days in March on Amity do. The sun rose a little higher, and I unbuttoned my flannel shirt collar. I took the faded red fisherman's hat off and set it down on the deck to wipe the sweat from my brow. Mr. Quint and I finished installing the new davit arm on the swivel mounted at the back of the mast. Longer and made of a heavier wood, this davit arm swung off to either port and starboard and held a tremendous amount of weight.

Too early for the hunting season to begin, my captain emerged from his winter of solitary confinement with a plan to go after the larger sharks. To chase them down south in the late fall, when the warm waters retreat. With all the rigging and rope, and now a heavier boom, the Orca was ready to haul onboard just about anything the sea could throw at her.

The captain was getting old. The long winters of regret and alcohol were taking their toll. Amity had a way of aging everyone who lived year-round on the island. There was no escaping it. Even at thirty-five years old, my hair grayed, and deep lines tracked across my face. Mr. Quint was grayer and slowing. I believe he was born in late 1916. He never told me his exact birthday, but through many conversations, I put the clues together. He was going to turn fifty, and already a decade and a half living on the island—his body broke down. Amity Island always wins in the end.

The next project was to make it so we could remove the fighting chair and stow it below decks during barrel encounters with larger sharks. To work the barrel, lines, and harpoons, Mr. Quint wanted more space. We removed the fighting chair from the pedestal. A heavy piece of furniture—over two-hundred pounds of bronze metal and dark teak wood. The captain rigged it, so it came apart in two pieces to be carried down to the forward berthing compartment inside the Orca.

As we lifted the chair from the mounting bracket in the deck, I heard a pop. Mr. Quint never made a sound when he dropped his side of the chair. The right arm went limp, and he grabbed hold of his elbow. I never saw him show signs of injury before. Except his dropping tools from time to time. He always said it was nothing and went back to work. That's just what he did on this day.

An hour later, Mr. Quint stood under the fishing shack and worked a piece of steel. His coal forge glowed brighter in the cold air. Its black smoke highlighting the glowing embers from every strike of the heavy hammer against the anvil. I was on the flying bridge and applying an extra layer of paint in spots that needed some touching up. I heard the shout, and the hammer dropped to the floor. The captain knelt, doubled over and holding his right arm.

I climbed down from the flying bridge and ran up the dock to his side.

"What is it, sir? You want me to get the doctor?"

"No. Heaven's, no. That guy has no idea what to do other than handing out aspirin."

"But your arm?"

"It comes and goes, boy. Nothing much."

Mr. Quint picked the five-pound mallet off the floor and raised it with his right hand. A hesitant look my way and he held out his arm to straighten it. When his right arm extended, his hand let loose and dropped the hammer. The heavy mallet head landed with a loud thud and scared me. He looked over at me and shrugged.

"Just the old arm-wrestling injury, boy. Always trouble extending it ever since. Nothing to be worried about. Just can't put too much pressure on it for a few days, is all."

I picked up the hammer and set it back on the table next to the anvil.

"Don't worry about the forge, Hershel. That piece won't work. We need a section of pipe that will fit inside the hole for the fighting chair bracket. To cap it off, so water doesn't get below decks. Back at the graveyard. The merchant ship. The big rusting steel one that we walked through. On its main deck, starboard side, there are fuel tank vents. Take a hacksaw and go get one of those. I can make one of those work."

I nodded and went to the pickup truck. Maybe I should've gone to the doctor instead.

The graveyard cove still scares me. Right into my eighties, I won't go back there alone. Like the Orca, it's a place filled with regret and despair. It is fitting that she was born there.

He sent me back to that place, and I obeyed. His arm hung at his side in pain. I wanted him to rest, so I drove to the cove myself without objection.

I navigated the beach of stranded boats to get as close to the merchant ship as possible. I shut off the engine and walked the rest of the way.

The vessels laid strewn around the waterline in such a way; they became a cavernous path of maritime failure. A labyrinth of rotting wood and rusting metal hulls. Above them all, I saw the lofty upper deck of the merchant ship.

The ocean had a way of rustling the detritus of lost memories. As quickly as they appear, a storm will pass over to wash those memories away. You could not go to the cove and see the same thing twice. The boats shifted and deteriorated at their own pace. It was alive and breathing—this graveyard. The lost spirits cling to the hulls and hide there. I was sure of it. The ghost stories we told as kids were not too far off. This place waits for you and then draws you inside, and that is when they have their way with you.

Outside of the merchant ship, I glared. Three levels of wilted steel decks towered above me. Down in the sand, it caught my eye. A little white figurehead stared back at me. I knelt and dug away at the sand. A metallic figurine of a sailor man dressed in white—a child's toy. The kind I remember the kids having in the 30s. Was this dropped here by some child who came to play and met their doom? Or was this a gift from a former sailor on this ship? Maybe a father looking to bring home a surprise for his son and he never arrived—only the toy washed ashore. I held the little metal figure in my hand and looked around. A feeling of being watched. The silence. The terrible loud silence all around me. I never mentioned the little toy sailor to anyone until right now. All these years, it scared me to talk about it.

With my other hand, I dug a hole in the sand. Deep enough to where the sea water from the cove leaked in to fill the hole. I looked into the face of the sailor and wondered how long it had been here. My nervous hands placed the figure down into the hole and buried it with the sand. I'm not sure why I did that. Maybe I didn't want to be the one to take its curse upon my shoulders.

On the top deck of the merchant ship, I laid down on welded steel next to the fuel fill valves and vent pipes. I ran the hacksaw back and forth. The blade of the hacksaw ate through the weakened rusty metal with ease. Holding onto the goose neck top of the vent pipe, the last few bright shavings of metal spit from my saw and the pipe broke loose.

I sat and looked the beach over. In the distance, I saw the three schooners near the tree line, where we salvaged the mast for the Orca. If I listened to the silence close enough, I thought I heard voices of the crewmen working the decks of the boats below me. Their voices were faint, but real. Maybe my imagination? The voices echoed off the rock outcroppings and the thin pine trees of the cove.

A large ship engine rumbled. Its groan ran through the water and amplified against the steel hull of the dead ship I sat upon. I jumped to my feet and crept around the side of the superstructure.

There, in the center of the cove, the large dark ship dropped anchor. Black smoke howled from the giant aft stacks. A hull black as pitch, painted with runs of rust where the whales were processed. Men hustled across the ship's deck. Large industrial workings busy filleting the dead whale. The blubber being stripped from its body. The smell. That terrible smell of rotting whale met me on the shore when the ocean breeze kicked up.

On the stern of the ship, I read the name:

GOLIATH

A large thirty-foot mechanical steel boom hung off to the port side of the Goliath. It launched a smaller boat from its decks. The smaller boat waited below for the loading of the first of many black barrels that lined the deck. There it was before me. The same boat covered in black steel that we saw years ago. They returned, and I was the first to see them. I had to tell the captain. He always knew they were in our waters during the summers. Their illegalities, hidden by the island. Their wake of death and carcasses calling the sharks in. I tried to not make a sound and give away that I had seen them. When I found the sand of the beach, I ran as fast as I could to the pickup truck.

I busted through the door and around the wooden pylons of our fishing shack.

"Mr. Quint, I saw it. I saw it!"

With the vent pipe in my hand, I ran down the dock towards the Orca. He stepped out of the wheelhouse to see me.

"Hershel, slow down before you trip yourself right into the water here."

"The cove. They are there. But I don't know how long."

"Who is there?"

"The whalers. The men in the black boat we saw years ago. They are part of the larger ship like you thought, sir. I watched them work one of those whales. Black barrels too. They were offloading them."

Mr. Quint reached out and took the vent pipe from me. He listened while he walked over to the fighting chair mount to measure the pipe diameter for a perfect fit.

"Alright, boy. They drop some whale meat in the water and stink up the place. The big sharks come back, and we make some money."

"The Goliath."

He stopped and looked at me when I said it.

"I thought you would want to know the name of the ship, sir. I saw it. It's called the Goliath."

The captain stood up to his feet. His left arm reached over and squeezed his right elbow. The pain still lingered. He didn't speak and turned to the harbor. Amity Point bustled with activity. Life seemed to be normal except on the deck of the Orca. Mr. Quint gauged the clouds in the sky and the sight of the open ocean in the distance.

"Hershel, get the wet gear loaded up. We're getting underway."

38   THE LAW

While getting underway, Mr. Quint emerged from the fishing shack, wearing the usual. A light blue Navy work shirt and his old green service jacket. I started the Orca's engine. As always, he walked down the dock mumbling his checklist of items while shouldering his packed green sea bag. Sometimes, I'd see him trading with the army-navy store in town for old military surplus shirts and such.

Every sailor has his superstitions. Once, I met a sailor who never left a half turn on a cleat. Said it was bad luck—always finished it with a full turn and once around the base. There lived a lobster boat captain further down on the same side of the harbor as my old shack on the hill. He insisted his traps get stacked end to end, never side to side. Said it was bad luck.

I always assumed Mr. Quint's uniform for working in the Navy became his tradition. The one for heading out to sea. The heavy sea bag was his way of packing everything he owned in case he never returned. Maybe he felt it was bad luck to leave anything on shore—tempting the fates. My captain confided his belief in never coming home from the sea when he took to the Pacific during the war. His body came back, but his mind was still out there.

On this day, he walked with a solemn stride. When he stepped down into the Orca, he looked around at the fishing shack and the harbor like it would be the last time he would see it. I never headed out to sea with him without that green sea bag stowed below. Today, he packed it solid.

"How long we headed out for, sir?"

"As long as it takes, Mr. Salvatore."

"Takes for what?"

"To find what we're looking for."

Mr. Quint tossed a cryptic smile back towards me. He moved with some urgency and untied the mooring lines himself. That was his signal that we were out of time.

Like her captain, the Orca cruised out of the harbor with a confident stride. The row of five yellow barrels standing at attention on the bow like soldiers at parade rest. The red stripe down the side of the black hull glowed in the waning sun. On the horizon, dark storm clouds clustered and rolled towards the light.

The white hull of the United States Coast Guard boat approached the Orca at the inlet of Amity Point harbor. I stood in the wheelhouse next to the captain to watch it get closer. Mr. Quint groaned and took off his jacket.

"Look at these clowns. What do they want now?"

The way their boat steered towards us meant they wanted to talk. He eased back on the throttle when one man aboard the Coast Guard boat leaned off the side and waved his hand.

"What do you think they want?"

"Nothing much, just checking us out. Let me do the talking, boy."

The forty-four-foot motor lifeboat slowed and pulled alongside the Orca. A crew of four men stared down at me when I stepped out of the cabin door and looked over their new boat. The newest in 1960's life saving technology, the lifeboat stretched out into a gleaming white steel hull. Streamlined and heavy to punch through giant waves, it carried an impressive look. The boat's coxswain sat at the controls and kept her steady while the crew tossed me a line. I took a turn on the port side stern cleat, and they pulled in closer to us. The two boats touched, compressing the rubber fenders they rigged off the side to protect their shiny hull. Our old battle-damaged wood hull from the past rubbed along the gleaming white painted steel hull of the future.

"Are you the captain?"

"No, sir. Captain's inside," I said while looking over their futuristic vessel.

The Senior Chief Petty Officer watched in silence as the two junior petty officers leaned out and looked at the aft deck of the Orca. Mr. Quint cut the Orca's engine and emerged from the wheelhouse.

"Are you the captain, sir?" asked one of the petty officers.

"That I am," said Mr. Quint.

"Request permission to come aboard for a safety inspection, Captain."

"Do I have a choice?"

"Not really."

"Well, don't let me stand in your way."

The two petty officers, baby faced and full of energy, stepped from the gunwale of their motor lifeboat and dropped into the Orca. Mr. Quint looked their new vessel up and down. He read the classification numbers and title printed on the stern.

"44-321 Amity Point, huh? This is the new boat for the station?"

"Yes, sir. We just got it delivered."

One of the petty officers made his way inside the pilothouse for a look around while the other talked to Mr. Quint. The older coast guard sailor, the senior chief, stepped down and walked across the aft deck to look at the bloodstained wood in the aft corner. Random red streaks baked into the fibers from years of chum buckets and bait lines.

"Headed out to do some fishing, Captain?" asked the younger petty officer.

"Always fishing."

"What's your catch?"

"Maybe some Marlin. Stingray. Stripers."

Mr. Quint rolled up his sleeves and knew they didn't believe his nonsense. He didn't care too much for them knowing his business. They were outsiders to an island that he considered his. The government completed the Amity Point Coast Guard life station back in the late 1950s and only staffed it part of the year. With all the ruckus being created by Larry Vaughn, the town requested a new ferry line to be scheduled from the mainland. Tourists were certain to follow in droves. The federal government wanted a detachment out on Amity that could patrol the local waters. Our history of havens and coves serving smugglers and criminals became well-known lore. The first traces of law and order manifested itself on the island. We still didn't have a year-round police officer, and the population hadn't boomed yet. The law had to be established sometime, and these Coast Guard boys were the first I had ever seen of it. This stop was the first brush with the law I ever experienced. I'm almost certain it was not Mr. Quint's first time.

"How about the row of yellow barrels in the rack on the bow? What are those filled with?"

"Just air."

The petty officer paused and looked up at Mr. Quint, who just stared right back at him.

"What's the matter, Petty Officer? Something illegal about transporting air?"

Before the junior man answered Mr. Quint, the other petty officer emerged from below decks and went over to the senior chief, who sat on the transom, observing the back and forth.

"Senior Chief, there aren't any life jackets onboard, no maritime radio installed, no ship's bell or sound making devices and the boat hasn't been registered. No registration number on the bow. You want me to order a return to port?"

The older man shifted the Coast Guard cap on his head and stood up. He was tall, about the same height as the captain, but with larger shoulders. He raised his hand to stop his petty officer from talking.

Mr. Quint already turned and faced the senior chief from the center of the aft deck. The low rumbling of the motor lifeboat's twin diesel engines is all we heard.

The senior chief pointed to Mr. Quint's left forearm tattoo.

"You were on the Indianapolis, Captain?"

The captain was reluctant to answer but squared up to the question.

"Yeah."

"You are the one they call Quint, right?"

"I am."

"I've heard about you. Seen this vessel docked in the back of the harbor. You fish for sharks. You ever get any?"

"A few."

The senior chief looked down at the bloody stains on the deck and returned a slight smile.

"We heard stories about large sharks around Amity. But nothing ever verified. You and your first mate have been in these waters longer than us. You know anything about large sharks?"

Mr. Quint never broke his deadpan gaze.

"Only what we've read in the National Geographic."

"What about dead whales? Some fellas here are saying bodies of whales have shown up over the last few summers." The senior chief looked over at me. "You men know anything about that?"

I held still and looked towards my captain. He shook his head 'no' and shrugged off the line of questioning.

"There are two reports of a large white shark that got into some fishermen's nets off long island this month. Turned them into Swiss cheese. Almost scuttled one of the small boats out there. Might be headed this way. You know anything about that?"

Mr. Quint stood up straight to answer.

"This is the first I've heard of it. A little early for those types to be around here."

"I won't assume to know more about sharks than you, so I'll take your word for it."

The senior chief raised his voice a little.

"I think we are about done here, boys. Captain, you have a nice day."

The young petty officer stepped forward.

"But Senior Chief, there are quite a few violations. We haven't even inspected the hold—"

"We are done here, Petty Officer Beaumont." The senior chief's voice, direct and firm. "This man can do whatever he pleases in these waters while I am in charge. He's earned it."

The senior enlisted man stared down the younger one with an intensity I had only ever seen from my captain. I knew how that kid felt. Been there too many times myself. The two young officers turned to disembark the Orca. After a brief pause, the senior chief turned back to Mr. Quint.

"You'll have to please excuse my subordinate, Captain. He doesn't understand his naval history."

Mr. Quint nodded. The gray clouds swallowed the last remaining beams of sunlight from the sky. Dark shadow fell across the two men when the seas picked up. The two boats rocked with a rolling swell of water.

"There's a storm brewing, Captain Quint. You be safe out there."

"Thank you, Senior Chief. You, the same."

I tossed them their line, and the two boats separated. The Orca pushed forward with Mr. Quint at the helm. Through the aft wheelhouse window, I watched the Coast Guard motor lifeboat rumble towards the harbor. The senior chief never took his eyes off us until we turned west and escaped into the open Atlantic Ocean.

39   THE CHASE

The heavy rain pummeled the Orca under the sweeping light of Amity Harbor lighthouse. The rain fell hard against the glass windows—impossible to see the channel makers just ahead of us. I propped the window open in front of the helm to help the captain's view. The seas calmed inside the harbor, but we had to inch ourselves along to make sure we stayed in the channel and not run aground.

Mr. Quint saw it right away. Moored in the same spot, the small, black-hulled utility boat from the Goliath. We drifted by to get a closer look. The rain pounding on the metal deck making a distinct sound as loud as the Orca. More rust and weathering graced the rivets and steel plating of the thirty-foot boat since we last saw it. I looked around the harbor for the black barrels.

We slipped the Orca against an open dock. I pulled my orange rain slicker on and jumped outside. Soaked by the heavy downpour, I tossed a line over a misshapen wooden pylon.

Mr. Quint leaned out of the cabin to yell. "Not all the lines, boy. We won't be here very long."

I nodded, then tended to the stern line. Mr. Quint stepped out with his heavy-weather trench coat and Sou'wester hat. The dark navy-blue vinyl ran with the downpour of water off his shoulders and back. I pulled my waxed leather fishing cap down to my eyes.

Mr. Quint walked up the pier of Amity Harbor, firm and confident. I followed. His raincoat flowed behind him in the heavy gusts. The sagging hat shrouded his identity. A fury raged inside him.

Off to the far side of the harbor, a truck parked around the rows of black barrels. Two men struggled in the rain to push the dolly cart loaded with one barrel into the truck as we approached. The rain muffled the potent smell—now reduced to a faint stench hanging in the air.

"Where's the manifest for these barrels?"

My captain spoke strong and direct.

The two men paused and looked over at Mr. Quint, who moved around the barrels and closed the distance towards them. He seemed to grow over them the closer he stepped.

"I'm going to ask again, but not a third time. Where is your shipping manifest for these barrels?"

"We don't have one. Talk to the fella in the red Dodge. We just go where he tells us."

He gestured to the parked 1966 Dodge Charger across the street. The driver's side door opened and out stepped the man we had seen in Amity Point a dozen times over the years. Vaughn's lackey with the necktie and glasses. He opened an umbrella and pulled up the collar of his tan trench coat. Mr. Quint didn't waste any time and walked toward the car.

"Mr. Quint. It's a little early to be meeting. We take care of our business on the other side of the island."

"Our business has changed. Where are these barrels headed?"

"Now, Mr. Quint, I don't see Mr. Vaughn approving any conversation of these. This is part of a bigger project that I'm not allowed to discuss."

Patience outside of hunting big fish was never a strong suit for my captain. There always came a point where his fuse burns short—where ability to reason becomes useless. In the driving rain, with the water pouring from his hat over the ever-lingering scent of deceased whale, Mr. Quint lost all decorum.

He lunged for the thin man and grabbed the collar of his raincoat. The umbrella dropped to the asphalt. The two bodies slammed against the parked Dodge. Rain pounded on the shiny red metal roof next to the man's face. His black horn-rimmed glasses laid crooked and covered with water. The captain stared into his eyes while holding his collar tight.

"Listen to me, you weasel. I don't like being used. I know what you are doing, and I want to know what's in it for Vaughn. You are going to tell me right now before I work you over and toss you in the harbor. We are on an island out in the middle of the ocean. They'll never find you in time. Do you understand?"

The men loading the truck dropped their barrel from the commotion and scrambled into the cab. Its engine started, and the truck drove off.

The businessman shook and held his hands up in surrender.

"It's whale oil. Spermaceti. Sperm whale oil."

"I already knew that. You can smell it all over the island. Where's it going?"

"Nye Lubricants. Vaughn has a deal with them. The owner John Hammond sells it back to the government. Big money for this stuff."

Mr. Quint squeezed on the neck of the businessman a little harder.

"Don't bullshit me. I'm not in any mood for it."

"No, I'm not! Don't hit me."

"What's the government want with whale oil? This isn't 1905."

"Not just whale oil... sperm whale oil. It never freezes. NASA uses it for their equipment. Rocket technology. The space race with the Soviets. They pay unlimited funds for lubricant that doesn't freeze in sub-zero temperatures."

Mr. Quint leaned into the man.

"And what's with the Goliath?"

"A contract ship. They find the whales for us."

"You tell Vaughn it's over. I'm putting a stop to it."

The businessman looked in disbelief.

"You can't stop it. They'll just go somewhere else. Things are in motion that you can't understand. Mr. Vaughn will not be satisfied with—"

I watched the captain pull the man forward and then slam him back against the car. The rainwater shook off from the impact.

"I don't care about Vaughn, and I don't work for anybody but myself. It's over. If he doesn't like it, he knows where to find me."

Mr. Quint released his grip. The man dropped into the shallow pool of standing water collected under the car. I turned and followed my captain. He wasn't done.

The door to the tavern opened and everyone inside paused from the rush of cold, damp air. Mr. Quint and I stepped from the failing gray light of late afternoon and into the orange glow of hanging lights. The fireplace in the corner sent a warmth over the room that couldn't compete with the breeze and rain entering alongside my captain.

I closed the door behind us and watched him remove his hat. They all huddled around the table in the corner. The crew of the black steel boat. Five men, leaning back in their chairs, turned to face us. With his back to the wall, the silent captain stared with dark eyes and watched. These sailors were not small by any means. All well-built men who lived at sea for most of their lives. They reminded me of Mr. Quint. For that moment, the tavern stayed silent. Amity was too small an island for these men to exist together. Someone would have to leave.

Mr. Quint walked over to the table and bumped into it. The table lurched a few inches, causing the beer in their glasses to spatter over the sides. Two of the sailors rose to their feet. Their captain remained silent and looked up at Mr. Quint. He wore a wicked smirk under his dark mustache and unshaven face.

The bar tender pushed aside a few bottles on the bar and leaned over.

"Now, hold it right there, Quint. I don't be needing any more trouble. This place was just fine before you came in."

"Shut up, Charlie. I'm not here to cause trouble. I'm here to tell these fellas they are leaving the island. Their ship is getting underway tonight."

Mr. Quint glared at the seated captain, who looked back with an unbroken gaze.

"They don't speak English, Quint. They can't understand you."

"Sure they can, Charlie. They can understand me just fine," said Mr. Quint, without looking away from the Portuguese captain.

Nobody moved. Mr. Quint stood tall. Water dripped from his soaked rain slicker and collected on the table.

"Get your dishwasher out here, Charlie. The little guy. Portuguese kid, isn't he? Maybe he can help us with some translation. We don't want any confusion here."

A few seconds turned into an eternity. Another one of the Portuguese whalers stood with caution. Mr. Quint eyed the three standing men one at a time. Neither of them wanted to make the first move.

A young sweaty kid wearing a white t-shirt and apron emerged from a backroom and approached the table. He looked nervous.

Mr. Quint looked down at the short dish washer.

"Say, boy. You speak Portuguese?"

The boy nodded his head. "Yes, sir."

"Translate for these gentlemen what I'm saying."

The other people at the bar moved away from the confrontation in the corner.

"Tell them they aren't allowed back to this island. Whatever business they have here is finished. This was their last shipment."

The young kid paused, then turned to the men and spoke in the foreign language. When the kid finished, Mr. Quint continued. He stared into the eyes of their captain while the boy translated.

"I can smell it on you. You stink of whale and fear. You know about me, and you know who I am. If I see you around here again, you will deal with me at sea, and you'll never return."

The boy paused and looked at Mr. Quint.

"Finish it, boy. Tell them what I said."

The table next to them cleared out, and some people left the tavern. Most stayed motionless in the silence that followed the boy's Portuguese words.

We turned and walked back towards the door. Their captain looked with a steel gaze. The smirk dropped from his face when his crew looked down at him and awaited his orders.

Mr. Quint swung open the front door and walked into the cloud of rain.

The last remnants of winter winds swept across the docks of Amity Harbor. The rain came at us from the windward side. I was nervous, for I didn't know what the other crew was going to do.

Mr. Quint walked to the fuel pumps. On the side of the small shack, a fire extinguisher and a heavy ax mounted to the wall. He grabbed the ax and marched back up the pier.

"Mr. Quint, what do you want me to do?"

"Nothing. Stay with the Orca and start the engine."

I followed his orders and stayed back with the Orca. I climbed up on the flying bridge to see the captain storm back into the row of black barrels. He leaned forward and pushed through the surging rain and heavy winds. The Dodge was gone, and the large delivery truck never returned.

The crew of the Goliath marched down the pier towards their steel boat. They watched as Mr. Quint wielded the fire ax and swung into the black steel barrels. Puncturing holes in the sides, he kicked the barrels over. The heavy drums crashed and rolled, emptying the putrid smell of their oil contents across the pier. The crew of the Goliath didn't wait around. Their captain barked at them while they all moved to the small transport boat. The engines started and the boat moved away from the dock. Before leaving, they watched the captain thrash away a year's worth of work, countless miles around oceans, and heaven only knows how many lives of whales taken. The sounds of the heavy ax crashing into the metal drums pierced the silent harbor, only to be drowned out by another gust of howling wind.

Night fell over Cable Junction. We left Amity Harbor and sailed to the small island of rocks. The destroyed metal enclosure at the south end of the island made me smile. I smirked at the memory of the fireworks but was glad I didn't have to see them again. We hadn't been back here in years. The sea wreaked its havoc on the little wooden dock and washed up more debris against the rocks during our absence. But it wasn't much different from when we left it.

Six hours passed since we left the pile of destroyed oil drums and lost sight of the black hull of their boat. The rain passed over and swept out to sea, leaving a chilled night air. I changed my shirt and dried off inside the Orca while my captain went aloft. The Orca took refuge on the leeward side of Cable Junction. Mr. Quint stood on his lookout platform and studied the shipping lanes to the east of Amity. He became a bird of prey. Standing above the world and watching. Thinking and planning. A hunter waiting for his target.

We never spoke a word. I decided it was best to just stay out of the way. There was more going on than I could understand.

"There they are, boy. Just like I thought. These types are all predictable." He stepped into the wheelhouse. "Shut the light off."

I reached up and flipped the switch on the lamp hanging over the table. The Orca went dark. We didn't have any running lights outside either. We became invisible. On the horizon, a series of lights from the Goliath moved left to right.

"Is that the Goliath?"

"Yeah."

"How do you know it's them, sir?"

"It's them all right. They're headed to Boston."

The Orca tracked the Goliath from a safe distance away. Running dark, we stayed a few miles off their wake and out of sight. The captain chased their running lights around Nantucket Island and to the north. In a few hours, we moved past the coast of Cape Cod and around Provincetown. The Goliath stayed in the international shipping lanes and turned toward Boston Harbor.

This was the farthest I had ever been away from Amity. I was in uncharted territory once again, with my only sense of safety and salvation being the Orca and her captain. For the rest of my life, I would never look at Saint Patrick's Day the same way again.

40 KNOCKO NOLAN'S

The Goliath dropped anchor in the Gulf of Maine. Right on Boston Harbor's doorstep. We watched them launch their captain's steel-hulled transport under the bright work lights of the larger ship. The Orca stayed dark and observed the smaller vessel speed away from the Goliath and into the harbor.

Mr. Quint lit up the running lights and pushed the throttle forward. He cast the bait back on Amity and they bit. They led us right to him.

I stood outside the cabin door and watched the lights of the big city get closer. Never saw a sight like it. Lights and life all along an endless coast in all directions. Boston Harbor was a minefield of ships, boats, and debris. Mr. Quint navigated them with ease. He knew the right lanes to be in and which buoy lights to put off the bow at just the right time to stay the course. I got the idea he sailed these waters before.

We followed the Portuguese boat right into the Boston waterfront of shipping piers, fancy boats, old beaten down wharves, and fireworks—lots of fireworks. The closer the city pushed towards me, the more I shrank back into the Orca. A fish out of water never feels comfortable. I wanted to go back to my shack on the hill. My hands shook with nerves. The captain didn't speak at all—steering the boat with his eyes locked on their prey.

He saw them tie up to Battery Wharf and kept our distance. They exited the boat, climbing up on the rotted planking of the dock and walked towards the brick buildings along the waterfront. The Orca found a construction barge with its steel spuds buried into the seafloor. The barge nestled tight against a seawall construction site. After securing the lines, the lights shut, and the engine killed.

Mr. Quint and I climbed onto the seawall and headed into the city, following the five men from the Goliath.

The night of Saint Paddy's Day in Boston might as well be a New Year's Eve. I never saw so many people crowded in the streets. The Irish showed up in force. They spilled out from the bars and onto the sidewalks. The traffic— oh Lord, the traffic. Not sure how anyone could drive in such a place. I walked a step behind my captain. He seemed to know where he was going. I had enough work dodging the drunken sailors and streetlight posts along the busy sidewalk.

A street sign that said Battery Street guarded a sea of illumination. Neon lights and glowing bulbs advertising the world—diners, a bookstore, bottled liquors. A place called *The Playland Cafe* that said it served 'Fine Food'. The *Golden Nugget Dine and Dance* lit the sky in a yellow hue. Colossal buildings stood over us, making me feel even smaller.

The damp coldness of March mired the night air. A day's rain melted most of the snow, leaving small mountains of white in the corners of the concrete and blacktop.

Mr. Quint turned the next corner, down a side street and there I saw it. A large neon display of letters—glowing red:

He unbuttoned the top fastening to his dark Navy pea coat and turned towards me.

"Look, boy. You just stay by my side. I won't let anything happen to you. Should've done this a long time ago."

I responded with a nervous nod of my head.

We stepped forward through the last melting snow and walked up the front steps.

The Irish band in the back corner of the Knocko Nolan's bar hustled their instruments and drove the room wild. A tavern larger than anything back on Amity and cloaked in polished wood trim. Long and narrow, with a second level to the far back. A long bar constructed of old ship timbers extended from the right side of the front door and ended somewhere further down.

The crowd jammed in shoulder to shoulder, blocking me from seeing deep inside. Sounds of fizz and cheers stifled the music—beer flowed, and glassed mugs clinked. The men were loud and the women even louder.

Mr. Quint stepped inside, and I closed the door behind us. The door hit a ship's bell and some heavy shouldered merchant marines leaned back on their bar stools to witness a living legend.

The bartender leaned over, whispering to a few others at the far end. More than a few recognized Mr. Quint. The music never stopped and most of the crowd carried on with their celebration of Irish festivities. To the more experienced and weathered of men, they knew this was a moment to remember; Mr. Quint had returned.

We moved through the narrow establishment. As we passed the bar, some sailors turned and tipped their hats to the captain. Others kept a hateful eye on him. They looked at me as well. I didn't know how to feel. Victorious or cautious? Nervous or triumphant? It was all of these at the same time.

Behind the bar, a cavernous shelf stretched to the ceiling, lined with bottles of alcohol and exotic drink from all over the world. The smell of pipe tobacco and whiskey cut through the haze of exhaled smoke and sweaty heat from the musicians clamoring away at their instruments. Mr. Quint kept his eye on the stairs leading up to the wooden door and windows of the second floor.

Once through the crowd, we saw them. Four crewmen of the Goliath, seated at a special table next to the stairs. The other tables packed with revelers, pounding their beer glasses against the wood and stomping their feet to the driving Irish music.

The crew of the Goliath saw Mr. Quint and stood up.

Above our heads, the wooden door opened. Out stepped the captain of the Goliath along with the owner of this establishment—this sliver of the Boston netherworld.

Knocko Nolan leaned over the railing, looked down at Mr. Quint, and smiled. Mr. Quint never moved. He turned the collar down on his coat and removed his hat. I looked around and many of the crowd back at the bar began their whispering and gestured our way. The band continued.

He walked down the steps with a confident stride. His energy and the way he carried himself mirrored my captain. Knocko Nolan stood broad shoulder to broad shoulder with my captain. They matched each other's height and build. A head of graying red hair with an unshaven face. His voice—a gravel filled growl.

"I never thought I'd see you again in my life, Quint."

"It's been a long time, Knocko. How's your father?"

"He's dead."

"I'm sorry to hear that."

"No, you're not."

The Portuguese captain of the Goliath walked down the stairs and stepped towards his crew. His eyes never left Mr. Quint's.

Knocko looked over to the anxious Goliath crew, leaning and ready to pounce.

"You know how much money you cost me today?"

Mr. Quint shrugged off the question.

"It's over, Knocko. I don't want to see your ship anywhere near Amity Island ever again. It's my island now."

Knocko reared back in a heavy laugh from his bellows. "You are going to just sail into my city and tell me which island is yours? After disappearing for years? You belong in the asylum, Quint. You really do."

"This isn't a request or a discussion," Mr. Quint said.

"You and your Pa never could stomach the hunt and the killing. Always chasing the damn marlin… thinking you gonna catch the big one and win the sweepstakes one day."

Mr. Quint stepped in closer to Knocko to speak over the music.

"We both chose to do what our father's done—nothing more, nothing less. Your industry was dying. The smart money was in the marlin. You chose wrong."

"No. It's you who chose wrong. There's more money than ever in whale oil. Because now it's rare. If my ship doesn't go out and get it, someone else will. You think you go out and survive the war, come back, kill a few sharks, and now gonna play the hero? That's not how it works, Quint. Yeah, I heard about you and what you've been doing. You are nothing special. You gotta atone. Everything you touch dies."

"I've come here on a mission of warning," said Mr. Quint, while pointing at the Portuguese sailors. "If I see them working off Amity again. I'll kill 'em."

The unshaven face of Knocko Nolan grimaced with intensity.

"Not if I don't kill you first—here and now."

Mr. Quint looked over his shoulder. The music died away, and the crowd went quiet. Some of the larger sailors from the bar stepped forward to get a better view. A side door next to a glass window swung open. Two young ladies dressed in green stumbled inside. They saw the tension-filled room and backed out into the side alley to move along.

Knocko looked to save face and put Mr. Quint on the spot. The heavy Boston accent projected across the room.

"Ladies and gentlemen, the great and legendary Captain Quint returns to stake his claim on the north Atlantic. This is history in the making. He must have a way of settling the score. Did he bring any weapons? Of course not. This is a town of laws. There must be some way of deciding this impasse."

"I'll wrestle you for it," said Mr. Quint.

The crowd snickered. Some men turned further in their chairs and strained to listen.

"You'll wrestle me for Amity Island?" asked Knocko, while tapping his chest with a chuckle.

Mr. Quint shook his head. "No. I'll wrestle him." He pointed to the captain of the Goliath.

Knocko looked back at the Portuguese captain. A slight smaller than Mr. Quint while thinner in the chest and neck. Knocko shook his head.

"It's been a long time, but not long enough to forget about that arm of yours. No. If you want Amity, you lock arms with the first mate—Fausto."

The large man stepped out from the back of the table. Fausto, the first mate of the Goliath, took up enough space for two men. His chest stretched across the room. Overbuilt forearms bulged the sleeves of his black whale oil-stained wool overcoat. The captain of the Goliath looked over at Fausto and nodded. They understood English just fine and knew what was happening when they smiled their wicked grins back at my captain.

Mr. Quint looked up at the giant first mate. He responded in the surest of voices.

"Get the whiskey."

The room erupted in a cheer, and the band played. Tables moved, and the crowd closed in. Some of the smarter ones took their coats and left. Knocko Nolan directed a table to be placed with towels for padding. The unexpected highlight of this year's fading Saint Patrick's Day night—an antique arm-wrestling match.

Mr. Quint took me to the side door. His fist crossed the edge of the bar and snagged a bottle of Irish whiskey. He filled a glass to three fingers and pounded it back, then turned to me.

"Listen, Hershel. Take my coat."

Mr. Quint removed his coat and handed it over to me.

"Mr. Quint, sir. You can't arm wrestle that fella. Your arm's busted."

"Shut-up and do as I say, boy. Take this coat and wait outside. If I don't come out of here, I want you to take the keys to the Orca and sail her back to Amity. You will be her captain."

"But sir. Where will you go?"

"No time to explain. Just go outside."

Mr. Quint took another stab of whiskey from the bottle and turned towards the table. The awaiting crowd rustled up a roar. The big sailor, Fausto, stood his ground and scowled with menacing, dark brown eyes. His arm flexed. The biceps—a piston of steel ready to fire.

My captain strode up to the uneven wooden legged table and leaned in. The two men locked their right hands. They worked to gain an edge on the grip of each other's fingers. Another sailor stepped in and held their hands tight. Speaking in Portuguese, he yelled for them to hold steady.

Knocko Nolan climbed a few creaking wooden steps to look down on the action. He took pleasure in the situation. The crowd closed in even more.

For the first time in my years of sailing underneath him, I disobeyed my captain's orders and stayed inside. I climbed onto a chair by the side door and peered over the cheering arms of the late-night revelers. Mr. Quint's heavy pea coat held tight to my side.

They had yet to start. I saw my captain pulling on the arm of the giant to get his hand closer. I could see the giant pull back even harder. They pulled against each other to gain the advantage.

The crowd began the countdown…

"Three…"

"Two…"

"One…"

The man released his hand on the clenched fists of the two combatants.

With all the strength and speed summoned from his soul, Mr. Quint harnessed the moment. With Fausto still pulling back with all his strength, my captain thrust both of their hands up into the giant's face. The added momentum allowed Mr. Quint to convert their white-knuckled right hands into the hardest punch I'd ever seen. I heard the crack of skull and Fausto's nose exploded in blood. The table tipped over. The giant dropped back to the floor in a crash of glass and wood. Next, Mr. Quint lunged for the captain of the Goliath with a massive left hook. Another pop of facial muscle and bone and the captain of the Goliath went falling backwards—his face a bloody ruin.

The tables cleared. Knocko Nolan's erupted into the greatest bar fight the city of Boston had ever witnessed in all the three-hundred and thirty-six years of its existence. Wars had been nothing new to Boston, and this was just another one to be fought on her streets.

I lost sight of the captain and fell back off my chair. The side door opened with the non-fighting types spilling outside and running away. The stampede of the crowd pushed me out into the cold. I moved to the large window and wiped away the cloud of condensation on the glass to look for my captain.

The sailors who tipped their hats to Mr. Quint when we first walked in rushed to his aid. They each wrestled and threw punches at Knocko's men. Some dropped chairs onto one another. Glass bottles broke across heads. A crescendo of swearing, agonizing screams, and breaking bones replaced the music.

In the middle of it all, I saw him. Mr. Quint held his ground and swung haymakers into anyone who dared to rush him. A fighter with nothing to lose, he moved with a calculated experience. An experience obtained through a lifetime of bar battles in dives all around the world. The forest of hired heavies and thugs, already a night's deep in the bottle, hadn't the first idea how to subdue the barroom warrior chopping his way through them.

Knocko Nolan cursed his fury and moved to the side. More of his henchmen blasted out of the illegal gambling backrooms and scrambled down the stairs to wade into the fray. The bodies were too many. The confusion of chaos and carnage, too great for any mortal.

Mr. Quint never saw the large man swing a steel spittoon from the floor. The Damascus steel rim buried in the top of his forehead. Through the glass of the window, I heard my captain's skull dent, and he fell backwards. He struggled back to his feet. Blood poured down his face from the gash just above his hairline. Mr. Quint raged against his attackers, who now outnumbered him.

I didn't want to watch anymore and shrunk away from the window, hearing his screams and shouts inside. I can't tell you what they did to him on that night, because I wasn't there to witness—only heard the sounds. They beat my captain. Too weak and scared to do anything about it, I hesitated. He told me to stay outside, and I did. I walked to the other side of the alley and looked at the side door to the bar. The glass windowpanes fogged up against the night air. Silhouettes of the warring bodies projected across the ceiling inside. At that very moment, I felt the loss of my father. Against the far brick wall of the alleyway, I shrank into shadow.

The side door busted open, and three men fell out carrying my battered and broken captain. They struggled to their feet while Mr. Quint laid motionless in a large pool of melted snow and gutter water. Knocko Nolan stumbled out the door, then stomped down the short, lopsided steps.

"Get back inside, all of you. Leave him there."

Knocko bled from a split lip and a deep cut under his left eye. His knuckles bleeding, the large man leaned back against the wall to catch his breath. The three others, all bruised and worn, clothes ripped and soiled, didn't object to their boss's command. They each shuffled back up the steps to find the ice chest inside.

"Dammit, you sonofabitch. You son of a…" Knocko couldn't find his breath. "Don't nothing ever change? Still gotta do things your way."

Mr. Quint rolled over and pushed himself up to his knees. He wobbled and rose to his feet, one leg at a time. His face swollen and contorted into an unrecognizable, bloody mess. He wiped the blood from his brow. With the torn sleeve of his white Navy thermal undershirt, he cleared his eyes.

Silence fell between the two men. Knocko stepped forward. The golden light from the window illuminated the bloody shirt of Mr. Quint. The neon sign out front flooded into the alleyway to wash Knocko Nolan in a red haze of sweat and anger.

I stood in silence and held my breath.

Knocko reached behind his back and pulled out a handgun. The menacing man pulled the slide back and charged the weapon with a bullet. Mr. Quint heard the gun slide snap forward and looked up at the barrel.

"You gonna kill me, Knocko? Do it. It's not gonna change the past. If you don't, I'll just keep coming back here until you leave the island."

The handgun shook and then steadied. This wouldn't be the first time Knocko Nolan delivered a bullet to an adversary in a back alleyway of Boston.

Knocko spit a mouthful of bloody saliva across the antique cobble of the alley floor.

"If Maureen chose me, she'd still be alive. Do you know that?"

Mr. Quint looked down at the water collecting along the stone curbing and nodded in agreement.

Knocko continued, "You failed her. You always have been a failure, Quint. Everything you touch dies. Just like her. Just like your Pa."

Knocko lowered the weapon to his side and wiped the corner of his mouth with his sleeve.

"Go on and keep your shit island in the middle of nowhere. Take your ass back to Amity and live the rest of your days, knowing you'll be nothing in this life but a loser."

Mr. Quint just stood with his head hung. He never responded.

The aging Irish Boston warlord, Knocko Nolan, turned and took two steps up to open the door. He paused and never looked back towards Mr. Quint.

"If I ever see you in Boston or catch a glimpse of you on the docks, I'll send you back to Amity, unable to walk."

The door opened and Knocko disappeared inside.

Mr. Quint exhaled a cloud of warm breath. The pain of a broken rib knifed him in the side, and he hunched over. I stepped out from the shadows to hand the man his coat and take my captain home.

41 TARGET SHIP

"Right here. Go drop the anchor."

I didn't understand what he said. His jaw, misshapen and bruised, worked to spit sounds from a swollen mouth. The words didn't get out right. I paused and stared at him. Mr. Quint directed me from the helm of the Orca. He bent over in pain while holding his left side. His left hand held a towel to his head to stop the bleeding. The beaten man pulled the fuel stop to kill the engine, then slumped over the table inside the cabin, falling into the corner bench seat. His back hit the aft bulkhead, and he groaned.

"The anchor, Hershel. Gotta drop that anchor or we'll drift right into it."

Understanding the muffled order the second time around, I rushed outside and scurried around the wheelhouse to the bow. In the chilled night air of Cape Cod Bay, I looked up at its massive shape. We drifted so close; it blocked out the stars off the horizon.

Well after midnight, I got my captain to the Orca before the police arrived. We shoved off and got out of Boston Harbor—never to return. My first and last time I ever saw a city. I heard some are even worse than Boston. You can keep them all. I'll take my lonely island any day of the week and twice on Sunday.

At the bow, I fumbled through the storage compartments to remove the Orca's anchor and chain. The charts showed high tide, and I knew we needed extra chain. They hurt my captain. He couldn't pilot the boat back to Amity in his condition and running at night was dangerous enough. We headed south into Cape Cod Bay, where he knew of a refuge to drop anchor.

In the looming presence, I looked up at its black shape. A massive dark wall of nothing. The only visual references to gauge its size were the constellations in the sky. They added a backdrop of light so I could make out its silhouette. I dropped the anchor into the dark water of the bay. The chain rattled while feeding over the splash guard of the bow. Deeper than I thought, the chain let out a few shots more than expected.

Back inside the Orca's wheelhouse, I stepped into the waning warmth of its heater core. The captain sat at the table under the hanging light bulb. The lonely source of light shone down on him. His troubled brow blocked the light from his busted eyes, both swelled and blackened. The Orca's engine rumbled at idle below my feet.

"I turned her back on, boy. I forgot about the cold on this bay."

Mr. Quint tried to smile, but it hurt too much. His face fell back into a grimace.

"You are missing a tooth, sir."

"I am, huh?"

Mr. Quint examined his mouth and found the bloody space. The base of the cracked tooth jutted from the upper gum line, a few spots to the left of his front teeth. It must have been painful in the cold air.

"I forgot to keep my chin tucked to my chest. That's what I get for not following the proper etiquette."

Mr. Quint fiddled with a metal contraption on the table. About the size of a soda can—a collection of metal springs, tubes, and bushings. His bloody-knuckled right hand pushed and prodded the springs, then pressed a release. The contraption clicked. This went on in a steady rhythm while he sat in silence.

"You should get some rest, sir. You need to lie down."

"My head is so pounding, I don't think I'll wake up if I do, Hershel."

"You could die? Does that happen after a fight?"

"Sometimes."

I shifted with nerves. "Well, we need a doctor then? What are we doing here?"

"Relax, boy. I know what to do," he said while lowering his left hand from his head to check the bloody rag. "Already dry. Always was good at clotting up to stop the bleeding. I still got it."

Another wry smile touched his swollen lips with a tinge of pain.

"Why did you do it, sir? Why not just let them do their whaling?"

He didn't look at me. The metal contraption snapped and clicked a few times over while he thought of my question.

"Knocko's dad and my dad were friends. We grew up together, running along the New Bedford piers, waiting for them to come back to port. The

Nolan's were always chasing the dollar, and my father didn't want me to turn out their way, so we up and moved. My dad always preached the nobility of the fisherman—the mariner. Two thousand years of history and an ocean cathedral. He was the best there was at reading the tides, the winds, temperatures of the water. The big fish—he taught me their migration patterns. We moved out here on the Cape, where we battled the swordfish. Giant marlin. The Nolan's stuck to the whaling, even after it became illegal. They couldn't give up the killing. They never were good at hunting. So, they took the easy way out."

Mr. Quint pressed a spring release inside the metal contraption under his hand. It snapped once more.

"Maureen's family ran grocery stores. They stayed their summers here in Wellfleet. In winter, they moved back to New Bedford. We all grew up together as kids. As teenagers, we never were around at the same time. Nothing like a pretty girl to bring about the rivalry in boys. When I was sixteen, I argued with my dad and didn't go out with him to fish. It was about Maureen. Her family headed back to town where Knocko was, and I didn't want to stay on the Cape. I wanted to move out and go on my own. Get a boat myself. He said I wasn't ready. I wish I could take back some of those words I said. I ran out. He struck out on his own that morning and never came back. When the news spread how we found him... the skeleton of the giant marlin alongside his boat. My dad laying across the transom with one hand on the boathook, still trying to land the fish even in death. The sharks ripped it to pieces. He lost his life and not even a pound of fish to show for it. News spread fast, and everyone asked where I was. Why wasn't his son on the boat with him? The town blamed me for it. They didn't need to. I blamed myself. They were right. Had I been there, he would've lived."

The gentle sway of the Orca in the bay water created a rhythmic creaking of its wooden decking.

"Mr. Salvatore, be a good mate and fetch me that bottle of whiskey and a cup behind your shoulder. I need a drink."

I nodded and reached for the bottle. Under the hanging light's sway, I helped him pour a cupful. With caution, Mr. Quint took a painful sip of the whiskey. He stared at his blood left on the rim of the cup.

"If you grew up around whaling, you know its smell. The first summer in Amity, I knew it was going on. It's been that way for decades. It didn't take many cycles to read the big sharks coming in for easy food. Dead whale brings in the biggest ones. When you said the name of the ship was The Goliath—the same name as Knocko's father's boat, I saw my father's heart break in heaven. I had become what he didn't want—one of them. For once in my life, I didn't want to let him down. Had to make things right. So, I ended it. We won't be seeing them near Amity after tonight."

I thought of Amity Point and the cove, then wondered out loud. "Larry Vaughn's been making money—hired them out? Letting them use the island?"

"He's another one. We cut off his money supply tonight. Men like Vaughn stayed back and made a business in sending boys off to the war to die. They never cared about the results of their actions. Watching him suffer will be heavenly."

"And the sharks? Do they disappear now?"

"They will for a while, but they never forget. The big ones always remember where their best meal was. They'll be back. We'll be waiting."

Mr. Quint raised his cup to the air and smiled. Another drink to drown his thoughts.

Another click of the metal lever pitched from inside the device on the table. "What do you have there, sir?"

"This? A minor project I stowed under the bench here and forgot about. I figured it's time to finish it."

"What's it called?"

"When I left the Navy, they said I could take anything I wanted. This was one of those things I had to sneak out of there. Pistol firing mechanism for a mark five Naval ordinance—depth charge."

"Depth charge? Those bombs they tossed at submarines during the war?"

Mr. Quint nodded his head. "The power of water. Explosions below turn water into a weapon. Destroys anything within six feet."

Another long drink from the bloody cup to numb the pain of speaking.

"This last winter I suffered through a dream. I had it before, but this time I saw the whole thing. Couldn't forget it. I'm getting eaten by a giant shark. Much like the ones I killed in San Francisco. A white shark... but this one is big. A real porker. Massive. I'm letting him swallow me 'cause I gotta bomb in my hands. And when I'm almost all the way in his mouth, I pull the trigger. I woke up before the explosion. Don't even know if it worked. I can make this work, though." Mr. Quint tapped the metallic assembly on the table. "I'm going to find the largest shark on the planet. Maybe him and I will go out together."

The metal firing pin snapped forward, and I flinched from the sound. My captain wasn't thinking clear. I tried to change the subject.

"My mother always told me I was on this planet for a purpose. God had a plan for me, and life is supposed to be about finding that purpose. What's your purpose, Mr. Quint?"

My captain finished the whiskey in his cup and looked up at me. He looked older with the missing tooth. The dried blood in the crow's feet of his eyes aged him. His eyes, black with shadow from the swaying light above his head. The sight of him reminded me of those old fishermen telling ghost stories on the wharf.

"Some have to die to find that out. I have no idea, boy. Right now, my purpose is to get some sleep and relish in denting the local politician's bankbook."

Mr. Quint slid out from the bench seat. He struggled to his feet, then opened the seating storage to place that metal contraption inside.

"But sir, your head?"

"It's fine now, Hershel. The pounding has stopped. The whiskey helped some."

He never looked back when I moved forward to help him find the steps to drop into the forward berthing compartment. His body collapsed into the lower starboard rack. A thin gray mattress of pinstriped ticking and a rolled sea bag would be the night's grave for the captain. I sat down on the rack opposite him and watched. He blacked out, flat on his back. The snoring meant he was still alive. The noise didn't bother me. I fell asleep, comforted that he was still breathing.

I awoke the next morning to the sounds of the gulls. A slight breeze through the porthole touched my head from above. A gray light shone outside.

Mr. Quint was silent. He had rolled to the side and turned to the bulkhead. The same position I found my mother in when she died. His body laid motionless and turned away from me. My heart jumped. I startled awake and twisted off the rack, falling over to my captain's side.

"Mr. Quint. Captain, sir. Are you sleeping?"

He didn't make a sound.

I thought him dead, and panic struck me. Had I lost my family once again?

His torso rose, and he rolled onto his back. Still locked into a slumberous hold, he exhaled a breath. I sat back on the deck of the berthing compartment in relief. That feeling told me I was not ready to be on my own again.

A silent rise to my feet, I stepped into my boots to go topside and look around. The thick fog bank had swallowed us whole. The windows of the Orca filled with a misty white eeriness.

How could I forget about it? I opened the bench seat and there it laid. The metal contraption. The odd assembly of springs, levers, and pistons felt heavy. In my hands, it was innocent and useless. In his hands, it would be a weapon of death—his death. He would take his own life with it, given the opportunity. Maybe my purpose was to save his life. I could do it right now. Send this thing to the waters below and never mention it again. His snoring from below seemed in tune with the idle of the Orca's engine—still asleep. Now's my chance.

I stepped outside into the dank morning fog. The device clutched tight to my chest with my left hand. I pulled myself along the outside of the Orca and moved up to the bow. A few more steps to the end of his shark hunting pulpit. I leaned into the railing and looked down at the water below. The fog broke in the slightest of ways and I saw it.

The massive ghost ship stretched far over my head and dwarfed the Orca. I couldn't see the ends of the rusted metal hull, for it reached a hundred feet in both directions and disappeared into the fog. I only heard stories of this place, but never thought it would be this big. My captain anchored us along the port side to protect from the ocean winds coming into the bay.

They grounded the SS Longstreet in the bay after the war. For the last twenty years, the government used her for target practice. Bombing runs by fighter planes had taken their toll. The once youthful and glorious hull, now riddled with holes and dents. The waterline of the hull plagued with hordes of crustaceans and seaweed. Her only purpose was to accept abuse and destruction from those who had borne her. Until the tides take the hull apart and commit her to the seafloor forever. Some sailors back home said they could hear the bomb explosions from this place if the sounds caught the winds right and carried them over to Amity. With the fog, she was no longer a mere target ship, but a ghost ship. A dead relic of the past. Underway in an eternal oceanic purgatory. Never to return to port.

I stood at the Orca's pulpit and held the metal device out over the water. Just a simple release of the fingers. I could save him right now.

The old target ship's red and orange rusted plating lorded over me. I looked at the destruction and heard the voices of the men who served aboard this ship. All the living and dying that took place within this hull. We are all target ships in the end. Useful and young, until life sets you aside, where you are to wither away from the abuse and neglect. The ghosts aboard this ship were watching me. The Orca watched me. Who am I to play God and decide what fate the ocean will have over the captain? My hand shook, and I couldn't do it. I am a coward—too scared to tempt them. What were they? Spirits, angels, ghosts? What was I so frightened of? I'll never know.

Overwhelmed by it all, I pulled the metallic contraption back into my chest and retreated from the Orca's bow. Still asleep below, I put it back, so he never knew. I never mentioned this moment to anyone in my life until now.

42   DROUGHT

"You are a stupid man, Mr. Quint. I had high hopes for you."

I hadn't seen him around in a great while. Until now, we were dealing with the emaciated neck-tied lackey to bring the payment for the sharks. It didn't take long. Only a few days back in port, and there he was. Larry Vaughn pulled up to the fishing shack in the shiny red Dodge. Every time I saw Larry Vaughn, the car he drove only got bigger and fancier—the same with his bravado. Some gray hair now, but tanned and fresh looking. He stormed down the dock towards Mr. Quint, who stood inside the aft deck of the Orca.

"That's one hell of a stunt you pulled in Boston."

Mr. Quint waited for this moment. He never liked Vaughn, never trusted Vaughn, and never respected Vaughn. To get the last laugh made it all worthwhile.

"Mr. Mayor, that sure is a fancy car you got there. What brings you this far up-island?"

The captain stepped over to the dock to meet the frustrated politician head-on. Vaughn got close and saw the bruised and cut face of Mr. Quint. Calculated and tactful, he looked around. Other fishermen in the nearby shacks were watching and listening. He lowered his voice.

"Let's cut to the chase, Mr. Quint. You knew what you were doing. You must be allergic to money. Because you lost it all."

"You knew the whaling was bringing the sharks here. You let them process the hides on the north side of the island. Out of sight from the shipping authorities. You brought me in to get a handle on the large sharks while you kept it all going."

I leaned in to listen from my vantage point on the bow of the Orca. Vaughn didn't know I was there when he continued the back and forth.

"Whaling has been going on in these waters for a hundred years. What's a few more?"

"And the people? You have blood on your hands when one goes missing."

"You sure are on a high horse. I understand that. I know what happened to you in the war. Some of us don't need a tattoo on our forearm to prove we know what these fish can do. You aren't the only one who's known someone killed by one. Just call them missing and move along. I'm turning this place around. Building a new world for these people. If a few fishermen have to go missing, or befall an accident out there, then so be it."

Larry Vaughn stood back and gathered himself. Running his fingers through his hair, he straightened the flashy royal-blue suit jacket over his shoulders and fastened the top button.

"Won't happen now. I invested in you years ago. Got the best fisherman for the job and he took care of it," said Vaughn while looking over at the Orca. "Kill them all. You sure as hell did. Cleared these waters right up and just in time."

"Just in time, huh?" Mr. Quint's eyes searched the politician.

"That's right. The ferry terminal just finished on the other side of town. We cut the ribbon last week and ferries start running around the clock next month. This summer the population of this island is going to triple with the tourists and summer folk. A whole new wave of paying customers looking to escape the world and enjoy our beautiful sandy beaches. It was about time to get out of the oil business. I'm going to make ten times the amount of money from all the realty rentals and sales over the next decade."

"Not if I don't call the newspapers. Let them into my shack to see the jaws. There are still sharks swimming out there."

The aging politician laughed. His glorious grin of white teeth flashed.

"What do you have inside there, huh? A couple of sets of teeth any tourist in Cabo San Lucas could pick up at a Five-and-Dime. You have any proof there are sharks off Amity? Any photos? Anyone who's not a drunk ready to vouch for you?"

There was a pause and Larry Vaughn knew he had Mr. Quint dead to rights.

"See here, Mr. Quint. I'm about to be elected mayor of this island. People around here seem to think I'm a swell guy. I take pictures with their babies. Hand lollipops out in the town parade. Cut ribbons with scissors. But you. In you they see a disgruntled, beaten down, washed-up has-been who is nothing but a failure."

Vaughn smiled and waved to a couple of fishermen. They started their engine to move on down the harbor.

"Your one success—the eradication of the mythical fish population of Amity Island will always be just that—a myth. A tall tale. A drunk fisherman with his arms out wide, trying to convince anyone who will listen that the catch was *this big*. We, the board of selectmen for the town of Amity, thank you kindly for your service."

"The Goliath. Nye Lubricants? The oil? Reporters will have a field day with that story," said Mr. Quint.

"All handled in cash. Hammond and I go way back. We didn't get to where we are by letting the town drunk scoop us on a story. As always, I'm afraid you lost on this one. Again."

Vaughn winked his checkmate grin at my captain and turned to walk away.

"This will never be your island, Mr. Quint. This is my island, and I allowed you to be here. Never forget that."

The captain just stood and watched the future mayor light a cigarette and walk to his car. Larry Vaughn was correct. This was his island.

The summer of 1966 it began. The longest drought Mr. Quint had ever seen. We never caught a single shark off Amity Island. Vaughn was right. My captain was the best. He did the job Vaughn hired him to do, and he did it well. Too well. He hunted and killed them all. Cut off their food supply and made them disappear. For the last fifteen years, he honed his craft and worked the sharks with a ferocious, unyielding vengeance. Much of the island's new generation of children grew up here, never knowing what a shark was.

Ferries brought them to the island in droves—tourists. They placed Amity Island on the ferry schedules out of Cape Cod and mainland USA. We became the third stop on the line. An official summer destination island after Nantucket and Martha's Vineyard. Because of this, 1966 and 1967 brought the greatest changes to Amity the island would ever see.

I never witnessed so many cars on the island. New cars meant more roads. Paved roads and parking lots blotted out the natural dunes and forested areas of the island. I watched landmarks I played on as a child become extinct overnight. A gavel from the board of selectmen followed by a bulldozer and my island became unrecognizable in parts.

As long as they stayed away from Amity Point, I didn't care. I was powerless through it all.

Larry Vaughn won his first election as mayor of Amity in the fall of 1966. Over ninety percent of the vote was his, after they tallied it all in the Amity town hall. He became a local hero. The man who brought electricity to the island. The man who started it all. Spending his own family money to invest in the island he grew up on. The newspapers ran stories of Mayor Vaughn from Amity Island to California. I even heard whispers of a future as Senator Vaughn—if the war in Vietnam would simmer down first.

I never saw him in Amity Point again. He stayed down-island in town and had a big house on the eastern shore, overlooking one of those high-end white sand beaches. Mayor Vaughn ruled with a free rein. The other selectmen passed every decision he made.

The five selectmen all established businesses around the island and made out like bandits. One had hotels. Another had a bicycle rental business, which later turned into car sales. The monopoly of grocery stores and gas stations was owned by another. Vaughn had the property and landholdings. The last guy had the waterfront docks and shipping contracts. All of them became millionaires. They owed it all to Vaughn and would do whatever he asked. They were the law.

The police from Nantucket sent over summer deputies to keep an office in town. The Amity police department was a part-time hustle. Two police cars and a phone. Nobody came here for trouble, so it was the duty a monkey could do. Just sit in an office and answer complaints about cars double parked and kids lighting bonfires on the beach.

The island changed. They pushed the local town fishermen to the side after overcrowding Amity harbor. Many of them migrated out west to Amity Point, and our little harbor packed them in like sardines. But they didn't complain. The fishermen made more money than ever before. With the whispers of the 'nutty captain' having killed them all off, the older boats got brave and ventured into deeper waters. They invested in larger nets and cast them out all along the coasts. The size and quality of the catch off Amity became all anyone talked about.

Everyone seemed to make money. Except Mr. Quint and I. We lost it all.

With the repeated assault of tourist tidal waves hitting the island, the prices of everything spiked. Paint, liquor, fuel, blood and guts for the chum lines—all doubled in price. Fixing a leaking hull, or a busted bearing, no longer accomplished by trade or a good deal—you had to come with the cash. We ran out of it right quick. Everyone on the island found profits off Mr. Quint's work, except the man himself.

My captain became the ultimate outcast. A recluse—symbolic of the old ways. A living representation of the despair that Mayor Vaughn pulled everyone out of. When the real islanders in town saw my captain and me walking down the street, we reminded them of when they had nothing. For that, they gave us no quarter. I found myself an outsider in the only place I ever called home.

After a second summer and nary a shark seen in the waters, Mr. Quint threw all he had back into the Orca. We resorted to fishing for big game far offshore. A few marlin on the lines helped pay the bills, but nothing steady. Too much competition now with the new fishing boats arriving to the island. More restaurants opening meant higher prices paying out for the fish. Some even moved their operations from Nantucket to Amity to haul in the profits—an unheard-of move ten-years prior.

The Orca showed signs of her age. Locals fished closer to shore, increasing the demand to go farther out and for longer times. The hull leaked. The engine tired. She needed to be dry-docked and overhauled. Mr. Quint insisted we do it ourselves. We pulled the Orca out of the water during the late summer of 1967 to scrape and sand her down. Fixed her hull and repainted every inch of planking. An engine overhaul devoured great gulps of cash. I remember watching the tourists walk by while we were working. Some had never seen a boat before. They never knew this island existed five years earlier. Amity became the flavor-of-the-month vacation spot for what seemed like the entire country.

Like my captain, it also filled me with resentment. I didn't want to hate, but I sat my mornings on the deck of my little shack on the hill with dark thoughts. I watched the harbor below, packed to the hilt with new boats full of young, strong fishermen. The Papov's now had three boats. One for each of them.

This wasn't the way it was supposed to be. Everyone was supposed to be hailing us as heroes. My captain was the only one brave enough to face the monsters that lurked the dark waters, and I was his first mate. We did something none of these boats had the guts to do. Nobody noticed us. We were dead to them all.

Until the summer of 1968. It all changed.

43 CHARTER

September brought about the last month of a lingering tourist season on Amity. A third summer of misfortune extended our economic downturn while everyone around us prospered. I had to convince him to change our business plan. The marlin season was hit-and-miss, leaving us with just enough to cover the cost of fuel.

"Get that thing off my boat, boy."

"Mr. Quint, now hear me out. I've been asking around. There's easy money to be made. We just gotta follow the rules."

He didn't want to admit it, but I was right. We watched most of the boats around us give up the daily hassle of a fishing routine during the summer months. They switched to charters—renting out their boats to tourists willing to pay an inflated buck for the experience of fishing on the high seas. Everyone up-island was doing it and making more money than they would for an entire year fishing with their nets or lobster traps. Three months of charters was enough to keep you alive for the rest of the year, with some to spare.

It took us to the last gasp of summer, right on autumn's doorstep in 1968, to realize it. I was the first to break and went asking around. The rules stated a boat needed a registration number with the Coast Guard for a charter license. That was easy. I added the vinyl decals **MS 15 LF** to the Orca's bow and made it official. Mr. Quint didn't have a problem with that.

He also didn't care for, but agreed to, the stack of life jackets I stowed below in the berthing compartment. He hated life jackets. I was never sure why the anger and resentment towards them. Something happened during the war involving life jackets. He didn't talk to me about it, and I never asked. A man's darkest thoughts are his business.

The Coast Guard regulations said we needed enough life jackets onboard as we would have crew. I went out and found six. The captain didn't object as long as they got stowed somewhere where he didn't have to look at them.

Next was advertising. I took a brush and white paint to the black Chevy pickup. On the door, in my best lettering, I painted: **QUINT**

Across the utility boxes along the side: **BOAT FOR CHARTER**

Of course, I added a little drama to pull in the tourists. A painted outline of a giant shark across the black steel door. Mr. Quint saw my handwork and said I was missing a gill. Sharks have five, not four. A quick correction and we had our advertising.

The last piece to the puzzle was the one Mr. Quint resisted the most. He hated it from the first time I stepped on board carrying it.

"I don't care about the rules. I don't want one onboard."

"Without one, we can't get underway as a charter boat, Captain. We are down to the last tank of fuel. It's gotta be done. Mr. McQuitty, let me take it for free," I said when I handed over the small electronic CB marine radio. "And this needs to get installed somewhere up there."

Mr. Quint took the whip antenna from me and looked up at the mast.

"This is only for show. If we get into trouble out there, there will be no call for help. No distress signals of any kind. Got it?"

"Yes, sir," I said with a smile.

"Put it in the pilothouse off to the side. I'll install it when I have time."

"You better get to it soon. We have a charter scheduled at twelve."

"At noon?"

Mr. Quint hated the thought of tourists on his boat. The idea disgusted him. He spit at the mere mention of them on his lips. The realization that the world changed, and money had to be earned this way made him reach for the bottle of apricot brandy—his last one.

"How many?"

"Three of them. Look like college kids from New York City. They stopped me at the pier this morning and asked about the sign on the truck. We just take them out to the deep water, grab some bluefish, and come back. Three hours and we are sixty bucks richer. That's all there is to it."

Mr. Quint took a swig from his little tin cup of brandy.

The shiny white AMC Rambler station wagon drove past the fishing shack and skidded to a stop. It reversed back to where the passengers inside saw the Orca at the end of the dock. They arrived thirty minutes late and bailed out of the wagon with the fanciest clothes I've ever seen for a fishing expedition.

Their corduroy trousers and white canvas sports shoes seemed as alien to the docks of Amity Point as their combed back hair and turtle necked sweaters. The beautiful seventy-eight-degree September afternoon didn't mean it was warm out on the ocean. The three men laughed and jumped with excitement. They brought a young college girl in a fancy striped dress and knee-high white leather boots. All four stumbled down the dock and pointed all around towards the different boats. I stepped up from the Orca and met them.

"I thought there were only three in your party?"

"Well, yes, originally, but we met Judy here at lunch…"

"It's Jill." The girl tapped his shoulder.

"Yes, Jill. Jill said she had never been, and we should show her what she's missing. I'll throw in an extra forty to cover her," said Bobby while pushing his red feathered hair out from his eyes.

I nodded my approval.

"Great! George and Henry here, you already met this morning. Jill, this is the captain of our boat here." Bobby leaned over to read the lettering across the stern. "The, uh, Orca."

"No, no, I'm just Hershel. The first mate. The captain is up there."

I pointed up to the mast. All four youngsters looked up at the blue sky and the man watching them from above. They said nothing and looked back at me.

"Is he going to stay up there the whole time?" asked Jill.

"He's just making some adjustments to the new radio antenna before the trip. He'll be down soon. Come aboard and let's get all your bags stowed below." I grabbed the few expensive leather duffels they set at their feet.

These people had no business being on the water. I knew it. The captain knew it. But a hundred bucks is a hundred bucks. Bobby handed me two fifty-dollar bills, and the kids started climbing all over the Orca. Henry climbed up to the flying bridge and yelled for everyone to get around the fighting chair so he could take a picture.

Mr. Quint watched the group in all their naivety and took his time climbing down. I started the engine to the Orca, and she let out a loud rumble with a cough of black exhaust. George yelled from the bow.

"Hey, guys. You gotta come see this!"

The kids all laughed and shimmied around the wheelhouse to the rack of yellow barrels. They each took turns walking to the end of the pulpit for a photo. Never saw anything like it. They smiled about nothing special. Just happy to be alive. Was this what I missed from the mainland? And the photos. I never saw someone snap away at one of those new cameras so many times. What was he going to do with all those photos? They were fish out of water on the Orca but proud of it.

Mr. Quint climbed down from the mast and then back in the wheelhouse. He checked the gauges on the Orca and tossed back another two drinks of brandy. This was torture for him. He seemed to be unimpressed with the antics but kept his cool. If he didn't have to talk to any of them, he'd survive.

I untied the mooring lines, and we shoved off from the dock. The kids stayed on the bow while we taxied out of the harbor. More photos. The camera never stopped clicking. This was to be the longest three hours of our lives.

The Orca cruised ahead at trolling speed about one mile south of Amity. We went out just far enough to the open ocean where the bluefish ran. Striped bass bit too. I rigged the transom with a rack to hold multiple fishing rods and we had five baits cast off the stern. Three rods on port, and two on starboard. The kids sat on the gunwales and transom, talking about everything but fishing. Music, movies, life in New York City—nothing of importance. I never heard so many words spoken with nothing said.

Mr. Quint stayed inside. Steering the boat and drinking more brandy was his way of running a charter.

When a rod bent over, the kids rushed to grab it, then act like they were hauling in a whale. They reeled in the bluefish and laughed. More photographs followed. My job was to step into the fray and take their catch to put in a plastic box of ice. Rig another bait and set it out for them to try again.

"First-Mate Hershel?"

"Yeah, Bobby?"

"Can I try this groovy chair? It says Rockaway on it. Like Rockaway beach back in New York."

"Hey, didn't we see the Beach Boys there? Or was it Jan and Dean?" asked Henry.

"You guys seen just about everyone. So unfair," said Jill.

I stepped in and looked around.

"Well, this chair is important to the captain and…"

"C'mon, it will be a great photo. My dad would love to see this stuff. Here's an extra ten bucks."

How could I argue? I gave him the nod. We baited up another rod, cast it off the stern, and set it into the holder under the chair's armrest. Bobby sat down and unzipped his leather jacket.

"Henry, take a photo of this. I'm going to do my Steve McQueen stare."

I shook my head and stepped back inside the wheelhouse.

"Captain, I can't adjust the arm rests for one kid on the fighting chair. He's short like me. The back has to come up some for him."

Mr. Quint groaned and pulled the throttle control back, then clicked the engine into neutral. He stepped out from the cabin with his green military jacket and canvas fishing hat pulled down to his ears. The kids didn't know what to make of him. They all fell silent as he stepped over to the chair and pushed, then pulled the metal latch to adjust the back for Bobby.

"Thanks, Cap. This is just like our boats back home," said Bobby, with a wink at his friends.

Mr. Quint turned back around.

"You done much boating before?"

"Yes, I had two first-place finishes on the yachting team back in school. I spent some time on the water."

I listened to the exchange through the open cabin door and worried the captain would lose control.

"Captain Quint, what are those yellow barrels for on the bow? The ones in the rack?"

"Don't bother him with ridiculous questions, George. It's extra fuel for the long days at sea," said Bobby, then looking up to the captain for approval.

Mr. Quint just glared at them all and walked back inside the wheelhouse.

Jill stepped forward. "Gosh, he sure is creepy. What's his deal?"

Bobby's pole twitched and then bent forward.

"Oh, I got a bite! First-Mate Hershel, I gotta big one here!"

The young man grabbed the pole and shoved its handle into the mount in the center of the chair. He placed his feet up on the footrest of the fighting chair and pulled the rod back as it fed out the line. The lightweight pole twitched and then stopped. The other kids cheered.

"C'mon, Bobby. Reel that whopper in!"

"Get your camera, Henry. You getting this?"

"I got one more shot!"

"Well, make it count. I'm gonna land a tuna."

I stood behind the chair and watched Bobby crank on the fish. The pole was bent over some, but not too bad. The kids all laughed and hollered at the anticipation.

Jill and George leaned on the transom to look over the edge.

"We don't see anything yet, Bobby. Keep cranking!" said George with a smile. "Henry, give me the camera. I'm going to take a photo of the fish on the surface."

Jill squealed with delight.

The line snapped taught, and the rod bent over, almost to a full arc.

George aimed the camera and pressed the trigger. The shutter snapped.

"Hey, I got it!"

The monstrous head of the great white broke through the surface and lurched for the Orca's transom. Jill and George screamed, losing their footing and falling backwards into the aft deck. I never saw a head that big in all the hunting I'd done with the captain. I stood speechless. Bobby let go of the rod, and it took off from his hands. The great white shark bit down hard on the large striped bass in its mouth and slammed back into the water. The rod and line snapped over the side of the boat, following the great fish into the deep.

Mr. Quint heard the screams and pushed open the cabin door.

The five other rods in the bracket along the transom bent. One after the other, they snapped.

"What the hell was that?" asked Bobby.

"Did you see those teeth?" asked Henry.

"I want to go home!" said Jill, laying on the deck with a bloody knee.

The rods shook and flew out of their holders. The shark raged against the hull of the boat and the bait lines that followed it.

"Hershel, get the line to the first keg and bring it aft. Quick, boy!"

Mr. Quint lunged for the pole spear rigged to the side of the wheelhouse.

Clutching it hard, he leapt up onto the transom and jabbed at the massive fish just below the surface.

"Captain, what's going on? Is this part of the charter?"

"Shut your mouth, Bobby, or George, or whatever one you are. The charter is over." Mr. Quint yelled while plunging the spear into the water. "Sit down and stay out of the way. All of you!"

I shuffled back from the bow with the barrel line in my hand. Mr. Quint jabbed at the shark, which rolled itself in a tangled mess of fishing line and broken rods. Its gigantic crescent tail swung wide. A wave of water dumped into the aft deck, soaking all the charter guests. The girl screamed from the shocking cold saltwater bath.

"My hair!"

"This coat is suede, dammit!" Bobby slammed his fists down and tried to scramble to his feet on the slippery deck.

George and Henry just watched the captain stand above the shark, sending the tip of the spear down into the water, trying to find a target.

The thrashing shark rolled under the boat and hit the hull with a loud punch. The kids flinched at the noise.

Mr. Quint jumped off the transom. A few massive strides and he disappeared into the wheelhouse. The boat shifted in the water. The shark hit the hull again. Another splash of water broke across the starboard side and drenched us all. The giant fin of the shark cut the water with razor blade precision. It circled back and headed towards the Orca.

I looked down at the kids.

"Hold on to something. All of you. Hold on!"

The shark breached along the port side. Its pointed snout ramming and feeling for anything it could bite down on. The kids shouted and crawled to the other side of the aft deck.

Mr. Quint barreled out of the cabin with his harpoon rifle loaded. He tossed me the clip on the end of the steel leader line and shoved a clean harpoon over the barrel. In one fluid motion, he cleared his body of the excess leader wire, moved over to the port side and drew down on the great white. My fingers flipped the rope and tied a bowline on the end of the barrel line. I set the clip.

The shark turned and slapped the water, baring the triangular dorsal fin and its back to Mr. Quint.

The rifle fired, and the kids covered their ears at the noise.

Blood exploded on the surface of the water when the harpoon buried itself into the great white shark. It pumped its massive tail and kicked water over the side one last time. The great fish converted the aft deck into a sloshing sea of blue fish, ice, rotten bait, and soaking terrified twenty-year olds.

The shark ran out and the yellow barrel launched from the rack on the bow. The keg took to the air, then fired across the surface of the water. In all the yellow barrels my captain buried into sharks, this was the fastest I ever seen one fly across the ocean's surface.

The captain climbed the ladder and charged to the upper controls of the Orca. He cranked the wheel hard to port and laid into the throttle. The boat screamed and dug into the water. The hull tilted far to port on the spinning maneuver the captain put us in. I held onto the fighting chair and watched the water, ice, fish, and kids all slide across the aft deck. Two of the boys went head over heels and bashed into the inner frames of the port side gunwale. Jill screamed once more. She had the screaming part down and reminded me of the radio monster shows we sometimes picked-up from the mainland when the weather was clear.

The captain jumped on the same track as the yellow barrel. The shark picked up speed. He had the throttle down full and closed the distance. I could see him shouting at the ocean winds that flew through his hair. My captain's lust for revenge had awakened.

The great fish dove deep. It pulled the barrel just below the surface waves. With the bow of the Orca only a few feet out of reach, the yellow shape vanished under the churning water. The strength of this great white was unlike anything we had ever seen.

Mr. Quint dropped the throttle down and looked all around.

He lost the barrel.

Bobby found his footing and held his shaking hands on the ladder leading up to the flying bridge.

"Captain Quint. Take us back in right now. This was not the charter we had in mind."

"Go down below and take a nap, Bobby. We are staying out here until we find that barrel."

I remembered the fuel gauge from earlier. We had nothing to spare.

"Captain, we don't have the diesel to stay out. We gotta go in," I said.

Mr. Quint looked down and realized I was right. The Orca would soon be on fumes and the great white headed out to deep water. After a few moments of scanning the horizon, he turned the wheel towards Amity and pushed the throttle down.

44   CAPTAIN McVAY

I didn't even have time to finish tying off the stern line to the cleat, and our charter guests already had one foot on the dock. One of them leapt from the Orca and promised never to go on a boat again.

Mr. Quint looked down from the flying bridge to watch the commotion.

"My father knows a few selectmen back in town, Mr. Quint. I can assure you, he'll be hearing about all of this," said Bobby, while gathering up his leather duffel bag.

The captain nodded his head in a dismissive gesture.

"Yeah."

Bobby was the last to step off the Orca. Dried streaks of salt marbled his leather jacket. His clothes, doused and ruined from the ocean.

"You know what? You're certifiable, Quint. Do you know that? You're certifiable."

"Yeah. Yeah."

Mr. Quint waved the boy off with his hand and turned back to the controls of the Orca. In a squeak of soggy shoes, Bobby turned and stormed up the dock to follow the others. The doors of their AMC slammed, and the car spit sand with an aggressive turn.

"That was unexpected, sir."

"Aye. That was the biggest porker I ever seen. He's got our barrel now. I shot him in the back, missed the head. He's strong enough to pull one down. We go find him and bury a second harpoon in his head. No way he stays down."

"We made one-hundred and ten dollars, Captain."

"Lost seventy-five in fishing rods and tackle. Doesn't matter. We land that shark and bring him back in one piece—the mayor is finished. No tourist will want to set a toe in these waters if they see the monsters that swim out here."

"Maybe we'll get our island back?"

"We might, Mr. Salvatore. We just might."

Three hours passed, and the sun began its fall into the horizon. The captain and I squared away the aft deck and rigged the ship for getting underway.

"Respectfully request permission to come aboard, Captain?"

Mr. Quint turned to see a single man looking down at him. From inside the cabin, I crouched to look out the window and see who was talking. My first thought was that someone wanted to charter the boat. An older man, dressed in a tan summer sports coat. I remembered his chiseled jaw outlined from the sun sneaking under a dark brown straw fedora hat.

"Captain McVay?"

For the first time since I had known him, Mr. Quint's demeanor changed. He squared himself up and seemed unsure in how to react to the man on the dock.

"I'm gonna have to salute you first, sir," said Mr. Quint. "Let me give you a hand. This low tide makes for a bit of a drop."

Captain McVay steadied himself with one hand on the dock's pylon, and stepped down to the transom, and another step down into the Orca and met Mr. Quint with a salute and a solid handshake.

"Just turned seventy in July, Mr. Quint. I still can manage."

"I sure see that, sir. This is the surprise of my year. You looking to charter a boat? Here on vacation?"

"Oh, no. I wanted to pay you a visit, is all. It's been quite a few years."

McVay appeared refined in the way he talked and moved—an elder statesman. I could tell that from inside the Orca. Already, I knew this was an important meeting. I stepped down below and kept out of sight.

"It's not a simple task to find you, Mr. Quint."

"To be honest, Captain, I didn't think anyone would find me here."

"Even in retirement, I still have my sources."

McVay nodded and looked around the Orca.

"How about some coffee, sir? I have a stove in the cabin."

"Coffee will be fine right about now."

Something was off about the older man that boarded the Orca. The pleasantries he spoke didn't match his gaze. This man stood troubled, with eyes that hadn't caught sleep in years. He focused on the smallest details of the Orca and touched everything.

Mr. Quint stepped inside the wheelhouse and lit the portable stove, then shook some coffee beans out of the metal storage can into a hand grinder. He looked as if he wanted to say something more but stopped himself. McVay stepped next to the fighting chair. He brushed his hand across the teak back rest, pausing his fingers on a series of scars and chips in the wood. Some quick spins on the grinder, and the filled coffee percolator set over the flame.

"Come on in and have a seat, sir."

"If you don't mind, I'd like to have a climb up to your flying bridge, Captain? This is an intense operation you have here. I'm impressed."

Mr. Quint nodded and smiled.

The old man climbed the ladder to have a look around.

I climbed up a step from below and kept my voice low.

"Mr. Quint. Who is that guy?"

"Captain Charles McVay. The captain of the Indianapolis when we sunk. I thought he was a ghost when I turned around. He's been through a lot. We all were, but not like him."

"What does he want?"

"To have a word."

I nodded and went back down below.

About five minutes later, the old captain climbed down the ladder with steady hands and stepped into the wheelhouse. Mr. Quint set down two cups on the table and poured some coffee.

"This might not be as good as the coffee onboard the Indy, sir."

"It'll do, Mr. Quint. It will taste gourmet. Everything does these days when you reach my age."

McVay took a sip and sat back in the Orca's booth under the aft window. Mr. Quint moved around to the other side of the table and sat facing his captain.

"That's great coffee. I want to appreciate the finer details. The things we take for granted. Like this cup of coffee. The beans roasted, you ground them by hand... the fire that boiled the water. These minor parts of life that make it so... special."

McVay looked down at the marks on the Orca's wooden cabin table.

"This is a beautiful grain pattern here."

Mr. Quint sipped his coffee. He searched the old man for clues about how he should engage in the conversation.

"Eight years ago, I saw many of the survivors back in Indianapolis. The reunion in 1960. They surprised me with the invitation. I looked for you, Mr. Quint."

"What surprised you, sir? You did nothing wrong. If we all disappeared on June 29th, 1945, they wouldn't have bothered to write so much as a letter of inquiry."

"July 29th," said McVay with a smile.

"It was July, wasn't it?" Mr. Quint smiled at the memory lapse. "We all told the Navy to shove it for what they put you through. Every man on that ship would sail with you again."

"The deceased might beg to differ."

"No, they wouldn't. We were at war. We all knew the risks."

"I appreciate your sentiments, Mr. Quint." McVay took another sip of coffee and gave a weary smile. "I looked for you at the reunion for two reasons. The reasons I'm here now. I wanted to say thank you for your service to me and the Navy. I remember what you did at your battle station off Okinawa on that morning. The kamikaze. He would've killed me and many others on the bridge had you not reacted the way you did. I planned on putting you in for a medal and with all that happened, I never did. I'm sorry."

Mr. Quint shook his head. "Sir, there's no need to—"

"Yes, there is, Mr. Quint. Yes, there is. I want to set some things right. I've searched for most of the survivors. The ones who were not at the reunion, I'm trying to find on my own. Louise, my wife, died seven years ago. Cancer. I should've done this then. I procrastinate on the little things in life. That's my sin. Just so much to do and never enough time. I remarried. Vivian... she has a farm in Litchfield, Connecticut. I moved there, and it took a few years to get to this point. A point where I told myself to do it. Go find them and tell them. The survivors and the families of those who died."

Below in the forward berthing compartment of the Orca, I held my breath and listened.

"Tell us what, Captain?"

"I am sorry for letting you all down as captain of the USS Indianapolis."

"Captain, you had no control over that Japanese submarine. Those torpedoes."

"No, not that. You are correct. The trial showed they'd hit us no matter what maneuvers the ship ran. Yes, a tragedy I had no control over. I insisted on the destroyer's escort. I did. Regardless, I was the captain, and I was derelict in my duty, and I need to apologize."

"Apologize for what, sir? What duty did you have when the Navy sent us out there alone, on secret orders?"

"For not going down with the ship. I want my entire crew to know that I am truly sorry."

The words caught Mr. Quint off guard. His hand shook like he wanted to get a drink of something—anything but the coffee in front of him.

"You have any nightmares, Mr. Quint? Do you dream about them? The sharks? Our crew's screams and splashing? The dead bodies floating all around?"

Mr. Quint nodded his head. "Yeah, Captain. I sure do."

McVay continued. "Lately, the dreams have narrowed down some. It's been me in the raft. The men I'm with look at me with black eyes. They won't talk. The sharks are circling. Waiting for me to fall in. I wake up screaming in a sweat. Vivian can't stand it and tells me to sleep in another room. I don't blame her. The dreams never stop. Never."

Mr. Quint took another sip of coffee to clear his voice.

"Yes, sir. They changed for me over the years. I can't tell if I'm dreaming or awake. It's all the same. I see them when I stare down into the water. Their faces… when they look at you and realize it's their time to go. I remember waiting for my turn and thinking about who I will look at when I go. What will be the last thing I see as I leave this planet? In my dreams, it's the mouth of a shark—the last thing I see."

They both sat in silence. McVay took a long sip of coffee from the ceramic mug.

"This is the best coffee I had in ages, Mr. Quint."

The older captain searched through his pockets. He pulled out his car keys and set them on the table. Next, he removed a small, folded stack of papers wrapped with string from his jacket pocket. His solemn fingers untied the string and searched through the letters. Slipping on a small pair of reading glasses, he looked one letter over.

"This is from a couple out west. It's a letter from a Christmas card they sent me. *Dear Captain McVay, I hope you are enjoying the Christmas season. Our son, James, would be forty-two years old this year had you not failed to do your job and bring him back alive. When you play with your grandchildren around the Christmas tree, think of the grandchildren we do not have because of your negligence. James would have been a great father.'* They send one like this every year."

"They're wrong," said Mr. Quint.

"No, they're not. Maybe one or two, but I get a hundred just like them every year. Louise used to hide them from me when they first starting coming in. I didn't know how many there were until she died. Then I saw the full load. And that was fifteen years after the sinking. It's been twenty-three and they still come in—especially around the holidays."

"They got lied to, Captain. The Navy had no business with the court martial."

"I got what I deserved because I failed in my duty. It was difficult at first, but I understand that now. I've responded to every one of these letters—you should see the stacks of them back at the farmhouse. The phone calls. It's the phone calls that hit the hardest. I made a promise to myself that I would answer every one and never hang up first. They deserve it, for what they gave... who they lost."

The troubled captain fiddled with his keys. He thumbed a figurine attached to the ring.

"Every Thanksgiving, give or take a day, one of the regular calls. A grieving widow calls me. She asks my name and introduces herself. Her husband was an officer under my charge. She introduces herself and just cries. When she first called me, she was holding a crying baby. I sat on the phone and listened to them both cry. Every year the same call. The baby must be twenty-three now. The widow still calls. Sometimes, it's a few minutes. Other years, it's half an hour. I just sit and listen. She can't get the words out. The grief is too much. Every year, the call ends the same. She gathers herself, and whispers, 'I hate you'... then the line goes dead. Every November, I think of the first phone call she made... baby crying on the other end. A baby crying for a father who'll never come home, and I was responsible. November makes me cold inside... because I know the calls are coming."

McVay held up the little metal figure on his key chain. The shivers raced down my spine when I saw it from my vantage point below deck. The metal figurine of a sailor, dressed in white. I buried the same one in the sand at the cove.

"The night when we got hit. I pulled my clothes on and looked at my desk. Of all the things to take, I grabbed this and shoved it in my pocket. A toy from my father, the Admiral McVay, given to me when I was a boy. It stayed with me throughout the academy, the war, the sinking and the rescue, the trial, and it's here right now on your vessel. I saved this little piece of metal but couldn't save eight-hundred seventy-nine souls and a forty-million dollar ship."

McVay set the tiny sailor on the table. He looked at the chipped paint of the toy sailor's cast iron face and continued to speak.

"Please understand, I meant to go down with the ship. That night. The Indianapolis rolled to starboard, completely on her side. I pulled myself along the decks, trying to reach the radiomen, while ordering anyone I saw to get their life jackets and abandon ship. I made it as far as the number three turret on the afterdeck and the ocean... the surge ripped me away. Twelve minutes. All happened so fast. Sound asleep and twelve minutes later, I'm in the water and staring up at my ship—the stern pointing at the moon. The port screws chopping away at the air... coming towards me. The screams of the men jumping into them. Their bodies are tossed like rag dolls. Please believe me, Mr. Quint. I wanted to go down with her... I did. I was supposed to die. The ship was falling on me. I closed my eyes and waited for it. If not the impact, then the suction of the hull, pull me under and drown me. I closed my eyes and... nothing. The hot oil burning my neck. Another wave of water and she was gone. She left me alive."

Mr. Quint leaned over the table. "Many of us jumped from port, Captain. Our training told us to go from the high side during a sinking. So, the ship doesn't roll on top of you. All we found there was burning oil and bodies. The rafts and most of the floater nets went down with the ship or went off the starboard side. We had nothing, sir."

"The ocean mocks us all, Mr. Quint. Twisting our fate. That night, I prayed and expected to meet God. All that I found was not one, but two life rafts— one atop of the other. And a crate of potatoes. They just rose from the water right next to me. Then the voices. The other men shouting in the blackness. Calling for help. I reacted as any captain would and wanted to save the men. Quartermaster Allard heard my voice, and we used the rafts to collect anyone we found floating. I was the one who wanted to die, and I had enough space for twenty men to get out of the water, while you and the Doctor Haynes group had six-hundred-fifty and not even enough lifejackets—only a few hundred yards away in the darkness of it all. The ocean and its mockery."

McVay broke a soft smile from his weary and troubled face. He picked up the little sailor toy and examined it.

"This was supposed to bring me good luck. My father said it would. I meant to pass it on to my five-year-old grandson when he got older. Three years ago, he died of a brain hemorrhage. That little guy meant everything to me. This was supposed to bring me good luck."

McVay smiled at a few memories but kept silent. The toy sailor figure, along with his keys, disappeared into his pocket. The old captain finished his coffee and slipped out of the bench seat. He stepped to the helm of the Orca.

"This sure is a fine vessel you have here, Mr. Quint. You are a captain now. Captain Quint. That is a great responsibility."

Mr. Quint took another sip of his coffee and rose to his feet. He stood next to his former captain and looked out the windows at the harbor.

"Captain McVay, for what it's worth. We all died out there. None of us came back the same. I read the newspapers—the crew stood together and told the Navy we had complete faith in you and would sail again under your command. You weren't guilty."

"Yes, I was. Guilty of not following the code."

My captain's voice raised with his frustration at the moment. "What code? The sharks didn't care about a code. The Japanese didn't care about one and our Navy sure as hell didn't when we got back."

"It's the code you and I both take when we became captains, Mr. Quint. Some of us need to die, so that others may survive. It's not that my death would've saved lives—my death eliminates the blame. The sea swallows a ship, her captain, and the crew—humanity shrugs its shoulders and moves on. Been that way for a thousand years. The captain goes down with the ship. That is how it's supposed to be for men like us. Captains don't die for our ego. We die for the families who trust us with their sons and husbands. That part of the story is missing here. It's why they write these letters and make the phone calls. I don't blame them, it's not their fault. They can't heal because I broke the code. We die with our ships. It is the only way. And twenty-three years of condolences and handwritten letters to the orphans, the widows, the grieving parents—it all doesn't matter when its words from the man who should be resting with their loved ones at the bottom of the ocean."

McVay turned and stepped outside of the cabin. Mr. Quint followed in silence.

"She sure is a fine boat, Captain Quint," said McVay as he looked over the rugged fighting chair. His voice dropped into a painful whisper. "Why didn't she pull me down with her?"

A blast of an air horn from a lobster boat leaving the harbor broke the silence of the moment. McVay stood up straight and drew a deep breath of salt sea air into his lungs. He placed his straw fedora on his head and turned to face his former gunner's mate.

"Captain Quint?"

"Yes, sir?"

"Request permission to lay ashore, sir?"

Mr. Quint smiled and held out his hand. "Permission granted on one condition."

"What is it?"

"That you come back and let me take you out fishing. It would be an honor, sir."

Captain McVay smiled, and the men shook hands.

"I'd like that. Thank you."

The seventy-year-old man stepped up onto the dock and looked around the harbor.

"Where are you off to now, sir?" asked Mr. Quint.

"I'll catch the late ferry back to the mainland. I have a few more visits to make while I'm in the area."

He placed his hand on his jacket pocket to pat the stack of hate mail letters burdening his side. The solemn man turned to walk away and paused.

"One more thing, Captain Quint."

"Yes, sir," said Mr. Quint, staring up from the aft deck of the Orca.

"That was a tremendous cup of coffee. I'll appreciate it always."

"You come back for another round. I'll be here, Captain McVay."

With a friendly nod, Captain Charles Butler McVay III turned to walk up the dock. The setting sun shone across his back.

45 BEACHED

The longer I live this life, my cemented realization in that there are no coincidences sets. I've seen too many things happen in such specific moments in time where one second earlier or later changes lives. I leave nothing in this life to chance. There's a higher purpose to it all.

There are many such examples to note from my time as first mate to a legend. If you were to ask me what the greatest example is—I'll think of this one morning. The next day, after the troubled captain paid Mr. Quint a visit on the Orca. No way in God's grand design was this by chance. This was a sign.

When I ponder it all, I see there was no turning back at this point. My captain's destiny was at hand. The machine of fate already working hard, and I became a minor cog, turning and doing my part.

I did not go to my shack on the hill that night. We prepared to get underway to look for the yellow-barreled shark that swam out there somewhere. Onboard the Orca, Mr. Quint and I removed the fighting chair and stowed it below—rigging the deck for a full-on fight with a monster. Hooks and lines were no longer logical for a shark of size and strength to take a barrel down with him. A war of attrition would soon begin. Who would give up first—my captain or the shark?

The money from our lone charter was enough to handle the fuel dilemma. Our bait of blood and cow parts had run low. I paid Mr. McQuitty a visit to clean out the rest of what we had in his deep freeze locker. He let us take space in the back to freeze anything we wanted. Aside from the fresh imported coffee he tossed our way, the space in the giant freezer proved the most valuable. In the last few years of money running low, every scrap of bait needed to be preserved.

I awoke to the small transistor radio on the table of the fishing shack. The chimes of the Cascades and their tune *Rhythm of the Falling Rain* tapped across the wooden walls. I slumped further into the hammock and wondered why I didn't light a fire. The damp air chilled my nose. The witching hour—right before the sun breaks the horizon. A moment before a fisherman's call to head down to the docks and get underway, I felt that familiar sense of dread. It had been a few years. I thought it was gone, but this morning it returned.

Out the back window, I could see the mast of the Orca reaching to the dull gray opaqueness above. The mast watched us inside the shack. It stared down at me. If I didn't move, maybe she would think I still slept. I closed my eyes and didn't want to see her in the window. Something terrible was about to happen. I felt it.

The radio announcement broke at the end of the song:

"Five AM now on Cape Cod with another brisk morning. A special bulletin. Coast Guard and local authorities are asking boaters and swimmers to proceed with caution along Nantucket's Cisco and Surfside Beaches, also South Beach on Amity Island. Unexplained beaching of pilot whales has occurred, and the area is unsafe for now. Local authorities will notify us once they re-open the areas to the public."

I sat in the hammock and looked up. Mr. Quint stood at the top of the steps and listened. The light of dawn illuminated the shark jaws along the large cross beam of wood in front of him.

Low tide carried a September fog bank across the dunes and eel grass of Amity's south shore. I walked these sands for all my life. If you do it as often as I had, you'd see the ocean will deliver gifts and treasures when you least expect them.

Before us, the fog lit white from the sun above. The Orca dropped into a slow drift. It approached the beach, and we saw them. The black bodies of dead pilot whales dotted the sands as far as my eyes could see. Hundreds swam themselves into the shallows during the night, right onto the sand and rocks of South Beach. I've heard of it happening before in other places. This was a first in my lifetime for Amity Island.

"Hershel, come with another sounding there. I'm flying blind. Need them steadier, you hear?"

"Yes, sir, right away."

I stood at the pulpit of the Orca and tossed the heavy lead weight into the misty air in front of us. I watched the wet rope uncoil from my hand and follow the weight into the water. The illuminated white fog made the sands of the beach glow. Dark-bodied blackfish stood out like ink blots on fresh paper. The Orca crept forward at a snail's pace. The rope stopped paying out when the lead weight hit the seafloor. I pulled in the slack and eyed up the colored marker on the line.

"Eight feet, Mr. Quint. By the mark, eight feet now."

"Very well. You keep on sounding. We're getting close. Don't run me aground now."

"I won't, sir. You can count on that."

At a steady pace, I pulled the line in and coiled it into my hands. The lead weight, back from the depths, dangled by my side. I looked back. Through the haunting mist, above the mounted jaws of the tiger shark, my captain stood at the flying bridge controls. We pushed in closer to shore. Not a soul in sight. Most of the commotion—the Coast Guard and townsfolk were at the other end of the beach, about six miles to the east. The Orca moved into the shallow low tide waters.

The ocean had an eerie calmness to it. South Beach sat absent from its usual wild surf and pounding waves. This morning the water issued a gentle lap against the sand. The drop-off is more gradual in this area. While in others, a few steps and half-dozen strokes will find yourself in thirty feet of water. South Beach can be tricky like that.

Another toss of the lead line.

"Seven feet now, Captain."

I looked ahead and could see them not twenty feet away. The fog broke here and there, revealing more of the beach further down the coast. The silent corpses of dead whales. Their black skin was already drying in the salty air. Still too fresh to gather sand flies. All sizes and ages. What possessed them to do this? An entire community rammed themselves to certain death—high and dry, suffocated under last night's full moon.

I took another sounding and looked at the whale closest to me. Its eye, glassed over and open. What was he thinking about while feeling the last of the water leave him—the weight of his body crushing his lungs? They are intelligent animals. There is no reason for such a suicide. What did he think about in those last moments? There could have been so many more corners and caverns of the ocean to explore in the years he had left. This noble animal had an entire life ahead of him. To end it all, so definite like this, without reason or purpose— a waste. I'm sure he had some regrets in those final breaths of pain. Wasn't there a single treasured experience in his deep-sea life he longed to partake in once more?

"Six feet. By the mark, six feet off the bow, Captain."

"Six feet, aye."

I've never seen such a loss of life at one time like this. Certainly, they all couldn't have been suicide. Most were following the one in front or to the side of them. Just doing what they had done their whole lives. There is an order to all creatures. These pilot whales were as organized and friendly a community as anyone could find and look how it all ends. Mass death in a moment of poor judgment and miscommunication.

One of them, though. There must have been one that didn't plan on exiting this life. One that saw the sands, felt the rocks rub on his belly, and heard the calls of terror from the others. The noises telling him death was only a few feet away. It was in the last moments, a decision. Turn around to face this cruel ocean on his own or go out with his family. He decided to die with the family. Nobility or madness? I could not decide.

I tossed the weighted line once more.

"Five feet! By the mark, five feet, Captain."

Mr. Quint inched the throttle back and dropped her into neutral.

The water still held the warmth from the southern currents and summer months. Chest deep in the ocean, I walked with my arms held overhead. My boots and socks left back on the Orca and stripped down to my undershirt and trousers. I didn't care. There would be an extra change of clothes in my sea bag back on the boat. This wasn't the first time I had to get wet to help my captain.

A few more steps to reach hip-deep water. The Orca sat broadside to the beach with the davit arm hanging off the port side and pointing towards me. I looked back and gave a good tug on the line Mr. Quint payed out from the aft deck twenty feet away.

"Go to that big one right in front of you and lash it around the tail."

I lost him in the foggy haze, but the outline of the Orca and the sound of her engine gave me a bearing. His voice carried across the beach.

I sloshed my way to the dead pilot whale. The massive body felt icy to the touch. The skin was a tough rubbery hide, dried and starting to wrinkle. I didn't want to look into its eye, which stayed open and stared back. A few turns around the trunk of the tail and I locked it off with a timber hitch, doubling the end of the rope back on itself. I weaved the knot and gave a good tug to make sure it held fast.

"Okay! Rope it in, Mr. Quint."

My voice wasn't as loud as his, but it did the job. I heard the squeak of the sheaves on the blocks as Mr. Quint pulled out the slack. The line went taught and the black tail of the porpoise pulled.

"Hold!"

I moved to the next blackfish corpse. Another coil of rope slung over my chest which had to be undone and rigged. He wanted two. While rigging the second one, something moved on the beach next to me. I jumped at the motion. The tiny tail slapped the sand. A little one—just a baby. It twitched and let out a weak flutter while nestled up to a larger one—maybe its mother. I froze and stared at the little whale. It watched me as my hands held the rope tying off the line to the dead porpoise I claimed. It's hard to ignore something like that. I felt it watch me and blame me for what had happened. I thought about saving it by walking it into deeper water. Would I then sentence it to an even more gruesome death by a predator, without its family's protection? Who am I to play God? If I was still asleep back at the shack, this little guy would've died looking at the fog. Instead, he looks at me as if to ask, 'Why?' My eyes fought to look away.

"Hershel! Get that blackfish rigged up, yet?"

His voice sobered me up, and I pulled the second knot tight. Two ten-foot-long pilot whales rigged and ready to be salvaged. I stepped into the water to walk towards the Orca and never looked back through the fog to the little one on the beach. Not a day in my life goes by that I don't think about it.

46   BAIT

October entered with an intensity. Not the weather. The lingering Indian summer warmth held Amity Island in a comfortable blanket. Warm water greeted the tourists still flooding in for last-minute ocean swims. Some leaves still held their green. The weather tricked the island into thinking the summer would last forever. Even the birch trees and red maples that stood watch over the harbor—not a leaf fell to the ground.

All around my feet, rivers of blood ran steady. Mr. Quint and I processed the two pilot whale cadavers right under the fishing shack. In order to keep the rot and smell down, we worked for forty-eight hours straight. The blubber and muscle filleted into large rectangular sections and then loaded into Mr. McQuitty's freeze locker for preservation.

Mr. Quint took the two carcasses and rigged them alongside the Orca to sneak them out of the harbor around midnight of the third day. He believed the large great white still lurked our waters. With one barrel weighing it down, it would have no other choice. My captain theorized this worthy adversary could not stay deep and wouldn't attempt an open-ocean run to southern waters with the yellow barrel in its back. He believed this thing returned for the taste of whale flesh—the big sharks never forget where their best meal occurred. The whale bait handed to us on the foggy low tide last month was just what he needed to find the great white.

The Orca towed the gutted and stripped blackfish bodies out to sea, dropping them south of the island. In the weeks to follow, Mr. Quint took the boat out on his own, sometimes for days at a time. The Orca became a silhouetted sentinel—a permanent fixture on the horizon off Amity Island.

During this time, I stayed at the shack while he sailed the Orca on his own. I had two jobs. The first was to get a new batch of frozen whale blubber and meat from the deep freeze. A required thawing of the blackfish, I then had to grind it into a putrid pulp. A little dash of fish entrails for some seasoning. In a few hours, another four buckets of chum were ready for my captain. Sometimes, he would come back for a shower and a shave. I'd load the buckets and the spare fuel canisters. He'd shove off and head right back out to lay another chum line down on the horizon and wait. We were a regular shark hunting pit crew. How couldn't we be after seventeen years together?

The shark became a wraith. Something that flashed for a minute and then disappeared in a crest of a wave. Other boaters came back with reports of a yellow barrel seen in the trough of the turbulent waters kicked up by a passing storm cloud. Most reports I heard were of a man standing atop a mast of a boat far out to the south and west. I knew that was my captain at the watch.

Most fishermen left and returned to port with steady hauls of bluefish, redfish, and nets full of whatever seasonal catch they could pull in. They laughed and mocked my captain while he sat out on the water, patrolling for endless hours. A race against time. A desperate search for one of his precious yellow barrels. They didn't know what he went through to find those barrels. What those barrels meant and what function they served meant nothing to these outsiders.

At McQuitty's coffee shack in the mornings, I heard other fishermen speak of Mr. Quint in jest. They didn't see me. I was around the side, feeding the seagulls with bits of leftover toast. These men didn't know that Amity even existed a few years prior. And here they were, making sport of the only man who provided the comfort and security in the waters of which they worked and earned their money.

I had enough and became confrontational, choosing to wade right into their forays of laughing and jest. If Mr. Quint could take on an entire bar of goons back in Boston, then I sure as hell could stand up for his name to a bunch of fishermen ignorant to the honor of their craft. I remember reaching up and grabbing a funny guy by the collar and pulling him down to my level. He clammed-up right quick after Mr. McQuitty had to come around and pull me off the guy. It was a losing battle. I couldn't fight them all. Under my breath, I prayed to God that Mr. Quint found that giant shark and sailed its massive body right back into the harbor to show everyone that we weren't the crazy ones. My captain is the hero of this island and I, his first mate.

October drew to a close. My captain only returned to port for three things: Fuel, chum, and alcohol. The last part was my second job at the shack. After the latest round of chum buckets prepared, and the blood, oil, gristle sprayed off the deck and cleaned, the distiller had to be checked and tended to.

Money was tight, and we only had enough for fuel. We only ate what small fish we caught from the sea. No time to schedule charters. No patience for them, either. My captain turned down opportunities to catch and sell giant marlin. Instead, we hocked whatever held value. We sold many of the power tools we used to overhaul the Orca. The belt sander and an electric drill were all we had left. I never liked that drill. The brace and bit were more accurate. Only enough money for fuel. Nothing extra for my captain's usual order from Harborside Liquor store back in town.

Over the last year, Mr. Quint built a crude distillery in the lower portion of the shack. He learned a recipe for moonshine from another recluse who lived a few minutes away. With a small harvest of plums from the farm on the north shore, Mr. Quint developed a process for distilling them into a vodka of some sort. He called it vodka, but it might as well have been lighter fluid. I could get a fire started in a second with that stuff towards the end of October when the nights turned cold.

A small collection of empty whiskey and apricot brandy bottles sat in crates against the wall. I kept the still running and bottled up the illegal alcohol. Mr. Quint lived off this stuff while underway. Many times, with vision blurred by the effects of this poison, I'll bet he missed the barrel as it pulled right by the starboard side. There were other reasons he drank. I knew he saw horrors that you or I could never imagine. He sometimes screamed in his sleep at night. Calling for and taunting an attacking shark, which never reached him in the bad dream. He'd wake up and wrestle himself back to sleep.

After the visit by his old captain a month ago, he got less sleep. Something had awakened within him. A hatred, a fear, or maybe a little of both. A determination to will another leviathan from the deep and settle the score. I filled the bottles with the clear liquid and thought of him on the Orca by himself, with the strength and odor of this alcohol as his only reprieve. His only escape. I bottled the alcohol and wept. I'm not sure why I cried. Maybe it was because I knew if the sharks didn't kill him, this stuff sure as hell would. It was only a matter of time. I wanted to ruin it all and dump it into the harbor. I thought of smashing the still with the sledgehammer in the corner, but I did not. Too much of a coward to go ahead with it. Too afraid of his wrath, or his disappointment, to act and protect the man from himself.

I wish I had more courage. Maybe things would have been different.

I miss him so much.

All Hallows' Eve fell over the island in a dark overcast sky. Wisps of cold air broke through the warmth and I felt the hunt was lost. It had been over a month since we first saw the monster, and my captain darted a barrel into its hide. The large sharks hate the cold water and this one sure wouldn't stick around anymore. With the clouds of autumn giving us a show, the sun could not keep our waters at the high temperatures we experienced.

Mr. Quint and I loaded the Orca with buckets of fresh chum. We only had enough frozen whale parts left for another week of chum lines and patrols.

"I might have to go south, Hershel."

"Where will you get the fuel for that, sir?"

"I don't know."

He wasn't thinking straight. Too many days in solitude. His mind—lost in the hunt's focus. Endless hours, day and night spent reading the winds, the tides, the temperatures—a toll being paid. It had been forty days with no sight of the barrel.

"Mr. Quint, maybe you should stay in. Let me secure the spring lines and rig the Orca for winter. You need rest."

A boat pulled around from the other side of the Orca. The crew of three stood in the well deck and stared at us as if we had murdered their dog. I never saw them before. They weren't inhabitants of Amity Point and didn't have a slip anywhere along the harbor. Maybe they were just here to work the waters?

Their burly captain stepped out from the pilothouse and barked with a heavy voice.

"Are you Quint?"

My captain turned from me to face our visitors.

"That I am, captain."

"We heard you might be interested in this," the large man said, then motioned to his crew to pick it up and display it for us.

The three men held the torn and tattered remains of a fishing net in their arms. Three large sections were missing. Holes the size of a compact car torn out and missing. The crew looked at us with somber eyes. I felt their hatred.

The captain continued in his gruff voice, "Five-thousand dollars for this net. Brand new. We had the catch of the year right off our stern. At least two-thousand dollars' worth trawled in. That's when it hit us. The boat pulled backwards. We saw white water, and the shark took it all. Chewed it up and took them all. A yellow barrel dragged behind it. Biggest damn shark I ever seen."

Mr. Quint looked down at me with determined eyes.

"The guys in the boat out in the harbor said you might want to know," said their captain.

"Where did you see it?" asked Mr. Quint.

"It attacked us due west. About one mile out."

"I'm sorry for your losses. Thank you for taking the ride down here to give word."

The captain motioned to his crew to drop the net.

"Just thought you might want to know," he said, while stepping back into the wheelhouse of his fishing boat. The vessel moved away as if leading a funeral procession.

Mr. Quint looked over at the chum buckets overflowing with whale oil and meat.

"Mr. Salvatore, there will be no shutting this operation down for the winter until we get our barrel back. Keep the distillery running and get another case filled. I'm headed out. I'll be back in a few days."

The somber cloak of dread fell over my soul. Something didn't feel right. This shark was desperate and took to that net in a way the captain had never seen. It scared those crewmen ghost white, and they blamed us. I know they did. I turned and climbed onto the dock to untie the stern line.

The sudden urge to beg my captain to stay back hit me. Tell him to not go out there.

The Orca's engine lit off in a cloud of black diesel exhaust and growled at me.

47 ERASED

He stayed out for an entire week. The Orca pushed out of Amity Point harbor on Halloween night of 1968. I kept watch from my little shack on the hill. On the eve of the seventh day, the familiar diesel rattle of the Orca's Ford Lehman engine echoed down the harbor shacks and met my ears. I jumped from this bench on my deck and leaned over the railing from my lookout above the harbor.

It was the Orca with my captain at the helm. The setting sun highlighting the mast. The patina veneer of its brass letters glowed orange across the stern. I remember hitting the screen door open with an excited force and the loose rocks of Harbor Hill Road crumbled under my heavy steps. My strides, ungraceful and wide, took me to the dock before the Orca could make the turn and back down to her usual spot. I was there with the mooring line in hand like a good first mate should be.

He looked as if he had been in a fight with a hundred ghosts and lost every one. His face was pale and gaunt. Mr. Quint stepped out of the cabin and looked around the harbor. His voice, hoarse and weak.

"Nothing. Dropped chum lines for seven days straight to the south and west. Nothing."

I pulled the line tight and took three turns on the mooring cleat.

"I was worried, sir. No man should stay out at sea that long. The Orca is not fit for long range."

Mr. Quint started pulling the empty chum buckets from the aft deck and setting them on the dock.

"I'll tend to those, sir. You go in and get some sleep. That shark is long gone. Time to winter over."

"No. No, it's not. Have you got another round ready?"

I stood on the dock and looked at the man. He stood in the aft deck of the Orca. They both looked bruised and beaten—the captain and his boat. His green military jacket, wrinkled and decorated with damp sweat and dried salt stains across the back. His face: thin and unshaven, with unkempt sideburns fit for a pirate. The dead man's fishing hat, given to him by the souls who sailed this vessel years ago, sat on his head in a crooked slouch. He stood before me; a man possessed by the allure of vengeance. It wasn't just a hatred of the mayor that fueled this man. There was more. The demons he fought were dark and mighty.

"You want to kill yourself, Captain?"

He did not answer.

"Because if you go out there again, without proper rest, looking for a shark that size—"

"Do not presume to lecture me on my limits, boy. You get the next round of whale down here on the double and top off the fuel tank. I'm shipping out at dawn."

"It's the last of it, sir."

"Last?"

"We are all out after this. No more whale. We used it all. Only four buckets left. No more money. We have nothing left to sell other than some tools that nobody wants. There's enough fuel for maybe two days at sea."

"I'll shut the engine down, drift with the tides, and get four out of it then."

Mr. Quint stepped off the Orca. He took his military coat off and draped it across the gunwale.

"You are being a good first-mate, Mr. Salvatore. I understand your concern. If I never sail again, I'll be proud of you being the last I sailed with. Do not worry about your captain. That bastard shark is the one that should be worried." Mr. Quint rolled up his sleeves as if to get back to work.

I smiled and nodded my head. Strong words backed his weak voice. I didn't enjoy seeing him in such a state.

"Hey, boy. Come down to the corner store, and I'll buy you a coke. I have three soggy dollar bills in my pocket and they gotta go somewhere. Might as well get some provisions. We'll get the boat ready when we get back."

I looked at his green military coat hanging over the gunwale. The setting sun cast shadows across the ridges and pockets of the jacket as it dried in the cool

November air. The Orca held his coat and stared back at me. Unsettled and intimidated, I turned to follow my captain.

Everything on this island is small. The corner store on Amity Point, not too far from our fishing shack, was just big enough to be called a store. When inside, it felt more like a closet. Just a small room with one shelf in the center. Wooden shelves along the walls held anything the owner, Walter Mishkin, could keep in stock. With the winter fast approaching and the waves of tourists receding, the shelves were full.

A delivery truck idled out front. A younger man wrestled a dolly cart of boxes into the store by the time Mr. Quint and I walked up the front steps of the wooden porch. I held the screen door open for him so it wouldn't catch him on the backside.

It was at the register where it happened. What if the guy said nothing? What if we were five minutes earlier or later? Would my captain had ever found out?

I still think about it to this day.

That delivery guy stood talking to Mr. Mishkin and reading the afternoon edition of the Boston Globe. Mr. Quint stepped up to the counter and paid for a few boxes of crackers, two bottles of Coca-Cola, a bottle of aspirin, and a loaf of bread. He reached out with his left hand to pay the three dollars and the young man stared at his forearm.

"You were on the Indianapolis? You must be glad then."

Mr. Quint was too tired for pleasantries and the man's words took him aback. My captain just stared and ignored the few cents in change Mr. Mishkin was trying to return to him.

"The tattoo on your arm. Indianapolis? Sunk in the Pacific by Japanese torpedoes. Your former captain did everyone a favor and put a bullet in his head yesterday," said the man as he handed Mr. Quint the front page of the Boston Globe.

A dreadful silence and Mr. Quint read the newsprint. I stepped forward to see the paper.

The man continued in his nonchalant ignorance.

"That McVay guy sounded like a piece of garbage. The coward saved himself during the sinking and let all those men die. Good riddance."

Mr. Quint dropped the paper and lunged forward. His large hands grabbed the man's throat, and the two bodies went crashing into the wall. With a deep-seated rage, Mr. Quint tossed the man into his dolly cart. A shelf tipped over, sending books and stacks of newspapers across the floor. The crash tore the screen door off its hinges with both bodies falling outside. I rushed over and grabbed at the shoulders of Mr. Quint, who towered over the fallen man with clenched fists, ready to inflict pain and damage.

"Mr. Quint don't do it! Let's go. Let's go."

The delivery guy crawled out from under the captain. He wobbled to his feet and jumped into the large truck, locking the door and rolling up the window with shaking hands. Mr. Mishkin emerged from the store, hollering up a storm over his broken door hanging from the bottom hinge. People looked on from down the street towards the noise and commotion. Mr. Quint grabbed the wrinkled newspaper from the ground and stormed off in his anger. Left to apologize, I pled for understanding. I went back inside and grabbed our bag of groceries, along with another copy of the newspaper, and moved on down the street.

Around the corner, I lost Mr. Quint. He walked too fast.

Out of breath, I leaned against a bench next to the harbor seawall and scanned the front page of the paper. My hands still shook at the sudden violence. My eyes searched the newsprint. Nixon named the new President of the United States. The Paris peace talks failed for Vietnam. On a side column, with the smallest headline:

INDIANAPOLIS SKIPPER KILLS SELF

Yesterday morning, on November 6th, Captain Charles Butler McVay III, dressed in his khaki Navy uniform and stepped outside the front door of his farmhouse in Litchfield, Connecticut. He raised his service issued revolver to the temple of his head and pulled the trigger. The paper said the gardener heard the shot and found his body. McVay left no explanation. No notes of any kind. All they found in his left hand—a toy sailor he carried around for good luck. He died at seventy years old.

Night had fallen on Amity Point. The streetlight clicked on and buzzed over my head.

It was an hour before I mustered up the courage to enter the fishing shack. I waited down the street and even thought about going back home to my little shack on the hill. Maybe give him the night to cool off? But what if he doesn't make it through the night? The evening grew cold, and my hands shook. The shaking in my fingers confused me. Was it from the air's chill or the nerves over what I should say to the captain?

The article described how eight hundred and seventy-nine men died during the ship's sinking. Mr. Quint would be one of the three-hundred and sixteen survivors who lived in the water for five days. Deadly thirst and shark attacks took the rest of them. He never told me any of this, and I never asked. I must have read that article a dozen times, trying to learn every detail. Right before opening the door to the shack, I understood my captain's screams during the nights when he slept. The large barrels collecting and storing fresh rainwater under the shack. The constant drinking. It all made sense.

I stepped into the blackness of the shack. The light above the table hung dark. Only a lantern's flicker illuminated the large wood table to the center of the wide-open room. The shark jaws all along the walls and cross beams appeared even more menacing now. The horrors they inflicted on my imagination were more vivid than ever.

My eyes didn't focus on the jaws and teeth hiding amongst the shadows. They could not look away from the center of the table. I crept in and got closer. A metal cylinder the size of a paint can posed in the flickering lantern light and stared back at me. The cylinder's brim welded and sealed. A metal switch protruded from the top, next to a welded D-ring. I saw the switch with a pinned ring on the mechanism and recognized it. My conscience cursed itself for not dropping it in the ocean when I had the chance. The dark energy of the moment hit me. There were ghosts here. I felt them.

"Don't touch that."

His voice made me hold my breath. I felt more nervous than when I first met him. The man that stood over me, looking down from the top floor of the shack. I didn't recognize this man. He wasn't the same man I worked for over the last 17 years. Decades of guilt and pain seemed to change his face.

"Get away from the table, Mr. Salvatore. That's live. A tidy sum of TNT packed into that. You pull that pin and we all cross over."

Mr. Quint leaned over the banister and looked around the room. He held a bottle of the clear liquid poison. I looked down at the metal canister.

"What are you going to do with this?"

"Depth charge. Homemade. One of a kind. I'm gonna kill that bastard shark with it. Great white death."

"How are you going to do that, sir?"

"I don't know. Might just have to use myself as bait."

Mr. Quint smiled and raised the bottle. The remaining liquor drained down into his gullet.

"That sure is a lot to drink in a short while, Mr. Quint."

"Good. I need to be good and drunk for what we must do… what you have to help me with."

"What is that sir?"

Mr. Quint dropped the whiskey bottle from the second floor, and it hit the wood deck next to me. The sound made me flinch. The heavy glass bottle bounced and rolled to the side on one of the uneven planks. He slumped down the steps and looked at me. He already removed his shirt and prepared a small workbench next to the wood-burning stove. His broad shoulders and white skin glowed from the moonlight through the windows.

The stove burned hot, stoked with extra wood. Its searing iron squealed at me as I stepped closer to my captain. On the workbench; two towels, a clump of rags, another bottle of alcohol—all next to the Shop Chief US Industries portable belt sander.

The belt sander connected to the electric drill. Mr. Quint picked it up and pressed the trigger. The machine motor screamed a high-pitched whine and spun the heavy-grit sandpaper belt. I used that thing for a few weeks when we took down the hull of the Orca to bare wood and resealed and repainted her.

"What do you need that for, sir?"

"I want you to just hold the trigger down and don't let go. I'll do the rest."

He looked down and held his left forearm in the moonlight. The faded black lettering USS INDIANAPOLIS was never more apparent than this night. The eagle's wings. Once a symbol of duty, pride, and camaraderie to this man—became a branding of guilt and despair over a side column headline in a newspaper.

"I need this removed, boy. It's coming off tonight."

I backed away at the gruesome realization of what was about to happen.

"Mr. Quint, no. This is not a good way to be, sir."

"It is the only way, Hershel."

Mr. Quint picked up the wrinkled front page of the Boston Globe and looked at the article. The name of his former captain in black ink. He whispered to his foreboding collection of shark teeth along the wall.

"A captain goes down with his ship."

He crumpled up the paper, opened the stove door, and tossed it inside to stoke the flames. The heat overwhelmed the shack. My flannel collar soaked with sweat.

His powerful hand reached out and grabbed my shoulder. With the tug of his right arm, I pulled into the table. The belt sander laid on its side.

"I'm ordering you to depress the trigger and hold it down. Look away if you don't have the stomach, but you are not to let go. You got it, boy?"

He pressed the trigger, and the belt spun. I smelled the leftover remnants of white oak dust from the Orca's hull. It kicked into the air in a bleak cloud of white.

The Orca—she was here. I tasted her wood on my lips when I breathed in. I looked out the back window. There she stood, under the moonlight, looking at us inside. Terrified and lost, I backed away from the table. Mr. Quint let go of the trigger and looked at me with angry eyes.

"Where are you going?"

"Mr. Quint, it wasn't your fault. I heard everything you and Captain McVay talked about. This isn't your fault, what he did and all. You are drunk."

He stood tall and approached me. This wasn't him. This wasn't the man I knew.

"You little runt. For once in your life, you need to be a man. Face the music and pull the trigger. Men went to war and had to do stuff they didn't like. Now get over to this table and do your part."

"No."

"Are you disobeying an order, boy?"

"No, sir. I don't want to see you hurt yourself."

Emotion took me over, and I cried. My hands shook with fear. He towered over me—a menacing silhouette approaching.

"You little coward. No wonder you never left this island."

Mr. Quint grabbed my flannel coat with his left hand and struck me across my head with his right. The impact rattled my skull. I only reacted by holding my hands up to my face so I couldn't see his eyes.

"Stand up and become a man, boy! This place will kill you before long. Now get to that table and pull the trigger! You hear me?"

"It's not your fault, sir. I read all about it. The Navy didn't come find your crew because the mission was a secret. You couldn't have saved them. This isn't you right now. It's everything else. This place. It's the Orca. The sharks. It's not you talking right now."

Another swing and the impact hit my ear. I felt the burn of the blood rushing to the smashed flesh on my left side. My red fisherman's hat fell to the floor. He tugged at my jacket and pulled my body back to the table. A third strike by his massive forearm landed across my head.

"Press the trigger, boy. Erase this once and for all. It's an order."

He reached for the bottle of alcohol and pulled off the top. I watched the liquor funnel into his body. I clung to the table and wanted to collapse. The strikes to my head left me in a daze.

"Alright, sir. You want to ruin yourself? You go right ahead," I said through tearful eyes.

I straightened myself up and leaned into the table. My hand grabbed the handle of the belt sander and pressed the trigger. The machine screamed and the heavy grit belt spun, shaking the table with its violence.

He bit down on a leather belt and grabbed his left fist with his right.

As if guiding a piece of lumber, Mr. Quint leaned into the machine. With his left arm bent and flexed, his right hand pushed down on the white knuckles of the clenched left fist. The leather belt muffled his screams. The tattooed skin of the forearm met the spinning grit of the belt and sheared off. I watched the blood and flesh spray off the machine and onto the floor. Mr. Quint dragged his left forearm across the belt sander in three slow and methodical swipes. In the moonlight, the blood appeared black. The decking under the table stained black. The table looked as if it wore a spattering of black paint.

I let go of the trigger on the machine and he pushed the table out of the way. He leaned his bloody forearm into the searing hot iron stove top. The smell of cooking flesh and burning blood hit me in a wave of horror. I backed away and leaned against the wall. I lost myself in the horrid insanity of it all.

Through drying tears, I watched him try to wrap his forearm in a towel and then take a lasting pull from the bottle. After seven days alone at sea, learning the loss of his captain, and the excruciating pain in erasing the memory on his skin—his spirit gave out. Mr. Quint collapsed on the floor of the fishing shack.

Over his unconscious body, the shark's jaws hung open and hungry. They claimed another soul.

PART III

48 NOMANS LAND

"Mister Quint!"

The accented voice of Yuri Papov echoed across the harbor. The growl and shouting grew louder with every word. Amity Point was known for decades as the quiet haven at the other end of the island. On this morning, it was anything but quiet.

"Quint! I know you are in there. Come out and face me like a man!"

Yuri screamed from deep within the chest. His unshaven face burned red. Neck muscles strained, he steered his small fishing boat next to the Orca's dock. The aged fisherman, with white hair and a swollen red alcoholic's nose, leaned out from the pilothouse of his boat and stared up to the windows of Quint's fishing shack.

"Where are you, you bastard? Look what you've done!"

Quint stirred from the noise down below. His forearm pulsed with the burn under a blood-soaked wrapping of dirty rags. He opened his eyes. The dried wood of the floorboards to the shack felt cool on the side of his face. Above him, the large back window to the shack remained open through the night. The white canvas shade, yellowed by years of salt air mornings, rolled down to block the seagulls from flying in. A torn corner twitched from the slight breeze.

He remembered the pain and smell from the night before. The scent of burning flesh still hung in the air. His blood dried on the wood deck and smeared across the grinder. He remembered everything in great detail.

The angry shouts jarred him, and he reached with his right arm. Quint pulled himself up by the back windowsill. The hangover pounded at his brain. With a quick strike, he pulled the canvas blind away from the window and the cauterized patch of skin on his left forearm stung. The sea breeze rushed across the exposed nerves and stabbed at him.

"There you are. You did this to us!"

Quint straightened his back and looked down at the boat in the harbor below. He knew the old man. He saw him and his two sons working from their dock a few shacks up the way every day since he arrived. This time, there was only the man and one son standing in the boat looking up. Yuri Papov's eyes burned with anger but swelled with defeat.

"Your shark. It hit our net this morning. We tried to haul in the catch. My son, Stefan. His arm caught in the line, and it pulled him in. Look at Andros. Look at his hand!"

Andros Papov stepped forward. His right arm held up the bloody ruins of a hand. Bandages wrapped the exposed knuckles and missing finger. The boy stood in pain. Losing his brother hurt the most.

"The yellow barrel! One of yours!" Yuri pointed to the rack of four yellow barrels on the bow of the Orca—a space in the rack for the missing one. "That was the last I saw of him. The tail of that shark. The white water. Your yellow barrel and my boy, disappearing below the waves."

"Where?" asked Quint.

"It's doesn't matter anymore. We searched for hours. My boy is dead and there's nothing you can do about it!"

Quint leaned forward and pounded on the open window's wooden frame.

"You want revenge? I ask you again. Where did you see the barrel?"

"Eleven miles to the Northwest. Nomans Land. It's there."

The adrenaline made him feel alive. Quint turned and looked—the depth charge on the table. He threw on his light blue Navy work shirt, pulled on his canvas fishing hat, and grabbed the metal canister. A stiff kick opened the back door, and he marched down the steps of the shack. Quint looked over to the Papov's boat while walking down the dock. He untied the stern and bow lines and stepped over the Orca's gunwale.

The old fisherman would not turn away. The shouting through a thick Russian accent continued when the engine of the Orca ignited to life. Quint ignored the grieving fisherman, threw on his military green M51 field jacket and climbed up to the flying bridge.

"Before you, this place was normal, Mr. Quint. You are a curse on this island. The Coast Guard men. They say my Stefan is an accident, but we know better.

You did this to us. I hope you die out there. It is what you deserve! You did this. Your shark took my Stefan. I curse your name on this day!"

Yuri's language switched to Russian in his curse of obscenities. The grieving father fell over from the guilt and rage. A father who watched his son die and the other maimed. A father who stood and watched it all while paralyzed in the fear of facing a nightmare.

Quint shoved the throttle forward on the flying bridge controls. The Orca pushed off from the dock. Its wake rocked the Papov's boat. Quint never looked back.

Captain's Log–November 8, 1968.

I don't know if I'll come back alive this time. I'm prepared to die to kill this shark. May this be the only record of detail if that is the case. I left Amity Point sometime around eight in the morning. The Russian fisherman and his kid. Their faces reminded me of the others in the water on the first night of the sinking. Disbelief in the reality of what happened, yet ignorant of what horrors the future has in store. He isn't the first father to lose a son to a shark. Just another in a long line. The guy must be seventy years old. I'm surprised he didn't learn it yet. Life is loss. Get used to it.

Quint steered the Orca down the harbor towards the inlet. He looked up at the little shack on the hill. Hershel stood on his deck and watched him as he passed by. Quint saw the weathered and worried face of Hershel and didn't know how to react. Hershel raised his hand to wave. Quint returned a wave of goodbye.

I never had time to apologize to Hershel. A loyal first mate—with me from the very beginning. I wish I could tell him why I did all that last night. After I passed out on the floor, he stayed and stocked the Orca. I noticed the four buckets of whale chum loaded next to the transom. Even the spare fuel tanks filled. If I make it back, I owe him an explanation. If I die on this day, may this captain's journal be just that—I'm sorry, boy.

The Orca reached the widest part of the harbor, and Quint turned the steering wheel to the correct course. The nautical compass shifted in a northwestern direction. November winds on the open Atlantic Ocean bit hard against his face. He climbed down the ladder and moved to the helm inside the pilothouse. The engine sped up and white water churned off the stern at full speed ahead.

Nomans Land Island came into view within the hour. A small uninhabited island in the middle of the open sea—last remnants of land before a stretch of ocean. Quint pulled the throttle back and looked around the wide windows of the Orca.

You're still here. The barrel is getting heavy. You're used to it by now, but it feels better to let it drag on the surface. So, you'll stay up high, won't you shark? Just give me that chance. One flash of yellow and I'll be on you for good.

Quint looked off the port side. He reached across the helm to his collection of nautical charts.

I never get out this far west. Haven't been to Nomans Land since I was a teenager.

A chart unrolled on the dining table inside the Orca. At first glance, he saw it and his instincts kicked in.

Block Island. That's where I'll trap you. The waters are cold up north. You won't head to the Vineyard or the Cape. You want to go south, but that barrel is heavy. Too heavy. So, you will just keep going west. Try to work your way down the coast? You just fed on that load of fishing net, so you don't need food. But you will. You can't go deep—the weight of that barrel won't let you stay down long. Burning up more energy than ever before and you need easy food. You'll be hungry around Block Island, and I'll be waiting.

After a few measurements and calculations, Quint spun the steering wheel hard to port and set a fresh course. The seas tossed with a three-foot chop. The winds whisked water from the whitecaps under the overcast light.

I got lucky this year. Still can't believe how warm it stayed. The water, the air, everything—many degrees above normal. But it's changing, the icy winds are moving in. The seas kicking up as well. Only a few days left to land this fish.

Block Island is forty miles to the west. The seas are a three-foot chop. Head wind is solid. At full throttle, I can be there in two and a half hours. A chum line dropped between the island and this fish will bring him right to me. I must stay throttled down. If the Orca lets me abuse her, I'll outrun the shark and beat him there.

Two hours passed, and Quint felt the pangs of hunger. His mouth, sticky and dry. He looked around the cabin.

Dammit. I never took the provisions. There might be some dry stores down below. A few crackers maybe. The water tank is empty too. I used it all last week looking for this shark. I never should've left that fast this morning. That Russian's shouting rattled me. I wasn't thinking straight. It doesn't matter. Maybe this will be a one-way trip after all.

After a quick search around the cabin and the forward berthing areas, all Quint found were three small packages of crackers and two bottles of the homemade alcohol.

Six crackers and two bottles of the good stuff. I'm thirsty. I should've taken the water. It doesn't matter. I'll kill this shark and be home by tonight.

The crisp air cleaned his visibility. The Southeast Lighthouse of Block Island winked at Quint from ten nautical miles off the starboard bow. A flash of green light in his binoculars every five seconds gave him all the information he needed.

Quint cut the fuel supply to the engine. The Orca dropped into silence. Just the gentle rocking and last momentum of her keel cutting the sea.

Five miles off Block Island. Gotta get to work. I have three hours to sunset.

Quint fastened the buttons of his work shirt and jacket. His body moved with a newfound youthfulness. The hunter slid and pulled his way along the Orca, making multiple trips to the bow. He positioned two yellow barrels aft next to the transom. One in each corner. A coiled rope attached to a steel leader wire rigged to a harpoon dart perched on top of each barrel. Forward, on the bow, the other two barrels, rigged with the same set-up, stayed in the barrel rack.

He lifted the storage seat to check on his homemade explosive ordinance. It sat secured from rolling free. The seat closed and Quint assembled the Greener rifle at the Orca's table. A pocket full of rifle ammunition, and he was ready to begin.

The first chum bucket smelled more rancid than any of the ones he had used in the last month. The clean November air made the smell more potent. It stood out in his nostrils with every scoop of the small frying pan Quint used as a ladle. The thick puree of whale blubber and shredded muscle fibers coagulated in the cold. A putrid jelly that made his empty stomach acids churn.

I only have four buckets of this slop. I have to make every one of them count. I'll never get used to the smell. Nothing worse than rotting whale in the morning. Such an evil stench can only attract a demon. These sharks have no soul.

With a methodical timing and the patience honed by three decades of shark hatred, Quint dug into the chum bucket—one scoop at a time. The gelatinous feel on his fingertips reminded him of the bodies and carnage on Iwo Jima. He closed his eyes at the red liquid of bubbles and blackfish skin mixing with white fleshy swirls, designing the top layer like an abstract work of art.

Am I any different? Look at the way the white trails of flesh skim on top of the water when it lands. Look inside this bucket of blood concoction I play in during these last days. The way it feels. Iwo Jima. The stomach of that Japanese fella felt the same way. He came at me from the tree line on the beach. I was looking at the water, but I heard him first. His tired footsteps. That running stumble gave him away. He stabbed me good on the side, but I was stronger. Do you remember how many times you dug your knife into his belly? For that very moment, you had no soul either. We were both doing what we were told to do. Had I never heard him break from those palms, would he be staring into a bucket of mess decades later— thinking about the way my stomach felt as he stabbed me to death? Where is your soul, boy? You lost it in the Pacific, remember? You and the shark are no different.

Quint dropped another chum marker into the water halfway through the first bucket. He watched the tall stick bounce on the water. The yellow piece of fabric tied to the top snapped in the breeze. Its foam base resting in a red ocean and drifting off.

I gotta conserve fuel. No more engine until I see the shark. I'm down to my last five chum markers. Should be enough to tell where the tide is taking me and the chum line. The sun will set soon. No way I can head back now. I've come too far. He's here. I know it. One scoop at a time. Lay this trail out nice and wide.

After two buckets dispensed into the ocean, Quint made a steady climb to the flying bridge. He looked around and smelled the air. The headwind died into a slight breeze, and the waters flattened. Hand over hand, he pulled himself up the mast.

No use getting out the tackle—gotta get another barrel in him first.

I spent the last hour of daylight aloft. The wind dropped, and the cold was tolerable. The surface currents weren't as strong as I expected them to be. I could see the trail of blood and the chum markers well off into the distance. The ocean drifted the Orca a few miles to the west.

The chum line meandered from the Orca's stern in an erratic pattern. Quint watched the cloud of red suspended against the dark black of the deep water and lead off to the outline of Block Island on the horizon. The yellow colors of the chum markers told him what direction he started in.

A highway of blood starting way back there. That bastard shark will come cruising right down it. He's coming. He has to.

I faced west and watched the sunset in front of the Orca. The clouds moving in. I'm thirsty. I promised myself I would never be thirsty again after they pulled me out of the Pacific. On the wing of that PBY, you promised yourself. Look at you now. Twenty-three years later and you're begging for water. How could you fail at something so simple?

49   ENDEAVOR SHOALS

The night covered the Orca in a thick blanket of darkness. The overcast blocked all traces of celestial light from the heavens. Quint sat at the table inside the cabin and waited. He put to sea almost every day since burying the harpoon in the back of the great white shark. The isolation never bothered the weary sailor when work distracted the mind. It was the darkness that unsettled him—the waiting. Only on nights like this when the ghosts from the past paid him a visit.

I'm losing my patience—maybe my mind. I sat for an hour in the dark cabin. On the table in front of me, a bottle of the good stuff. I couldn't see it, but I sat and stared at it. I didn't switch the running lights on. Invisible and adrift. Must save the batteries. Can't start the engine. I don't want the noise to ward him off. I want it to think I'm drifting helpless. The pot at the end of the blood trail I laid out for him. They feed off the helpless—the stranded and the beaten down. He thinks I am wrecked.

Quint reached up to the swaying lamp above the table. His fingers ached when they searched for the switch. A click and the bulb glowed with electricity, warming to a yellow light. He leaned back into the red vinyl cushions of the bench seat and exhaled. The lamp shade of tin spoke in a soft squeak while rocking side to side. He watched the bottle's shadow move with the ocean's cadence along the grain of the chipped wood tabletop.

He sat right here. Captain McVay looked at the grain on this table only a few weeks ago. He already decided before his visit. What is it like on the other side? I wonder if he found his solace. The thirst is burning. Just take one drink from the bottle. It's right there. The shaking in your hands will stop. But the dehydration will speed up the desire. Do you want to die out here? Does it matter? McVay is waiting for you.

The dead sound of the first bump against the hull amplified throughout the Orca. Quint watched the shadow of the bottle twitch on the table from a second vibration. Another strike sounded from below.

The shark made first contact close to midnight. It's here. I have no visibility out there right now. Not sure I can get a clean shot even with the working lights on. The water is black. He is invisible. The shark has the advantage right now. I'll keep him close until dawn. The fish doesn't sleep, and neither shall I. Tomorrow, one of us will die.

Quint sat at the table and stared with the intensity of a predator. The alcoholic temptation faced him from behind clear glass. It danced back and forth with the gravity of the Orca's movements. For a moment, the Orca tempted him. She called him to the bottle. To drown the ghosts of guilt with a little liquid strength.

He rolled up the sleeve on his left arm and unwrapped his bandages. The burned patch of missing skin had glazed over into a thin leathery scab.

Another bump. This time, towards the bow. The yellow barrel dragged along the Orca's chipped wooden hull at the waterline. Quint's eyes followed the sound it made while moving down the port side.

Quint slid from the booth in the cabin and stepped outside. In the black of midnight, he took three scoops of chum from the third bucket and tossed them over the side. Ambient light from the hanging lamp inside the Orca guided him back to his seat at the table. Before he entered the cabin, he could hear the sweep of its tail kicking through the ocean surface of fresh bait.

Captain's Log–November 9, 1968

I didn't sleep the entire night. At the top of every hour, I chummed the water with three scoops. Made the third bucket last until I saw the first light of dawn. Down to the final bucket of bait now. Have to rig the deck for landing this fish.

The red light of the overcast sunrise cut across the horizon. The seas remained calm, giving the Orca a gentle rock as a mother would a cradle. Quint looked to port, then starboard, and couldn't see the yellow barrel. The red sunrise reflected off the waves and kept the water black as oil. He looked into the deep and remembered the oil slick of the Indianapolis. Five days of bathing in this blackness.

"Red in the morning… sailor, take warning."

Quint smiled at the childhood rhyme, which crept into his head and brought him comfort. For the moment, he forgot about his thirst.

Forward lockers tossed open, and the aft deck filled with yards of fresh line. Two-sheave blocks and large landing hooks of pitted iron taken from stowage and piled at the ready. A chain hoist, grips, and personal slack blocks—anything he might need to rig the weight of a giant. He carried the last plastic bucket of ground pilot whale and blood to the port side. Quint preferred working from the port side on colder days. The Orca's muffler, mounted to the exterior of the port aft cabin bulkhead, radiated warmth. Comfort at the cost of errant gulps of diesel fumes when the wind shifted.

With its lid still sealed, trails of red streamed down the sides of the bucket and collected in a crimson ring on the decking. Quint lashed the bucket's handle to a shackle, then rigged it to a set of blocks which suspended from the davit arm on the Orca's mast. He pulled out the slack, and the bucket lifted into the air. The working line locked off to a side cleat, and Quint left the bucket to sway back and forth with the slight ocean swells. Inside the cabin, a large, sharpened hunting blade of steel mounted to the wall. He gripped the machete and marched back to the aft deck.

"You are hungry, shark? Haven't eaten in over a day. You're waiting down there for something."

Quint's voice cracked with fatigue.

I rigged the last bucket to the gin and slashed it up with the machete. Get the fish surfaced. Just one chance is all I need. One clean shot and get two barrels in him. No way he stays down with two barrels.

Large swings of the machete buried its blade into the bucket. The whale blood and oil spewed from the wounds in the scratched white plastic. Quint pushed on the davit arm. It pivoted to the port side, and the bucket swung over the water. The dripping blood rained down and the calm ocean surface came to life in a dance of red droplets from above. The stench of dead whale mixed with the salt air and filled his nostrils with an eye-watering sting.

Dawn arrived. The sun began its creep over the horizon. Quint looked at the orange light while untying the working end of the line. He remembered being alone at dawn in the morning—waiting for them to take him. The memory enhanced his thirst for revenge.

Come and get it, shark. You may be a clever fish. You outsmarted the lines, the nets, and one barrel. Let's see how much fight you have left.

He released his grip. The rope slid through his calloused palm and weaved through the blocks. The suspended bucket lowered into the water. Quint pulled the rope back and forth and the bucket bobbed up and down on the surface, releasing a cloud of blood and fragmented blackfish. The seagulls collected in the air above the bucket. Their screeching madness unsettled him. He looked at the bucket and saw his friend. Herbie Robinson in a gentle float—bobbing up and down, eyes open and staring back from the black and red water.

Quint leaned over the gunwale to get a closer look.

Right under his chin, the yellow barrel emerged in silence, causing Quint to draw back.

The violence and sound stole his breath when the large great white shark exploded from the black water four feet from his face. The giant jaws flashed their rows of serrated white triangles. Its black eye looked into Quint, then rolled back into its skull, showing white. The menacing upper jaw of teeth extended from the shark's mouth and the fish bit down on the white bucket. The entire half of the shark rose in the air and turned to face Quint. He saw the dorsal fin's distance to the head and imagined it all a dream—the largest white shark he had ever seen. The great white seemed to hang in the air, suspended in time. Bloody water spit from the five wide gill slits stretched across its shiny skin. Its impact on the water shook the Orca when the enormous belly of white caught gravity then smacked the surface waves. The giant fish landed with a thunderous sound, sending a layer of cold seawater to cover Quint.

The davit arm's polished wood flexed at its attachment point to the mast when the rigging shook back and forth. A surge of power and the monster's jaws bit down on the bucket a second time. Intense thrashing of the shark's head, shaking above the surface, broke the lid from the bucket. Quint spit the salt water out of his mouth and dried his face with his sleeve. The bucket's integrity gave way inside the powerful, crushing mouth of the great white shark. Blood and chum spit from behind the protruding teeth, teasing the shark but not satisfying its hunger for sustenance.

There's your chance. Bury this animal.

Rehearsed a dozen times in his mind, Quint did not have to think—he reacted. He moved with the speed and agility of a trained soldier in a fight for his life. Quint reached over and took up his rifle from the deck. The sharpened harpoon, already loaded upon the rifle's barrel. Steel leader line tethered to the rope of a waiting yellow keg—a sentry ready to defend its fortress.

The shark shook the remnants of the bucket out of its mouth as Quint raised the rifle, sighted in, and pulled the trigger.

Through the cloud of gun smoke and the intense crack of the rifle's recoil, Quint watched the harpoon bury into the top of the shark's dark gray head just as it rolled to the side. The harpoon dug in at an angle and the fish kicked its powerful tail to launch its body forward. The dart wrenched out of its sandpaper hide from the force of its titanic body cutting into the chaos of churning water.

Quint watched his harpoon pull from the body and drop into the depths, to hang from the side of the Orca by the steel leader wire. He launched to his feet and ran forward to get ahead of the great white, which pumped its tail along the surface of the water. With one hand holding the rifle, Quint pulled himself along the port side of the Orca. He rushed to stay ahead of the giant dorsal fin. A quick few steps along the ledge of the cabin and a jump into the boat's bow. He ejected the spent cartridge from the rifle's chamber while grabbing a new one from this shirt pocket. In one fluid motion, Quint chambered a fresh round, slammed the locking handle of the rifle home, grabbed another harpoon from the top of a racked barrel, and moved to his hunting pulpit.

The head of the great white moved fast under the surface of the water.

Don't lose the dorsal fin. Stay ahead of it.

Quint left the Orca's bow and side-stepped down the thin planking of the pulpit while shoving the next harpoon dart over the rifle's muzzle. He looked back and saw his first yellow barrel drag in the water along the hull of the Orca. The great fish turned in the water and cut underneath his hunting pulpit. A quick spin to starboard—Quint swung the rifle to the opposite shoulder. He leaned over the railing of the pulpit and stretched. The dorsal fin passed under his feet, letting him know to target the head of the shark out front.

His left hand squeezed.

The trigger pulled.

A shot rang out, and the rifle kicked back into his shoulder in another blast of warm smoke. A streak of gleaming steel launched and found its target. The harpoon buried deep into the shark, causing the fish to surge into the dark water. Quint reached back and grabbed the steel leader line that ran out behind his legs. He tossed the wire over his head and clear from his body at the very moment it snapped taught. The rope payed out. A yellow barrel erupted from its rack and pulled over the bow.

Take it and run. Let's see how far you can get with two holding you up.

The two yellow barrels raced across the water's surface. They bounced and danced together in a strange unison, twisting and turning against the ocean. Both barrels tried to dig down into the water, becoming half submerged and leaving a wake of white foam on their trail.

Quint marched back down the pulpit, heading aft. He never took his eyes off the yellow shapes heading away from the sunrise and towards the dark horizon.

I put the second barrel in the great white a little after sunrise. Their speed told me the fish was tired. The second barrel made it angry, and it swam in heavy strokes towards the west. Block Island was far out behind us. No way could the shark pull the barrels down and submerge. It couldn't swim faster than the Orca. Not a chance.

With confident strides, Quint navigated the starboard ledge while pulling himself along with his free hand. He slipped into the cabin and stepped to the helm. The fuel stop jammed down, and he fired the engine start switch. The Orca whined and waited for the teeth of its starter to catch the gearing. Its engine turned, compressing the injected diesel mist. The fire exploded through the engine cylinders, and she called out in a triumphant roar of black smoke.

Quint rushed over to the navigation charts and slid one across the table, knocking the bottle of untouched alcohol onto the deck. The bottle met the wood with a dead thud and rolled starboard with the pitch of the latest wave under the hull. Quint's fingers searched while he leaned in to examine the details of the chart in the dim ambient morning light.

Where are you headed, huh? West. You want to go west and into deep water. The deep water has calmer seas. Less drag on the barrels. You are feeling how heavy they are. And you can't handle any turbulence.

His finger dragged across the chart of known depths and found a name.

Right here, this is where I'll take you. Endeavor Shoals. The depths go shallow. From one hundred fathoms to sixty. You won't know what hit you.

His finger slid over a few inches more on the same heading. He knew this ultimate battle would end there.

The shallows off Montauk point. This is where you won't be able to out swim the drag of those barrels. This is where I'll herd you and watch you drown.

Quint raced out of the cabin to gather the missed harpoon and leader line hanging from the Orca's aft port side and toss it on deck. Making sure the davit arm pulled back to center, and all lines were out of the water, he bounded up the ladder in three quick pulls.

The Orca dug itself a handful of ocean as the torque of the engine caught the drive shaft. The propeller blades cut into the water with a ferocious aggression and the stern dropped into the waves. Quint felt the boat rise and lurch forward. He pressed the throttle down hard. The bow corrected and aimed at the twinge of spinning yellow fifty yards out.

I tracked the fish for ten miles. Whenever it tried to veer south, I sped up the Orca to get on top of the great white and push it back on its western course. The shark found itself in shallow waters. It wasn't long before we were over the shoals and the waves picked up. The water turbulence kicking off the shallow bottom. I could see the barrels slow. The shark was tired. I felt weak and tired. My hands shook when the adrenaline of the moment wore away. The cold. The wind on the flying bridge, damp and piercing. I didn't dare take my hand off the throttle. Ahead, the blinking of Montauk Point lighthouse. To the right is where I want it to go.

The shallows—I corralled that porker right down the line. Checkmate, you devil.

Montauk Point loomed off the port bow, and the seas carried an unpredictable turbulence. Quint steered his boat and kept close to the yellow barrels. The bow of the Orca bumped into them, letting the shark know it was being hunted.

Quint watched the waves breaking on rocks off in the distance, and he backed off the throttle. He set the trap. They reached less than ten fathoms where the waves grew heavier. The ocean pulled and grabbed at the yellow barrels, cutting the great white shark's momentum.

A feinted moment and Quint felt victorious.

This trophy will ruin Vaughn.

A smile broke from the corner of Quint's mouth. It receded when the yellow barrels turned and headed straight for the Orca.

50 CHECKMATE

Quint reacted and put the vessel into an evasive maneuver. The Orca flinched when the transmission jammed into reverse. The yellow barrels, now locked together in an embrace, homed in on the Orca. Their tether lines twisted ten feet below the surface. They moved at an uncanny speed.

The great white locked in on the sound of its tormentor. The large dark shape that herded it into the shallows. It listened to its clumsy machinery. The engine's drone struck across the shark's lateral line of sensory receptors. It hated the mechanical chop of the propeller. Exhausted and out of any deep-water escape, the great white turned to defend itself. Mechanical sounds grated on its brain, sending instructions to kill the source of that menacing noise which followed it here. The weight of the barrels pulled on its wide body, but it didn't care. The fish stroked its powerful tail with enormous force. Predatory survival instincts overriding any thoughts of logic or self-preservation. The shark washed in the enthralling hatred of the sounds from the dark shape. The muscles of the fish flexed. It attacked with a violent fury.

Hard to port and pushing down full throttle, Quint watched the shape of the shark go deep and disappear from the surface. The Orca shook with a fury at the prop wash pushing under her hull. Her stern crashed forward and tried to spin out of the way.

The two barrels pulled beneath the waves made by the reversing Orca. Quint looked in all directions for any sign of the monster.

Where did you go? You bastard shark.

Behind the Orca, the ocean regurgitated the barrels in a geyser of white water. Quint heard them and sensed the impact a second before it happened.

He pulled the throttle back and took the transmission into forward gear, but it was too late.

It struck from below and hit the propeller hard with the force of a freight train. The hardened snout crashed into the forged blades; jaws locked onto the rudder chain. Violent and thrashing, its body kicked and slammed into the rudder. The Orca's stern careened to the side from the impact.

On the flying bridge, Quint lost his footing but caught himself before falling. He pushed the throttle forward. Nothing. Two of the three blades on the propeller, bent by the impact, rendered useless by the blunt force trauma. The surging shark pulled the rudder chain from its attachment, and Quint lost the steering wheel from his grip.

With two more kicks of its crescent-shaped tail, the shark dove back into the shadow of the Orca. The tether lines of the barrels followed it and swung into the spinning propeller. Quint saw the barrels at the stern of the Orca and pulled in the throttle to bring the boat back to neutral. The lines twisted like spaghetti on the surface of the water and disappeared under the boat.

I knew by the sound of the engine that there was resistance on the prop shaft. The shark attacked out of the Montauk Point shallows. Something I didn't expect. It fouled the Orca in the barrel lines. Two kegs are off the stern, pinned to the hull. The shark is somewhere below. We are over the shoals, adrift and paralyzed.

The engine fell silent, and Quint climbed down from the flying bridge to assess the damage.

From the aft stowage in the transom, Quint removed a rusty length of pipe as long as his arm. A sight glass installed at one end, a gooseneck angle with a second sight glass at the other. He looked around the water for the dorsal fin. The yellow barrels nudged the hull of the boat. He leaned over the transom with a cautious eye.

The barrels bobbed on the surface below his chin. They carried scars of black where the abuse of the ocean scraped and scratched at their painted surfaces. Quint focused on the streaks of missing yellow and thought of Hershel painting many years ago outside the fishing shack.

With silent movements, Quint pushed the barrels to the side and leaned out over the water. He slid the rusty pipe past the brass letters that wept green patina. The gooseneck sight placed into the water. He peered into the top sight glass.

Built for checking to see if the sharks on the other end of the barrel lines were dead over the last decade of hunting, the underwater viewer surveyed the damage. A mirror inside allowed him to see at an angle under the boat. He turned the pipe in his hands towards the rudder. Through the hazy green surface light, he looked past the floating oceanic particles. He saw the problem. The Orca's rudder, a large square of Corten steel, swung loose from its chain and pinned against the propeller. The barrel lines wrapped in a tangled mess around the shaft just behind the bent and disabled prop. Both lines pulled taut and extended down below the Orca. Quint pivoted the sight glass back around to get a better view.

The massive maw of the great white flashed its teeth in the sight glass, and Quint recoiled in shock.

The shark hit the viewing pipe and bit down hard, ripping it from Quint's hands. Its monstrous head rose from the ocean, missing Quint's arm by inches. He watched the muscular white underside of its lower jaw flex and pump. The eyes rolled back to a dull, fleshy white. His hands pushed off the cold metal of the Orca's lettering. Stomach muscles burned when Quint flexed his body to pull himself up onto the transom. The head of the fish continued to chew on the viewing pipe when it vanished below the sea foam. The thrashing of the tail kicked water in his face. Quint rolled and fell back into the safety of the aft deck to catch his breath.

The damage is severe but not paralyzing. It's fixable. I must get in the water.

No other options. Our drift in the ocean means we will be on the rocks in less than an hour. The Orca will break apart and wreck. The shark played its last move. If I can get below the Orca? Untangle the lines, connect the rudder chain, and we can get underway. That shark will rip me to pieces down there.

If I force the shaft into gear, the lines get severed and the shark is free. If I wait out this fish, we wreck on the rocks. I am dying. I know how long I can go without food and water. It's been over forty-eight hours since my last drink. My body is weak. I can feel death around the corner, but I will not let this fish go. If I let it go, Mayor Vaughn wins. If I die, Mayor Vaughn wins. I supposed this is a checkmate. Well played, Mr. Mayor. I'll see you in hell.

"Amity Point Light Station to Orca. This is Amity Point Light Station on Coast Guard hailing and distress frequency channel sixteen. Come in, Orca."

Quint pulled the depth charge canister out of the storage space in the bench seat of the wheelhouse and looked over at the radio. The voice through the speaker scratched with the static of the distant tower's faded signal.

"Come in, Orca."

He set the depth charge down on the table. The sun broke through the overcast clouds and lit up the wheelhouse's interior from the glass windshield over the helm.

Just answer the radio. Call for help and they'll send a boat out. Not a chance. Where was the distress signal for the others? For Machado? Who came to help Troy or Herbie? The captain goes down with the ship, boy. Captain McVay is watching. They all are. Maureen. She's watching too. Your father. You don't deserve a rescue. You failed for the last time, boy. Time to face your fate like a man. Get along with it.

The beaten captain stood tall inside the Orca and looked around his world. If he should die on this day, he would not object.

"Get along with it, boy."

Quint gazed down at the metallic cylinder on the table. His face wore a gentle smile. He decided.

"Amity Point light station to Orca. Come in, Orc—"

The radio ripped from its wires and mounting on the shelf inside the wheelhouse. With a long sweeping sidearm of strength, Quint threw the radio console overboard like a discus. He watched the piece of modern-day electronic temptation spin in the air and land into the ocean beyond.

"The captain goes down with the ship," Quint said to the mark of disturbed ocean, where the radio met its fate.

He dressed as the Navy told him to. When the call went over the ship's sound powered speakers for emergency quarters, the men battle dressed their service uniforms. Sleeves rolled down and fastened. Shirt buttoned to the top, keeping hot brass and shrapnel from falling down the collar. Jackets and coats, secured and strapped for extra layers should you go overboard. Quint emerged from the cabin of the Orca in full battle dress. He pulled on the waistline of his fastened green M51 field jacket and straightened up. It comforted him to remember being in battle dress and waiting with his team for enemy planes. He was a free man then. Free from the sharks. Free from the guilt.

The waves crashed on the rocks of Montauk point just ahead. The Orca's engine remained silent while the boat drifted towards an impending doom.

Not much time left. This is a general alarm. Get to your battle station, boy.

In the minutes prior, he rushed to secure the end of a working line to a port side cleat. The rest of the rope unraveled along the decking. He fed it down into the water, walked it under the stern, then pulled the other end up on the starboard side to secure it. The rope looped under the hull and pulled tight, giving a way for Quint to pull himself to the fouled propeller. If he had a hold of the rope, he could hold fast to the bottom of the boat and fight against the current.

Next, he removed the shoulder sling from the M1 Garand and fastened it to the welded eyelet on the metal canister. Quint slipped the sling over his head and left arm. The fifteen-pound weight slung against his field jacket and reminded him of the artillery he loaded on the Indy. He looked down at the homemade bomb. The fabricated switch, with a circular safety pin fastened to it, shimmered in the sunlight that broke from the clouds and beamed down upon the Orca's aft deck.

My insurance policy. No matter what happens, I'll have the last laugh. You might have a mouthful of me, fish, but I'll see you detonate from this ocean while you're at it. Not a bad run, to be fair. Fifty-two years. That's a few more than the rest of the guys had.

I consider myself the lucky one.

Quint collected the bottle of alcohol, which moved along the deck when the Orca rolled to starboard. He stepped to the gunwale and took a wider stance to balance himself. He unscrewed the cap and emptied the bottle's contents into the ocean. The alcohol met the water in a flickering stream of white sunlight. The old sailor imagined the souls who departed him and buried at sea. Would they partake in a drink with him on the other side?

"Save a round for me, boys. I'll be there soon."

Quint looked around into the water. It glowed a dark green. The clouds appeared more beautiful than ever before. The sunlight—its warmth on his face. His eyes closed. He blessed himself with the sign of the cross. He hadn't done that in decades, but at that very moment, he remembered his grandmother from half a century ago and felt he should do so. The faded images of her handing him a piece of candy during a service at Saint Patrick's chapel in their fishing village played for him. He remembered the rice paper thin skin of her hand.

This must be the angels. Is this how they come to free me from this place? I'm ready.

He placed both of his legs over the side and held the rope with an iron grip. His body lowered into the sea. The rush of cold water filled his jacket and shirt, causing Quint to hold his breath. Ever so careful to not disturb the metal cylinder hanging under his left arm, he allowed himself to drop the rest of the way in. The wound on his forearm screamed with pain when submerged in the salt water. The horrors of the Indianapolis hit him alongside the pain. A tattoo memento, now a scarred physical reminder of it all. From his field jacket pocket, he pulled the glass bottle he emptied earlier.

He held the bottle above the surface to shake out the ocean and turned it to his eye. Placing the body of the bottle into the sea, he peered into the finish.

Through the clear glass portal, he watched his feet dangle over a vastness of deep green. All around, a cloud of particles and silt kicked up by the ocean currents. With the sea floor only sixty feet below, visibility reduced to ten feet. He looked for the barrel lines. The morphing shafts of sunlight beamed down through the water all around. The Orca's hull cast a giant shadow over the green depths. Quint saw the other ends of the barrel lines, taut and moving. They extended down into the Orca's shadow and disappeared.

The shark was alive. It lurked below, swimming in circles. He could tell this from the motion of the two barrel lines that dropped into shadow.

A few deep draws of air to fill his blood with oxygen and stretch his lungs. The bottle tossed back into the aft deck of the Orca and Quint settled into the cold water. Another series of rapid breaths, and he was ready.

Quint took in a massive gulp of air and stretched his chest to the fullest capacity. He looked at the clouds above and dropped below the waves.

No time to think. Just get to work.

Hand over hand, he pulled himself along the hull of the Orca by the working line he tied earlier. He felt the waves sweeping in and the current try to wrench his body from the hull. His hands gripped tight and worked their way to the center keel. He felt the large plate of Corten steel. The rudder's metal exterior had pitted from the years of saltwater corrosion. Quint felt the divots and imperfections. He opened his eyes. Tolerable was the saltwater sting on his already bloodshot corneas. He pulled the rudder away from the propeller, then secured the rudder chain to the hull with a new shackle—a miracle the chain remained in one piece. His lungs felt strong. Still plenty of oxygen.

He moved to the propeller and worked his way towards the shaft. The barrel lines tangled around the shaft just behind the prop. He looked down to the lines pulled taut and moving in slow circles. The shadow of the Orca loomed wide, reaching deep below him. It swallowed the other ends of the barrel lines. The green sunlit water outside the Orca's hull lent enough of its ambiance to give him guidance. Quint pulled down on the blades of the propeller, turning the shaft counterclockwise. His hands worked to pull the ropes from their fouled nest. A few inches at a time, with every quarter turn of the prop, the lines pulled free.

His lungs ached. It had been over a minute. Almost there.

He felt a presence and spun around.

A small pilot fish cruised in to see what offerings the commotion may serve to it. Quint turned back to the propeller and pulled down hard to work another quarter turn. He pulled on the barrel lines with his right hand, and they released from under themselves, drifting free from the dark shape of the Orca.

Quint felt relieved and wanted to surface for a breath. He turned away from the Orca's hull in triumph.

The black eyes of the great white shark glared at him an arm's length away. The great fish, almost three times his size, broke from the Orca's shadow and closed in from below. Quint's eyes widened and strained to look through the churning Atlantic at the monster's slow, nightmarish ascent. He no longer had a concern for air. He let go of the line on the Orca and reached for the depth charge explosive that slung across his chest. The white shark's jaw dropped in slow motion. Great jaws of terror flashing rows of teeth with a snarl. The shark's tail stalled.

Both opponents, suspended in ocean and time, faced each other. Quint looked into the lifeless eyes before him. He shouted the rest of the air from his lungs in a stream of bubbles and muffled noise. His fingers grabbed for the safety ring on the firing trigger, and he kicked towards the light above.

He punched through the surface of the water. His chest ached from the stretching for more air. Quint threw the sling from his shoulder and pulled the pin, releasing the trigger. The metal cylinder began a series of timed clicks inside.

He steadied himself and waited.

The dark gray skin of the great white's head broke the surface. Quint saw its scars—healed gouges and battle wounds from its life of hunting and killing. The shark remained motionless.

"No!"

Quint slapped at the massive animal. "Fight me, fish!"

He cursed it for denying him the fate he saw in a thousand restless nights. His mind—a reactionary void of irrational thought. The man prepared to die, while his soul wrenched back from the white light by a failing fish.

The shark hung on the surface of the water. Its great dorsal fin and wide body slumped over. The fish died and rolled into the Atlantic.

Out of time, Quint pitched the clicking metal canister further out to sea. The weighted mechanism hit the water and erupted with an explosion just a few feet below the surface. The blast of a white oceanic mist hung thirty feet in the air. He felt the shock wave of the distant pressure on his chest. The exploded water returned from above in cold droplets across Quint's face and the vast white belly of the dead shark next to him.

51 SECOND CHANCE

It took all the strength left in his soul to pull himself up the rope and back into the Orca. Quint collapsed on the deck. His muscles convulsed in a series of tremors. He crossed his arms and embraced his shivering upper body, pulling in tight. The cold never felt so painful to him before.

I was reborn. The cold, the pain, the fatigue—they all let me know I was still alive. No way in hell does a ghost feel this bad. I should have removed the wet clothes and gone inside. No strength. Just lay on the aft deck and breathe. I stared at the clouds. The air never tasted so sweet.

I am human. My rejoice in life only lasted a minute. An anger builds inside. The words from Vaughn playing in my mind: 'Nobody cares because there is no proof.' I got your proof right here, Mr. Mayor. The tourists will have a heart attack when they see it.

Quint sat up and leaned over the gunwale. The white underside and pectoral fins of the shark's carcass sat atop the chopping waves. The barrel lines snaked across its body and strewn about the surrounding water. A wave brushed over the shiny skin and pushed on the body. The ocean looked to reclaim its warrior—the shark began to sink.

Get up and get to work, boy! Move!

He pulled at the zipper of his sullen jacket and ripped the water weighted coat from his shoulders. The chill of November hit him hard. Adrenaline would keep him moving and warm for now. Quint threw the long boat hook across the water. The pole was long enough to reach the first floating barrel line. He hooked the line and pulled it to his outstretched fingers. Hand over hand, he moved with a clumsy speed. The cold water from the rope fibers numbed his touch. His fingers cramped and wanted to seize like rusted machinery without oil. Every movement, no matter how small, hurt the desperate captain.

The first barrel pulled up over the gunwale and Quint let it roll to the starboard side of the aft deck. As he pulled in the slack around the forward port cleat, he watched the last of the great white slip below the surface. The shark's gleaming white underside, now a glowing shape of green below the waves.

Pull dammit! Pull it in and lock it off. You are losing him.

His arms had the strength of an eighty-year-old. He was so tired. His mouth burned from the thirst and tried to curse his body's lack of strength, but only a slur of sound escaped past his swollen tongue.

The first line went taught, and he took three figure-eight wraps on the cleat.

That harpoon won't hold two tons of shark. The sea is picking up. Sun is hanging low. It must be late afternoon.

While Quint boat-hooked the second barrel line, he watched the shape of the shark to make sure it didn't fade from view. The great white body suspended a few feet below the water's churn. He recovered the second yellow barrel and pulled it into the aft deck. Quint worked with a newfound fury. His target of revenge shifted. No longer did he see the shark as the enemy. The fallen beast would be his greatest triumph. The war over the politicians was still worth the fight. He hated the politicians just as much as the sharks. They tormented Captain McVay and hung him out on a yardarm. He pulled in the second line and took a few turns on the cleat mounted at the transom. He smiled and the nerve from his missing tooth winced from the icy breeze. The thought of using the largest shark he ever killed to sink the career of a crooked politician amused him.

The Orca rose with a surprise swell, and Quint saw the rocks just beyond the bow. Breakers exploded in white foam under the hunting pulpit. He rushed to the helm inside the pilothouse and fired up the engine. No time to idle. He locked the transmission in reverse and pushed the throttle forward. The engine roared and coughed. A slight tremor under the hull from what little water the damaged propeller could push.

Those harpoons won't hold that weight forever. The shark is just below the surface, and I can reach it. Gotta hook the fish and rig it close to the hull. The rocks of Montauk are off the bow. Only one good fin on the prop and the Orca is in a crawl at full throttle. There's still time.

With master seamanship, Quint secured the steering wheel inside the cabin with a rope sling. A few quick knots and turns around the pipe housing for the upper controls, and the Orca's rudder locked amidships. The Orca could stay moving backwards while he worked the catch.

Quint emerged from the cabin and took a set of blocks from the deck. He hoisted one large two-sheave block above his head and clipped its forged iron hook onto the end of the davit arm. He reached down and snatched the massive landing hook from the deck. A quick bowline to secure the end of a heavy heaving line to the hook, and he moved to the port side.

The Orca pushed backwards and groaned when the waves tossed it around. Cold water splashed over the side of the aft deck, and Quint took a wider stance to lock in his footing.

I left the helm of the Orca amidships and in full reverse—pushing with little speed against the growing seas. The longest five minutes of my life. The boat listed to port with the four-thousand pounds of shark hanging from her cleats. No telling how long those harpoons will hold in its hide.

His eyes searched along the white outline of the fish, stopping at its head. Quint peered down past the surface bubbles to the mouth of the shark. He gripped the large landing hook with a fist, as a warrior wields a sword into battle. The Orca pitched forward. The turbulent seas assaulted the hull from all directions.

A white-knuckle grip on the mooring cleat with his left hand, Quint slung his body over the side of the Orca and reached down into the water. His right hand, clutching the iron hook, searched along the mouth of the great white. His fingertips felt the teeth on the inside of its mouth. The mouth hung open, just out of reach. Quint sucked in a chest full of air and stretched out his left-arm hold on the Orca's port side. His head and right shoulder dropped into the water. The massive white lower jaw of the capsized shark hung a few feet from his face. He reached his hand into the mouth of the great fish and pulled it closer to the hull. His fist sliced open on a sharp tooth and bled. Quint inserted the hook into the mouth to where his forearm pushed inside the animal.

His arm sunk into the cavern of teeth and reached inside the shark, just behind the right corner of the lower jaw. Feeling for the corner of the enormous mouth, he pulled the hook forward and watched the sharp point of iron pierce the white flesh of the jowl. The hook set deep into the thick muscled mandible and anchored against the skull. Quint pulled his hand free from the mouth just as the entire shark shifted.

A rogue wave sent the Orca aloft, and Quint felt the gravity of the moment. The great white shark lifted into him. He pulled on his left arm as the Orca came crashing down into the sea. The momentum of the fall tossed the captain onto the aft deck like a rag doll. The monster fish slammed against the hull and the harpoons buried in its body broke free from their hold. Another wave broke over the starboard side. A battered Quint sprawled across the deck, doused with water. A loose yellow barrel rolled into his head. The impact clouded his thoughts. He heard the engine groan as the one-blade prop grabbed water to pull through the heavy seas.

I saw it. The line rigged to the landing hook in the shark's mouth. It payed out. The waves hit hard. The shark broke free from the barrel lines I tied off to the Orca. I watched the rope feed over the gunwale. The sea was taking it from me.

Quint refused to fail. That moment, every adversarial thought and deep-seated guilt summoned up from his soul in the few feet of loose rope that snaked away from him along the deck of the Orca and disappeared over the side. He envisioned the weight of the shark dropping its body into the shadowy depths to be lost forever.

The words of Knocko played in his mind: *'You always have been a failure, Quint. Everything you touch dies. Just like her. Just like your Pa.'*

Quint lashed out at the escaping last few feet of rope. He screamed a wild rage from deep inside and seized the running fibers with his right hand. His grip became iron. A half century of labor-fueled muscle fibers and tendons wrenched down. He squeezed with every grain of resentment from his life. His right arm pulled and locked. Quint dropped onto his back and swung his left arm over to the large, heavy two-sheave block that laid on the deck. He screamed and felt his body stretch when the weight of the fish jammed against his hand. The rope slipped through his fingers and the Orca took another wave across the stern. The crash of cold water fell across his face and the boat pushed backwards, the rope pulled and extended Quint's arm even more.

He screamed in painful horror as his hand lost all feeling. The nerves. His right hand. The upper arm. Quint remembered protecting Harold on the net. The pounding on the shark's head with his right fist. The big Chinese fella pushing down and destroying his right arm on the table. It returned. His arm failed. All sense of feeling left his hand and his grip loosened.

The Orca pitched to the stern from a swell and the rope went slack for a moment. Quint circled his forearm, taking two wraps of rope around his dead wrist and hand. The boat leveled out and the rope bit into his skin. The flesh tore and blood seeped between the fibers of the nautical line.

Another scream of pain. Quint clutched the large block with his left hand and laid on his back across his deck to keep his body from being pulled into the water with the fish. Both arms drawn to the side and stretched. He stared up at the sky. The clouds began their turn to orange in the low hanging sun. The muscles in his neck strained. His shoulders burned.

Quint looked over at the gear lying next to the gunwale. The small hoist the line foreman had given him over a decade ago rested in the mix of gear laid across the deck. His left hand reached for the hook on one end. The turbulent ocean pulled the heavy shark another few inches and the rope bit into the bones of Quint's lower right hand. He felt them twist. The warmth of the blood on his skin alarmed him. He was sure it would sever his hand on the next rogue wave.

His left hand set the hook of the soft pullers into the large block on the deck. The brass grip clipped to the other end reflected the setting sun. Quint pulled it over to the line around his right hand. With his free hand, he pushed the grip open and set its teeth around the tightened hook line just beyond his bloody fingers. The grip bit down onto the rope. Quint grabbed the working end from the slack blocks and pulled.

Locking them off, he released the tensioned blocks, and they sprung into the air, catching the weight of the shark. The large two-sheave block lifted off the deck and the davit arm flexed in shock from the massive pull against its rigging. Quint's right arm dropped when the blood-soaked line wrapped around his hand slacked. The shark was once again his.

I should be dead. The shark expired a few feet from me. Another few beats of its heart... maybe two strokes of its tail and I'd been up to my hips in teeth. I'm sure of it. We both would've gone up in that explosion of water. That's not such a bad way to go, is it?

It took me another hour to rig the shark to the Orca with only one good arm. My right hand crushed and bleeding. Still no strength in my right arm. I'm used to it.

I secured the shark's head with the hook in its mouth from the davit arm off the port side. The entire fish stretches all the way to the stern. I roped a tail line around the thick part of its hind end and fastened it to the stern cleat. Another line around its midsection to keep it righted and snug to the hull.

Check my charts. Seventy-two miles from Amity Point. I don't know how I'm going to make it.

Quint turned the wheel and pointed the Orca's bow due east. He pushed on the throttle and felt little movement. He watched the landmarks of Montauk point drift further away. Using the visuals and the years of boating experience, he calculated the top speed of the Orca was now three miles per hour. The damage to the propeller coupled with the fifteen-degree list to port from the four-thousand-pound great white lashed to the side made for a new fight. A fight against the sea and time. The shark hobbled Quint and his boat.

They found themselves at the mercy of a vengeful ocean.

52   CURSED VICTORY

For the first time in days, Quint allowed his mind to be at peace. Only time stood in his way. For that, there was nothing he could do but wait. The Orca limped forward with following seas. The last time he checked his charts and worked the math, with an almost-three knot top speed, Amity Point harbor sat a long twenty-four hours away. He topped off the fuel tank with the reserve fuel canisters and double checked the lashing on the steering wheel inside the cabin. Locked in full throttle and the wheel secured from spinning aside, the Orca pushed on herself. He rested.

Hauling two tons of shark on a propeller with one good blade. I could row faster than this slog.

Quint stumbled through the cabin doorway and slumped into the port side gunwale. The glorious sunset to the west warmed the right side of his face. He had seen many sunsets during his time at sea. All over the world, no two were ever the same. He figured this one might be the most beautiful. The crisp autumn air from the north smelled clean and offered the clearest visibility. The color of the water, the mysterious clouds dispersed across the orange beams of light, the endless horizon in all directions. All these factors played second fiddle to the main reason he thought this sunset was the most beautiful. This was the first sunset he thought he'd never see. He felt the warmth on his face—grateful to be alive.

He looked over at the fallen warrior. The giant shark was too heavy to bring out of the water. He pulled as much as he could and only got its wide back to the surface. The sixteen-foot inanimate body of the shark cut through the water below. The regal dorsal fin towered above the slight wake flowing from the Orca's bow.

Quint looked at this shark differently than all the rest. He remembered the men he killed in battle. The Japanese soldier defending the beachhead of Iwo Jima. Hand to hand combat, and he watched the other man's life leave his body. The shark went the same way. He watched life leave its body. The difference was in the eyes. A man's eyes have life behind them. He knew when the other guy died. Quint looked down at the pitch-black eyes of the great white just under the surface. Even in death, it still looked at him with a haunting stare. It watched him. He was sure of it.

The tired captain leaned out and placed his left hand on the dorsal fin of the great white. He dragged his fingers across its dark gray shine. The slight grit of its skin—microscopic teeth catching and cutting the very tips of his fingers.

I scraped my pruned fingers across the dorsal. Saw a small piece of my skin left hanging on the gray sandpaper hide. The ultimate warrior—even in death, taking the fight to his killer. May I have the strength one day to be such a fighter?

His throat swelled from thirst. Quint shuddered at the memory of long ago. He needed to get something in his body. The swelling in his right elbow kept him from straightening his arm out. Only the thumb and index finger worked on his right hand. The crushing of the rope reduced it to a bloody mess, which he held close to his body.

Quint reached his knife over the gunwale and plunged the blade into the back of the great white. Just under the dorsal fin, he sliced into the thick, muscular trunk. He watched the water run over the base of the fin and rinse the bloody section of missing meat. Legs weak and back sore, he didn't have the strength to move into the cabin and prepare the shark meat. Instead, Quint slumped back down onto the deck and rested with his back to the dorsal fin.

He held the bloody fillet of shark in his hand. A small piece whittled off its back, and he ate his first meal in many days. The rubbery rawness and salty taste—an award-winning steak to a starving man. He sucked and savored the juice before swallowing, then watched the blood of the shark mix with the dried blood of the rope burns on his hand.

The mayor has no idea what is coming for him. You hear me, fish? I'll have to find myself a serious taxidermy man. Back in Amity Point, you will be the biggest tourist deterrent an island has ever seen. Nobody's going swimming when they see the likes of you hanging over the shack.

Quint looked to the west. For the moment—a first in his life. The warm sun set upon the cracked skin of his face and Quint felt victorious. A triumph over impossible odds. A life of loss and pain. Failure and anger. All a distant memory. Tomorrow he'll enter the harbor a conquering hero. It will be his finest hour.

He took another piece of shark meat into his mouth and breathed through his nose. Quint felt alive and believed nothing could take this moment from him. The captain, who lived an entire lifetime and never felt success, won at last.

This is how it feels to win. It sure is the most beautiful sunset.

Behind him, the dorsal fin moved.

Quint sat, chewing on his dinner of raw shark and never saw it. Another twitch, and a slight splash. He could not hear it over the low rumble of the Orca's engine reverberating below his legs. Another flicker behind him. The glare of the setting sun reflected off the shiny fin's movement and into the corner of Quint's eye.

He turned around and watched the body of the great white move. He held his breath and understood what was happening.

I should've remembered—they come for you first when you are alone. They attack at sunrise and sunset. They found me.

Quint propped himself up by his left arm on the gunwale's edge and peered over the side. A section of the great white's body was missing. The wake of the Orca washed away the shredded dark gray skin and bloody meat, leaving a trail of red streaming towards the stern.

A large oceanic whitetip shark surged from the deep north Atlantic water and hit the body of the great white. The carcass of the dead shark shifted and shook as the smaller predator bit down with an evil fury—another hunk of flesh taken. Red foam clouded the ocean around the port side of the slow-moving Orca. Quint watched the feeding frenzy from the safety of his platform and remembered them doing the same to his Indianapolis shipmates. He screamed in a wild rage. The once-triumphant captain looked with eyes of disbelief as the demons from the past swarmed him to take his victory, one bite at a time.

The captain descended into madness. Fury and adrenaline mixed with fear, then cemented by the screaming memories of those he saw get eaten alive. Quint stormed into the wheelhouse and emerged with the M1 Garand rifle and a large metal ammunition box. He didn't feel the cold air. Nor did he care for his swollen tongue and emaciated body. Only hatred focused his eyes. These demons from the deep couldn't die fast enough.

The haunted man ignored the pain of his arm, and shouldered the rifle, taking aim into the red churning waters around the great white. He fired eight shots into whatever dorsal fins moved and circled the bleeding carcass. Oceanic whitetip sharks flinched and retreated. Some took rounds into their hides and vanished below the waves. The empty clip ejected from the top of the rifle and Quint dropped to his knees to execute a perfect battle load with a new clip of eight rounds. He rose to his feet just as the next wave of oceanic whitetips closed in. With precision firing, he made every round count. If the sharks dared surface, he sent them back to the depths. They did not care, for their numbers were many. They responded to his rifle in waves of attack.

Another ping sounded out—an empty metal clip sent into the air. Quint dropped to reload, ignoring his ringing ears and sinuses filled with gun smoke. He lost all sense of reality. This was a nightmare he'd seen before. He battled the relentless wave of oceanic terrors. They followed him and waited. They heard the struggling sounds of his propeller and the slow-moving drone of the engine. These sharks knew when to attack. He hated to be outsmarted by them. Despite his knowing this fight to be insurmountable, he fired his rifle and emptied another clip.

The sharks moved in a pack and learned. They learned the surface was death, so they stayed deep and attacked from below. The white underbelly of the great white offered an endless feast for their starving bodies. One last splendid meal before their long migration south to warmer waters.

Quint's damaged right hand squeezed and fired the last few rounds into the deep. It was worthless, and he knew it. The bullets were useless after a few feet of water. The sharks were too deep. A final clip left the rifle in a smokey trail of warmth, and he was out. He looked down at the deck of rolling brass cartridges. The empty casings swarmed around the overturned shallow ammunition box and hot metal clips. He dropped to his knees. The rifle met the deck of the Orca with a dense thud. A stream of smoke still rising from the barrel.

The rifle's kick reduced his shoulder to jelly. The bruising inside left him with an even worse right arm than before. It had been decades since he fired so many rounds in such a short time. He collapsed backwards onto the hot brass— hands shaking and chest heaving for air. The exhausted man listened to the hull. Through the engine's rattle, he heard their thrashing subside. The bumps and pounding of the feeding frenzied bodies against the hull faded with the sun from the sky.

The last of the orange light left the clouds above his head and the sharks retreated into the darkness below. Quint just laid there and looked at the heavens. His heart pounded the inside of his chest. The inner ear, assaulted by gunfire, muffled the sounds of the surrounding ocean. He only heard the blood pump through his skull and felt the engine's heavy reverberations beneath him.

The Orca continued to lumber east and never stopped.

53   LAST STAND

His brain shut down with the gentle sway of the deck under his head. The Orca rocked him and sang to him with the steady sounds of her injured propeller on the ocean. No dreams or memories of happier times dared to enter his mind. Only a deep fragment of missing time that is sleep for a man worked to his body's physical limitations.

The darkness of the ocean swaddled him until a cold snapping wind gust shook him back to life. He opened his eyes and stared into the scratched surface of a wood plank. The dim white light of the moon and stars made the droplets of blood on the deck visible. The night sucked any color of red out of them, reminding him of the black oil leaking from an engine's valve cover. His aging mind could not process where he was. Was it all a dream? Was this life after death? He imagined the Orca—his Charon, taking him to Hades.

With a brutal fury, all thoughts of his situation fired through the synapses of the brain and Quint erupted from the deck of the Orca. His heart raced and pumped the adrenaline-fueled blood through his body.

The whitetips. Fight them. Fight them now!

The panicked sailor scrambled across the deck of empty brass casings and endless turns of uncoiled rope. He rolled a stray yellow barrel to the side and reached for the port side gunwale.

Please, let it still be there. Please, God, let there be something left to defend.

Quint pulled himself up and peered over the side. They reduced the large carcass of the great white by a third. Its length was still intact, but the girth of the animal eaten away by the marauding horde with white-tipped fins. The dim light of an impending dawn allowed him to see the level of destruction.

Look what they did to you, fish? Look at what they took from me? No, they didn't take it all. Still enough here to prove you exist.

I'm out of ammunition. If only I had brought more clips—and water. No more time. Curse my body for falling asleep. No idea how long I was out. The Orca is moving as fast as she can. Every straggling fish and night feeder had taken a piece of the great white. Still enough there to show the size. There must be a chum trail for twenty miles behind us to the west. At sunrise, they'll come calling.

The sky turned to a light shade of gray. The moon and stars began their retreat to the heavens. Quint moved with a tortured body. He readjusted his rigging on the great white. The port list of the Orca was not as extreme, telling him the sharks took off at least a thousand pounds of weight from his catch. He wanted to get the dead animal out of the water. Quint rigged a rusted but well-oiled chain hoist between the mast and the working line from the block that suspended the head of the great white. He cranked on the chain hoist, taking the fish higher with every click of the handle. The wood of the jib arm flexed with the added pressure—a feather's weight from snapping.

That's all she's got. The jib will give way with another click on the hoist. Can't get the fish anymore out of the water than the top of the head. The tail's eaten away. I fixed the line at the stern, but the lower half of the shark is submerged. They will return. I don't know how long I can hold them off. Almost sunrise, and Amity Point is still ten hours away.

The sun cracked the linear horizon of blackness and added color to the ocean. Quint raced back and forth to collect every spear, harpoon head, knife, and stabbing weapon he would need. He double checked the turns on each cleat to make sure they would hold.

To take the rest of you, they will have to come to the surface and take what's left. I will be waiting.

He went inside the cabin and fastened his antique military jacket. The fabric tag with his stenciled name had frayed. The left breast pocket had torn away at the inside seam next to the zipper. This jacket had been through a lot, and now he needed one more fight out of it.

Quint checked the Orca's bearings and then stepped back outside with the first light of dawn. The warmth of the sun and the slight chop of the seas. It would be a beautiful day under any other circumstances.

He looked down into the moving water at the great white. The magnificent dorsal fin, drying and wrinkled in the cold air—a monument over the water sliding down the hull. Exposed above the surface, the giant head of the shark. Its pointed snout aimed forward. The head cut through the water and left a wake of its own. Suspended by the ropes and lashings, it still cruised through the water on a hunt.

I don't know what I hate more. The thought of feeding them with you. Or the thought of losing you and the mayor getting away with it all. You were the first one I ever saw take two barrels and still fight. You had me dead to rights but couldn't close the deal. Maybe you and I are the same, fish? Two hunters with bad luck. Your luck just ran out first. I'm sure mine will run out soon enough. Not today, though. On this day, I'll send as many of them to their deaths as I can, fish. Or are they your revenge on me? All of this—the ocean telling me there will be no winner in this fight. Have I tempted the seas enough?

The tiger could have taken me just as easily as it took Troy. With a flick of its tail, a second swing of its head—I'd been pounding and screaming in its mouth down into the deep. What made the shark take him instead of me? There are no coincidences. What made you die an arm's length from your attack on me? There must be a purpose to it all.

"Maybe they forgot about us, fish."

No sooner had the thought verbalized from his mind, did the first shark emerge from below. Quint stood as praetorian guard for the remnants of the great white. The sun emerged above the horizon and its rays of orange turned to bright white, illuminating the deep green of the chilled North Atlantic. The Orca trudged ahead, with only twenty more miles to go.

Quint hovered above the gunwale with his pole spear raised as an Olympian wields a javelin.

A brown head of an eight-foot oceanic whitetip bit into the body of the great white just behind its gills. Quint took aim and plunged the eight-foot handle down into the attacking shark's head. He missed his target, but the shark let go and disappeared with a partial mouthful of meat.

I missed, dammit. No strength. My arms are shaking and unsteady. Don't fail me, you wretched body. If this is how you take care of me, then to hell with you. I'll get every drop of worth out of you or you can die right here. The choice is yours.

A tail slashed the surface of the water, and another oceanic hit the great white's frayed flesh. A thrust of the spear with all his strength. He felt the tip hit the cartilage vertebrae right behind the skull and sever it in half. The shark went limp and rolled off into the Orca's wake.

"Not so deadly when you come to a fair fight. You hear me, you demons? I know you're down there. I'll leave a trail of you in my wake. Come and try me."

The water around the great white erupted into chaos with a swarm of white-tipped fins and slashing jaws. A feeding frenzy had begun. The sharks stayed on the far side of the great white and gnashed their jaws of triangular razors with a zombie rage. They fell into their trance. Miles ago, they locked onto the blood and smell. They no longer felt pain or fear, just the ecstasy of flesh inside their mouths was their concern.

Quint jabbed into the thrashing and splashing cloud of bloody green Atlantic. They were too far out to reach. He stepped over the gunwale and onto the back of the great white. With one hand holding the tackle from the davit arm that held the hooked head of the giant carcass, Quint took a firm stance on the mound of dark gray skin and worked the spear into the enemy sharks. The heads of the sharks dodged and bit. Some exploded in bloody geysers from the punctures. The captain stood his ground and felt the cold sea water cover his feet. He no longer cared.

He saw their yellow eyes and remembered the deadly cat-like stare of the oceanic whitetip shark. For the last ten years, he took his fair share of them at the end of the yellow barrels. Two decades passed since he locked into hand-to-hand combat at the water's edge with them. With every stab of his spear, he remembered the details of long ago. The bronze color their skin takes in the sun. The maniacal way the yellow eye burns into you and watches your soul. Their numbers grew. The largest of them emerged to claim their revenge.

A ten-foot oceanic leapt from the ocean and went for Quint's leg. Quint drew his leg back, and the shark missed. Holding himself by a firm grip on the taut ropes from the hanging block, Quint kicked his leg and buried his foot into the gills of the shark. Another head broke from the water and clamped its jaws onto the pole spear. Quint struggled to free the spear, but the violent thrashing force from the frenzied fish ripped it from his hands.

The water exploded at the tail of the great white. An oceanic whitetip targeted the tail rope that secured the massive carcass to the Orca's stern. Quint saw the shark clamp onto the rope and twist its body in the boat's wake. He stepped up to the gunwale from the back of the great white and pushed off the shaking block of the taxed davit arm.

The sharks continued to rip into the great white. The ocean became a misty cloud of shredded flesh. By the hundreds, Oceanic whitetips had their way from underneath their dead cousin. The body of the great white shook and pulsed with the repeated hits from the shiver of sharks. Even with full bellies, the attackers relished in their victory and continued to feed.

Quint bounded across the aft deck towards the transom. He picked up a short-handled machete and flopped over the gunwale with both arms. The fatigue of battle sent his hands into a series of wide slashes against the shark. He cut into the body of the fish, and it let go of the rope. Another slash into its back, Quint felt the backbone sever. The wounded attacker whipped its tail and kicked into the green depths. Frayed fibers of the damaged rope twisted and shook while trying to hold the weight of the great white's stubbed and chewed tail.

Brown heads slammed against the body back towards the great white shark's gills and distracted him. Quint failed to see the next oceanic when it breached from underneath the transom and aimed its jaws at his arm. The shark's mouth caught on the frayed rope—blocked from biting down on the exposed right arm of Quint. The sudden surge caused him to rear back and throw a defensive swing of the machete into the shark's side. His blade buried in the glistening bronze skin and stuck deep. The shark released the rope from its mouth and dropped. His weakened fingers could not hold fast, and the machete handle ripped from Quint's hand. The whitetip disappeared under the waves with the blade buried in its side.

The fibers on the tail rope gave way from the shaking and snapped. Quint reached down with his left hand and grabbed. He caught the rope in his grip and pulled with all his strength. The immense weight of the half-eaten tail almost pulled him overboard. Quint screamed and surged backwards. His back muscles strained. The lower back tore at his spine. He pulled with all the power of his soul and lifted the tail enough to pin the rope over the edge of the gunwale and hold it down for leverage. The rope locked against the wood. His hand would have to come off before he let go.

Another surge of oceanic whitetips hit the great white and whittled down the body even more. Quint strained across the deck for a hand coil of rope less than a foot out of reach. He felt the tail rope surge against his left hand's grip from an additional weight. A wave of water kicked over the side and doused him as the next large oceanic whitetip struck. The muscular jaw extended from its skull and the fish bit down hard, adding its weight to the rope. The soaked fibers bit into his hand. Quint felt the skin on his palm tear and the warmth of the blood leaking from his fist. The shark shook its teeth into the white fleshy trunk of the great white's tail and the rope that secured it to Quint's hand.

He looked down at the oceanic whitetip and saw its yellow eyes. The dilated slit of black zeroed in on him. The shark tugged and pulled, shaking from side to side. Quint leaned hard to his right, grabbing for the short-handled baseball bat from its clip on the inside gunwale. His damaged right hand gripped the bat to swing it over the side. He clubbed the shark in the head, and it wouldn't release its grip. Quint swung the wooden bat again, and the weapon met its target. He felt the hardened cartilage of the shark's skull collapse and soften. The shark's eyes stayed locked on him. It never let go. Quint lost all strength with a barrage of strikes down on the head of the animal. The oceanic rolled into the water and hung from the great white's tail—its mouth locked in death. The added weight broke the frayed rope under the waterline and Quint fell backwards into the aft deck.

In the Orca's wake, the entire backside of the great white broke free and swung down into the depths. Strained wooden fibers of the davit arm creaked from the shifting weight of the half-eaten body hanging by its last few lashings of rope around the head and the hook in the corner of its jaws. The Orca groaned and rocked from the commotion along its port side. Her damaged propeller doing all it could to push ahead.

Quint's mind boiled. The defeat summoned a blind rage. He raced along the port gunwale and stopped above the suspended head of the enormous great white. It stared up at him with the soulless black eyes from the water churning with bronze fins. Quint gazed into the animal. Its massive mouth hung open and slack. He threw every spear he had left. When he ran out of stabbing weapons, he leaned over the side and clubbed the water. The wood of the Orca's gunwale dug into his ribs while he strained to reach. He looked into the black eye of the dead great white—only inches from his face.

Below the waterline, Quint saw the feeding frenzy rip the great white to pieces. Exhausted, his body devolved into a ballet of flailing desperation. He smashed at the water with the club in his hands. The splashing cold sea covered his face and the head of the monster next to him.

The white-tipped dorsal fins and tails never ceased. They invaded the Orca and took everything from him.

54   THE RETURN

On the third day, with the late afternoon sun's warmth across the stern, the Orca returned to Amity Point. The harbor laid silent and watched her pass through. Windows of houses and shacks shut at the sight of the beaten boat. The townsfolk averted their gaze. Nautical superstitions and dark tales of doom had preceded her—a cursed vessel and one to be avoided.

The engine's voice dwindled with an uneven sound of a damaged prop fighting to pull water. Her captain, reduced to a misshapen figure inside the cabin, slumped over the helm. Quint stared ahead. His eyes, bloodshot and unable to focus through the delirious haze of fatigue. He looked at the other shacks and vessels. Most fishermen ignored him and only waited for him to pass until they went about their day. Some of the braver ones looked upon his boat and peered through the dried salt haze clouding its glass windows. He felt their eyes of disdain but didn't care.

His head dropped into a subconscious nod, and he fought the temptation to pass out. Quint snapped his head back and adjusted the steering wheel. The Orca lurked towards the back of the harbor. The red tower of the fishing shack came into view. He looked off to port. There, up high, he saw Hershel at the deck of his little shack on the hill.

The Orca made its final push towards the dock. With the engine throttled down, it drifted, bow first, right into the back of the fishing shack. Its bow set into the wood of the dock with a slight nudge, as if to whisper she was home. The long hunting pulpit stretched across the seawall and reached to the steps of the fishing shack. The engine idled, then cut to silence. The exhausted captain staggered out of the wheelhouse. High tide kept the boat's port side gunwale above the dock, and the tired man reached for a weathered pylon. Uncoordinated muscles and a broken spirit, Quint stepped across the gap and laid ashore. He felt the quiet serenity of the land anchoring the pylon. He clutched the wood with both hands and collapsed to his knees. The stillness of the land underneath confused him. He fought hard to remember who he was and what he needed to do.

Hershel raced out to the dock from between the shacks. Out of breath, he stopped and recoiled from his reaction at the sight of his captain. He never saw Quint as broken and gaunt as what appeared in the crumpled mess of a man kneeling in front of him. Hershel looked to the davit arm extended over the space between the hull and the dock. Its block and tackle hung loose with a disheveled rigging of frayed ropes. The bloody mess of pulp and skin resembling the colossal head of a shark was all that clung to the Orca. The aft deck of chaos—yellow barrels and steel wire mixed with empty buckets of foul-smelling whale chum and severed ropes.

"Mr. Quint. I thought the worst had happened, sir."

Hershel fought back the tears in his eyes. Only minutes earlier, at the sight of the Orca returning to port, he realized he avoided the heart-breaking grief of losing another father to the sea.

Quint looked up at the weathered face of concern on Hershel. The wound of the missing tattoo on his arm stung with infection. The aged captain pulled himself back to his feet and leaned into the dried split wood of the pylon.

"Hersh, you've always been a faithful first mate. If I searched for a lifetime, I'd never find another like you. Follow me this one last time."

"Captain, I'll follow you to the ends of the Earth. You are the only family I got."

The sailor and his captain exchanged a nod. A single tear in Hershel's eye was the greatest salute the captain had ever received. The nod of approval returned to Hershel from his captain was the greatest fatherly hug he ever felt.

"Next time, you take the helm."

"Aye aye, Captain."

"Throw a stern line on her and get the pickup started. We are going into town."

"Yes, sir."

"No need to call me 'sir', boy."

Hershel jumped into the aft deck of the Orca.

"Yes, sir."

The captain straightened and pushed with his legs. He careened into the wooden barrels of fresh water under the shack and collapsed onto the rim of the largest one. His cracked hands shoveled the water in desperation. He drank for the first time in days. Life emerged from his insides with every gulp. Thoughts of settling the score returned to him.

Quint reached to the wall for a five-foot rope sling and a carving knife. Back to the Orca, he knelt on the dock and leaned over to work what they left of the great white's head. The body separated by its weight during the frenzied attack at sea. The chewed remnants of the massive carcass broke free between the cracked vertebrae behind the skull and sank to the depths many miles back. Devoured to the base of the skull, only the pointed snout and wide mouth remained.

His knife pierced the white flesh under the snout. Quint carved the blade across the top of the upper jaw line. The size of the teeth reminded him that only one day ago, this was the largest fish he ever caught.

"If only this island saw the whole of you, fish. What a different story they would tell."

He smiled at the thought of talking to the fish.

They are certain to think you as crazy now. Good. They haven't seen madness yet. These people of Amity don't know what's coming for them.

Quint threaded the center loop of the rope sling under the jaws and pushed it back through the space he carved under the shark's nose. He wove the two ends back through the loop to secure a hold on the upper jaw with a girth hitch. With the rope sling clamped inside his fist and holding the weight of the jaws, his weakened right hand struggled to carve into the flesh and tendons around the shark's mouth.

He hadn't been this tired in decades, and he forgot how every movement is a struggle. The simplest tasks become exhaustive conflicts. He pushed and worked the blade until his right arm gave out once more. The jaws of the great white broke free from the cavernous head when Quint's right hand released the knife. Quint shouted in pain and watched the blade disappear into the green harbor waters. Only his left hand worked. He adjusted his grip on the rope sling and heaved the massive set of jaws up from the Orca's hull.

The air from the windows of the pickup truck was cold but felt good. Quint pulled his Navy chief petty officer shirt over his shoulders. The dark navy-blue wool appeared black in the setting sun that reflected off the side mirror and illuminated Quint's face. He sank into the passenger side of the bench seat, watching the sand dunes and eel grass of South Beach race by.

Hershel looked over at his captain and wanted to ask questions. He knew there would be time for questions later. He stayed silent and just drove.

The pickup truck found an empty main street in the town of Amity. The tourists had all vanished. Only the owners of the businesses remained to count their summer-dollar profits. They too would soon be gone to abandon the island until spring. A cluster of late 1960s cars gathered in front of a large white building of antique architecture. Hershel brought the pickup truck to a halt further down the street and looked at his captain.

The truck doors slammed, sending rusted metal flakes to the pavement. The two men walked side-by-side, down the sidewalks of new concrete.

Quint's right arm dangled at his side—limp and useless. His left hand held the leash of the trophy tight against his hip.

The large bloody jaws of the great white flopped and bounced with every step. The raw gristle of decaying shark skin reeked and drew the sand flies in. Women revolted in horror while averting their children's eyes when the two sailors strode past. The shopkeepers hollered at the trail of blood and slime left down the center of the sidewalk when the jaws dragged behind Quint for a spell.

Their scowled dankness split bright-colored clothes and optimistic pedestrian smiles. They waded right through them all. Quint scoffed at the people and glared his eyes at the approaching sign of the large white building—Amity Town Hall.

"Before we move on to general business, I just wanted to remind everyone the Selectmen voted unanimously today to issue four more motel permits in the wake of our biggest summer season yet. These permits will start in the spring for the 1969 season and be good for ten years."

Mayor Larry Vaughn sat at the head desk with the other four elder statesmen. The governing body of selectmen looked over a full community room of fifty people. Store owners, hotel managers, real estate brokers, and concerned Amity residents sat and listened. The small council chambers ran out of chairs, leaving many standing and annoyed. They huddled close together to listen to the mayor speak.

Vaughn continued. "We are awarding these permits to those who apply and can verify they meet the required codes. We have granted the first to Mrs. Taft, who's sitting down in front next to Mr. Taft. She already runs one motel and is looking to expand onto the existing footprint. Congratulations to her."

A smattering of applause and a few whispers back and forth.

"If they can make more money, then what about shop permits? I could open another location."

"Extra tourists? Where are you going to put them? I don't want cars parked in front of my store?"

The rustle of the crowd grew louder. Some sat and listened with their patient hands raised. Other called out their concerns.

The mayor's gavel fell against the wood of the desk to control the noise.

"Now these are all valid concerns, and nice ones to have. This means we are growing. All things that happen when communities become successful. So, let's keep it all in proper perspective. There will be enough time to handle each of these concerns in the coming months—"

"What is that smell?"

"Do you smell that too? Did someone drag a dead animal in here?"

"Someone, open a window."

The murmur of the crowd filled the small chamber room. Larry Vaughn pounded on the desk with his gavel to bring order. The standing crowd behind the seated citizens backed away. Mayor Larry Vaughn paused his gavel when he saw him through the parting crowd.

In the back of the room, next to a green chalkboard full of notes and plans for the Amity town expansion, Quint sat in silence with his head down. Next to his chair, the flies buzzed over the glistening red pile of teeth, cartilage jawbone, and hanging white skin. A pool of blood and sea water leaked around Quint's soiled deck shoes and collected in the seams of the varnished wood floor.

Larry Vaughn rose to his feet to see the excessive mess of unrecognizable fish carnage everyone stared at.

The other selectmen, their vantage point blocked by those seated in front, also stood to get a better view. Voices from the crowd bounced across the room.

"Who's that?"

"It's the one from Amity Point."

"I heard about him."

Mayor Vaughn shifted the talk of the room in a concerned tone.

"Alright, folks. It's getting late, and that beautiful sunset outside should be enjoyed. We will adjourn for today and resume tomorrow afternoon."

Vaughn clacked his gavel one last time. The seated crowd grumbled and gathered their hats, purses, and windbreakers. Those closest to the door in the back of the room already filed out while holding their noses. Mrs. Taft stood up in front and shifted her horn-rimmed glasses while looking at Quint.

"Is this some kind of joke, Larry? I don't think that's funny at all."

The mayor never took his eyes off the man in the back of the room while responding to her concerns. "Alright, Mrs. Taft. Nothing to be concerned about."

"But we had the parking zones to discuss."

"We will go over everything in full tomorrow. You go home and get some rest."

Mrs. Taft held a handkerchief over her nose and stayed on the far side of her husband while they both exited the room with the crowd. One by one, the people passed Quint. Taking a long step over the growing pool of blood and oil seeping off the pile of shark mess.

One selectman, Harry Keisel, leaned over to Vaughn.

"You want me to call the constable in from Nantucket, Larry? This looks like trouble. I told you we should have a full-time police officer."

"No, Harry. No trouble at all. You fellas clear on out and let me handle this. I'll be fine."

The four older gentlemen filed out of the room and left the mayor standing at the desk by himself. Hershel stood outside in the long hallway and watched the selectmen leave, whispering their concerns.

Quint sat and stared at the floor. The setting sunlight shone through the windows behind the mayor and smeared across the reflective hardwood surface. He watched the pool of blood from the shark's jaws extend further and touch the sunlit shine on the floor. His tired eyes blurred. They focused on the tiny particles of dust floating in the rays of light.

Larry Vaughn was the first to break the tension.

"What do you have there, Mr. Quint?"

"Proof."

"Proof of what?"

"That you lied to these people. You never told them the full story of this island."

Larry Vaughn laughed in a rehearsed manner and gathered himself. He ran a hand through his hair and scratched the back of his head while contemplating the Rolodex of responses flipping through his mind. Quint looked up and saw Vaughn searching for words.

"You are nervous, Mr. Mayor. I can see you're rattled."

Vaughn shook his head and pulled out a cigarette from his fashionable brown suit jacket.

"My wife says that I should quit these things. Says these will kill you. There are a lot of things that will kill us these days. But we still do them."

Quint stayed slumped in the metal folding chair and watched the mayor light a cigarette. Vaughn stepped out from behind the long wooden arc of the town selectmen desk and made his way to towards Quint.

"You see, Mr. Quint? The one thing nobody taught you—presentation. It's not whether you have proof. It's how you present the proof that matters to these people."

Quint remained silent. He burned inside with rage, but his body lacked the energy to stand. The mayor looked him over.

"What do you have there?"

"The jaws of a great white shark. Sixteen-footer. This was attacking fishing nets out west. Been here a few times over the years."

"Yes, that may be true. But what they all saw was a broken, crazy old fisherman who stinks to high heaven sitting in front of piled fish guts. You can't even see the teeth through all that gristle. Presentation, Mr. Quint. It goes a long way."

The mayor exhaled his cigarette smoke through the orange rays of setting sunlight.

Quint held his right arm to his stomach. It pulsed with pain.

"There are reports to the Coast Guard in Amity Point," said Quint. "A fisherman out there lost his kid to this thing."

"Hearsay. Stories. Accidents happen. Let me tell you one."

Larry Vaughn flipped a chair from the back row around and took a seat to face Quint. He paused while looking down and then moved the chair over a few inches to make sure the puddle of blood didn't touch his brown leather shoes.

"Years ago, two kids go out for a swim off Avril Bay less than a dozen yards from the shore. They get tired and make a deal to race back and see who wins. The younger kid, who never has won anything before, gives it his all. He's going to swim as fast as his body would allow and he does. He slams the water until his shoulders burn, reaches the shallows, and sprints back to sand. Out of breath and laughing, he turns and... nothing. Not a trace of the other boy. What was a small childhood victory turns into fear then grief. I hate these animals more than you would ever know. My older brother always beat me in the water. The one day he let me take the lead. Just being a good big brother and all—and it took him. He disappeared. They called it an accident. A drowning with undercurrents taking his body out to sea. I knew better. I saw the fin. My mother, God rest her soul, knew better. They have always been here off Amity. There were only a few hundred of us who lived here back then—forty years ago. All these people don't have a clue because they weren't here."

Quint interrupted the mayor. "It was the whales. Your family has been luring them here all this time."

"That's right. My father called it an accident. He knew the money was more important. I went on and swore if I ever get control of the business, I'll get someone in here that will kill them all. And I did."

"That's impossible. This is a great white. They get a taste of whale, and they never forget."

"The whaling is done. It's over. Nothing this size will be around here again."

"I'm going to let everyone know."

"Know what? That you killed a bunch of fish? They won't care. The fact is the water is safe and cash is king."

Larry Vaughn laughed and sat back in his chair to take another drag of his cigarette and loosen his necktie.

"Mr. Quint, I am the elected mayor of this town. These people you just saw in here stand to make hundreds of thousands of dollars over the next decade. They will listen to and believe in whatever I tell them. I present to them hope and a future with a five-hundred-dollar suit and a smile. You bring them doom and gloom in the stink of rotting fish and a wardrobe from the Nantucket Army Navy shop."

"It's politicians like you who I hate as much as the sharks, Mr. Mayor. You never care about the ones you step on to get what you want. Politicians like you sold us out during the war. Blamed us instead of yourselves. I'm not leaving this island until you get exposed."

Mayor Vaughn nodded his head in the challenging words from Quint and stood to his feet. Looking down at the captain, he finished his cigarette.

"Before you go threatening the mayor of this island, let's remember one thing here. You are on this island because of me. You did your service to this country and the community, and I will honor that by allowing you to stay. But don't think for one second that I won't use every bit of my power to drive you from our shores should you ever try anything like this in the future."

Vaughn looked over at Hershel in the doorway.

"Now you both take your stench back up-island where you belong. I never want to see you in this town hall again."

Quint wore a tired smile and stood to his feet as a chess player does a stalemate. He straightened up his Navy CPO shirt and tucked in the front of his blood and salt-stained light blue Navy work shirt.

"Mr. Mayor, this is my island. The newspaper knows where to find me. I promise you this. If you ever see me in this place again, you'll have a much bigger problem on your hands than myself."

With his one good hand, Quint reached down and took the ends of the rope sling. He yanked the slimy jaws from the floor, nodded to Larry Vaughn, and turned. Quint slouched down the long hallway of the Amity Town Hall, with Hershel following. A trail of blood and debris smeared the floor in their wake.

Captain's Log–November 11, 1968

Last entry of the year. Preparing the Orca for the long winter. Hershel made a deal and found some cheap rods and reels. I'm not sure how to adjust to the charter business, but if it means I'll stay living long enough to see the mayor take the fall, I'll do it.

We haven't seen the last of the sharks. It all happens in cycles. The people of this island will come calling and I'll make sure it hurts their wallet as much as their egos.

Under the light of dawn, Quint lit a fire around the large steel drum on the beach next to the fishing shack. The wide ring of kindling struck up in flames surrounding the barrel. Through the cloud of warm breaths, he watched the water simmer inside.

Hershel walked back and forth inside the Orca and swabbed the aft deck. He paused on every pass to look over to his captain on the shore, and the smoke of the fire rising into the frosty morning sky.

The fifty gallons of water boiled over the rim of the metal barrel. Quint watched the vapor leave the boiling surface and escape to the sky.

With gloved hands, he reached down and took the rope tethered to the jaws of the great white and lifted them to his chest. He placed the gigantic set of teeth down into the boiling water and listened. The water sizzled and screamed when touched by the oils, skin, and cartilage.

The mayor can't outrun his past. None of us can. I don't know what my purpose is in this life. I am alive and on this island for a reason. Impossible to have all the answers. Winter is rolling in. Another long one. I'm tired and ready to sleep.

Later that day, inside the shack, Quint raised his trophy to the back window of the fishing shack. The jaws of the great white, now boiled clean and dried wide open, as he remembered them in the water. Large triangles of terror looking into him, ready to devour his guilt and pain. Quint tied the tether line around a nail above the window frame. The suspended jaws tapped against the thin glass pane. Through their large opening, between the rows of serrated teeth, the captain saw his boat. The Orca waited for him at the dock.

EPILOGUE

"This is the last known photo of the fishing shack before the fire. I took it myself before leaving the island."

Rebecca turned her eyes from the aged color photo on the late 1970s Kodak stock paper. She looked down at the space among the fishing shacks lining the harbor below.

"There's so much history here, Mr. Hooper. Your collection is enough for a museum."

"Not my collection. Your collection."

Rebecca closed the over-sized leather cover of the photo album resting on the railing of the deck.

"Come on. I have a bag and a half of clothes in that rented jeep down there next to a vacant lot I only found out I owned a year ago. The taxes on storage must be enough to sink anyone around here."

The old man smiled under his white beard. His kind eyes scanned the harbor, and he breathed in the October air from the sea. Rebecca looked at him, puzzled at his smile and confidence.

Hooper walked a few steps down the deck of the tiny cottage and gazed across Amity Point.

"In my old age, I get emotional at just about everything. Any old movie can drag a tear out of my eye. I understand the emotions when I saw you hand me that photograph of your grandfather earlier. Tears of sadness and relief. When I last saw him, I was young and had my entire career ahead of me. He had so much to teach, and I had so much to learn. In my desire to be accepted by him,

I failed to ask questions. When he died, I spent the rest of my life trying to learn from him."

Rebecca listened to his words and realized this man was her only family.

"Tears of sadness and relief, Rebecca. A part of me still grieves at what I could have learned from him. Not one photo of him existed until today. I saw his eyes and remembered my grief. Then I saw you, and there's closure. My whole life has come full circle, beginning with him and ending with you. I'm so relieved to pass it on to you."

Her eyes watered, for she never felt a father's love. Rebecca's voice shook.

"You know, I thought I hated the ocean. It took everything from me. My parents... my fiancé. My grandfather and great grandfather. I swore I was going to move to a farm in Nebraska and run far away from the water. But I still love it... the ocean. It takes and gives, doesn't it?"

Hooper saw how tired she was from her travels. Rebecca's heavy eyes searched the orange horizon.

"You had a long trip. How about you get some rest in your house?"

"I was going to look for a hotel back in town... my house? You mean the vacant lot down there?"

"No, the main house up there."

Hooper pointed up to the top of Harbor Hill Road. The large windows of the extravagant house shone orange with the reflected sky. The lights of the expansive garage illuminated the winding drive leading to the estate.

"I said this place was all yours, Rebecca. Didn't mean just the barn in the back with all your family history. I meant this place."

"I don't understand, Mr. Hooper?"

"Your grandfather had ten-thousand dollars in reward money from 1974. I took that and invested it in his last name, with myself as executor. It went all into tech stocks, then those turned to bonds and shares in... well, let's just say, it's fifty years of compounding interest in 'lectric toothbrushes."

Hooper broke out in a quiet laughter. Rebecca smiled back.

"I don't get it?"

"I'll explain it to you later. It's funny that there's a fortune with your last name on it, made through phones and gadgets, started by the guy who hated it all. I loved that man. Yes, it's all yours."

Hooper gestured to the massive house on the hill, then waved his arm over the harbor.

"Amity Point is yours now. Most of it. I lost track after sixteen. Bought all these little shacks up over the years as the fishermen passed on. I didn't want this place to change… wanted to remember him by it. I'm signing it all over to you, Rebecca. Your grandfather was a great man. His legacy deserves to live on. With you it will."

Rebecca Quint fell speechless. Hooper reached out and handed her a set of keys.

"You'll never have to worry about taxes again, Miss Quint. The ocean takes and gives. It's all yours. I'll stay here in this little shack on the hill and maybe you can come by tomorrow and tell me about Dutch Harbor."

She nodded her head. "I can make you coffee."

Rebecca smiled, and Hooper found a daughter.

"I'd like that very much," said Hooper. "Just one more thing before you go get your jeep."

"Yes. Anything, Matt. I can't thank you enough."

"Fifty years, trips across the country and countless hours sifting through antique file cabinets. Never found his name, just his initials… RSQ. His full name? I gotta know."

Rebecca smiled and looked down at the photo of her grandfather and the house keys in her hand.

"Robert Samuel Quint."

Matt Hooper sat down on the small bench of the ancient deck.

"Thank you, Miss Quint. Thank you."

APPENDIX

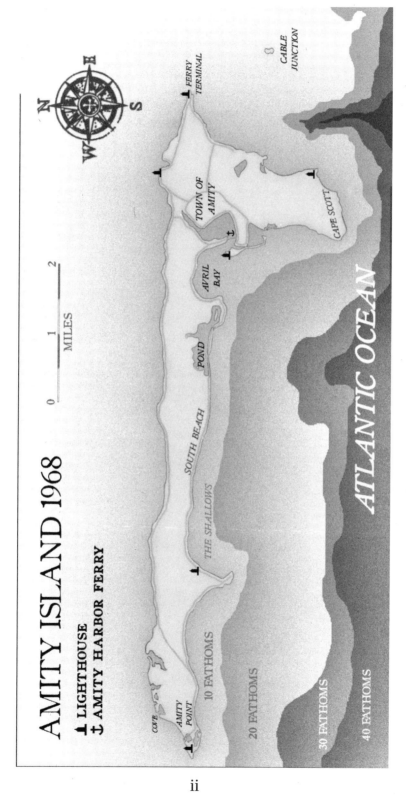

AMITY ISLAND 1968

🛆 LIGHTHOUSE
⚓ AMITY HARBOR FERRY

MILES
0   1   2

N
W   E
S

FERRY
TERMINAL

CABLE
JUNCTION

TOWN OF
AMITY

CAPE SCOTT

APRIL
BAY

POND

SOUTH BEACH

THE SHALLOWS

COVE

AMITY
POINT

10 FATHOMS

20 FATHOMS

30 FATHOMS

40 FATHOMS

ATLANTIC OCEAN

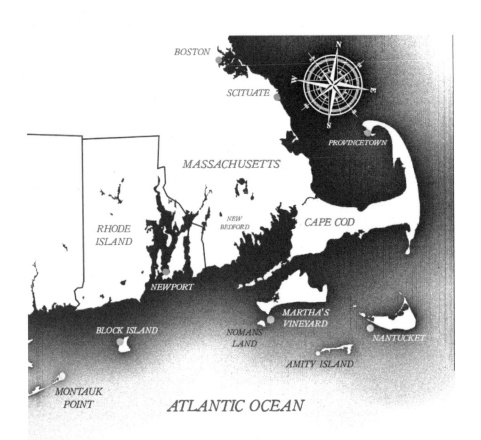

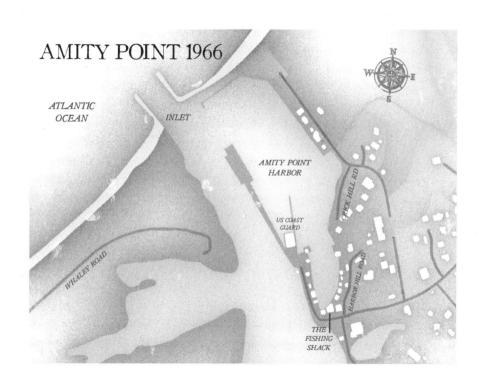

AMITY POINT 1966

ATLANTIC
OCEAN

INLET

AMITY POINT
HARBOR

US COAST
GUARD

CRICK HILL RD

WHALEY ROAD

HARBOR HILL ROAD

THE
FISHING
SHACK

N
W E
S

The Orca 1966

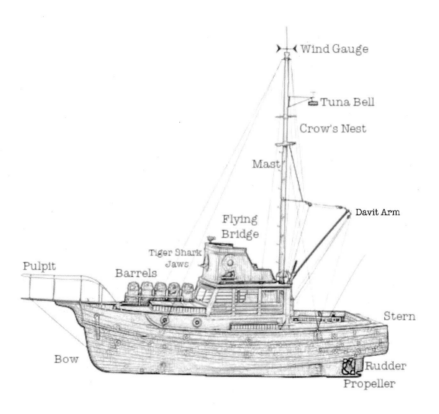

Wind Gauge

Tuna Bell

Crow's Nest

Mast

Flying
Bridge

Davit Arm

Tiger Shark
Jaws

Pulpit

Barrels

Stern

Bow

Rudder
Propeller

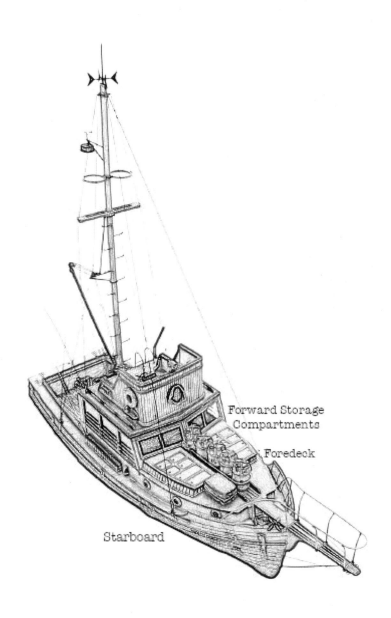

Forward Storage
Compartments

Foredeck

Starboard

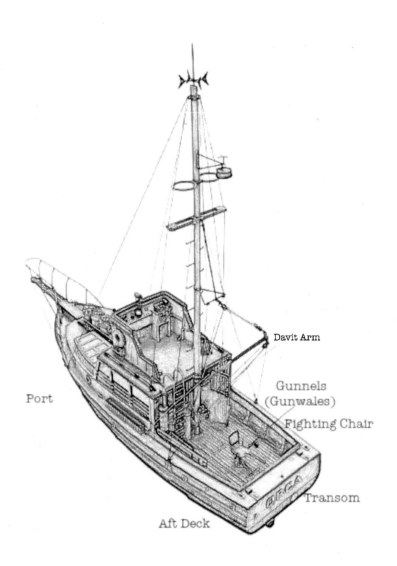

Davit Arm

Gunnels
(Gunwales)

Port

Fighting Chair

Transom

Aft Deck

Harpoons & Gaffs

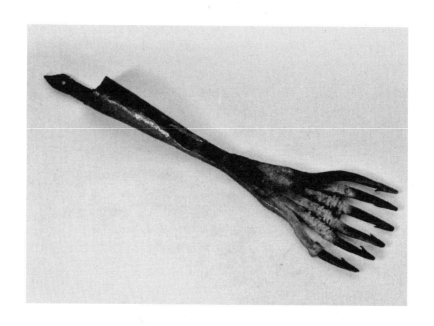

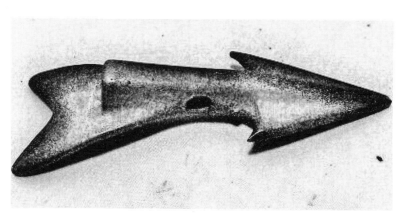

ix

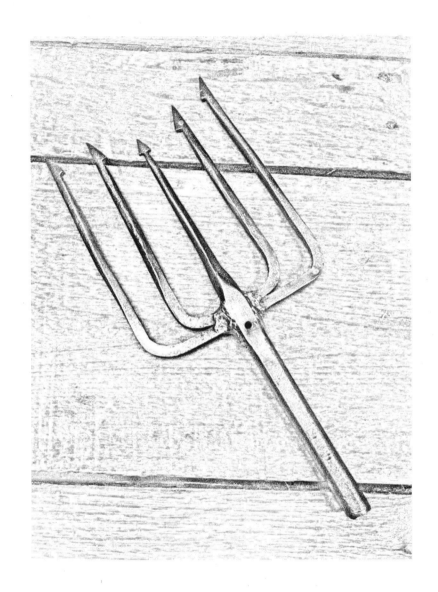

Blocks and Rigging

Two-Sheave Blocks

Soft-Pullers/Slack Blocks

Grip

ACKNOWLEDGMENTS

The Book of Quint would not be possible without the contributions by technical advisor, boat builder, fisherman, and Orca specialist: Jon Tedder.

Fielding an untold number of late-night phone calls by myself, Jon brought a wealth of information to the research and planning of this book while sacrificing countless hours. His knowledge of the Orca and the world of Quint is astounding. You can search the entire planet and only find one Jon Tedder. His dedication and efforts into the accuracy and feel of this book played an important role. From the map of Amity Island to the Orca font, the *Jon Tedder Effect* is felt throughout these pages. Throughout the writing, I have gained a lifelong friend and confidant in Jon. The intensity surrounding this book, with his Orca Rebuild project (Orcarebuild.com) and my broadcast of the Jaws Obsession, was an adventure unto itself. It was all worth it. Thanks, Jon.

Without support, a mission cannot be a success. My wife Tatiana was the greatest source of support throughout this book's 28-month creation. She tolerated my Jaws fascination and never said this project wasn't possible. For the first fourteen months of research, she encouraged me. During the one year of writing, her taking care of family and daily life allowed me to forge ahead. I discovered so much about life while writing this book. Re-discovering how much spiritual faith and guidance Tatiana brings to my life is the greatest gift the writing of this book has taught me. Anything is possible with her.

My three children: Alex, Katya, and Stasya. Giving up two years of spending time and breaking our little routines together to lend their father to this project wasn't easy. Books are forever, and I hope they can pick up this novel for the rest of their lives and realize their sacrifice was worth it. I look forward to getting back to spending time together.

My mother and father: Rosemary and Zenon Dacko. Summer trips to Cape Cod and purchasing untold numbers of shark books to satisfy a child's shark obsession in the early 80s were ground zero for this book. Their support and encouragement four decades ago built the foundation that gave me the confidence to tell this story.

Mike Currid of the Edgartown Tour Company: I realized many ideas in this book while riding in the tour van of Mike's Amity Island Tour. His passion for the history of Martha's Vineyard and the production of Jaws came into my life at the perfect time. It was on his 3-hour tour during October 2020, when I realized all of this was possible; there was so much history to Quint that needed to be told. It was one of those moments in life where two paths cross, setting you on a trajectory into the unknown. Tatiana was there to witness it. I encourage everyone to see Mike and find out where your Jaws obsession takes you. (Edgartowntours.com)

Peter Benchley was writing *Jaws* one-half a century ago in 1972. He completed the final draft in January 1973. For those who listened to me throughout the writing of this book, a significant source of focus was The Peter Benchley Timeline. That one man at a typewriter could create a ripple effect lasting decades into the future never ceases to amaze me. It was of great importance to complete this book near the 50th anniversary of Peter Benchley's writing of *Jaws*. That's where it all started.

The Men of the USS Indianapolis CA-35: These men gave the ultimate sacrifice for their country. 879 lost their lives at sea while the 316 survivors fought a new battle over the rest of their lives. The fictional story of Quint is rooted in the reality of the new battle these survivors fought. With wars being waged during our lives, all survivors of these conflicts will continue to fight for the rest of their lives. They need our support.

Captain Charles Butler McVay III went down with his ship twenty-three years after it dropped into the ocean. May he rest in peace.